THE DREAMER

Wolves of the Northwoods
Book 2

A.J. MANNEY

Revised 2022

Edited: Caryn Pine
Cover Design: Germancreative
Interior Design: Manney Resource Solutions

WOLVES OF THE NORTHWOODS

Book 2
The Dreamer

Wolves of the Northwoods Series

Book 1- The Finder

Book 2- The Dreamer

Sicario Clan Series

Book 1- Darken the Trux

Book 2- Defy the Tyrant

Book 3- Defend the Throne

The True Marks Series

Book 1- Red Rose Rising

Book 2- Courses Clashing

Book 3- Hope Dawning

Book 4- Allies Ascending

Book 5- Christmas in Cascadia (Novella)

Leave a Rating and Review

If you enjoy *The Finder*, would you consider leaving me a review on Amazon? Reviews are so important for an independent author like me. I would greatly appreciate a review! Thank you!

Discover Your Next Escape
at AJManneyBooks.com

Sign up to be in the know for upcoming books, release dates, teasers, and bonus content at AJManneyBooks.com.

Chapter One

Talya zipped her backpack shut and threw it over her shoulder. She was going to be late if she didn't get a move on. She glanced at herself one last time in the mirror and eyed herself critically. She was short. Too short. It wreaked havoc on her figure. She eyed her long blond hair that reached almost to her waist. She had wanted to cut it for a long time, but Brandon wouldn't let her. A lot of the girls envied her for it, but it often gave her headaches because it was so long and heavy. The one feature she did like were her eyes. They were a pretty blue and her best feature. Today, they popped because she was wearing a soft blue sweater with jeans. After slipping on her Chuck Taylors, she was ready to go.

She walked out into the living room. "Breakfast is in the kitchen, sweetie." Talya turned towards her grandpop sitting in the recliner reading the newspaper.

"Thanks, Pops; but I'm good." She didn't tell him that she couldn't eat the toast or bagel or whatever other carby food he had put out for her. Her grandparents never understood that she couldn't eat any of those foods. "Is Grams still in bed?" she asked.

Grandpop looked up at her. "Yeah. She wasn't feeling well this morning."

Talya glanced towards the closed bedroom door, worried for her grandma. She wasn't doing well. She needed more medicine, but the medicine cost a fortune. Talya tightened the strap on her backpack. She would have to ask Joe, her manager, if she could pick up more hours at the diner. "Don't you worry, Talya; she'll be okay," Grandpop said with a smile.

Talya smiled and bent to kiss his cheek. "Have a good day. I'll be back late tonight after my shift gets done."

"You work too much," he grumbled.

Talya didn't respond. She was going to be late if she didn't get going, and she knew better than to think Brandon would wait for her. Sure enough, she heard him honk before she opened the door. Sighing, she opened the door and made her way to Brandon's mustang. "Hey baby," Brandon said and leaned over to kiss her on the cheek. Talya ignored the comments from the guys in the back seat. Mitch and Trevor were Brandon's best friends. The three of them were worse than girls; they were never apart from one another. They had grown up together, and now they played football together and were incredibly popular. Brandon was the star quarterback, and he looked every inch the part. He was tall and muscular with shaggy brown hair and brown eyes. He captured all the girls' attention wherever he went. Mitch with his blond hair and Trevor with his reddish-brown hair were both pretty much the same way.

All three of them had ignored Talya her entire life until her sophomore year. Suddenly, she was on Brandon's radar. He asked her to the prom that year, and they had been together ever since. She had initially been excited to be Brandon's girlfriend. The excitement had faded over the years, especially after she had seen his mean side. And boy, did he have a mean side. Her ribs had felt it one too many times. She knew she should probably dump him, but she was terrified of doing so. Instead, she put up with him. Most of the time he wasn't too bad, just demanding. Her grandpop made no secret about the fact that he didn't like Brandon, so Talya tried to not bring him home much.

"You excited for the game tonight?" Brandon asked her as they squealed out of her grandparent's driveway. Talya just nodded; it was pointless to try to talk over the noise of the engine and the wind blowing. She hated that Brandon always kept the top down. By the time she got anywhere, her hair was always a mess. She had told him that once, and he had told her in choice words that she needed to deal with it. Since then, she never complained.

Talya watched the scenery pass and tuned the boys out as they talked. Thankfully, the drive wasn't long. They parked in Brandon's usual spot, and Talya climbed out of the car. She tried to smooth out her hair; no doubt it was all tangled from the drive. Brandon grabbed her arm and pulled her along with him as they walked towards the school building. Thankfully, she only had to endure first period with him.

With a kiss goodbye, Brandon left her with a promise to see

her in a few minutes. He had something to take care of. Emma began making her way to her first class. "Hey Talya." Talya turned and saw Stephanie wave at her. Talya smiled and waved back before continuing on her way. The problem with dating the school QB was that she never knew who her real friends were. Well, she did have one real friend. She smiled her first real smile of the day when she saw Sage.

Sage was quiet and incredibly sweet. Talya had taken her under her wing when Sage transferred into school in their junior year. Since then, they had been close. "Morning, girl. You ready for this Physics quiz?" Talya asked.

Sage shrugged. "I hope so." Talya just grinned. Sage would most likely ace it. She was just that smart. They were walking towards their Physics class talking when somebody fell into Sage and Sage went down hard. Talya turned instantly.

"Oops, sorry," Brittany said. "I didn't see you there," she said with a smirk.

"Do you need glasses?" Talya snapped at her.

Brittany turned her glare on Talya. Meanwhile, Sage tugged on Talya's hand. "It's fine. Just let it go. Come on." Talya turned back around and helped Sage off the floor.

By the time she turned back around, Brittany and her giggling minions were gone. "I hate girls like that," Talya said. Brittany was the lead cheerleader, a position Talya had once held before her grandma got sick and she had to take on more hours at the diner. Sage grinned at her. "Not a word," Talya said. She didn't need to be reminded that she had once been just like that. Her friendship with Sage had helped to mellow her out. With a sigh, Talya turned around and started towards class again, lost in her own world. That's why she didn't see the man coming out of the classroom. With a grunt, Talya ran smack into a hard chest. She would have fallen backwards, but two strong arms grabbed her arms, steadying her.

Talya looked up and up. "Holy muscles," she whispered. Then caught herself when the insanely gorgeous man in front of her smirked at her. She couldn't even stop her response to him. She just stared at him. He was insanely tall and built broadly. She could see his muscles through the shirt he was wearing. He had blond hear that was perfectly gelled and a beard that looked more like scruff. She itched to run her hand through it and see if it was soft or scratchy. His eyes were a startling blue that she felt she could get lost in.

"I'm Sage, and this is Talya," she heard her friend say. Sage's voice was like a glass of cold water to the face. Talya got ahold of herself when she realized she was staring at this man and practically drooling over him. Well, he was drool-worthy, but... she shook her head. *Focus, Talya.*

"Talya," his insanely sexy voice said, and Talya practically melted on the floor. Talya looked up at him and was surprised to see his eyes boring into hers. He was staring at her in awe, like she was a fresh piece of meat and he hadn't eaten in days. "I love it," he said, his rich warm voice melting her insides.

"Me too," she said before she caught herself. She felt her face redden. "I mean, I like it, my name, that is," she stumbled to a halt and could have slapped herself. She needed to escape this guy before she said something more stupid than she already had.

"My name's Liam," his sexy voice said. Talya memorized it; it seemed like the smart thing to do. *Liam. His name even sounds sexy.*

"We need to get to class," Sage said, pulling her towards the open door. "Your *boyfriend* is probably wondering where you are." Those words got her attention like nothing else could. It would not bode well for her if Brandon saw her talking to this gorgeous man.

"Right," Talya said. "It was nice to meet you, uh, Liam. We will just be going now," she stumbled over her words. Talya looked up at the man and was shocked to see anger on his face. He blinked, and it was gone. Talya wondered if she had imagined it.

"I'll be seeing you," Liam said. With a nod to the two of them, he disappeared down the hall. Talya watched him go until Sage pulled on her arm.

"We're going to be late for class," Sage said. Talya allowed Sage to pull her into the classroom. She sank into her chair, while Sage sat directly behind her. Thankfully, Brandon wasn't there yet.

Sage leaned forward. "You okay?" she asked softly.

Talya turned to look at her. They hadn't started class yet. "Yeah, why?" she asked, confused.

Sage shrugged. "I've never seen you respond to a guy like that before?"

"That was no guy; he was like a Greek god or something," Talya whispered.

Sage laughed. "Wow. Well, get it out of your system now before Brandon gets here," she said seriously.

"You're right. I don't know what I was thinking. Sorry," Talya said, feeling embarrassed. She had totally acted like she'd never seen a good-looking guy before. She had a boyfriend for goodness' sake.

"It's okay, Talya. You're too hard on yourself," Sage said quietly.

Talya didn't say anything in response. Brandon had just entered the classroom. He came towards her with a big smile on his face. He planted a kiss on her cheek and dropped into the seat next to hers. Sage leaned back against her seat. She always kept her distance when Brandon was around. Talya opened her book to try to cram a few last minutes of studying in. Brandon didn't. He laughed and talked with the guys seated around him who worshipped him like a god. Talya ignored all of it, so she could study. It didn't matter how hard she tried to focus, though. She couldn't get her thoughts off of a certain tall, gorgeous male. She wondered what he was doing here. He couldn't possibly be a student, and she hadn't heard of any new hires. Her thoughts were pushed aside when their physics professor arrived. Talya had to mentally focus, so she could pass this quiz.

The class dragged on, and so did the next two. Finally, it was time for lunch. Talya couldn't help the pep in her step. She wondered if she would see Liam at lunch. She walked into the cafeteria next to Brandon and quickly scanned the room. Disappointment flooded her when he was nowhere to be seen. She grabbed a tray and walked through the buffet line. She put some salad on her plate with some grilled chicken and light Italian dressing. She grabbed a water bottle and made her way over to where Brandon sat. She slid in next to him and across from Mitch and Trevor. She ate her salad quietly while her mind wandered. When she was finished, she sat and waited for the guys to be done.

The next two classes passed quickly, and Talya found herself making her way to her last class of the day—her most dreaded one. P.E. She had found out at the beginning of the year that she was missing P.E. credits and she would have to take the class this year. She hated it. The only bright spot was that Sage took it with her. She had heard of Talya's misfortune at the beginning of the year and signed up to take it with her. Talya was so thankful for her.

She and Sage quickly joined the other girls and changed in the locker room. "Come one. Let's get this over with," Sage said. Talya couldn't agree more. That is, until they walked into the gym. Talya froze when she saw who was standing with their P. E. teacher.

Chapter Two

Talya stared at Liam. He turned his head as if he felt her stare and locked eyes with her. Talya felt like she couldn't breathe. Only when Sage nudged her did she break eye contact with him and finally feel like she could suck in some oxygen. "What's he doing here?" she asked in a whisper to Sage.

"I have no idea," Sage mumbled.

Great, Talya said to herself. She studied the man again briefly and scowled. As if he didn't look good enough in what he was wearing earlier, now he was wearing a gray hoodie that was sleeveless. It showcased his muscular arms. Talya made herself focus on something else, anything else.

Talya started walking with Sage at her side. She didn't make the mistake of looking at Liam again, but she could feel his eyes boring into her. She startled when the whistle blew. She joined the other girls moving towards their P. E. teacher but stayed towards the back of the group with Sage. Talya looked warily at their teacher. "Ten laps." The whistle blew, and they all moved.

Talya fell into an easy pace next to Sage. She didn't mind running. It was relaxing to her. If all she ever had to do in this class was run, she would be fine. It was the other stuff like basketball, baseball, and all the other sports she hated. She had been good at cheer, but that was about it as far as her athleticism went. But seeing as their P. E. teacher was also the men's football coach, it was hard to avoid a lot of those sports.

Talya tried to push Liam out of her mind, but it was difficult to do with him standing in the same room as her. When they were finished running laps, she grabbed a drink of water and made her way to where the other girls sat. They waited for a few stragglers to finish up. "All right," Coach Stanley said. "You may have noticed we have a newcomer here today."

"How could we not notice?" one of the girls muttered. Several of the girls giggled.

Coach seemed not to hear her because he continued. "This is Liam Graves. He will be working with us the next few weeks. He will be teaching self-defense. He has the power to pass or fail you, so listen up and work hard." With that, Coach Stanley turned and left the gym.

Okay, then, Talya thought to herself. No worries. She just had to endure the next couple of weeks with her new teacher. No big deal. Then she glanced at Liam once again and nearly groaned out loud. It was totally going to be a big deal.

"All right," Liam's rich, warm voice assaulted her. "We are going to get started with a few simple moves." He spent the next few minutes talking, but Talya really didn't hear a word he said. A few minutes later, they were supposed to pair up and practice the move he had just taught them. Talya paired up with Sage.

"What are we supposed to do?" she asked Sage.

Sage grinned at her. "Did you hear anything he said?"

"Nope."

Sage laughed. "All right. Come on. I'll show you." Thankfully, Talya was able to focus on the moves they were working on. It was pretty simple, basic defense. After that, Liam called them back in.

"The next thing we are going to work on is your response when somebody grabs you. I'm going to need help with this. Talya, do you mind helping me?" he asked.

Talya didn't move for a moment until Sage elbowed her. That prompted her into moving. She walked slowly towards Liam, ignoring the scowls on other girls' faces. When she got to him, he was all business. "Talya, go ahead and face out with your back to me. I am going to show you how to escape when somebody attacks you and grabs you from behind," he said to the class. A moment later, she could feel Liam at her back. He wrapped his arms around her and locked her into place. Talya blinked and was suddenly overwhelmed as panic shot through her and memories resurfaced. She froze. She heard Liam talking; she could feel his chest rumbling from where it was tight against her back, but she couldn't focus on anything he was saying. Panic had completely taken over her mind, and she couldn't move. She squeezed her eyes shut and tried to draw in a breath, but she couldn't. She was really panicking now. She couldn't get any air into her lungs. Just when she thought she would pass out, she was suddenly released. It was enough that it broke through her panic. She greedily sucked in air. She felt Sage's hand on her back, rubbing it and soothing her.

"Just breathe," Sage said softly. Talya greedily sucked air into her deprived lungs. Her legs felt shaky, like they wouldn't hold her up.

She vaguely heard Liam giving directions to the rest of the class. Soon everyone had moved away, giving her space.

"Is she okay?" she heard a low voice ask.

"She is, but maybe you should just keep your distance," Sage said as politely as possible. She didn't hear if he responded or not. Her head was buzzing, the after effects of her panic attack. She just wanted to get out of there. "Do you think it would be okay if we left now?" Sage asked.

"Yes. Of course. Please take Talya to the school nurse and make sure she's okay," she heard Liam say.

"Okay," Sage responded sweetly. Then they were walking. After what seemed like an eternity, they finally made it to the locker room. Talya staggered over to the benches. She put her head between her legs and focused on taking deep breaths. "Are you okay?" Sage asked, sounding worried.

"Yes," she rasped out. Sage, being the good friend that she was didn't say anything more. She simply sat next to Talya and rubbed her back. After a few minutes, Talya felt composed and embarrassed. "I'm sorry," she mumbled.

"There's nothing to be sorry for," Sage said in her sweet voice. It was quiet for a few more minutes. "Did something happen to you, Talya?" she asked softly. Talya felt her stomach tighten in response. She couldn't respond. "It's okay if you can't say anything."

"I," Talya stopped. "I can't talk about it," she finally got out.

"That's okay," Sage said. Her hand rubbed Talya's back again. "You don't ever have to tell me if you don't want to, but if you ever want to talk, I'm a good listener."

Talya wiped at the sudden tears in her eyes. "Thank you," she whispered.

"Do you want to go to the nurse?" Sage asked.

Talya shook her head. "I really don't."

"That's fine," Sage said. "We only have ten minutes of class left anyways. Let's just change and get ready to go." That sounded good to Talya. She finally stood up and started getting changed back into her school clothes. A few minutes later, the door to the locker room opened and the girls came flooding in. Talya backed out of the way and tried to pretend she was busy getting dressed. Finally, the room emptied out and it was just Sage and Talya once again. "You ready?" Sage asked.

Talya nodded. She grabbed her backpack and threw it over her shoulder, grateful she had packed everything earlier so she didn't have to go to her locker now and run into anybody. Brandon had practice right after school, so hopefully he wouldn't be looking for her either. She could catch a bus and get to work and put the whole episode behind her. She led the way out of the locker room with Sage behind her. She stopped short and Sage bumped into her, jolting Talya.

Liam straightened from where he had been leaning against the wall. "I checked with the nurse, and she said you never showed up," he said, looking down at her in concern. "Are you okay?" he asked. Talya was so shocked that he was standing there, talking to her, that she didn't know how to respond. He took a step closer and Talya automatically backed up. He froze as his eyes tracked her movements. "I would never hurt you, Talya," he said in a low voice.

"Yo, Talya babe." Talya tensed at the sound of Brandon's voice, but that was nothing compared to Liam. He straightened to his full height and stood perfectly still, his eyes locked on something behind her. There was something to it that made Talya shiver, almost like he was a predator seeking its prey. Talya shook the thought off.

Brandon came and stood next to Talya, putting his arm around her and pulling her flush against him. He turned questioning eyes to her. "I was waiting for you," he said accusingly. "I'm going to be late to practice now," he complained.

"Sorry," Talya mumbled.

"Who are you and why were you talking to my girlfriend?" Brandon asked in an aggressive tone, turning to look at Liam.

Talya didn't look at Liam. She could feel her face heating up. "I'm teaching self-defense to the P.E. class," Liam said easily.

Brandon made a sound, but Talya couldn't interpret it. "Well, make sure you keep your distance from my girl," Brandon said.

Mortified, Talya put her hand on Brandon's chest. "Stop," she said quietly. She stole a glance at Liam and saw he wasn't looking at her. He was staring at her hand on Brandon's chest. She quickly dropped her hand. She glanced up at Brandon, then at Liam. She couldn't help comparing the two. Brandon was good-looking, handsome even. But Liam was in a category all his own. He was several inches taller than Brandon, though both of them were built about the same. She dropped her eyes when Liam turned his gaze to hers. Now was not the time to think about it.

"Well, I have to take off. I'll see you in class on Wednesday, Talya and Sage," Liam said. Then without another word, he was gone.

Brandon turned to watch as he left. "I don't like that guy," he said. Talya kept her mouth shut. "Don't be late again. I can't afford to be late to practice." With that, he bent and kissed her on the lips. He left her and went in the direction of the guys' locker room, and Talya was finally able to take a deep breath.

"All righty then," Sage said and Talya turned to her. "That was fun," she said with a grin.

Talya managed a small laugh. "You have a weird sense of humor. Thanks for staying with me," she said sincerely to Sage.

"Of course. You'd do the same for me. I'll see you tomorrow," Sage said and gave Talya a quick hug.

Talya began walking towards the bus stop. Her mind was whirling while she waited for the bus. It had been a crazy day, and it wasn't finished yet. She still had a six-hour shift at the diner to get through.

Thankfully, her evening went much better than her day. It was a fairly easy night, nothing out of the ordinary. A few minutes before she was supposed to clock out, two men in suits came in and sat in Talya's section. With a sigh, Talya moved towards them. *So much for getting out of here on time*, she thought to herself. Forcing a smile to her face, she moved towards their table.

"What can I get for you tonight?" she asked cheerfully.

Both men looked up at her and Talya fought a feeling of unease in her stomach. She felt like a deer in headlights. She pushed the thought away and forced herself to remain calm. *They're just customers,* she told herself.

Chapter Three

The first man glanced up at her. "I'll have a black coffee and a bowl of whatever soup you have." Talya busied herself with writing it down.

"And for you, sir?"

"Same," the second man said without looking up at her.

"Okay, I'll go grab that for you. I'll be back in a few." She turned away quickly and forced herself to keep her steps even as she walked towards the kitchen. "Hey, Joe?" she called out.

He turned from where he was currently manning the grill. "What's up, sweetheart?"

"Do you mind serving these two guys in my section? I don't know what it is about them but they're creeping me out."

Joe frowned. "Sure. You leave 'em to me. Why don't you go ahead and clock out and go out the back door? I'll take care of them."

Talya breathed a sigh of relief. "Thanks, Joe."

"Sure," he said easily. "Have a good night. Be safe going

home."

"Thanks, you too." With that, Talya untied her apron from where it hung around her waist and clocked out for the night. If she hurried, she could catch the 10 o'clock bus; usually she had to wait for the later one. She pushed the door open and stepped out into the chilly air. Spring was supposedly here, but it was still cold. She shivered as she made her way to the bus stop. Thankfully, it pulled up just as she got there.

Talya put her headphones in and rested her head back against the seat, enjoying the few minutes of calm before she got home. She ignored the texts she saw from Brandon. When she got home, she let herself inside quietly; she didn't want to wake her grandparents. She slipped past their room and saw they were both sleeping. That was good; they both needed it. Neither of them slept well, especially her grandma with all her health problems. Talya lingered for a moment outside their door. She had forgotten to tell Joe she needed more hours. She would have to tell him tomorrow night. With a sigh, Talya made her way to her room and got out her homework. Two hours later, she finally finished and pulled on pajamas and crashed in bed.

The next morning, she got dressed quickly after taking a quick shower. She did her hair in an easy up-do for the day. She passed her grandpa, sitting in his usual chair. "How's Grandma today?" she asked, bending to kiss his cheek.

Grandpop sighed. "Not very well. She had another hard night." Talya frowned and turned towards her grandma's room. Tonight, she was definitely asking for more hours. "Don't you worry, kiddo. She'll be okay. You get to school and have a good day."

"Love you, Grandpop." Talya made her way outside to where Brandon was waiting with the guys.

"You're coming to the game, right?" Brandon asked when they pulled into the parking lot at school.

"I forgot about it, but I'm sure I can make it," she hurried to say, so as not to risk Brandon's wrath.

"Game's at 7 p.m. You need to be there no later than 6:45, in your seat, with your jersey on," he said as if Talya hadn't been through this a million times before.

"Got it," she said. She inwardly sighed. She would have to find someone to cover her shift so she could leave early, and she would have to find time to run home and grab her jersey with Brandon's name and number on it. *So much for more hours,* she thought to herself. The only positive was that the season was almost done. She just needed to get through this game and maybe one or two more, depending on how they did.

"Are you coming?" Brandon asked impatiently. Talya grabbed her backpack and climbed out of the car.

Sage sat behind her in first hour. Talya waved to her but didn't say anything. She really wasn't really into her classes today. Luckily, she was acing all of them; so, she didn't have to focus too hard. The day passed quickly. At work, she was able to find someone to fill in for her so she could leave early.

Talya slipped into her seat at 6:45 on the dot and sighed in relief. She had made it. She put her headphones in and closed her eyes, relaxing for a few minutes before the game started. Hopefully Sage would get here soon. Being the good friend that she was, she always came to these games to keep Talya company. Talya started to relax and unwind from the stress of the day, until she felt a tap on her shoulder. She opened her eyes and was shocked to see Liam standing there. She pulled the headphones out. "Hey," he said with a grin.

"Uh, hey," Talya said lamely.

"Is this seat taken?" he asked, pointing at the one next to her. Talya panicked slightly.

"You can't sit there," she blurted out. Brandon would freak if she watched his game sitting next to another guy. He cocked his head to the side, watching her. "My friend Sage is going to sit there," she said quickly.

"Okay," he said. Then he stepped in front of her and slid into the seat on her other side. She turned to him, her eyes wide.

"You can't sit there either," she said.

"Is somebody sitting here?" he asked.

"Well, no but…" Talya started.

"Then I think I can," he said with a wink.

Talya stared at him, desperately trying to figure out how to get rid of him. If Brandon saw him, she would be in so much trouble. Who knew what he would do to her or even Liam? *Probably cause a huge scene,* she thought to herself. She really needed to figure out what to do.

"Talya," Liam's warm voice wrapped around her. "What's wrong?" Talya didn't look at him; she was still trying to control the mini panic session she was having. "Talya, look at me," Liam said in an authoritative voice.

Talya couldn't resist the power of that command. She turned

her head to look at him. He was close, too close. She tried to move backwards in her chair to create space between them. "Hey, Talya." Talya heard Sage's voice and was never more grateful for her friend.

"Sage," she said enthusiastically, turning her head to look at her. "I'm so glad you're here. I was wondering when you'd get here." Sage narrowed her eyes at Talya's overly enthusiastic greeting. Talya ignored it and quickly stood up. "You can sit here. That way I don't have to crawl over you when I go to the bathroom or get a drink or a snack," she said, rambling. She practically shoved Sage in the seat she had been sitting in and slid into the next one. Now, Sage sat between Liam and Talya. Talya drew in a breath of air and tried to relax. Before she could fully relax, the music kicked up and the announcer announced the away team. Then it was time for the home team. Talya stood up and clapped because that's what was expected of her. She watched Brandon run out onto the field. She saw the moment he laid eyes on her; because of that, she also saw the moment he caught sight of Liam. She watched him stiffen. She closed her eyes briefly. At least he wasn't sitting next to her. She couldn't even imagine what would have happened if he had been. When she opened her eyes, Brandon was jogging towards her as was his pre-game custom. She hated this part. She dutifully stood, though, when he hopped into the stands. He pulled her into his arms and kissed her. The crowd went wild. She was used to this public display, even though she hated it. What she wasn't used to was the aggression in Brandon's kiss. His hold on her was almost painful. He tried to get her to open her mouth, but she didn't. She wasn't going to do that in front of all these people. She gasped in shock when he bit her lip. He used her gasp to force his way into her mouth. Talya was so shocked, she didn't bother fighting him. A moment later, he pulled back. He grinned down at her for the sake of the crowd, but she could see the fire in his eyes. He bent down to her ear. "I'm watching you," he said. Talya shivered at his ominous words; then watched as he grinned and waved at the crowd before vaulting back over the railing and running across the field.

Talya slipped back into her seat, feeling numb. She forced back the tears that threatened and fingered her bruised lip. She wiped the blood there and refused to let her tears fall. Sage leaned in next to her. "Are you okay?"

Talya nodded. She couldn't talk right now, for fear she would burst into tears. When the game started, she sat up and noticed for the first time that Liam was gone. "He left after Brandon's kiss," Sage said by way of explanation. Talya sat back, lost in her own thoughts. At halftime when Talya turned to Sage, she saw Liam .He had obviously come back at some point during the first half. "I'm going to brave the line for the bathroom. Want to come?"" she asked.

"Sure," Sage said. Talya debated whether or not to say anything to Liam. She figured it was probably in her best interest to just ignore him. He stood up behind Sage, though, prompting Talya to look at him.

"Bathroom break," he said with an easy grin. Talya turned away and didn't say anything. She began working her way through the row of people and into the masses. After not getting anywhere for nearly five minutes, Talya started to get frustrated. Her height always made it hard for her to get through crowds of people. Suddenly, Liam was in front of her. "How about I lead?" he asked with an easy smile. "Hang on to my shirt, and I'll get us through this crowd." Before she could argue he turned back around and started pushing through the crowd. Talya decided to go for it. Her bladder felt like it was going to burst, and she would never get through this crowd on her own. She quickly grabbed Sage's hand behind her with one hand and Liam's shirt with her other.

Talya couldn't believe the way the crowd practically parted for Liam. In just minutes, they made their way through the crowd. Liam turned to her when they got to the bathrooms. "I'll wait for you," he said simply and moved to stand against the wall on the other side of the women's bathroom. Talya didn't say anything. When they came out, Liam came towards them. "Ready?" he asked with a smile.

He was so calm and relaxed, Talya couldn't help but relax around him. She gave him a small smile and nodded. He pointed to his back and Talya grabbed a hold of his shirt again. Sage clasped her other hand, and once again they made their way through the throngs of people to get back to their seats. Soon, they were back in their row, and Talya dropped her hold on his shirt. They made it back to their seats, and Talya settled in to watch the rest of the game.

The second half passed quickly, and Talya got lost in the game. Thankfully, they won. It was close, but they pulled it out at the end. Talya breathed a sigh of relief. That was good for her going home. Brandon was horrible when they lost. When Talya stood up to stretch, Sage turned to her with a grin. "That was a good game."

Talya agreed. "It was, and they won. So, my ride home will be happy."

Sage gave her a knowing smile. "Are you good if I take off?"

"Yes, thanks," Talya said and gave her a quick hug. Sage smiled at Liam and took off.

Liam came and stood beside her. "Want help navigating the crowd?" he asked. Talya glanced up at him, trying to read his face. She wasn't sure why he was being so kind to her, but she didn't see anything other than genuine kindness on his face. She glanced over her shoulder at the crowd. It was normally a feat to get to the guys' locker room where she was supposed to meet Brandon. She supposed it would be nice to use his height and bulk to get through easily again.

Talya looked up at him. "That would be great, if you don't mind."

Liam smiled down at her. "Not at all."

Chapter Four

Liam led her through the throngs of people easily. She directed him where to go, and soon they stood in front of the locker room. "Thanks for getting me here," Talya said, tucking a piece of hair behind her ear.

"You're welcome," he said.

"You don't have to stick around. Brandon will be out in a minute," she said. Talya didn't say it, but she figured Liam got the hint. She didn't want him around when Brandon came out. It wouldn't be good for either of them.

Liam looked down at her for a moment. Then he nodded. "Have a good night, Talya."

"Thank you; you too," she said. He turned and began walking away. Talya turned back to wait for Brandon. She was tired and ready to get home. She leaned against the wall and closed her eyes, hoping Brandon's team would be out soon. She heard footsteps but didn't open her eyes. It was probably just some of the boys' girlfriends.

"Hey beautiful, were you waiting for me?" an unfamiliar voice asked and she heard a few laughs. Talya ignored it; they obviously weren't talking to her. That is, until she felt a touch on her shoulder. Her eyes snapped open. She took in the three guys standing in front of her, and panic suddenly flared. She glanced around and saw that she was totally alone in the hallway. The first guy moved closer and brushed her hair over her shoulder. "You look lonely. We can take care of that," he said with a carnal smile.

Talya's heart was pounding in her chest. "I have a boyfriend," she said, trying to project confidence. "You're not going to want to be here when he comes out," she said.

All three of them laughed. The guy leaned closer and ran his finger down her cheek. "I think we'll take our chances," he said softly.

Talya was really starting to panic. There was no way she could get away from all three of these guys. They were obviously football players from the other team with the way they were built. Before she could say anything, she heard her name called. Her head snapped up when she recognized Liam's voice. She watched as the three guys in front of her turned towards Liam. "Is that your boyfriend, baby?" the guy in front of her asked, moving closer to Talya.

"Yes, and you'd better step away from her now." Talya's eyes widened at the threat she heard in Liam's voice. She couldn't believe it came from him; he'd been so easygoing every time she was around him. When none of the guys moved away from Talya, Liam reached out and grabbed the first guy and flung him against the opposite wall. Talya stared in shock. He had thrown that guy like he was nothing. This got the other two guys' attention. They both moved away from Talya.

"Okay, dude. We're moving away," the guy who had touched her said.

Liam moved incredibly fast and was in front of him in a second. "Don't ever touch her again," he said through gritted teeth.

"W-we won't," the guy said; Talya could hear real fear in his voice. Liam released him roughly and the three of them hightailed it out of there. Talya turned back to Liam. He was glaring in the direction the guys had gone. She took a step, and he turned his head towards her. His fierce stare trapped her, and she couldn't move.

"Are you okay?" he asked, his voice gruff, not his usual warm voice.

Talya couldn't think of what to say; she just nodded. He took a step towards her. Talya heard the locker room door open behind her, and she turned around in panic. She watched as the guys started coming out of the locker room. Brandon was one of the first few out. He saw her and grinned. Talya turned quickly to look behind her, but Liam was gone. Talya breathed out a sigh of relief. "Hey, baby," Brandon said as he moved towards her. "We won!" he said in a loud voice. Several of his teammates cheered behind him. Brandon picked her up and spun her around before kissing her hard to the delight of his teammates. Finally, he set Talya down. Her face flamed. She hated the attention.

"Can we just go?" she asked quietly.

Brandon ignored her and continued laughing and carrying

on with his friends. Brandon finally grabbed her hand and led her down the hallway and outside to the car. He and his friends were loud and obnoxious on the way to Talya's home. Brandon pulled into the driveway. "Are you sure you don't want to go out with us?" he asked her one more time.

"No. I've got homework to do. I'll see you tomorrow," she said. She opened her door and climbed out of the car before he could try to convince her to come with. She quickly made her way up the front porch and inside. Breathing a sigh of relief, she closed and locked the door behind her. Glancing at the clock, she winced when she realized it was after 11:00. She quickly made her way to her room, so she could start on her homework. She ignored her growling stomach. It was too late to eat. She would gain weight for sure. She finished her homework and quickly got ready for bed. She passed out as soon as her head hit the pillow.

The next week and a half passed quickly. Between work and school, Talya didn't have any spare time. With the extra hours Joe had graciously given her, she worked every night until 11:00 and helped with closing. She didn't get out of there until 11:30 each night. She also picked up extra hours on the weekends. The extra income was good for her paycheck, but the extra hours were killing her. She was exhausted between doing school and working and staying on top of her homework at night. She wouldn't complain, though. She knew why she was doing this. She just had to keep the big picture in mind.

Before she knew it, it was Friday night, and the last game of the season. Talya had somebody lined up to take her shift, so she could leave early to go to the game. She wondered absently if Liam would show up again. She hadn't seen him except in class. He hadn't singled her out again since the first day. The time passed quickly at work. Talya watched the clock, knowing she would be leaving soon.

"Talya," she heard from inside the kitchen. She had just dropped drinks off at her table. She walked into the kitchen. "Talya," Joe said. "Cally just called. She can't cover for you tonight; she's sick. Do you mind staying? We're understaffed as it is because Sam's sick." Talya stared at him. Normally, she had no problem staying extra hours, but tonight was the last game. Brandon would be furious with her if she missed it.

"Is there anybody else we can call?" Talya asked. "I normally wouldn't mind; it's just that tonight's the last game," Talya explained.

Joe looked at her in between manning the grill. "I know, honey. And I'm sorry. I just don't have anyone else to call."

"What about Carl?" she asked.

"Out of town," Joe responded.

"Jenny?" Talya asked.

"She's back at college," he said.

Talya closed her eyes. "I'm sorry. I wouldn't do this if I had any other choice," Joe said, apologetically. Talya nodded. She hated for him to feel bad. There was nothing he could do.

"It's fine. Brandon will understand," she said with a forced brightness. Even as she said the words, she hoped and prayed that somehow those words would be true. She forced the thoughts of fear from her mind. There was nothing she could do. She grabbed a stack of menus and moved to the table where a family had just sat down. She greeted them and took their drink order. When she had a free moment, she quickly texted Brandon. He wouldn't see it until after the game or maybe at halftime, but at least he would know she tried.

Talya: *Hey, I'm so sorry. I won't be able to make it to the game tonight after all. We're short-staffed at work and my replacement canceled. I know you'll play great and win. Good luck!*

After that, she quickly shot off a text to Sage, explaining what happened. Talya pocketed her phone and pushed all thoughts of Brandon and the game from her mind. There was nothing she could do about it.

Her shift passed quickly. Soon, it was 10:30. She kept an eye on the front door, wondering if Brandon would show up at the diner. She wondered if they had won. She checked her phone repeatedly, but nothing showed up. She finally gave in and texted Sage really quickly.

Talya: *Did they win?*

She kept working and waited until she had a short reprieve to check her phone. She saw a text from Sage.

Sage: *Not sure. I didn't go. Sorry you got stuck at work.*

Talya pocketed her phone again. She would just have to wait to hear from Brandon. Maybe the game had gone long; maybe it had gone into overtime. When 11:00 came and went and still no word from Brandon, she started to worry. What if something had happened? She helped Joe finish with closing. By 11:30, she left and headed to the bus stop. She didn't look at her phone on the way; she always paid attention to her surroundings because it was so late at night. Thankfully, the bus stop was close. When she got there, she only waited a minute or two before the bus got there. Once she got on the bus, she texted Brandon.

Talya: *Hey, I'm so sorry I missed your game. How did it go? Did you win?*

Talya sent the text and watched her phone, waiting for his response. When she got to her stop and he still hadn't replied, she got a bad feeling in the pit of her stomach. Maybe he was ghosting her because she hadn't made it to the game. She blew out a sigh of frustration. She couldn't do anything about it. Hopefully, he would cool down tonight and she could talk to him tomorrow.

No such luck. Saturday and Sunday passed without a word from Brandon, even though she texted him a few more times. She worked long shifts on both days, so at least she wasn't sitting home and thinking about it. When she climbed into bed each night though, her mind wandered. What would he be like in school on Monday?

Her answer came soon enough. Monday morning, Talya stood at the bus stop, furious. Brandon hadn't picked her up. Now she had to take a bus to school, and she was going to be royally late. She had texted him twice and even called him, but he didn't respond to any of it. She couldn't believe he was doing this to her, just because she missed his game. She was so going to have a word with him when she got to school, if she ever got to school!

When Talya finally made it to school, she had missed most of first hour. She didn't even bother showing up for the last ten minutes. She decided to wait outside the classroom, so she could talk to Brandon when he came out. When he came out, he was laughing with his friends. He didn't look her way once. She tried calling his name, but he ignored her. Talya stared at him for a moment before dropping her head.

Humiliated, she quickly made her way to her second class. She pulled out her phone and saw a text from Sage saying she was staying home today because she was sick. Talya sent her back a text and told her she hoped she felt better. Talya sat in her chair and tried to ignore the looks she was getting. She didn't know if word had spread that Brandon was ignoring her, but she was sure on the receiving end of plenty of curious looks today. She just wanted this day to be over.

By the time the bell rang for lunch, Talya was over all of it. She was just going to ignore Brandon. If he wanted to talk to her, he knew where to find her. She headed towards the lunch room. She wished she never had.

Chapter Five

Talya followed the crowd into the lunchroom with her head down. She was tired and frustrated and ready for this day to be over. When she entered the lunchroom, was she imagining it or did a hush descend on the lunchroom? Talya looked up and froze. She stared at the sight in front of her. Brandon sat with his boys at his usual table. That wasn't what caught her attention. What caught her attention was the girl seated next to him, practically on his lap. Talya couldn't move. The scene paralyzed her. When they finally came up for air, Brandon put her on her feet and stood up. He caught Talya's eye for just a moment before jumping up on the bench seat.

"Three cheers for our victory last night!" he yelled. Cheers and whistles broke out all across the lunchroom. "As is our custom, after the last game of the year, the quarterback announces who he will be taking to Prom. This year, I asked Stephanie; and she said yes." Cheers drowned out his voice. He pulled her up onto the bench and took her into his arms, kissing her disgustingly.

Talya couldn't breathe. She felt like she'd been kicked in the stomach. She saw people looking at her. Some of them were talking and pointing; others were laughing. A few had expressions of sympathy, but not many. Talya had to get out of there. She felt like she was going to puke. She turned to run and ran smack into a hard chest. Two arms came out and wrapped around her upper arms, steadying her. Talya glanced up and saw Liam. He wasn't looking at her, though. He was looking over her head. She didn't have to turn her head to know what had caught his attention.

"Excuse me," she said, her voice weak with tears. She had to get out of there before she made a complete fool of herself.

"Don't give him the pleasure of seeing you run away," Liam said in a low angry voice. He looked down at her, his jaw locked. "Turn around and face him. Hold your head high. Then walk away. And whatever you do, do not shed a tear for him." The sheer force of his commands made her hold back her tears. She swallowed, forced her shoulders back and turned to face Brandon. She was surprised to see him looking toward her, anger on his face. She crossed her arms and glared at him before turning and leaving the lunchroom. Her legs felt like they would give out on her at any moment.

"Talya," she heard Liam's voice behind her, but she didn't stop. She just kept walking. She was angry, hurt, and confused. She just wanted to go home. She knew she was a coward, but she just couldn't do this today. "Talya," she heard again, but she still didn't stop. A hand enclosed around her wrist, halting her. Liam turned her around, but she didn't meet his eyes.

"Please. I just want to go home," she whispered.

It was quiet for a moment. Talya was preparing to argue with him, but he surprised her. "Okay. Let me give you a ride home," he said. Talya was going to argue, but then she stopped herself. If he was offering, she might as well let him. She wouldn't have to wait for a bus that way. She wasn't sure if he would get in trouble for it later, since he was technically on staff but that was his problem.

"Thank you," Talya said, still not looking at him.

"Will you look at me?" he asked softly.

Talya finally met his eyes. He stared down at her, searching her gaze. She wasn't sure what for. "Please tell me you're not brokenhearted over this." He said it softly, but there was an edge to his voice.

Talya had no idea what to say. Her emotions were riding her hard. Was she sad Brandon had broken up with her? Not really. She had wanted out of the relationship almost since it started. But she was hurt in how it had ended. He had dumped her because she missed one game and then he chose someone else without even batting an eye.

"I see," Liam's voice broke into her thoughts. Talya looked up at him. She was going to say something, but she didn't know what to say. His face was void of emotion. "Come on. Let's get you home," he said. He started walking, and Talya assumed she was supposed to follow.

She followed him through the school. She stopped at the office to tell them she was heading home because she didn't feel good. Then she followed Liam outside. He led her to a car, a really nice, expensive car. She wasn't sure what it was, but she knew it was worth a lot of money. He opened her door for her and she slid into the seat. The interior was every bit as nice as she assumed it would be. It failed to excite her though. She stared out the window as Liam slid in behind the driver's seat and started the car.

It was quiet as they drove, and Talya was surprised when they pulled into her driveway. She didn't remember telling him where she lived but she must have and just forgotten about it. Before she could get out, Liam came around to her side and opened the door for her. She grabbed her bag and climbed out of the car. Turning to Liam, she said, "Thank you for the ride."

He looked down at her with a look Talya couldn't interpret. Then he nodded. Talya made her way up the stairs and into the house without looking back.

When she walked inside, she smelled tomato soup, and her stomach growled. A small smile lit her face. That meant Grandma was out of bed. Her grandma made the best homemade tomato soup. Paired with a grilled cheese sandwich, it was the perfect comfort food. Talya dropped her backpack on the couch and walked into the small kitchen. Her grandma turned from the pot she was stirring. "Talya? What are you doing home in the middle of the day? Do you feel okay?"

Talya couldn't help the smile that spread across her face. "Hey, Grandma, I'm okay. Just having a bad day. The school office said I could go home. How are you feeling? It's good to see you out of bed," Talya said as she walked over and wrapped her arms around her. She breathed in the scent of her grandma. It was the smell of comfort, of home. She couldn't help it when a few tears leaked out. She stood up and wiped her eyes quickly before her grandma saw.

"What happened?" Grandma asked, her sharp gaze missing nothing. Talya swallowed. Suddenly, she couldn't hold back the tears. She shook her head, and nothing came out. "Oh, honey, what happened?" Grandma asked.

Talya put her hands over her face as tears streamed down her face. She felt her grandma lead her to the small kitchen table. She sat down and continued to cry. She heard the back door open. "What's happened?" she heard her Grandpop's voice ask.

"I don't know," Grandma said as she rubbed Talya's back. "She hasn't said." Talya tried to stop the tears, so she could tell them she was okay.

"It's okay," she finally managed to get out. "I just had a really bad day at school," she said with a sniffle.

"Was it that boy?" Grandpop asked gruffly.

Talya sighed. There was no getting around this. She was just going to have to tell them. Before she could say anything, she heard a knock on the front door. Grandpop went to answer it. He returned a moment later with Sage trailing behind him. Talya looked at her in surprise. "What are you doing here?" she asked tearfully.

"Did you think I was going to let my best friend suffer all alone?" she asked.

The tears came back again. Talya stood up and hugged Sage. "Aren't you sick?" she asked. Sage just shrugged. "Nothing I won't live through," she said. Her voice was scratchy and her face was a little flushed. Talya felt bad she was here but so thankful.

"Would you like some soup, Sage?" Grandma asked.

"Ooo, yes please," Sage said. She knew how good Grandma's soup was. A few minutes later, all four of them were sitting around the table with steaming bowls of tomato soup and grilled cheese sandwiches.

"So, are you going to tell us what happened?" Grandpop finally broke the silence.

Talya sighed. "It's really not that big a deal; I'm just tired today," she said. When they all three just continued to stare at her, Talya finally gave in. "I had to work on Friday night, and I missed Brandon's game. He ignored my calls and texts all weekend. Then he ignored me after class today. When I got to the lunchroom today…" she took a shuddering breath. She looked at Sage. "He had Stephanie on his lap and was kissing her. Then he stood up and announced he's taking her to Prom," she said, utterly defeated.

"I'm so sorry, Talya," Sage said softly. "I'm so sorry I wasn't there."

"It's okay," Talya said. She looked at her Grandparents. They were quiet. Grandma looked sad, and Grandpop just looked angry. Talya sighed. "It's dumb. I wanted out of the relationship anyway; I don't know why I'm so sad about it."

"Because he's a jerk," Sage mumbled.

Talya couldn't disagree with her. She looked at Sage. "How did you know to come here?" she asked, confused.

"Liam called me and said he just dropped you off at your house. He said that you'd had a really bad day and probably needed a friend about now," she said.

Talya stared at her. "Really?" she asked. Sage nodded. "How did he get your number?" she asked.

Sage shrugged. "He's a teacher now; he probably has access to phone numbers."

"I can't believe he did that," she said softly.

"Who's Liam?" Grandma asked curiously, looking back and forth between the two girls.

Sage looked pointedly at Talya, but Talya didn't really know what to say. "He's a guy," Talya started.

"You don't say," Grandpop said.

Everybody chuckled. "He's an insanely gorgeous guy who is teaching self-defense at school, and he's totally into Talya," Sage said with a grin.

Talya felt her face heat up. "No, he's not." Sage shot her a disbelieving look. "Well, he's not."

Sage just shook her head. "Does he treat our Talya better than Brandon did?" Grandpop asked. Sage nodded. "Then I like him already." Grandma nodded her head in agreement with Grandpop's words.

Talya didn't have the heart to tell them he wasn't interested in her; he was just being kind.

Chapter Six

Talya's grandparents talked her into skipping school on Tuesday as well. She still worked her evening shifts; she didn't want to put Joe out. But she just wasn't ready to face everyone at school. By Wednesday, though, she knew she needed to face her fears and go to school. Grandpop drove her to school, and while it was slower than usual, it was a refreshing change. He dropped her off, and Talya started towards the building. A hand looped through her arm. Talya was never so grateful to see Sage.

"You ready for this?" Sage asked. Talya nodded. "I got your back," Sage said.

"Thank you," Talya said. She took a deep breath; she hated feeling this way. She wanted to feel confident again, but she feared it might take a long time for her to get back to that. She walked inside the building. When she got into the main hallway, she felt like everybody was staring at her. Maybe they were; she didn't look up to confirm whether it was true or not. She stopped at her locker and got what she needed before heading to first hour. When she got to the classroom, she froze. Brandon stood in the hallway next to the door with his arms wrapped around Stephanie. She felt Sage push her, and she allowed her stiff legs to carry her into the classroom. She was grateful to sink into her seat. Sage slid into the seat next to her. "Game face," she whispered.

Talya took a deep breath and pushed the emotions away. She would ponder them when she was alone. Right now, she needed to focus on making it through the next class without doing something stupid like crying or throwing something at Brandon. She wasn't exactly sure where she would land at any given moment with her fluctuating emotions.

Finally, first period ended, and Talya escaped the room quickly. The next three hours dragged before it was finally time for lunch. Talya was dreading lunch; she wanted to skip it, but Sage wouldn't let her. "Come on. You can do this. The first day will be the worst," Sage said. With her prompting, Talya made it into the lunchroom. Her eyes were drawn right to Brandon and Stephanie, but she quickly looked away. She could do this. She made herself focus on getting food. Then she and Sage found a table to sit as far away as possible from Brandon and Stephanie. Talya managed to get a few bites of her salad down. The rest of the time, she used to study for a quiz she had next hour. The next two classes dragged on; then it was time for the last period of the day—gym class. Talya was not in the mood, but she had no way of getting out of it. Besides, she didn't want to leave Sage hanging. She quickly changed and made her way into the gym. Her eyes immediately sought out Liam, but she quickly looked away when her eyes met his.

Coach made them run laps to get started. Then they moved towards the center where Liam was to teach them what they would be working on today. Before Liam could say anything, Coach started talking. "You have been doing a good job practicing on each other, but in the real world, your attacker isn't going to be somebody who has practiced with you and knows what to do. So today, you're going to be practicing with people who don't know what you've been working on. I've asked the football team to join us for today. They will be excellent practice."

Talya closed her eyes in dismay; she heard Sage make an angry noise next to her. Talya focused on taking deep breaths. She wouldn't let it bother her. She wouldn't show Brandon how much he had hurt her. She didn't glance at the door as the football team came strolling in. Soon, the entire football team had infiltrated their group. Talya worked on keeping her breathing calm. Coach Stanley addressed the team. "Boys, I've already told you what your job is today. You are going to be the bad guy in today's practice session. When I call your name, yell out the name of the person you would like to work with. If you don't have a preference, I'll assign you." He started calling names, and Talya's palms started sweating.

She closed her eyes when she heard, "Brandon."

"Talya," was his immediate response. Talya squeezed her eyes tighter, she immediately heard the whispering and giggling. Talya tried to remember to keep breathing. When she finally opened her eyes, Liam was in her eyesight; and he looked angry. Once everyone had been assigned a partner, Coach turned it over to Liam.

"All right. You know what to do. Do what you've practiced and you'll be fine," Liam said to the class.

Talya tried to find comfort in his words, but she couldn't. Liam blew the whistle and Talya knew she was officially out of time. It was time to face her fears. She took a deep breath and turned around. Brandon was standing not two feet from her. His arms were crossed and he was watching her with a cocky smile on his face. Talya walked towards him. She wished she could wipe that smile right off his face. "You ready for this?" Brandon asked her. Talya didn't trust her voice to work. So, she nodded instead. She turned around and faced away from him as he came up behind her. Before she could prepare herself for it, he grabbed her from behind and held her impossibly tight against his chest. "Try to get out of this," he whispered in her ear. His hold on her was so tight, it was causing her pain. She knew she would have bruises on her arms.

"You're hurting me," she said softly. She saw out of the corner of her eye that Liam's head whipped around to face her. She didn't know why. It wasn't possible he could have heard her soft words that far away.

"Then get out of the hold," Brandon sneered at her.

Talya's anger kept her from freezing up like she had the day Liam had grabbed her. For that, she was incredibly grateful. She began executing the steps she had practiced over and over, but no matter how hard she tried, she couldn't get his arms to budge. "Are you even trying?" he taunted in her ear. "Want to know what I did last night?" he whispered. Talya didn't. She tuned out his words. "Stephanie was more than eager to come into my bed, unlike somebody else I used to date." Talya ignored the jab. She just wanted this to be over with. She felt her willpower not to cry starting to give way. If she didn't get away from him soon, she was going to cry and that would just humiliate her even more. She blinked furiously. She was angry at him and angry at herself for ever getting into this situation in the first place. She tried again to get away from him, but he just tightened his hold on her. Suddenly, the whistle blew.

"Everybody gather around," Liam's voice commanded. His voice held an authoritative ring to it that nobody wanted to defy. Brandon was slow to drop his arms, but he finally did. Talya moved away from him quickly, rubbing her arms as she did. When she joined the others, she was near the back. "Talya and Brandon up front," Liam barked out. Talya startled. She wasn't used to that kind of voice from him. She moved forward without even thinking about it. Brandon came and stood next to her with a smug look on his face. Liam turned to glance at her. She saw his eyes drop to her arms. When his eyes met hers, they were darker than usual. Talya swallowed. He was furious. She could feel the fury rolling off him in waves. "Talya, were you able to break Brandon's hold on you?" he asked her in front of everyone.

Talya saw Brandon's smug smirk. "N-no," she got out, hating the catch in her voice.

Liam faced the class. "Talya is facing what some of you will face in real life. She's tiny, and Brandon's a big guy. She can't overpower him, so what does she do? What do you do when what you know to do doesn't work? I am going to be Talya, so

I can show you what to do. Brandon, go ahead and grab me the way you did Talya," he said. Talya glanced at Liam before looking at Brandon. She saw just the slightest hesitation on Brandon's face before his cocky smile took over. He swaggered towards Liam and wrapped his arms around his chest. He was a few inches shorter, so it made for an awkward hold. "Tighter," Liam said. Brandon made his hold even tighter. "Now," Liam said, addressing the class. "What do you do when what you know to do doesn't work? Improvise," he said. Not even a second later, Liam rammed his elbow into Brandon's stomach, hard before slamming the back of his hand behind him into Brandon's nose. Without missing a beat, he spun, grabbed Brandon's arm, yanking it upwards while he shoved Brandon to the ground, wrenching his arm painfully behind him. Liam bent over Brandon and looked at the class. He hadn't even broken a sweat, nor was he breathing hard. "See? You improvise." The class burst into applause, while the football team stared in shock at their quarterback who was currently shrieking on the floor.

"You broke my nose!" Brandon yelled. Liam pushed him back to the ground one more time as he stood up. As soon as he moved away from Brandon, Brandon was on his feet shouting obscenities at Liam. Liam just crossed his arms and watched him. Coach Stanley came over and stood next to Brandon.

"That's enough, Brandon. Trevor and Mitch, get him to the school nurse," he said cocking his head towards the door. Brandon's friends came along either side of Brandon. Brandon cussed one more time at Liam before walking away.

Talya was close enough to hear Coach say quietly to Liam.

"You better be glad football season is over." He moved away from Liam after his threat. He blew his whistle. "Class dismissed."

Talya was still standing there a few minutes later when everybody disappeared. "Are you okay?" Liam asked in a rough voice. Talya glanced up at him.

"Yeah." She wasn't sure what to say to him.

Liam motioned her towards the door. She turned around, looking for Sage. She found her standing right behind her. Talya started walking with Sage on one side and Liam on the other. Before they left the gym, Talya stopped. "Thank you," she said simply. He nodded in response. Talya frowned at him. "You shouldn't have done that, though."

"Why not?" Liam asked.

"Because you made him angry, really really angry; and believe me, that's not a good position to be in," she said with a shudder.

Liam stepped closer. "Does he hurt you when he's angry?" he asked in a low voice.

Talya ignored the question. "Just be careful, and watch your back. He'll be out for blood," she said.

"I'm not worried about him," Liam said.

Talya frowned. "Well, you should be."

Liam scoffed. "Brandon can't hurt me; I'm just worried he might retaliate against you. You tell me if he threatens you," Liam said with anger in his voice. Talya found herself nodding, just to appease him. "You'd better get changed and get to work," he said quietly.

That startled Talya out of whatever state she was in. "Yeah. Well, thanks again. I will say, it was fun to watch you break Brandon's nose like that."

Liam smiled a slow smile that made her stomach tighten in response. "Good," he said. Then he turned and walked away. Talya held in the sigh she wanted to make. She needed to get to work.

Chapter Seven

Thankfully, the diner was busy; so Talya didn't have to think about her life. She just had to focus on doing a good job. "Somebody just sat in your section, Talya," Jenny, one of the other waitresses said. "I must say, he is yummy." Talya just grinned; Jenny was forever checking out the males that came in. She shook her head and made her way to her section. Liam looked up when he saw her coming and smiled at her. Talya ignored the butterflies that erupted in her stomach.

"Liam, what are you doing here?" she asked, stopping at his table.

"Eating," he said with a grin.

Talya couldn't help but smile back. "What can I get for you?"

"I'll take a coffee and a water, and a double portion of meatloaf, a baked potato, and broccoli," he said.

Talya blinked and looked at him. "You want two portions of the meatloaf? One serving is pretty big," she said.

Liam grinned. "Yes."

Talya shrugged and wrote down his order. "I'll go put that in and get your drinks," she said. She moved away from his table. After she placed his order, she grabbed his coffee and water. "Here you go. Coffee and water. Do you want any cream or sweetener?"

"Just cream. Thanks," he said.

"Okay, let me know if you need anything else." With that, she left him and made her rounds at her other tables. Talya felt bad she did little more than deliver Liam's food and check on him once or twice before he finished, but she was just too busy. "Here's your receipt," she said as she handed it to him. She glanced down at the two plates she had brought him. "I would ask how was your meal, but I think the answer is pretty obvious," she said, gesturing to the two empty plates in front of him. He laughed, causing Talya to smile. He had a great laugh.

"It was good," he said with a smile. "I don't get a lot of home-cooked meals. This meatloaf was great; reminded me of my mom's meatloaf," he said with a smile.

"Do you not cook?" Talya asked.

He chuckled. "No, I definitely don't cook."

"Do you live by yourself?" she asked. "You don't have to answer that. That's not any of my business," she rushed to say.

Liam smiled easily at her. "I don't mind you asking. Yes, I live by myself, right now, anyway."

His answer was kind of cryptic, but Talya moved on. "If you would ever be interested, my grandma loves cooking for people. You should come over some time. She makes really good, home-made meals."

Liam looked at her for a moment, and Talya panicked. "I mean, you don't have to if you don't want to."

"I'd love to," Liam said, interrupting her.

"It's a date then," Talya said and then immediately regretted it. "I mean, not a date. It's not a date, date. It's just a..."

Liam stood up, towering over her. "It's a date," he said with a smile before walking up front to pay the bill. Talya watched him go for a moment, trying to catch her breath. She watched him pay his bill and then saunter out the door. Only when he was gone did she glance down at the table. Her eyes widened when she saw the hundred-dollar bill on the table. She snatched it up and ran after Liam. She ran outside, scanning the parking lot. She saw his tall figure and called out to him.

"Liam." He turned instantly towards her and began walking towards her.

"What's wrong?" he asked, intensely.

"Oh," Talya said, pulling back a bit. "Nothing's wrong, just you left this on the table," she said, handing the hundred back towards him.

He looked down at it then back at her, his eye brows pinching in confusion. "It's for you. It's your tip," he said.

Talya looked at him shocked. "It's a hundred-dollar bill," she said, stating the obvious.

He grinned down at her. "Yes, I know. I'm the one that left it."

"You can't leave a hundred-dollar tip," she said to him. "I didn't even hardly get a chance to serve you," she said. Then she frowned. "That sounded weird."

Liam laughed out loud. "Keep it. It's yours. You earned it," he said.

Talya frowned. "Well, only if you're sure," she said.

"I'm sure," Liam said.

Talya folded the hundred and put it in her apron pocket. "Thank you," she said.

"You're welcome. Come on, I'll walk you back inside," he said nodding towards the diner.

"Oh, you don't have to do that. I'm fine," Talya said.

"I want to," Liam said. He started walking, and Talya took a few steps to catch up to him. They walked back to the restaurant in silence. Liam held the door for her as she stepped in.

"Thanks, Liam," Talya said.

He smiled down at her. "You're welcome, Talya."

Talya smiled and walked back into the restaurant. The rest of the night was just as busy, but Talya didn't mind. It made the night pass quickly. When she finally clocked out for the night, she was ready to get home and get to bed. "Night, Joe," she called out.

Talya left the diner and began the walk towards the bus stop. When she got close to the stop, she noticed a guy waiting there already. Talya didn't pay him any attention. She put her headphones in and sat on the bench to wait for the bus. She noticed the guy move in front of her. She looked up and saw he was talking to her. She quickly pulled out her headphones. "I'm sorry. What did you say?" she asked.

"I just asked what time it was?" he asked.

"Oh, it's 11:15," Talya said. She moved to put her headphones back in, but the man talked to her again.

"What's a pretty young thing like you doing out so late alone?" he asked.

Talya looked up at him, trying to read him. The question seemed innocent enough. "I just finished my shift at work," she said with a smile.

"Work. Got it. Where do you work?" he asked.

Talya's smile dropped a little bit. "Not far from here," she said vaguely.

"You going home now?" he asked.

Talya just nodded. She looked around for the bus, willing it to get here soon. She went to put her headphones back in, but the man stopped her again. "I've seen you here before waiting for the bus. You ride it often late at night," he said. Talya didn't answer this time. She was starting to get creeped out. "You know, I have my car not far from here. I could just take you home; you wouldn't have to wait for the bus," he said.

It was official. Talya was really starting to freak out now. "I think I'll just wait for the bus. Thank you," she said politely but with an edge to it.

"Come on," he said. He put his hand on her arm. "Just come with me. It will be fast; you won't have to wait for the bus."

Talya stood up and took a step back. "No. I'm waiting for the bus," she said emphatically.

The man took another step towards her and Talya stepped backwards, right into a hard chest. "Hey baby, I was looking for you," she heard Liam's voice behind her. He slipped an arm around her waist and pulled her against his frame. "Come on, I'll take you home." Talya nodded blindly. Her heart was racing.

She watched the man in front of her scowl at Liam, but he wisely didn't say anything. Liam turned her so she was against his side. He wrapped an arm around her shoulders and began leading her away from the bus stop. They walked down the block a little bit and around a corner. She spotted Liam's car running, and relief flooded her.

Liam didn't say a word as he led her to his car. He opened the door and helped her in. He squatted next to her. "Are you okay?" he asked gently. Talya just nodded. She was still trying to calm her heart rate down. "I'll be right back. Lock the doors behind me," he said as he stood up.

"Wh-where are you going?" Talya asked.

Liam looked down at her. "I just have to deal with something. I'll be right back." There was no warmth in his gaze now.

There was no mistaking his intentions. "No, please," Talya said, reaching out to grab his hand. "Please, don't leave me. I just want to go home," she said.

Liam looked down at her for a moment before nodding. He carefully closed the door behind her and made his way around the front of the car. He slid in behind the wheel. Without saying a word, he put the car in drive and began driving. He turned around so they didn't have to drive on the street where the bus stop was. Liam reached out and took her hand in his. "You're okay, Talya. I won't let anything happen to you," he said. Talya glanced at him. He said the words with such confidence, she couldn't help but believe him. The trip home didn't take long, but by the time they got there, Talya had already begun to relax.

Talya turned to him. "How did you happen to be there?" she

asked, puzzled.

Liam shrugged. "Just happened to be at the right place at the right time."

"Well, thank you. I really appreciate it, and thank you for the ride." She reached out to open the door but Liam stopped her.

"Talya, I don't want you taking the bus home anymore this late at night. It's not safe for a beautiful girl like you," Liam said seriously.

Talya ignored the part of her that lit up hearing Liam call her beautiful. "I have to. It's my means of transportation."

"Not anymore it isn't," Liam said. "I'll pick you up and take you home each night. Give me your cell phone. I'll put my number in it," he said, putting his hand out.

Talya just stared at him. "You can't take me home every night," she said.

"Why not?" he asked.

"Well, because I'm sure you have more important things to do in life than play chauffeur for me," Talya said.

"This is something I want to do," Liam said. "Come on; give me your phone."

Talya watched him a moment longer before finally handing her phone to him. She watched him put his number in before handing it back to her. She looked down at it and laughed. "My sexy hero? Really?"

Liam just grinned at her. "If I'm going to be your knight in shining armor and save you from the bad guys, I gotta have a cool name," he said.

"And *My Sexy Hero* is what you came up with?" Talya asked,

incredulously.

Liam grinned again. "It's all I could think of in the heat of the moment."

Talya laughed at that. "Fine, My Sexy Hero. Thank you for bringing me home." She put her phone back in her pocket.

Liam nodded. "You're welcome."

"Try not to break any more noses, okay?" she said with a grin.

"Can't promise that," Liam said, matching her grin.

Talya laughed and climbed out of the car. She walked into the quiet house with a smile still etched on her face. It felt good to smile. Only Liam could make her laugh only a few minutes after she had been terrified. Talya shook her head. *That man.*

Chapter Eight

Surprisingly, it didn't take her long to fall asleep.

Talya walked through a field. The grass was as high as her waist in some areas, but it didn't impede her as she walked. Her eyes caught on all the wildflowers that appeared in all the colors of the rainbow. It was a beautiful sight. There was something so peaceful about the sight, Talya felt herself completely relax. She came to a huge tree. She decided to sit beneath it and rest in its shade for a few minutes. Her eyes were drawn to the creek that flowed nearby. She imagined taking off her shoes and socks and dipping her feet in the clear water. Maybe another day. Right now, she was content to just sit in the shade of this magnificent tree. Talya closed her eyes and rested her head against the tree.

Sometime later, she heard a sound. Opening her eyes, she startled to see a wolf not even a few feet from her. Before she could panic, a feeling of safety and warmth hit her. She peered at the wolf, not feeling threatened by it. "That's because there is nothing to fear from me," she heard a voice say. The voice was different. It was almost ethereal somehow. She looked around to see who had talked, but she saw no one. She looked back at the wolf. He moved closer to her; then sat on his haunches in front of her.

"Talya," she heard the voice say again. Talya looked at the wolf. Surely the voice wasn't coming from the wolf was it?

Talya stared at the wolf. "Are you talking to me?" she asked, feeling stupid for even asking the question.

"I am communicating with you," she heard. The wolf didn't move. His mouth didn't move, yet she heard its voice. Cleary she was losing her mind.

"The mind is a fragile thing. It only exists in one dimension. Yet there are other dimensions in which it can exist if one only but opens themselves to the possibility."

Talya didn't respond. She was trying to understand what in the world was going on. She didn't feel threatened by the wolf, but she definitely didn't feel as relaxed as she had a few minutes ago.

"Relax, and let your mind accept the possibilities," the wolf said.

"What possibilities?" Talya asked, confused.

"The ones that are coming," the wolf said vaguely. Then the wolf stood and walked away, vanishing completely from sight. Talya stared after it, bewildered.

Talya sat up, wiping the sleep from her eyes. "Okay, that was the strangest dream ever," she muttered to herself as she dragged herself out of bed.

After getting dressed in black leggings and a button-down denim shirt, she left her room and made her way into the kitchen. "Good morning, Grandma," she said with a smile.

"Hi, my sweet angel. Did you sleep well?" she asked.

"Mmm," came Talya's noncommittal response. She was still

mulling over her weird dream. "Hey Grandma?" Talya asked, the thought just coming to her mind. "Would it be okay if I brought a friend over for lunch on Saturday before my shift at the diner? He lives by himself and doesn't get home-cooked meals often."

"Of course. Bring him over," Grandma said. "Is he that man you told us about?" Talya nodded. "We'd love to meet him."

"Great! Thanks," Talya said. She bent and kissed her grandma's cheek. "I gotta run. Love you."

"Love you too, Talya," Grandma said.

Talya went out into the living room where Grandpop sat in his chair. "Love you, Grandpop."

"Love you, Tally-bear," he said, using an affectionate nickname he often used when she was growing up.

Talya smiled as she walked to the front door. She opened the door and was shocked to see Liam leaning against his car in the driveway. She shut the door behind her. "Liam, what are you doing here?" she asked.

He straightened. "I'm here to drive you to school," he said as if that was the most normal thing in the world.

"But why?" she asked.

Liam gave a small laugh. "You're a smart girl; you'll figure it out," he said. Then he walked around and opened her door for her. He pulled her backpack from her shoulders and threw it in the back seat. After shutting her door for her, he walked around the front of the car and slid in. Talya was still trying to figure out his cryptic comment.

"Thank you again for last night. I don't know what would have happened if you hadn't shown up when you did," Talya said with a shudder.

"I'm glad you're safe," was all he said.

It was quiet for a few minutes. "I had the weirdest dream last night," she said with a laugh, trying to make conversation.

"Yeah? What was it?" he asked with a smile.

"It was so weird. I was dreaming that I was in this beautiful place with tall grass and wildflowers. There was a creek and a huge tree. I sat down under the tree and closed my eyes. When I opened them, there was a wolf sitting in front of me," she said. Liam turned his head to look at her, but he quickly turned his focus back to the road. "Then I heard this voice; I couldn't tell where it was coming from. There was something so real about it," Talya said absently. Then she laughed. "Anyway, I told you it was a weird dream."

When Liam didn't say anything, she glanced over at him. He was frowning. "What did the wolf say?" he asked.

"What?" Talya asked.

"In your dream, what did the wolf say?" he asked again.

"Oh." Talya racked her brain for a moment. "I can't really remember. Something about how our minds are one-dimensional, but they're really not. Or something. I don't really remember." Talya glanced at Liam one more time, but he seemed lost in thought. She was content to just relax and look out the window. All too soon, they pulled into the school parking lot. Liam pulled right up to the curb. "Thank you so much for the ride. I'll see you tomorrow in class," she said with a smile.

"I'll pick you up after school and drop you off at work," he corrected her.

"You don't have to do that, Liam. I don't mind taking the bus," she started but Liam was already shaking his head.

"Not after last night. I'm taking you. I'll be here at 3," he said with finality.

"Okay," Talya said, not knowing what else to say. "Have a good day, then," she said.

His face softened, and he looked at her. "You too. I'll see you after school."

Talya smiled and shut the door and began walking towards the front doors. "Okay what did I miss?" Sage asked as she appeared out of nowhere next to Talya.

"You scared me," Talya said with her hand over her heart.

"Sorry, I didn't want to interrupt your private time," she said with a grin.

"Oh stop," Talya said.

"No seriously, what's going on with you two? He picked you up for school?" Sage asked.

"I had a bad experience last night. Liam rescued me and took me home. Because of that, he won't let me ride the bus anymore," Talya explained.

"What happened? Are you okay?" Sage asked. Talya filled her in on the events of last night as they walked towards their lockers, then first period. "Wow. That's scary. I'm so glad you're okay, and I'm so glad Liam was there to help you." Talya nodded. "That's kind of weird, though, isn't it?" Sage asked.

"Which part?" Talya asked.

"Well, the fact that Liam just appeared out of nowhere to save you. I mean, like what was he doing out and about at that time of night?" Sage asked.

"Well, he had eaten at the diner earlier in the evening. Maybe, he was just still in the area," Talya suggested.

"Or maybe, he hung out until you got done at work to make sure you got home okay," Sage reciprocated.

Talya laughed. "I don't think so. I think he just happened to be in the area."

Sage shrugged. "Maybe," she said skeptically.

Neither of them said anything more about it as they made their way to first period. When they got to the room, she saw Brandon and Stephanie again. Talya rolled her eyes and walked past them into the classroom. When they sat down, Sage looked over at her and grinned. "What?" Talya asked.

Sage leaned close and whispered, "You walked right past them without being hurt. You're getting over him, just like I knew you would."

Talya smiled. "Yeah, I guess."

"Of course, it helps that you're hanging out with Mr. Sexy himself," Sage continued in a whisper. Talya just gave her a small smile. "You like him, don't you?" Sage pushed.

Talya didn't say anything, but she couldn't keep the smile from her face. Her smile stayed on her face for the next few hours until lunch. Then everything went off the rails.

Talya was just about to walk into the lunchroom to meet Sage when Brandon, Mitch, and Trevor stepped in front of her. Talya looked up at Brandon and saw his black and blue nose. A small smile appeared on her lips. "What are you smiling at?" Brandon asked as he stepped into her personal space.

Talya immediately wiped the smile off her face. "Nothing," she said.

"You think this is funny? You think it's funny that idiot broke my nose?" Brandon asked, getting in her face now.

"No, I'm sorry your nose got broken, but I'm not sorry he put you in your place," Talya said, standing tall. "You were being a real jerk to me. He saw it and did something about it." She was tired of not standing up for herself and Brandon walking all over her. She was done with it.

Brandon glanced around the hallway and stepped even closer to her. She tried to back up, but she realized Trevor had gone to stand behind her, blocking her exit. She crossed her arms and looked up at Brandon. "He's not around now to rescue you, is he?" Brandon said in a low voice.

"I don't need him to rescue me," Talya said. "I can take care of myself." She was done being the victim to this guy. She had spent almost three years of her life giving in to him. No more.

Brandon stepped forward. "Can you?" He grabbed her arms and spun her around, trying to grab ahold of her like he had in class. Talya wasn't going to let that happen. She fought with him. "What is wrong with you?" she yelled at him. Fury erupted through her. Without even thinking, she kneed him as hard as she could in his groin area. He kneeled in front of her, gasping for her. She didn't stop there. She kneed him in the face, hitting his broken nose. He screamed in pain, and blood sprayed everywhere.

Trevor grabbed Talya from behind. Talya lost it. She was done taking hits from these guys. She turned on Trevor. She punched him in the face. She wasn't counting on him to shake it off, though. He came at her in a rage a moment later. He punched her, and Talya's head snapped back. She saw stars and stumbled backwards. She heard shouts and yelling. Suddenly, she was being pulled backwards. "What is the meaning of this?" she heard the principal yell.

"Talya attacked us," Brandon said. "We were on our way to lunch minding our own business. She did this to me," he said, showing his bloody nose to the principal.

"Is that true?" he asked in an angry voice.

"No, they..." Talya started.

"Did you do that to his nose?" he asked.

"Well, yes, but..." Talya didn't get to finish.

"My office. Now." He motioned her in front of him. Talya looked around for Sage but didn't see her in the crowd of people that had gathered. It was just as well. She didn't want her dragged into this. It was only as they were walking that Talya finally noticed she was dripping blood on her shirt and that it was destroyed. Several of the buttons were gone. She held the shirt together with one hand and reached up with her other hand to feel her cheek. She winced when she felt the cut. Trevor must have split her skin when he hit her. She hadn't felt anything in the rush of fighting, but now that it was done, she was definitely starting to feel it.

When she got to the principal's office, he held out a phone to her. "Call your parents for a ride. You're expelled for three days."

Talya looked up, shocked. "But I didn't..."

"Would you like it to be a week?" he asked.

"No sir," Talya said, dejected. She didn't bother telling him she didn't have parents to call. Luckily, she was good with numbers and had already memorized Liam's number. Hopefully, he would come pick her up. She dialed his number, hoping he would answer.

Chapter Nine

"Hey Talya," he answered. His warm voice instantly brought tears to her eyes.

"Hey, um Mom?" Talya said, trying not to cry and hoping Liam would play along.

"Talya?" he asked, sounding confused.

"Can you come pick me up?" she asked, trying not to cry.

"Talya, what's going on?" he asked.

"I got into trouble and the principal told me to call my parents to come pick me up. So, can you come pick me up?" she asked.

"Of course, but tell me what's happening first. Are you okay?" he asked. It sounded like he was moving.

"Yeah, just please come," she said, her voice breaking on the last word.

"Talya, what's going on? You're scaring me," he said, sounding desperate.

"I, I," she couldn't get the words out; a sob got caught in her throat.

"I'm on my way. I'll be there soon," he promised.

Talya didn't wait to see if he said anything more. She hung up the phone and gave it back to the principal. She needed to get out of his office, so he didn't know it was Liam that was picking her up. She wasn't sure if he would allow that or not, and she didn't want to take any chances. "She's on her way. I'm going to grab my backpack and meet her up front."

"No, you're not. You don't need your backpack. That's the whole point of expulsion. You get zeros in every class and every assignment, so don't bother with your backpack." He looked at her with his hands on his hips. "We have a strict no-fighting policy, and you just violated it. You're lucky you don't get kicked out. Push me, and we can make that happen," he said.

Talya pushed back the tears. "Yes, Sir. I'm sorry. It won't happen again." With that, she turned on wooden legs and walked out the door. She walked out right as the bell rang signifying the end of lunch. Talya felt mortified as she walked through the throngs of people holding her blouse closed, dripping blood. She kept her face tipped forward, trying to hide her face with her hair. She finally made it outside and sat on the concrete steps, waiting for Liam. She only waited a few minutes before his car came flying into the parking lot. Talya put her head down and waited for him to come to her. She didn't think her legs would carry her to the car.

Liam knelt in front of her. He gently pushed her hair back. He didn't say a word for a moment. Talya couldn't look at him; she was so humiliated. "Who did this to you?" Liam asked in a gravelly voice that didn't sound like him at all.

"Can you just take me home?" Talya asked.

"Talya, look at me," he commanded. Talya lifted her gaze to his. She shrank in fear at the anger she saw in his eyes. "I'm going to ask one more time. Who did this to you?"

"Please," Talya's voice caught on a sob. "Please just take me home. Please," she begged him.

Liam put his hand around the back of her head and gently pulled her to him. "Okay. Shh, it's okay. I'll take you home." He stood up. In one smooth movement, he bent and picked her up, cradling her to his chest. The movement startled Talya, and she grabbed at her shirt, trying to keep it closed. Liam didn't look down, though. He kept his eyes straight ahead. He opened the car door and deposited her gently in the front seat. He bent over her and buckled her in. Then he closed her door and jogged around to the other side of the car. Talya looked out her window and tried to keep the tears at bay. She failed at keeping the tears away, and one dripped off her face on to her blouse. Liam glanced over at her and put his hand on her knee. It was a comforting gesture that Talya found she didn't mind. "Talya, if you want to go home, I'll take you home. But I don't know if you're ready to face your grandparents. I thought maybe I could take you to my house until you're cleaned up and feel like you can face your grandparents. "

Talya looked down at her shirt that was torn and now had blood all over it and grimaced. "Yeah, that's probably a good idea," she said quietly. They drove a few more minutes. Soon Liam pulled into the driveway of a small house. He got out and came around to her side. He opened the door, reached in and unbuckled her, then pulled her into his arms and stood up. Talya didn't fight him. She just laid her head on his chest and let him carry her.

He carried her inside and took her right to the bathroom. He set her on the sink like she weighed nothing and looked her in the eye. "I've got a friend who's a doctor. I want to call him and have him look at your face to determine whether or not it needs stitches. It's still bleeding, and I'm worried it might. Is that okay?"

Talya nodded. She was starting to feel the after effects of everything that had happened. Her face was really hurting, her body ached, she felt sick to her stomach, and she had a massive headache building.

Liam face-timed his friend. "Liam, to what do I owe the privilege of this call?" a guy said.

"Hey Paul, I need you to look at Talya's face and tell me if you think she needs stitches," Liam said.

"Of course," the man said, now totally serious. "Let me look at it."

"Hang on just a second," Liam said. Talya watched in confusion as Liam put the phone down and in one smooth movement, tugged his shirt over his head. He put it over her head and pulled it down gently, being careful of her face. When he settled it around her, he picked up the phone. "Okay."

Talya was thankful for his thoughtfulness. She didn't have to worry about holding her shirt together anymore.

Liam turned the phone towards Talya. Talya looked at it and saw a good-looking man about Liam's age. "Hey Talya, I'm Paul, a friend of Liam's. I want to get a good look at your face, okay?" he said, sounding friendly and yet professional. Liam moved the phone around per Paul's request.

"That's a nasty cut, Talya," Paul said, still looking at her through the screen. "What happened?" he asked in a relaxed voice.

"I got punched," Talya said, unemotionally.

Neither man said a word. Liam just watched her. She wasn't sure if he was waiting for her to say more or what. "I don't think it will need stitches. Liam, if you properly dress it and keep it cleaned, I think it will be okay. Do you have all the supplies you need to do that?" Paul asked.

"Yeah," Liam responded. "Thanks, Paul. I appreciate it."

"Sure," Paul said easily. "Let me know if you need any more help. Be gentle," he said.

Liam nodded. "I'm trying," he said. "It's a lot harder than I thought it was going to be. Guess I should have been easier on Garrett," he said. Paul laughed. Then they both signed off. Talya felt like she had missed a lot in that conversation. "Give me just a second," Liam said. He disappeared for a moment and was back soon after wearing a shirt and carrying a first aid kit. Talya was grateful for the shirt. She didn't need the distraction.

Liam opened the box and pulled out some supplies. "Okay. This may hurt a little."

Talya groaned inwardly. Whenever someone said that, it meant it was going to hurt a lot. Liam dabbed at her cheek and Talya hissed. "Wow! You weren't kidding!"

"I'm sorry. I have to get it clean," Liam said apologetically. Finally, he finished cleaning it and started putting ointment on it and a bandage. "All right. That's the best we can do for now. Hopefully, it will heal naturally. I'm going to see if I have anything smaller you can wear. I'll be back in a minute." Talya closed her eyes while she waited for him. Her face was killing her. She just wanted to take some pain pills and lay down. Liam appeared a minute later with a shirt in one hand and a water bottle in another. He opened a pack of pain relievers and gave them to Talya. After popping open the cap on the water, he handed it to Talya. She took them gratefully.

"Thank you," she said.

"I think this shirt might fit a little better. It's the smallest thing I own; hopefully it will work. After you change, you can lay down and let those pain relievers kick in," Liam said. He left the bathroom and closed the door behind him.

Talya slowly worked at taking off Liam's shirt and removing her torn one. She took the other shirt Liam had given her and slipped it over her head. It was still big, but it would have to work. She rolled her shirt into a ball and threw it in the trash can since it was completely ruined. She picked up Liam's other shirt and left the bathroom in search of him. He met her in the hallway. "Here," she said, handing him his shirt.

"Do you want to lay down for a little bit and let your medicine start to work, or do you want me to take you home now?" he asked.

"I think I'll lay down for a little bit if that's okay. My head and face are killing me," she said. His face tightened, but he didn't say anything. He led her to the couch and moved the pillows around. Once she was laying down, he disappeared and came back with warm blanket. He put it on top of her. "Just rest, Talya," he said in a soothing voice.

"Please just wake me up at 3:00, so I don't miss work," she said. He didn't answer, but Talya knew he heard her. She lay down on the pillows, trying to get comfortable. Her head was pounding, and her face hurt something fierce. She tried to lay completely still and think peaceful thoughts so she could relax and fall asleep so her medicine could work. Her thoughts turned to the strange dream she had experienced this morning. A sense of peace overcame her, and she slowly drifted off to sleep.

Chapter Ten

Talya woke up sometime later, groggy and in pain. A quick glance told her it was not before 3:00. "No," she said. She stood up quickly and took a step or two forward before dizziness caused her to sway.

"Whoa," Liam's voice sounded. He grabbed her by the arms, steadying her.

"I'm supposed to be at work. Why didn't you wake me?" Talya accused.

"Talya, you're not going to work in the state you're in. I called your boss and let him know you were injured and wouldn't make it to work. He felt badly for you and said to take a few days off to rest up. Besides, you don't want to go to work with a bandage on your face, do you?" Liam asked.

"Well, no, but you should have let me decide," Talya said. She was feeling cranky and miserable.

"Are you hungry?" he asked, changing the subject. "I ran out and grabbed some soup from a restaurant nearby. I thought that might be easy to eat with your injury," he said.

"What time is it?" Talya asked, feeling disoriented.

"It's a little after 4:00," Liam said. He put his hand on her back and guided her to a small table. Talya sat while Liam grabbed a brown paper bag. He pulled out a container with a lid. "It's broccoli and cheddar. I thought that might be something you would like," he said, putting the container and a spoon in front of her. Then he pulled out a small baguette and handed it to her.

"You can have that; I won't eat it," Talya said absently. "Thanks for the soup. I love broccoli and cheese soup.

"Do you not like bread?" Liam asked as he grabbed another container of soup and pulled it out of the bag.

"Oh, I love bread. I just can't have it," Talya said as she blew on her spoon and took a small bite of the soup, being careful not to open her mouth too wide because it caused her cheek to hurt.

Liam sat down across from her. "Are you allergic?"

Talya looked at him in confusion. "To the soup?"

"No, the bread," Liam said motioning to the bread he was still holding.

"Oh, no I just can't eat carbs," Talya said.

"Why can't you eat carbs?" Liam asked.

Talya looked at him again. "Because look at me," she said.

Liam frowned at her. "I don't understand."

Talya rolled her eyes. "Look at me. Do I *look* like a person who should be eating carbs?"

Liam frowned even more. "I'm not following you at all."

Talya sighed. "Do I have to spell it out for you?"

"Apparently, yes," Liam said.

"I'm fat, Liam," Talya said bluntly.

Liam stared at her for a moment, then laughed. Talya put her spoon down and crossed her arms. Liam looked at her, and his smile instantly turned to a frown. "You're serious," he said. "You think you're fat?" he asked, incredulously.

"Well, I'm definitely not thin," Talya said.

Liam just stared at her. "Talya, you're not fat," Liam said emphatically.

"Right, I'm just curvy," Talya said using air quotation marks around curvy.

It was quiet for a moment. Talya sat back in her chair; she wasn't hungry anymore. "I think I'm going to just go," she said, pushing back from the table.

"Talya," Liam said.

"Thanks so much for taking care of me and for picking me up. I really appreciate it," Talya said, standing up from the table.

"Talya," Liam's voice sounded again, but Talya ignored him. She started to turn away, but Liam's voice stopped her.

"Talya!" he said with authority this time. Talya turned back to look at him. "Who told you you were fat?" he asked in a low voice.

"Liam, please stop. No one told me; I can look in a mirror," she said exasperated.

"Who told you?" he repeated the question.

"Liam, I..." she started.

"Who?" he demanded.

Talya fell back into her chair. "Brandon, okay? He always made me watch what I eat. He reminded me that I needed to watch my figure, especially since I was no longer a cheerleader. He reminded me all the time that I was fat. Okay? Do you feel better now?" Talya asked as she furiously wiped a tear from her eye.

"Is that why you never eat anything?" he asked, furious. Liam shoved his chair back from the table and walked over to the sink. He grabbed a hold of the sink and bent over it. She could see the muscles in his back and shoulders and arms bunching. She could tell he was furious. Talya sat in her seat because she didn't know what to do. "Liam?" she finally asked, unsure what was wrong. He bent his head and she heard him draw in a breath. Finally, he turned to face her.

Talya saw the anger in his eyes. "You have no idea how much I want to kill him," Liam said in a low, guttural voice. Talya's eyes widened. "Brandon?" she asked, incredulously. He nodded. Talya had no idea how to respond.

Liam took a few steps towards her. "Talya, you listen to me. You are *not* fat. Nobody in the world would call you fat. Do you have curves? Yes, and most men find that insanely attractive. You need to change your thinking and understand that you are not fat. Brandon is no longer a part of your life. You eat what you want to eat and eat until you're full. Do you understand?" he asked. Talya wanted him to calm down, so she nodded slowly. "Starting now."

Talya stared at him for a moment. She sat back down in her chair and picked up her spoon and took a bite. She was trying to just appease Liam, but when she tasted the soup again, she was reminded how good it was. She looked at the bread on the table.

"Eat the bread," Liam said in a gruff voice. Not wanting to make him any angrier, Talya picked up the bread and tore off a piece of it, dipping it in the soup.

She chewed it slowly, savoring it. "I haven't had bread in so long," she said. She took another piece of bread and dipped it. She ate that piece as well. "Oh, my word, that's so good." She looked up and saw Liam watching her carefully. "What?" she asked.

He leaned forward and brushed the corner of her lip with his thumb. "You had a little bit of soup there," he said quietly.

"Oh," Talya said, breathlessly. "Thank you." She looked down and focused on eating her soup. When she was full, she sat back. "That was so good. Thank you."

"You're welcome," he said.

"What kind did you get?" she asked.

"Beef stew," he replied.

Talya smiled. "Figures."

Liam looked at her. "How so?"

"You're a meat and potatoes kind of a guy, aren't you?" she said with a smile.

"Guilty as charged," Liam said. Talya noticed he was finally beginning to relax a little. Talya sat back in her chair, and the smile faded from her lips. "What am I going to do, Liam?" she asked softly. "I'm expelled for three days. I'm going to fail everything for the rest of the week. How do I explain this to my grandparents? They're going to be so disappointed in me. What if it throws off my GPA?" Talya asked.

"What happened?" Liam asked.

Talya looked at him but didn't say anything for a moment. Liam just waited. "I don't think I should tell you. You're just going to get angry again."

"I'm already angrier than you can possibly imagine, so just get it out," Liam said as he sat back and crossed his arms across his chest.

Talya sighed; he wasn't going to let this go. "I was walking to lunch and Brandon stopped me. I might have smiled a smidgen when I saw Brandon's nose," Talya said. "Well, as you can imagine that didn't go over too well. He said some stuff. I said some stuff. I kicked him in his groin and then kneed him in his nose. Well, of course, that started his nose bleeding again and he was screaming and wailing. The next I know, Trevor grabbed me from behind; so, I turned and punched him. He got angry about that, and gave me this," Talya said pointing to her face.

Liam sat absolutely still watching her. "So, Trevor gave you that?" he asked calmly. Talya studied him for a moment. He almost seemed too calm; it made him appear...dangerous, she finally decided. Talya nodded. "What did Brandon say to you?"

"Nothing," Talya said.

"Not a sufficient answer," Liam said.

"No seriously; he didn't say hardly anything. I did most of the talking," Talya said.

"Well, what did you say?" Liam asked.

"It doesn't matter," Talya said.

"Yes, it does. I need to know exactly what went down," Liam said.

"Why?" Talya asked.

"I just do. Now tell me exactly what you both said," Liam said in a tone that she didn't want to argue with.

"Fine," Talya said in exasperation. "He asked me if I thought it was funny that you broke his nose. I said no, but I thought that he deserved it and was glad somebody finally put him in his place for once. Then he said that you weren't around to protect me this time, and well…you know the rest of the story."

Liam shoved his chair back and stood up. Talya looked up and did a double take. His eyes looked different; they were lighter somehow. "There's one more thing I have to know, Talya," Liam said in a tight voice. "Why did you freeze when I put you in a hold in gym class?"

Talya felt dread build inside her. "I don't want to talk about that."

Liam stepped towards her. "There will only ever be the truth between us, Talya. And I need the truth," he said in a serious voice.

"I don't want to talk about it," Talya said, standing up and crossing her arms. "It's none of your business," she snapped at him.

"Your business *is* my business," Liam said, towering over her.

Talya scowled at him. "Trevor restrained me once for Brandon. Okay?"

"What did Brandon do to you?" Liam asked in such a low voice, Talya barely heard him.

"Nothing. I kneed him hard and told him if he ever tried something like that again I would tell his dad. He's terrified of his dad," Talya said by way of explanation. "Nothing happened;

but it terrified me for what could have happened," Talya said softly. "I guess when you restrained me, it brought back that memory and I panicked."

"I'm sorry that I did that," Liam said. Then he disappeared without another word. Talya sat at the table in silence wondering what was going to happen next. She didn't have to wait long. He came back a few minutes later. He walked over to the counter and grabbed his keys and phone. "Lock the door behind me. I'll be a few hours. When I get home, I'll take you to your grandparents."

"Wait, Liam. Stop," Talya said standing quickly and moving towards him. "What are you going to do?"

"My job," he said. Talya paused before saying anything. She took in what he was wearing for the first time. He was wearing black biker boots, black jeans, a black t-shirt, and a black leather jacket. He had gone from looking like and acting like the boy-next-door to...dangerous.

"I know what you're going to do," Talya said quietly, watching him.

Liam shook his head. "No, I don't think you do."

"Please don't do this," Talya said softly.

Liam shook his head. "I have to." He turned to walk away from her.

"Liam," she tried one last time.

Liam turned and strode over to stand right in front of her. "What Brandon doesn't understand is that I will always be around to protect you," he said in a dangerously low voice. "It's time he learned that." Without a word he turned and strode out the front door. Talya stared after him. After a few minutes, she finally made herself walk over and lock the front door. Then she walked on shaky legs back to the couch and sat down wearily. This was a mess. She had no idea what was going to happen tonight, but she knew it wasn't going to be good.

After sitting a little while longer, Talya finally decided to do something. The time wasn't going to pass if she just sat and watched the clock. She stood and made her way into the kitchen and picked up after their dinner. After that, she grabbed her phone and saw five messages and two missed calls from Sage.

She immediately dialed her number. Sage answered on the first ring. "I am so sorry," Talya said quickly before Sage could say anything. "I know I'm a horrible friend."

"Oh, you are right about that! I have been worried sick about you. I heard about what happened. I called and called, I went to your work, I even went to your grandparents' house," Sage vented.

"You didn't tell them what happened, did you?" Talya asked quickly.

"No, I made up some stupid excuse about needing a homework assignment from your room. What in the world, Talya? What happened? Where are you? Are you okay?" Sage fired off her questions.

"Okay, okay," Talya said. "First off, I'm at Liam's house."

It was quiet a moment before Sage said, "Tell me everything."

Chapter Eleven

Talya told Sage in detail everything that had happened since lunch. "I'm pretty sure Liam is going to kill them," Talya said, worried.

"No, he's not," Sage said calmly.

"Uh, you didn't see how he was dressed," Talya argued.

"I didn't say he might not break into their homes and beat them black and blue, but I'm pretty sure he won't kill them," Sage said confidently.

"Sage, that's not helping," Talya said nervously.

"Sorry," Sage said, but she sounded not the least bit repentant. "I can't believe you got expelled for three days," she commiserated. "These next three days are going to drag."

"I'm so sorry to ruin *your* life," Talya said sarcastically.

"You should be," Sage said teasingly.

"Seriously, though," Talya said. "You need to be careful these next few days. I don't know what's going to happen tonight, but stay away from those three at school. I wouldn't be surprised if they came after you to get back at me. Just watch your back, okay?" Talya said.

"I will," Sage promised. "How is your face?"

"It's definitely sore tonight, but I didn't need stitches. That's a plus. So hopefully it will heal in a few days," Talya said.

"Yeah. I'm glad you didn't have to go into work tonight. That would have been awful," Sage said. "I'm glad Liam called for you and got you out of it."

"Yeah. I wasn't at first, but now I'm really grateful. I can't imagine having to work all night," Talya said.

"What are you going to do for the next three days?" Sage asked.

"Well, if my face is healed enough that I don't look like Frankenstein, then I'll keep my hours at work. During the day I can see what Grandpa and Grandma need help with around the house. I never get a chance to do that normally."

"That would be nice," Sage said.

"Yeah," Talya agreed. "Well, I don't want to keep you from your homework. Thanks for checking on me. I'll see you in a few days."

"All right. Keep me in the loop, okay? Let me know what happens tonight," Sage requested.

"I will. Hopefully it's not that I have to go bail Liam out of jail," Talya said despondently.

"I don't think you can bail someone out of jail if they're there on murder charges," Sage said.

"Not helping," Talya muttered.

Sage laughed. "Okay, I'll let you go. Text me."

"I will," Talya said. "Bye." Talya hung up. "Now what?" she asked herself. She stood up and wandered into Liam's kitchen. He said he never gets home-cooked meals; maybe she could make one for him as a thank you for his help today. After looking in the cabinets and the fridge, though, that idea was out. Apparently, he really did eat out for all of his meals.

A few hours later, Talya was going absolutely insane with nothing to do. She couldn't focus on watching anything on Liam's TV because she was too nervous. She had none of her schoolwork, and she didn't feel like playing anything on her phone. "I'm officially going crazy," she muttered to herself. She glanced at the clock on the stove for the hundredth time in the last hour. It was after ten. She wanted to text Liam to see if he would be back soon, but if he really was hiding in Brandon's home, she didn't want to alert him to his presence. She sighed and flopped down on the couch again. She was growing more agitated by the moment, and the pain in her face wasn't helping. She finally decided to just lay down and rest. She propped up a few of the couch pillows she had slept on earlier and covered up with the blanket. She didn't think she would fall asleep because of her long nap, but she was wrong.

Talya found herself in the beautiful field again. This time, she took her shoes and socks off and waded in the clear creek. It was cold but invigorating. She laughed and splashed water around. She felt so carefree in this place. She caught a movement out of the corner of her eye and saw the wolf had returned. Talya climbed out of the water, grabbed her shoes and socks, and walked over to the tree. She settled at the base of the tree and just watched the wolf, wondering if he would say anything today.

Time passed, and Talya started getting impatient. She first started fidgeting with the blades of grass around her. Then she moved her feet around, unable to sit still. The entire time, she kept her eye on the wolf, waiting for him to speak. The wolf never moved. He just sat unnaturally still and watched her. It made Talya feel like she was back in grade school again under the watchful eye of her first-grade teacher.

"Okay, I can't be quiet anymore. Are you going to talk?" She finally asked. The wolf didn't move; he just continued to watch her. Talya finally gave up. She slipped her socks and shoes back on. "Well, it was good seeing you again," she said standing to her feet. She brushed off the dirt from sitting on the ground and was just about to walk away, when the wolf finally said something.

"It takes skill to be quiet, to sit still, to wait," the wolf said.

"Oh, good. I'm so glad you talked. I was beginning to think I'd made it all up," Talya babbled.

"Sometimes it takes a lifetime to acquire those skills, especially for humans," the wolf said.

Talya frowned and thought about it for a minute. "I guess wolves know how to be quiet and to sit still just by their very nature," Talya said, thinking out loud.

"It's in the stillness that you find strength," the wolf said.

"Riiight," Talya said, drawing out the word. She wasn't really sure how to apply that.

"You will need strength in the days to come," the wolf said. Then he turned and walked away, leaving Talya to stare after him, confused.

Talya sat up, breathing heavy. It took her just a moment to gather herself and remember where she was. She shook off the dream and glanced at the clock. It was 11:30. She wasn't sure when Liam would return. For all she knew, he could be out all night. She needed to get home and to bed. She quickly gathered her phone and purse. She unlocked the front door and walked out onto the front porch. She closed the door behind her and pulled up the map app on her phone. A bus stop was only two blocks away. She made her way down the steps and onto the driveway.

"Where are you going?" Talya gasped and spun around to see Liam approaching her from the side of the house. It was dark out but there was enough light from the moon to see that Liam was shirtless. She frowned at him, taking in his black sweat pants and bare feet. "Why are you out here?"

"Why are you sneaking around in the dark without clothes on?" Talya asked the first thing that had popped into her head.

Liam frowned and looked down. "I have pants on," he argued.

"Yeah, well that's all you have on," Talya said as she crossed her arms.

Liam shrugged it off. "Come on, let me just grab a shirt, and I'll take you home." He directed her towards the house. Talya was too tired to argue. He walked past her and disappeared for a moment. When he came back, he was wearing a t-shirt. "How is your face feeling?" he asked.

"It's sore," Talya said before letting out a huge yawn.

"Come on, let's get you home," he said gently. He put his hand on her lower back and led her out to the car. It was quiet as he began driving her home.

"Is Brandon still alive?" Talya finally asked softly.

Liam looked at her sharply. "Does it matter?" he asked gruffly.

"Of course, it matters," Talya responded.

"Why?" he asked.

Talya was exasperated. "Because I don't want to have to come bail your backside out of prison!"

"You sure that's the only reason?" he asked, his voice still gruff.

"What are you getting at, Liam?" she asked impatiently. She was tired and stressed from the day, and her face hurt.

It was quiet for a moment before Liam asked, "Do you still have feelings for him?"

Talya stared at Liam. "Seriously?" she asked. "Oh yes, I still have feelings for the guy who dumped me without telling me and started up with another girl and now harasses me *and* beats me. Yeah, I still have feelings for him. So please be careful with him," she said sarcastically.

Liam didn't say anything, and Talya didn't know what else to say. Neither of them said anything else. Liam pulled into her driveway and climbed out of the car. He opened her door for her but didn't say anything as they walked to the front door. Talya unlocked the door and turned to him. "Thank you for coming to get me today," she said quietly.

Liam looked down at her. "You're welcome. Get some sleep." With that, he turned and walked back to the car. Talya watched him go for a moment before stepping inside and closing and locking the door.

Talya opened her eyes groggily and rolled over to turn off her alarm. Her body ached, especially her face. Everything from yesterday came flooding back, and Talya held back the groan that threatened to escape.

She was still tired but she had set her alarm so she wouldn't worry her grandparents when she didn't get up for school since they didn't know about anything that had happened. Her plan was to keep it that way. She needed to come up with a story for why she couldn't go to school for three days *and* for the cut on her face. But that was a problem for later. Right now, she needed coffee. Lots of it.

She dragged herself to the kitchen, still feeling groggy. She froze in the doorway to the kitchen when she saw Liam sitting at the table talking to her grandparents.

He looked up at her and smiled. "What are you doing here?" she asked abruptly. Her mind wasn't working properly yet. She wondered how much he had told her grandparents. A quick glance at their faces didn't give her any indication.

"Talya, don't be rude," her grandmother scolded gently.

Liam looked up at her and winked. Talya ignored him and made her way to the coffee pot. She filled a mug of coffee and put a big splash of French vanilla creamer in it. It was one of the few indulgences she allowed herself. She took a sip and sighed. This was what she needed.

"Our Talya doesn't function well in the morning without coffee," she heard Grandma say behind her. "But you probably already knew that, didn't you?" Grandma asked.

Talya frowned but didn't turn around. "Not yet, but I'm still learning everything there is to learn about Tally Bear," Liam said.

Talya about spit out her coffee. She started coughing instead. When she had finally gotten control of herself, she turned around and narrowed her eyes at Liam. He just winked at her.

"Honey, maybe you should go put some clothes on, and then we could talk," Grandma said quietly. For the first time, Talya became aware of the fact that she had literally rolled out of bed and come out here. A quick glance down at her outfit confirmed her fears. She was wearing short shorts and a tank top. Her only salvation was that she had thrown a sweatshirt over her tank top, but it wasn't zipped. Talya pulled the sweatshirt around her and tried running her fingers through her hair. It was too late, though. The damage had already been done. She quickly glanced at Liam and saw he was grinning at her.

"Yeah, I'm gonna go change," Talya said, turning around and practically running from the room. She heard Liam's warm, rich laugh behind her. Talya shook her head as she hurried to her room.

Chapter Twelve

After turning on the shower, Talya walked over to the sink. She carefully took off her bandage. There was bruising around the cut now. Hopefully, she would be able to cover it up for work with some makeup. Talya took a fast shower. She had no idea what Liam was telling her grandparents, and it was dangerous to leave him down there unsupervised. She didn't want her grandparents to know everything that was going on. After her shower, she quickly dressed in jeans and a soft pink shirt. She threw her hair into a long braid and left her room.

Her grandpop looked up at her, and she could see the anger in his eyes. "Why didn't you tell us what was going on?"

Talya could have strangled Liam. "Because I didn't want you to worry," she said as she tossed a glare at Liam. He didn't seem the least bit bothered by her reaction. He was looking at her wound. His jaw was clenched tight, and Talya could see the anger in his eyes.

"Let me see your face," her grandma said as she moved close

to Talya. She shook her head. "I have some cream we can put on that. It should keep it from scarring." She put her hand on Talya's arm. "I'm so sorry for what you went through. You should have called us and told us. We could have talked to the principal," she said.

"No," Talya said right away. That was exactly what she hadn't wanted to happen. That was why she called Liam in the first place.

"I never liked that boy," her grandpop said in anger.

"Yes, dear. We know. But at least her boyfriend took care of it. It's a good thing she has him now," she said beaming.

Talya whirled around to look at Liam. *Boyfriend?* She mouthed to Liam.

He had the audacity to grin at her. "Yeah, now that Talya and I are official, I'll be making my presence known around school and her work more. Nobody will mess with her. Right, baby?" he asked, looking at her with an innocent look.

Talya stared at him. She was going to kill him. Fine. Two could play this game. "Hey, *sweetie*," she said, pouring the sweetness. He grinned. "I need to talk to you for just a moment. Can you come with me please?"

Liam stood and walked towards her, confidence in his swagger. Talya shook her head and turned to walk towards her room. "Keep your door open," Grandpop called after her.

"Oh, my word," Talya muttered, her face flaming. Liam had the audacity to chuckle behind her. Talya walked in and pushed the door almost all the way closed before turning to face him.

"Don't close it all the way, Tally Bear," Liam said still grinning.

"Don't talk," she hissed at him. "You have made a mess of everything! I didn't want them to know what was going on. Now they will just worry about me. Why did you even come here first thing this morning? And why would you let them think you were my boyfriend? We don't even hardly know each other!" Talya glared at him, crossing her arms over her chest. When he didn't say anything, she put her hands on her hips. "Well, don't you have anything to say for yourself?" she snapped at him. Liam just pointed to his lips. "Oh, fine. You can talk."

"Thank you," he said easily, but he was serious now. "The reason I came over first thing this morning was that I knew you wouldn't tell them what happened, and they needed to know."

"No, they didn't," Talya argued.

Liam stepped closer, serious now. "Yes, they did, Talya. They need to know so they don't accidentally do something that endangers you. What if Brandon shows up and asks to wait in your room for you? Or what if he did something to them?" Talya didn't say anything. He had a point. "As for being your boyfriend, I did that so they will understand when they see me coming and going, picking you up for school, dropping you off at night from work. I need to be able to come and go from your house easily in case of an emergency." Talya just stared at him. "The only thing I regret is making you upset. That was not my intention," he said, softening his approach.

Talya sighed and sat down on her bed. "This is such a mess," she said. Liam moved away, leaned against the wall, and crossed his arms. Talya noticed his arms absently. He was so relaxed and easy-going that sometimes she forgot to notice how incredibly muscular he was.

"What are you thinking?" Liam asked.

Talya's eyes shot to his. "Nothing," she blurted out quickly.

He gave her a small smirk. "Don't overthink it. It's not that big a deal. Are you going to try to work tonight?" he asked, changing the conversation.

"I don't know. What do you think about my face?" she asked.

"I think it's beautiful," Liam said totally serious.

Talya felt her face heat up. "That's not what I meant, and you know it. What do you think about my scar? Do you think I can go to work like this?"

Liam sat down on edge of the bed. He carefully held her chin, turning her head gently as he looked at her scar. He looked into her eyes. "It's not as bad as it was. Do you have makeup that could cover it up?"

Talya nodded. "I can try." He stood up and she moved into the bathroom. She walked over to the bathroom counter and began to put her makeup on. Liam stood in the doorway to the bathroom with his hands above the doorframe. Her eyes dropped down to where his shirt rode up, revealing his muscled stomach. She quickly looked away and focused on her makeup. She did the best she could to cover up the scar. "What do you think?" she asked. Liam came towards her and looked down at her face.

"I think it's okay, but do you need to go to work today? Can't you take today off to rest and recover?" he asked.

Talya shook her head. "No, I can't afford to take days off."

Liam frowned. "Do you need money because I can..."

"No!" Talya cut him off. "I don't need your money."

"Talya," Liam started.

Talya shook her head. "No, Liam. Now, you need to leave so I can get to work."

"What do you have to do? You don't have to go to school," Liam said helpfully.

"Thanks for bringing *that* up," Talya said sarcastically. "No, I'm going to use these three days to try to work on some projects for my grandparents that I don't ever get to because I'm too busy."

"I can help," Liam said.

Talya was already shaking her head. "No thank you. You need to go do whatever it is you do." She cocked her head to the side. "What *do* you do?" she asked, curiously.

"I work at a developing firm," he said.

Talya looked at him surprised. She hadn't expected that at all. "Really? I can't picture you behind a desk wearing a suit and tie all the time."

"I rock a suit," he said shamelessly. Now *that*, Talya could picture; but she kept that thought to herself. "Seriously, Talya. I've noticed some stuff around the house, mainly the outside of the house that needs to be fixed," Liam said. "Let me help."

Talya warred with herself for just a moment. Her pride wanted her to tell him no, but was that really fair to her grandparents? They could use all the help they could get. "Fine," Talya said.

Liam grinned. "Let me go grab some stuff out of my car. I'll be back in a moment." Talya followed behind him. She was curious as to what he brought. When he opened his trunk, her chin dropped in surprise.

"What is all this stuff?" she asked.

"I hit the store this morning before coming over," he said nonchalantly. He began picking up supplies and carrying them to the deck. Talya reached in, grabbed two paint cans and carried them to the porch. After they carried everything to the porch, Talya looked at Liam.

"So, what are we doing?" she asked.

"I thought we could start out front and work our way inside. The front porch, steps, and railing need to be re-stained. I'm also going to replace the boards on the stairs, so they are sturdy and safe. The front door needs a new coat of paint and a new door handle and deadbolt. I bought mulch for the flower beds and some plants. The shutters need a fresh coat of paint as well. That's enough to get started."

Talya blinked. "Wow, that's great. I don't have the money to repay you right now, but I'll pay you back as soon as I can," she promised.

"No," Liam said. Talya looked up at him. "You don't need to repay me. This is something I want to do."

"But what about your work?" Talya asked.

Liam shrugged. "I took sort of an extended leave," he said vaguely. "So, I'm all yours," he said, wiggling his eyebrows. Talya couldn't help herself. She laughed out loud. Liam smiled at her. "You have a great laugh. You should laugh more often," he said softly.

Talya turned away from him. "What do we do first?"

"You probably need to go change," he said nodding at her

outfit.

"Oh, good idea. I'll be right back. Do you need anything?" she asked. Liam was already going through supplies and getting stuff out.

"Nope, I'm good," he said.

"Okay, I'll be right back," Talya said. She hurried inside to change. She found an old tie-dye shirt in her drawer and an old pair of shorts. On her way back out, she told her grandpop that her and Liam were going to do some work. She didn't tell him what they were doing. She didn't want him to feel obligated to help. She slipped out the front door. "Okay, put me to work." Liam handed her a paint tray with a pretty blue paint in it. "Ooo, this is really pretty. What's this for?" she asked.

"I thought it would go nicely on the shutters," he said.

Talya smiled. "That would be perfect."

"Have you painted before?" Liam asked.

Talya scowled. "Yes, I've painted before. I'm not helpless."

"I know you're not," Liam said easily. He turned away and came back with a paintbrush and a roller. "Here you go."

"Thanks," Talya said taking them from him. She got settled over by the window and got to work. She taped around the shutters first. Liam pulled a speaker out of somewhere and connected his phone to it. Easy-listening music drifted out from the speaker, and Talya felt herself begin to relax for the first time in a long time. Talya finished with the first coat of paint on the shutters on the first window and went to work on the second.

"Have you had any more dreams about the wolf?" Liam asked after a little while.

"I did," Talya said. "One more dream, while I was at your house actually. I fell asleep for a little while on the couch. The dream wasn't very long. It was just as weird as the first one."

"How so?" Liam asked.

"I think he was trying to tell me I need to learn to be quiet," Talya said, frowning. Liam laughed out loud. When Talya looked at him, he had an innocent look on his face. "He said something about the quiet being a strength or something. I don't know. It's a good thing I don't believe in dreams," she said with a laugh. She didn't notice that Liam didn't say anything, or that he had a frown on his face.

Chapter Thirteen

They were both quiet after that. Talya finished both shutters and started staining the railing. She was amazed at how quickly Liam worked. He had the boards on the stairs replaced and a new door handle and lock in place before lunch. "What do you say we take a break for lunch?" he asked.

Talya shrugged. "I'm good to keep going."

"Let me rephrase that; I'm starving," he said dramatically.

Talya smiled at him. "I'll go find something for you to eat," she said.

"Nope, I brought sandwiches for us," he said. He walked over to his car and brought back a cooler. He opened it up and took out two wrapped sub sandwiches. He also pulled out two bags of chips and two water bottles. "Here," he said, handing her a sandwich. "I brought two for your grandparents too."

Talya stared up at him. Who was this man? She had never met anyone like him. "Thank you." She didn't know what else to say. He sat down on the steps and motioned for her to come sit next to him. She did so but didn't open her sandwich. He took several bites out of his before looking at her. "Aren't you going to eat?" he asked.

"I'm good," she said.

"Do you not like that kind? It's chicken salad. I thought you might like that, but you can have mine if you'd rather. It's an Italian, so it has lots of meat on it. And I might have gone for double meat," he said with a grin.

Talya smiled at him. "No this is perfect. Thank you." She opened up the paper and looked at the sandwich in front of her. It did look really good. Her stomach growled hungrily. She opened it up and took out a small piece of chicken. She chewed it slowly. After that she ate another small piece and then another.

"What are you doing?" Liam asked, frowning at her.

"I'm eating," Talya said.

"No, you're not. You're picking," he said.

"This is how I eat," she said.

"Why aren't you eating the whole thing?" Liam asked.

"I told you. I can't have bread, remember?" she said.

Liam closed his eyes for a moment. When he opened them, he fixed them intently on her. "Talya, you can't let Brandon continue to control your life. He's not a part of it anymore. He can't tell you what you can or can't eat."

"It's not him," Talya said. "I just can't eat certain foods or..." her voice trailed off.

"Talya," Liam growled at her. "We are not having this conversation again. You are not fat. You will eat the sandwich because you are hungry. That's what people do when they're hungry.

They eat," he said sternly. Talya looked down at her sandwich. She was really hungry and it looked so good. "Eat it," he growled at her again.

Talya took a deep breath and picked up the sandwich. She took a bite and the flavor exploded in her mouth. She closed her eyes and sighed. "Oh, that is good."

Liam smiled at her. "I'm glad. Now eat all of it or at least until you are full. Actually full, Talya. None of this stopping when you're still hungry," he said sternly.

Talya nodded, too content and at peace to argue with him. After a few more bites, she stopped. She couldn't eat any more. "I'm so full," she said with a groan.

"You didn't eat enough," Liam argued.

"I really can't eat anymore," Talya said. "I'll get sick," she said. Liam frowned at her, but before he could object she cut him off. "I really will get sick, Liam. I'm not used to eating much and certainly not bread."

Liam's frown deepened. "You need to start eating more, Talya," he said, concern in his voice.

Talya nodded. "I'm trying to listen to you. It's just really hard to undo the last almost three years."

"No more," Liam said fiercely. "You eat when you're hungry and eat until you're full. Do you understand?" he asked. "I'm serious, Talya. I'm going to be monitoring what you eat," he said. "And I'll get Sage's help when I'm not around at school. What time do you eat at work at night?" he asked.

Talya blinked. "I don't ever eat at work."

Liam took a deep breath and closed his eyes. When he opened

them, he seemed a tiny bit calmer. "Do you get a break to eat at work?"

"I do; I just don't ever take it," Talya said.

"Well, going forward, you will take it. Let me know what time your break is, and I'll eat with you every night so I can make sure you're eating," Liam said.

Talya opened her mouth to argue with him, but she shut her mouth. She knew he was just trying to help her. He had done so much for her and for her grandparents already. She could do this thing to make him happy. "Okay," she finally said.

Liam raised an eyebrow. "Okay?"

Talya grinned at him. "I can listen once in a while."

He huffed at that. "We'll see."

Talya stood up. "Thanks for lunch. Did you say there were sandwiches for my grandparents?"

"Yes," Liam said, standing fluidly. He handed her two sandwiches.

"Thank you for doing all this. That was really kind of you." She reached up on her tiptoes and kissed his cheek, surprising not only him but herself as well. She hurried inside before he could say anything. After delivering the sandwiches to her grateful grandparents, she got to work again.

The next few hours passed quickly; soon it was time for Talya to get cleaned up and ready for work. She changed out of her paint clothes and got dressed for work. She gave hugs to her grandparents and walked outside. Liam looked up from where he was working. "You ready?" he asked.

Talya nodded and they walked to his car. "You don't have to

take me, you know. I can catch a bus."

"I know," he said. He opened her door for her and closed it behind her when she got settled.

When he climbed in, Talya turned to him. "Do you think my scar is going to be a problem?" she asked.

He looked at her carefully. "I don't think so. You did a really good job covering it up." He smiled and rubbed a spot near her ear. "You have paint there," he said.

Talya laughed nervously. "Thanks."

The drive to work went quickly. Soon Talya was climbing out of the car. "Thanks for the ride," she said.

"Text me what time your break is," he said.

Talya nodded. "I will." With that, she closed the door and went into the diner. She found Sandy, Joe's wife, in the kitchen. "Hey Sandy."

"Hey honey, how are you doing? Joe said you had an accident. Are you okay?" Sandy asked her concerned.

Talya smiled. "I'm much better now. I was just wondering—would it be okay if I start taking a break now when I work?"

"Of course. We've been trying to get you to do that since you started. You need to eat more," she said pointing at Talya.

Talya grimaced. "So, I've been told."

"Why don't you take a break at seven thirty? Does that work?" Sandy asked.

Talya cringed inwardly but nodded. Eating at seven thirty at night would be disastrous on her figure, but she tried not to think about it. She quickly sent a text to Liam. *7:30.*

She grabbed an apron and got to work. It wasn't too busy for a little while, so she was able to help Sandy get caught up with some extra cleaning and prepping for the dinner rush. It wasn't long before the dinner rush was in full swing. Talya was doing a refill on drinks for a table when she noticed three men had been seated in her area. She dropped off the drinks and made her way to the table where the men were. When she got close, she realized two of them were the ones that had given her weird vibes before. The third one was new, and he looked younger. She took a deep breath and forced a smile to her face. "Hi, welcome back. Can I get a drink for you to get started?"

All three men looked up, but it was the new guy who talked. "Hey," he said with a smile. "We will all take a coffee, and what's the special for today, beautiful?" he asked.

"Shepherd's pie," Talya said forcing her smile.

"Great. We will all take that," the man said easily.

Talya forced herself to walk away from their table. Once she turned away, her head felt lighter. She shook her head trying to figure out what was wrong. She really got a weird feeling around those men. She quickly grabbed and filled three mugs of coffee. She steadied herself and prepared to return to their table. Her plan was to not look them in the eye.

She made it to their table and dropped off the coffees. She turned around to go back to the kitchen, but a voice stopped her. "Do you live around here?" the new guy asked.

"Not far," Talya said vaguely.

"I'm new to the area," the man said. "Any good spots to eat or visit that I should know about?" he asked conversationally.

"Um, well, this diner's good for starters," Talya said with a small smile. The man laughed.

"You've got spunk," he said with a smile.

Talya smiled. "Let me go check on your food," she said. She walked away from the table, feeling a little more relaxed. There didn't seem to be anything wrong with the new guy. Maybe the other two were just awkward. She felt badly about how she had responded to them. She checked on all her other tables before heading back to the kitchen. Her three shepherd's pies were ready, so she loaded them onto her tray and carried them out to their table.

"There's our favorite waitress," the man said.

Talya smiled and placed a hot dish in front of each of the men. "Okay. Let me know if you need anything else."

"Thanks, Talya," the new guy said with a nod at her name pinned to her shirt. "I'm Alec," he said.

"Nice to meet you, Alec," Talya said with a smile. The other guys didn't offer their names and she didn't ask for them. "Well, let me know if you need anything else," she said.

She took a step backwards, preparing to turn away when a hand caught her wrist. Talya looked at Alec in surprise. "Talya, you smell...different. It reminds me of someone I know," he said in a low voice.

Before Talya could say or do anything, a hand clamped down on top of the hand holding her wrist.

"Let her go now," she heard the icy words from behind her. She recognized Liam's voice but not his tone. She hadn't ever heard that tone before. The hand on her arm dropped, and Talya relaxed slightly. Liam moved close behind her and put an arm around her waist.

Alec smiled at Liam, but it wasn't the easy smile that he had smiled at her just moments before. "I would like to say I'm surprised to see one of you here, but I'm not." He leaned against his seat, relaxed and comfortable. "So, there's two of them now?"

Liam growled behind her. It sounded so real, she turned her head slightly to look at him. He glanced down at her for a moment, and she gasped. "Y-your eyes," she said softly. He quickly closed his eyes and took a breath. When he opened them, his eyes were back to normal. Talya blinked for a moment. His eyes had been yellow only a moment ago, almost like they were glowing. Had she imagined it? She had to have imagined it. She was just tired and really stressed.

Alec broke out into a laugh, but it wasn't a warm laugh. It was a cold, heartless laugh. "She doesn't know," he said.

"You've got some new friends, Alec," Liam said in a cold voice.

Alec grinned. "Yep. I found some friends whose goals align with mine. We're working together now," he said. "Who knew my little sister was such a hot commodity? Apparently, she's not *just* valuable in your world. Of course, now the price has just doubled," he said with a pointed glance at Talya. Talya shivered at the deadness in his gaze.

Talya wasn't stupid; she knew he was insinuating her. But the rest of the conversation was lost on her. Before she could ask what he meant, Liam pulled her away from the table. Talya let him lead her because she didn't want to have to be around those guys any longer than she had to be. He kept leading her and steered her right out the front door. "Liam, what are you doing? I have to get back to work." Liam just kept walking, steering her through the parking lot. "Liam, stop," she said, trying to stand still. But he just pushed her along. She turned around to face him. "Liam, I have to work." He didn't stop for a moment. He didn't even miss a step. He leaned down and swung her up into his arms and began striding forward. "Liam, stop. What are you doing?" she asked, louder this time. "Put me down now," she demanded.

This time, Liam looked down at her. Talya gasped at his eyes. There was no doubt about it; they were definitely glowing now.

Chapter Fourteen

"Put me down," she said in anger.

"I can't," he said in a voice that she barely recognized.

"Liam, put me down; you're scaring me," she said.

He didn't even respond. He strode to his car. "If you run from me, I will chase you and catch you," he said in a voice that left Talya no doubt he would do just that. He opened the door and placed her in the front seat. Almost before Talya could blink, she was buckled and he was around the front of the car and in the driver's seat.

What? She hadn't even had a chance to try to escape. Before she could reach out a hand to open her door, Liam pulled out of his parking spot and drove through the parking lot. Once they hit the road, he took off, tires squealing. Talya screamed. She was legitimately terrified. She glanced over at Liam. He didn't say a word. He just kept checking his rear-view mirror. "Liam, this is crazy. Let me out of the car," she yelled at him. When he didn't respond, she tried again. "I have to work. Take me back!" He didn't even respond.

Talya was getting ready to punch him and demand that he take her back when he suddenly cursed and the car shot forward. Talya's head jerked against the seat. She jerked her head to look behind her and saw a sports car behind them. She screamed when Liam jerked the wheel and they took a corner on two wheels. When they landed and shot forward, Talya quickly glanced behind her. The sports car was still right behind them. Talya glanced at Liam. He was totally focused; she would say he even looked calm except for the whiteness of his hands on the steering wheel. Talya shook her head slightly. What in the world was going on? She knew better than to ask that question out loud. Liam needed every ounce of his focus and attention on keeping the car from crashing at the speeds he was going. Talya couldn't believe there wasn't a policeman around to pull them over.

Soon, they were on the highway. Talya couldn't breathe; neither could she stop screaming each time Liam wove in and out of traffic. She was terrified they were going to crash at any second. "Liam, what is going on?" she demanded.

He didn't answer; he just kept driving like a maniac. While he was driving, he pulled his cell phone out of his pocket and handed it to Talya. Talya looked at him, confused. Then the phone rang in her hand. She jumped. "Answer that and put it on speaker," he commanded.

Talya waited for just a moment before doing as he said. "Kyle, talk to me," Liam spoke from his seat.

"Okay; you've got about ten miles before you hit a speed

trap. I'm looking for another route, so you can avoid the police and head in a new direction."

"No, just get me around the police and then back on the highway," Liam countered.

"Okay," the guy said.

It was quiet for a moment and Talya thought this would be a great time to interrupt. "Um, excuse me, Kyle? While you're helping Liam avoid the police, do you think you could call them for me and tell them that I've been kidnapped?" she said the last few words in a shriek.

Liam ignored her. "Um," she heard the guy say.

Then she heard a new voice. "He did what?" she heard a woman's voice now. "Liam? What did you do?" the woman asked.

"What? What did he do?" another woman's voice chimed in.

"Liam kidnapped Talya," she heard one of them say.

"Oh, my word. Liam!" another of them said.

"Talya, my name is Emma," one of the female voices said.

"And I'm Madison," the other female said.

"Uh, nice to meet you, I guess?" Talya said.

"Listen, I know you are probably as confused as all get out right now," one of them said.

"I'm not confused. I'm angry. He took me away from my shift at work, like legitimately carried me, threw me in his car and took off!" Talya bit out.

It was silent for a moment. Then two voices chimed in at almost the same time.

"Liam!"

"What were you thinking?!"

Liam shook his head. "This is not the time," he growled out.

Kyle's voice chimed in. "Okay, Liam, get ready to get off. The next exit is yours. How close is your tail?"

Talya closed her mouth for what she was about to say. She glanced behind her. "They're only two cars behind us," she said.

Kyle muttered something Talya couldn't catch. "You've gotta figure out a way to lose them, Liam," Kyle said urgently.

"Working on it," Liam said in a frustrated voice as he swerved around yet another vehicle. Talya slid in her seat before righting herself again. Liam floored it, and the car shot forward. "Talya, put your feet on the dashboard to brace yourself," he said.

Talya jerked her head to look at him. "Why? What are you going to do?" she asked.

"Just do it," he commanded. Talya glared at him before doing what he said. "Grab the handle above your head." Talya did it, scared of what was going to happen.

Liam was looking in the mirror and forward, back and forth. He slowed down and swerved into the right lane in between two semis and slammed on the brakes, turning the wheel sharply. "Hang on!" he shouted. Talya screamed as the car did a complete one-eighty. He gunned it and took the off ramp on two wheels. Talya screamed again as they almost hit a car. Liam swerved around it and onto the ramp. "Did they make the turn?" he asked.

Talya turned her head quickly. "No," she said breathlessly followed by, "I think I'm going to be sick."

"Go left," Kyle said.

Liam gunned it and went left. Kyle navigated him through town taking several turns along the way. Once they reached a road that stretched out straight, Liam floored it again. "Four miles on this and then you can get back on the highway, but do you want to do that if you don't know where they are?" Kyle asked.

"No," Liam said. "Get me across the state line; avoid the police and avoid the highway," he ordered.

"No," Talya said at the same time Kyle said, "On it."

"You can't take someone against their will, Liam. Take me back home," she said, trying to keep her voice calm.

"I can't," he said.

"What do you mean you can't? Those guys are long gone. Just take me back home and then you can just disappear and go do whatever you need to do," she said angry.

"If I take you home, those guys will just find you again," Liam said in a low, angry voice.

Talya threw her hands up. "So? They didn't even say or do anything. You're the one who grabbed me and took me away," she said almost yelling at him.

"You don't know who those men are," Liam said in anger.

"And you do?" she asked. Liam only nodded. "Then enlighten me," she said.

It was quiet for a moment. "I can't," he ground out.

"Why because I am a stupid, helpless female?" she asked angrily.

Liam spun his head to look at her and frowned. "No, that's not it at all."

"Then tell me what's going on," Talya demanded. She was so mad and getting angrier by the second. "Liam, I have a job. I have to go back to it and back to my grandparents."

Liam looked at her, a look in his eyes she didn't understand at first. It almost looked like...pity. "You can't go back," he said quietly.

Goosebumps broke out on Talya's skin. "What do you mean I can't go back?" she asked in a detached voice.

"It's too dangerous. You have to stay with me now. You can't go back, Talya," he said. This time she could clearly see the regret in his eyes.

Talya's heart rate picked up. "I don't know what is going on, but you need to stop the car this instant and let me out," Talya said. When Liam didn't say anything, Talya reached her hand towards the handle.

"Stop," Liam ordered in a scary voice. Talya didn't listen. She reached for the handle, only to find it didn't work when she tried opening it.

"Liam, turn this car around and take me home, or I will call the police," she said. She grabbed her phone and unlocked it. "I'm not kidding," she said.

Liam reached for her phone, but Talya was expecting this and moved it out of his reach. "Talya, stop. You're being unreasonable," he ground out.

"I'm being unreasonable?" Talya's voice went high. "You kidnapped me!"

"I didn't kidnap you," he responded angrily.

"Liam, that's exactly what this is. You won't let me go home.

Just stop the car; I'll find a way home." She waited a moment longer. "I will call the police, Liam," she warned. When he didn't stop, she punched in 911. Before she hit the call, Liam swiped for it again but missed.

"Liam, stop. This is not the way to handle this!" she heard one of the females say into the phone.

"It was Alec, Emma!" Liam said in anger.

She heard gasps on the other end. "What? Why? Why her?"

"I don't know," Liam said. "But he's with them now," Liam said in a resigned voice.

"With who?" Talya asked. "Who is Alec?" Talya asked in frustration.

"But why are they after Talya? That makes no sense?" she heard from the phone.

"Would somebody please tell me what's going on?" Talya yelled.

"Alec's my horrible step-brother," she heard either Emma or Madison say. "He's working with some really bad people, and for some reason they've set their sights on you."

"Who are they?" Talya demanded. It was totally quiet. "Somebody had better answer me right now or I am going to call the police!"

"They're vampires," Liam reluctantly said.

"Liam!" she heard from the phone.

"She needs to know," Liam said. "I saw how you reacted when we tried to protect you and not tell you everything. I'm not going to make the same mistakes Garrett did."

Talya's hand was frozen over the call button. She stared at

Liam. She waited for him to grin, but he didn't. He didn't look at her. "What? Is this a joke?" she asked.

Liam glanced at her. "No, Talya, it's not a joke. Those men are vampires, and they wanted..." he broke off, breathing heavy.

"Liam, you need to get help," Talya said. He had clearly lost it.

"Talya, this is real. Those men are really vampires," he said.

"Stop the car," she said in a quiet voice. Liam either didn't hear or was ignoring her. "Liam, stop the car," she said louder. When he didn't, she yelled at him, "Stop the car!" she screamed at him.

"Talya," she heard a voice speak from the phone, one of the women. "He's telling the truth. Those men are vampires, and they are incredibly dangerous. Liam is just trying to protect you."

The car was absolutely silent. Talya felt like she couldn't breathe. She was so confused right now. They were insane right? There was no such thing as vampires, right?

"Just think about it for a moment. Was there something off about them? Did you feel threatened when you were around them?" the voice asked from the phone.

Talya thought back to the first time she had served them. They had made her so nervous, she had asked Joe to take her table for her. "I don't know," she finally whispered into the phone.

Then a horrible thought hit her. "What about my co-workers? Will they hurt them?" Then a more terrifying thought hit her. She gasped and looked at Liam. "My grandparents!" she said. "What about my grandparents? I have to go back to protect them." Liam looked at her with that look of regret again and

Talya snapped. She reached for the door handle again. Then she kicked at the dashboard. "Stop the car!" she screamed. She hit the dashboard.

"Talya, stop. You're going to hurt yourself," Liam ordered. He reached across and put his arm in front of her, keeping her from thrashing around.

This only infuriated her. She pushed against him, but his arm was like steel. "I have to go home," she yelled at him. "Why are you doing this? Just let me go home." She pushed at his arm again, taking all her frustration out on him. "Liam!" she screamed at him. He didn't respond, nor did he move his arm. Talya fought until she wore herself out. A wave of defeat washed over her; then the tears came. Tears poured down her cheeks as the defeat crushed her. She was vaguely aware that voices were still talking on the phone, but she was past listening. She closed her eyes and let herself drift.

Chapter Fifteen

When Talya opened her eyes sometime later, she felt a weight across her body. She lifted her head and realized she had been sleeping on Liam's arm. It was still across the front of her body, from when he had restrained her. She looked over at Liam. He turned his head to look at her before removing his arm slowly. Talya felt bad; his arm was probably asleep. A quick glance at the clock told her it was past midnight. They'd been on the road for almost five hours. She wanted to ask where they were going and when they would stop, but she couldn't trust herself not to yell at him. In the end, she kept her mouth shut, choosing instead to look out the window.

"I'm sorry, Talya," Liam said quietly.

Talya didn't respond. Instead, she busied herself looking for her phone. She felt her pockets but didn't find it. She looked around the car and didn't see it. It was about that time that she realized she didn't have her purse either. She closed her eyes in defeat and put her head against the seat. She had no wallet, no license, and apparently no phone. Her grandparents would be okay until the morning, but she needed to find a way to contact them and an incredibly good story so they didn't worry about her. Sage, on the other hand, was probably already wondering where she was. She would have to find a way to reach out to her too before she called the police. Of course, the police didn't sound like such a bad idea right now.

Talya sneaked a glance at the gas display. Maybe they would have to stop soon and she could escape. She nearly groaned out loud when she realized it was almost full. Liam must have stopped while she was asleep. There went that plan.

"Are you hungry?" Liam asked. "I grabbed a sandwich for you when we stopped." Talya didn't answer him. She had nothing to say to him. "Are you just going to ignore me all night?" Liam asked. She felt his eyes on her, but she didn't face him.

She didn't feel like talking, but she also wasn't juvenile. "I'm not ignoring you. I just don't have anything to say to you," she said. It was quiet again. Liam turned on the radio.

The next five hours dragged by. Talya dozed off and on, but she couldn't really relax enough to sleep again. Her mind refused to rest. Liam never said a word, and neither did she. He didn't stop for gas; he didn't stop for coffee or snacks or anything. He was like a machine. Talya straightened when he took an exit a little after five in the morning. A few minutes later, he pulled into a gas station. "Want anything?" he asked.

Talya shook her head no. She waited until he got out to get the gas and watched him carefully. If he went inside, she would make a run for it. She waited anxiously as he pumped gas. As soon as he was done, he slid into his seat and took off again. Talya closed her eyes in frustration.

About an hour later, Liam glanced at her. "Are you awake?" he asked softly.

Talya nodded, even though her eyes were closed. "We're stopping in thirty minutes. We're meeting up with some of my friends," he said.

Talya turned to look at him, but he didn't say anything more. She went back to looking out the window. She blinked her eyes against the fatigue threatening to overtake her. She needed to stay alert; maybe she could slip away when they stopped. She would just have to be ready for anything. The next hour passed slowly before Liam finally took an exit.

Talya felt her heart rate pick up. They didn't drive far at all. There was a gas station immediately after the exit ramp. He pulled in and parked next to a black Land Rover. The Land Rover was on Liam's side. *That's good*, Talya thought to herself. Without a word, Liam climbed out of the car and stretched. He stood next to the Land Rover. The window rolled down and he talked to somebody for a moment, but Talya didn't pay attention. She watched as Liam walked away from the car and towards the gas station. As soon as he disappeared inside, she opened her door and started running for the restaurant next door.

She didn't make it ten yards before there was suddenly a huge guy in front of her. She turned to go the other direction, and there was another guy behind her. She gasped. Both men were massively built and equally terrifying. "You need to stay with us for your protection," the guy in front of her said in a deep voice. "Liam will be right back," he said as if he was trying to assure her. Talya glanced up at him. He was huge with dark hair and dark eyes.

"I'm trying to run away from him," she said pointedly.

The man's eyes showed his surprise for just a moment before a small smirk replaced it. Before he could say anything, she heard Liam's voice behind her. "Come on, Talya." Talya turned around to see him walking towards her. For just a moment, she almost felt sorry for him. He looked tired and defeated. When his eyes met hers, she looked away quickly.

"I'm not going with you," she said, looking at Liam. She lifted her chin defiantly.

Liam just kept walking towards her. He didn't stop. He bent when he got close to her, picking her up, and throwing her over his shoulder.

"What are you doing?" she cried out in outrage. She pounded on his back with her fists, but it did nothing. She thought she heard a laugh, but when she looked up, neither man was smiling. Liam opened the car door and dropped her into the backseat and closed the door. "Jerk," Talya muttered after him. She looked over and jumped slightly when she saw a man sitting next to her. He seemed just as surprised to see her as she was him.

A second later, his door opened and an angry Liam stood there. "Out." At his one-word command, the man slid out of the car. Liam handed him his keys and slid in the back seat of the car. Talya tried her door handle, but it was locked. Just as she was going to climb over the seat to go out the front, the front doors opened and the two scary men from earlier slid in. A moment later, they pulled out of the gas station. Talya looked behind her to see the other guy driving his car.

"Status?" the man in the passenger's seat asked.

"It's been quiet for hours," Liam said.

"What about on her end?" the man asked. Talya didn't have to be a brain surgeon to figure out he was talking about her.

"Nothing yet," Liam said.

"You know, I'm sitting right here," Talya said indignantly.

The man turned towards her to include her in the conversation. "Are you hungry?" Talya shook her head. She didn't hear Liam say anything. "We've got a good ten hours. Get some rest." With that, he turned around and everything was silent again.

Talya took a quick second to peek at Liam, but he was looking out the window. She went back to staring out the window. She had no idea where they were; she just knew it was a long way from North Carolina. She made it about two hours before she couldn't keep her eyes open any longer. Her head kept nodding. She put her head against the window trying to get comfortable. When that didn't work, she tried putting her head against the seat. She couldn't get comfortable in any position. As soon as she would start to fall asleep, her head would jerk and fall forward. She was so tired, she felt like crying. Just when she felt like she couldn't take it any longer, Liam unbuckled her seat belt and wrapped his arm around her, bringing her close to him. He pushed her head to his shoulder.

"Don't touch me," Talya snapped at him, exhaustion and the circumstances making her more snippy than usual.

"Come on, Talya. Just rest," Liam said with a sigh.

"I need to be buckled," Talya said.

"I'll keep you safe," he said softly. Talya wanted to argue with him, but she was too exhausted and this was the first time she had been comfortable in hours. She closed her eyes and let herself lean against him.

"Looks like you got your work cut out for you," Talya heard softly from the front seat.

Right before she drifted off, she heard Liam say, "Yeah, but she's worth it."

Talya woke up on and off for the next few hours, but thankfully every time she woke up, another hour had passed. Eventually, she felt the car slow and stop. She opened her eyes and sat up, taking in her surroundings. They had stopped at another gas station. She felt Liam move and she turned her head. His eyes opened and he looked down at her. Talya didn't move. They were caught in an intimate moment, and neither of them seemed to know how to respond. Talya was the first to react. She sat up and moved away from Liam, stretching. Liam opened his door and stepped out. Talya noticed for the first time she was the only one in the car. Cautiously, she tried her door and was surprised when it opened. She stepped out and looked around her, trying to figure out where in the world they were. She turned towards the gas station and saw the other man who had driven Liam's car leaning against the rear of the Land Rover. She grimaced. So, they *hadn't* left her unchaperoned. She shook her head.

"I'm going inside to go to the bathroom," she said to the man as she walked past him. He nodded. She was just about to pull the door open when she saw a car in the reflection on the glass door.

Talya's heart skipped a beat. It couldn't be. She turned her head slightly and gasped. She yanked the door open and went inside, looking for Liam. He had just come out of the bathroom. He looked up. When he saw her face, he immediately came towards her. "What's wrong?"

"It's them," she whispered.

His head jerked up. He cursed when he looked out the window and saw the car. The other two men joined them at the window, not a moment later. She heard a low growling sound, but when she turned she didn't see anything. "What are we going to do?" she asked.

All three men were quiet. She saw Liam shaking his head for a moment, but other than that, none of them responded. "Fine," Liam said. Talya frowned. She wasn't sure what his response was in reference to. "Talya, come with me," he said. He grabbed her hand and pulled her into the men's bathroom and bolted the door behind him. "I need your shirt," he said.

"What?" Talya asked incredulously. He shrugged out of his shirt and handed it to her.

"What am I supposed to do with that?" she asked.

"Wear it," Liam said. "I need your shirt."

"What's going on?" Talya asked.

"Listen, Talya, I know you don't trust me, but right now, I need you to do exactly what I say."

Chapter Sixteen

Talya didn't say anything at first. She really did want to return home, but the fact that those men, or whatever they were, had tracked them across how many states was really saying something. She had a feeling that if she wanted to stay alive, she was going to have to stick with Liam for now. "Okay," she said reluctantly.

"Okay," Liam said back to her. "Now, the first step is to take off your shirt and put on mine." He motioned towards the stall.

"Why?" she asked.

"My shirt will help mask your scent," he said.

Talya did as he asked. A moment later, she stepped out wearing his shirt and handed him her shirt. She had taken off the apron she hadn't even realized she had still been wearing. Liam reached into his pocket and pulled out his cell phone. He tapped on it a few times; then handed it to her. "You're going to follow these direction; it will take you towards where I live. You won't go all the way there. We will catch up to you, but that will get you moving in the right direction."

Talya frowned. "What are you talking about?" A knock sounded at the bathroom door.

"Liam," somebody called out.

Liam opened the door and took his keys from whoever was at the door. "Thanks," he said. He turned back to Talya. "This key fob unlocks the door and goes in the ignition. We are going to lead them away. Then you are going to run for my car and drive. Just drive. Even if you go the wrong direction, that's fine. Just get away from here. Once we've dealt with the threat, we will catch up to you. I'll call from Garrett's phone. That's my boss. He's the one who was riding in the front passenger seat, okay?" Talya blinked. "Did you get all that?" Liam asked, shaking her gently.

"Why am I going by myself?" she asked, confused.

Liam shook his head regretfully. "Because I have to stay with my friends and deal with these guys." He didn't say anything more, and Talya didn't ask. She was afraid if she did know just what kind of threat those guys really were, she would run away and hide. "Do you understand the plan?" he asked. Talya nodded. "Good. Now after I leave here, count to one hundred slowly then come out. If you don't see any of us, then run to my car and get out of here. If you still see one of us, then don't go out yet. Okay?"

"Why do you need my shirt?" Talya asked.

"So, I can lure them with your scent," he said with a grimace.

Talya felt sick to her stomach. "Okay," she whispered.

Liam put his hands on her shoulders. "I won't let anything happen to you. I promise. That's why we have to do this, so you can be safe. As soon as we've dealt with the threat, I'll catch up to you." Liam looked away from her for a moment. He shook his head. "This is a bad idea."

Talya took a deep breath. "I'll be fine. I don't have my license with me, so hopefully I won't get pulled over. If I do, you'll bail me out right? You won't leave me in jail?" she asked, only half kidding.

"Of course," he responded seriously. "I gotta go. Lock the door behind me. Count to one hundred, then run."

"Got it," Talya said. He looked like he wanted to say something more, but he didn't. He unlocked the door and left her by herself. Talya quickly locked the door behind him and started counting slowly. By the time she got to one hundred, her heart was pounding and her breathing was shaky. She unlocked the door and peered out. She didn't see anything. She stepped out of the bathroom and made her way through the gas station, keeping her head down, and made her way outside. When she didn't see any of the men, she broke into a run towards Liam's car. She hit the unlock button and slid in, locking the doors behind her. Her heart was racing as she pulled out of the gas station. She looked down briefly at the phone. Left. She turned left and picked up speed. She was able to get right back on the highway. She picked up speed but was careful not to go too fast; she didn't want to get pulled over. She wasn't kidding about landing in jail.

After a few minutes, her heart rate settled. She relaxed her position and eyed the car for a moment. She couldn't believe Liam was letting her drive this thing. It was amazing. She couldn't believe the speed and the get-up and go it had. Talya smiled. "I could get used to driving this," she muttered. Talya glanced in her review mirror and frowned. She looked back at the road in front of her, then back at the mirror again. She saw a black SUV a few cars back. It was probably nothing, but she kept an eye on it just in case. She pushed the gas and sped up. She passed a few cars in the left lane, then settled back in the right lane. She glanced up in the mirror and saw the SUV do the same thing.

"Oh, that can't be good." She sped up again; the SUV stayed right behind her. "No, no, no." Talya was starting to panic. She didn't know what to do. She needed to get ahold of Liam, but if she called his boss's phone what would happen? What if they were hiding and she alerted the vampires to their presence or what if they were in the middle of fighting? She bit her lip, undecided about what to do. She looked down at Liam's phone and an idea dawned. She grabbed Liam's phone and pulled up his recent calls. *There.* She hit the call button and put in speaker.

It only rang one time. "Liam, buddy, kidnap any more girls lately?" Kyle asked with a laugh.

"Um, this is Talya," Talya began uncertainly.

"Oh, sorry, Talya, uh what can I do for you?" he asked.

"I think I'm being followed and I don't know what to do. Every time I speed up, this black SUV speeds up. Can you do that thing you did for Liam and let me know if there are any police nearby so I know how fast I can go?" Talya asked.

It was totally silent for a moment. "Um, did you kill Liam and steal his car?" he asked.

"What? No! Liam and his friends are taking care of some vampires. Liam made me leave in his car. They're supposed to catch up to me after they deal with the vampires. I didn't want to call his boss's phone because I didn't want to get him hurt in the fight or distract him or anything," Talya rambled..

"Okay, give me a minute to get set up," he said, taking her seriously.

Talya gripped the wheel tightly as she passed somebody else. "Hurry," she whispered under her breath. She glanced in the mirror. The SUV was right behind her again. She sped up, but the car stayed right with her. She glanced in the rear-view again just in time to see the SUV shoot forward. It came right up behind her. "It's going to hit me!" she yelled.

"There's no police around for the next few miles. Floor it!" she heard Kyle's voice. She pushed the gas pedal to the floor, and her car shot forward. Talya gripped the wheel tightly, her knuckles turning white. "Have you ever driven at high speeds before?" Kyle's calm voice sounded.

"No," Talya said breathlessly.

"Okay, try to stay relaxed. You don't want to be too uptight or you'll jerk the wheel around. Liam's car is super responsive. Keep your eyes on where you want to go. Don't look down at the speedometer or anything else. When you're driving at these speeds, your car is going to go where you're looking. I'm going to try to patch Liam in, okay?"

Talya didn't say anything. She was focusing on trying to stay alive. She gave a quick glance in the rearview mirror. They were keeping up with her. She looked forward again, navigating around a car. Thankfully, there weren't that many cars. She tried to keep her movements calm, but she could see what Kyle was saying. She was struggling to keep her moves smooth at this speed. She felt like it wouldn't take much to lose control. Talya screamed when she felt the tap on her bumper.

"What happened?" Kyle's voice sounded.

"They hit my bumper!" Talya said. She hadn't lost control of the car, but it had certainly startled her.

Kyle cursed into the phone. She heard a ringing sound; then a man say, "Kyle."

"Put Liam on," Kyle ordered.

A moment later, she heard Liam's voice. "Kyle what's going on?"

"They found Talya," Kyle started. An expletive exploded so loudly that Talya jumped. Kyle kept speaking quickly. "She's on the line. I'm directing her."

"Talya?" Liam called out.

"I'm here," she said before pandemonium erupted. She screamed as she was rammed much harder this time. The car swerved for a moment before she got it under control. She heard Liam and Kyle both yelling. She floored it. "I can't do this," she yelled out over their voices. "I can't keep control of the car going this fast. I don't know what to do," she yelled in desperation.

"Talya, listen to me," Liam's voice came through the speaker. "Take a breath. You've got this. All you have to do is focus on keeping the car steady. Just stay calm. You can do this. You just have to evade them until I can catch up to you. Okay?" Talya couldn't respond; she was too focused on trying to stay alive. "Talya, talk to me," he commanded.

"I can't!" Talya yelled at him.

She heard voices. Liam was yelling at somebody to speed up. Then Kyle and Liam were talking. She blocked it all out and tried to focus. She heard another voice giving orders as well.

"Oh no," Talya said softly.

"What? What's wrong?" Liam demanded.

Talya stared ahead with dread. "There's two cars blocking the road ahead." Kyle and Liam both cursed. "What do I do? What do I do?" Talya yelled at them, panicking.

"Kyle, give her a road to take. Get her out of there!" Liam roared.

"There's nothing," Talya said, already knowing. "I have to slow down," she yelled. "I have to slow down!" She started slowing down. As soon as she did, the car rammed her from the back again. She screamed and just about lost control of the car. She jerked the car hard to the left, trying to gain control. She over corrected and ended up going off the road into the grass. She hung on to the wheel, trying to gain control. She heard yelling in the phone, but she couldn't process any of it. Without thinking about what she was doing, she pushed the gas again. Amazingly, the car shot forward through the grass. She found pavement again, turned and pushed the gas pedal to the floor.

"Talya!" Liam was still yelling at her.

"I'm okay," she said, shakily.

"Talya," Kyle said calmly. "I have you going the other direction. How are you going the other direction?"

Talya let out a shaky laugh. "I don't know. They hit me and I lost control of the car and ended up in a break in the median. I was able to get through the grass to the other side of the highway."

"Are they still following you?" Liam asked.

A glance in the mirror confirmed it. "Yes," she said. She had a head start but wasn't sure how long she could maintain it.

"Okay, Liam, she's heading towards you now. You will be able to cut the time down faster. You should be about ten minutes away from each other now," Kyle said.

"Talya, did you hear that? We're only ten minutes from you. You just have to stay ahead of them for ten minutes? Okay? You can do this," he said. She heard Liam talking to the other guys in his car.

Talya took a deep breath and glanced quickly at the clock, making a mental note of what time it was. Ten minutes. She could do this.

Chapter Seventeen

Talya sped up again, trying to keep a relaxed hold on the wheel. She focused on keeping her breathing even. A quick glance in the mirror showed that she still had an edge. If she could just keep it, she'd be okay. She heard the guys talking, well arguing, but she tuned most of it out.

Talya felt every painfully slow minute. Her muscles were aching from holding herself so tightly. A quick glance at the mirror showed that her lead was almost gone. She sped up again, wondering if she would be able to keep control of the car. The guys were still talking, yelling at times.

"Talya, you're doing great," Kyle said. "Stay calm; this is just about over." Just as the words left his mouth, Talya was hit from behind. She couldn't even scream this time. It happened so fast. She righted the wheel and increased her speed.

"They hit me again. How close am I?" she asked, desperate for this nightmare to be over.

"Talya, we're almost to you," Liam's voice came through the

speaker. She could hear the tension in his voice.

"Max, take the next exit," Kyle said. "Talya, you're almost there. You're doing great. Keep going. Guys, you're going to get there first."

Liam's boss started giving orders. Talya focused on keeping control of the car. "Okay, Talya, the next exit is yours. Slow down to take the ramp but not too much that they catch up to you. Go right when you come off the ramp."

Talya nodded. She couldn't respond; her fear was so strong. "Talya," Liam said. "When you come off the ramp, you're going to drive a little ways and turn right. There's a big red barn. You can't miss it. Once you turn, you will see us. Just keep driving. After you pass, we will close them off. Okay? Right and right, and whatever you do, don't stop. Just keep going." Talya nodded again trying to keep it all in her mind.

The exit appeared faster than Talya was ready for. She waited until the last possible second before turning and taking it, hoping they'd miss it. A quick glance told her they didn't. She came to the end of the ramp. Without stopping she took a hard right, the tires squealing. Then she floored it. The car shot forward. With eyes wide she looked for the barn.

"Awesome, Talya, just keep going. You're almost there." Kyle said. She no longer heard Liam or the other guys.

"I see it!" she called out. She raced for the road that she needed to turn on. She braked some; she would never be able to make the turn otherwise. That was a mistake. As soon as she started to turn, the SUV slammed into the side of the car.

Talya screamed and closed her eyes as the world around her

exploded. After what felt like minutes but probably was only seconds, the car finally stopped rolling. Talya heard screaming; she didn't even realize it was her still screaming. Her voice broke off, hoarse. She blinked, trying to take stock of herself. She couldn't feel anything. She didn't know if that was a good thing or a bad thing. She closed her eyes. She just wanted to rest; she was done.

Talya became aware of someone calling her name. She groggily opened her eyes, but she couldn't answer them. Her tongue didn't seem to be working, and her brain felt fuzzy. She closed her eyes again. Talya heard a terrible screeching sound; then she felt hands on her. "Talya, Talya!" she recognized Liam's panicked voice. She wanted to say something, but she couldn't. Somehow, she was conscious enough to realize she was upside down. Her buckle held her in place; that would explain why her brain felt fuzzy. "I'm going to get you out of here. I just have to check to see if anything is caught or broken or unstable before I move you," he said. Talya closed her eyes. She felt Liam practically on top of her. "Okay, I'm going to unbuckle you and get you out of here. You let me know where you feel pain," he said. Liam reached across her and unbuckled her belt. He caught her when she was released from her position. He crawled with her out of the car.

Talya blinked when he stood up, cradling her to his chest. She looked over his shoulder at the state of his car. She stared, unable to look away. She couldn't believe she had been in that. The car was upside down, the driver's door was completely torn away from the car. The glass was gone in all of the windows. The car itself was crumpled in on itself. Talya blinked and closed her eyes. She didn't think she would ever forget that sight as long as she lived.

She wanted to say something to Liam, but she couldn't. Her mind wanted her to speak, but her body couldn't keep up. "How is she?" she heard one of the men ask.

"Alive," came Liam's one word reply.

"Let's get out of here," she heard. There was more talking, but she tuned it out. Her hold on reality was starting to fade. The adrenaline that had flooded her system, allowing her to drive and survive the crash was quickly depleting. In its place came a feeling like being under water. Everything around her sounded muffled and far away. The last thing she remembered was thinking she was lucky to be alive.

———————

Talya opened her eyes, or at least tried to, but they felt too heavy. It felt like someone had sewn them shut. She didn't fight it. She just went back to sleep.

———————

Talya heard voices and speaking. She felt herself being moved. She heard voices she hadn't heard before. Then she heard one she recognized. "I'm right here, Talya. Everything's going to be okay. You're safe." She held onto those words as she slipped into the blackness once again.

Talya tried to open her eyes but couldn't. Panic flooded her. She tried to reach up to touch her eyes to see what was going on but she couldn't. "Easy, there Talya," she heard a calm, soothing voice say. "You can't open your eyes because they are covered to help them heal. I'm going to give you something to help you go back to sleep." She heard a crash and she jumped.

"Talya?" she heard a voice ask.

"Liam, let her rest. I'm giving her something to make her go back to sleep." She heard more talking, but she couldn't focus on it. She was already starting to float away to a place where there was no pain.

Talya slowly opened her eyes. She instantly became aware of pain. Everywhere. To distract herself, she took in the unfamiliar ceiling above her head and frowned. She turned her head slightly and looked around the room. She appeared to be in a hospital of some kind that was way nicer than any she'd ever been in before. She looked at the machine next to her bed and followed the tubes with her eyes to where they connected to her. She looked down at her arm and realized she was hooked up to an IV. She glanced at her other arm and saw it was in a cast, bent at the elbow and resting on her stomach. She lifted her head some and looked at the rest of her. A quick glance down the rest of her body revealed a cast on her leg. She closed her eyes for a moment and took stock of her body. Absolutely everything hurt. She didn't think there was a place on her body that didn't hurt.

She slowly turned her head to the other side of the room and was surprised to see Liam sitting in a chair. His head rested on the wall behind him.

Talya studied him for a moment. He looked terrible. His beard was overgrown and shaggy, his hair was a mess, his clothes were wrinkled and looked like he'd slept in them for a week. His eyes suddenly popped open and focused on her. "Talya," he breathed out. He was up and out of his chair and standing over her a moment later. "Are you in any pain?" he asked. Talya opened her mouth to talk to him but her tongue felt heavy. Liam put his hand on her shoulder gently. "Don't try to talk. You have stitches on your tongue. Just nod. Are you in pain?" he asked again. Talya simply nodded. Liam was quiet for a moment. "Paul will be here in a second."

The door opened and the man from the phone call after she had gotten hit at school walked in. He looked to be about Liam's age. He was tall and built similar to Liam. But he had dark hair, whereas Liam's was more blondish brown. "Talya, my name is Paul. I've been taking care of you. It's good to see you awake. You went through a nasty ordeal." Images of Liam's car ran through her mind, and Talya shuddered. "Now, I don't want you to talk because your tongue is still healing, but I'm going to ask you some yes and no questions. Just shake your head, all right?" "Do you remember what happened to you?" Paul asked. Talya nodded. "Do you have double vision or is your vision blurry?" Paul asked Talya several more questions. He asked her about her pain levels for each of her injuries. "You were pretty seriously injured, Talya. So much so that we weren't sure if you were going to make it," he said glancing at Liam. "When you got here you had a broken arm, a broken foot, two cracked ribs, a concussion, a deep laceration on your tongue, a scratch in your right eye, not to mention bruises all over your body." By the time he was done, Talya was exhausted.

"She needs to rest," she heard Liam say, but she couldn't seem to keep her eyes open. She felt his hand on her face, gently rubbing her cheek. "Don't fight it, Talya. Just let your body rest. I'll be here when you wake up." Talya wanted to tell him to go home and get some sleep, but she couldn't seem to get the words to form. She closed her eyes and let sleep take her away.

The next few times Talya opened her eyes were much the same. Liam was always there. He would talk to her for a few minutes, then she would fall asleep again. One good thing was that she was awake longer and longer each time.

Finally, she opened her eyes and felt like a change had taken place in her body. She didn't feel nearly as terrible as she had every other time she had woken up. She saw she was no longer connected to anything. That was good. She turned her head to see Liam in the same chair he always occupied. When he saw she was awake, he came and stood next to her. "Hey," he said softly.

Talya tried her tongue and realized it felt mostly normal. "Hey," she croaked out. Liam grabbed a cup of water with a straw and held it up to her.

"Here, try some of this," he said.

Talya drank greedily from the cup. She felt so thirsty suddenly. When it was empty, Liam filled it up for her again. "You look better; you have more color in your face," Liam said. "How are you feeling?"

"Better than I did every other time I woke up," Talya said, her voice still scratchy and her tongue thick.

Liam nodded. "That's good. Paul says your body is healing."

Talya finally had a chance to say what she'd been wanting to ever since the accident. "Liam, I am so sorry about your car," she managed to get out.

Liam blinked. "There's nothing to be sorry for."

"But I destroyed it," Talya said weakly.

"It's a car," Liam said. "You're way more important to me than a car. Cars can be replaced; you can't," he said sincerely.

Talya didn't know whether to blush or cry. She felt really out of control of her emotions right now. That must have been why the tears started tracking down her cheeks.

Chapter Eighteen

Liam froze. "What is it, Talya? Where do you hurt?" Talya couldn't respond. Reality was settling in, and she didn't feel like she could face it. She knew she would be in casts for several weeks. She had no idea where she was or what was going on, she was miles away from her home, and she was in pain. "Talya?" Liam asked again. Talya couldn't respond. The door opened and Paul walked in. "Help her," Liam demanded.

Paul came towards Talya. "Talya, are you in pain? I can increase your pain medicine," Paul said.

"I just," Talya choked out. "I just want to g-go home," Talya said, feeling utterly devastated. The tears continued to stream down her cheeks. She turned away from the men. She heard the rumble of voices and knew they were talking, but she didn't bother paying attention. A few minutes later, she felt the bed shift next to her.

"Talya," Liam said.

"Please, I just want to be alone," she said.

"Here," he said. Talya didn't turn towards him. She didn't want anything he had to offer. She closed her eyes tightly, hoping he would just go away.

"Talya, honey?" Talya heard her grandma's voice. She froze and turned her head. Liam had his phone out and the speaker on.

"Grandma?" Talya asked, her voice cracking.

"Oh, honey, we've been so worried about you. Liam told us you were in a terrible accident. Are you okay?" Talya felt her tears start up again. Liam handed her the phone and stood up. He walked towards the door and left the room quietly. "Talya?"

"I'm here," Talya said.

"Tally bear, are you okay?" her Grandpop joined in.

Talya smiled through her tears. "Yeah."

"Now we know from that man of yours that you're not okay, so no lying. How are you really?" Grandma asked.

"I've got a broken arm, a broken leg, broken ribs, stitches in my tongue—though those might have disappeared by now. I'm not really sure," Talya said.

"Oh, honey," Grandma said.

"I'm okay, really," Talya said, her voice wobbly.

"When can you come home?" Grandpop asked, his voice rougher than usual.

Talya just shook her head. She had no idea what to say. "I don't know," she finally whispered. She wasn't sure what Liam had told them.

"Liam will bring her to us as soon as soon as she's healed up," Grandma said confidently. "He told us that you needed specialized care, honey. That's why he took you to where he lives in Wisconsin."

"I don't know why she can't heal here," Grandpop grumbled.

Grandma sighed. "You heard what Liam said."

"How are you both doing? Staying safe right?" Talya needed to redirect the conversation until she and Liam could collaborate their stories.

"You don't need to worry about us; we're fine," Grandpop said.

"You don't know how happy I am to hear that. Have you heard from Sage at all?" she asked them.

"She's come over every day to check on us and to see if we've heard anything more from you or from Liam. Liam called her and told her what happened to you," Grandma said.

That was news to Talya. "He did?" she asked.

"Yes. She said it was a good thing too because she was getting ready to go to the police," Grandma said, chuckling. Talya smiled.

They talked for a little while longer. Talya smiled, listening to them. It was so good to talk to them, to know they were okay. "Talya, you do what you need to get healed up and get home, you hear me?" Grandma said.

"I will, Grandma," Talya said. "I love you, both of you."

"We love you too," Grandma said. "We took care of things at school for you. All the teachers are supposed to start emailing you your assignments. Sage gathered all your books for you and mailed them to Liam."

Talya felt grateful once again for her friend. They talked a few more minutes before Talya got tired. "I'll call again soon probably from this number. I lost my phone in the accident," Talya said. They said their goodbyes, and Talya hung up the phone with a small smile on her face. She put the phone down on the table next to her, so Liam could grab it when he came back. Talya laid her head back on her pillow and took a deep breath. She already had her chance to have a complete meltdown and pity party. Now it was time to stop feeling sorry for herself and do what she needed to get healed up and get home. The threat had been taken care of. All she had to do was heal; then she could get back to her life. It was a good plan. Her eyes drifted shut without her consent; soon she was asleep again.

When she woke up sometime later, she saw Liam working on a laptop. "You don't have to stay here all the time. I know you have a life," Talya said.

Liam's startling blue eyes met hers, and Talya fought the urge to look away. "I'm fine," he said. He closed his laptop. "What can I get for you?"

"What did you tell my grandparents?" she asked.

"I told them that you borrowed my car and were in a really bad accident. You needed special care, so they took you to Wisconsin to a specialized trauma center. Which is as close to the truth as I could get," he said unapologetically.

"But I can go home now, right? Because you dealt with them, right?" Talya asked. She couldn't bring herself to say *vampires* out loud. She still wasn't sure she bought into that whole story yet. She did believe, however, that those guys had been after her.

Liam shook his head. "No, I'm sorry. Not until we know why

they are after you. They could send more. You don't want to endanger your grandparents."

Talya sighed in frustration. "You're sure they're safe, right?"

"We've got two men taking turns watching them twenty-four hours a day," he assured her.

It didn't take away her worry, but it made her feel slightly better about the situation. "Is it possible for me to get a shower?" she asked.

Liam hesitated. "Let's ask Paul," he said. They didn't have long to wait. He came in a moment later.

"Talya, you want a shower?" he asked.

Talya frowned at him. She did, but how did he know that? She just nodded. "Yes."

"It might be difficult, but we can try," Paul said. "The hardest part is going to be keeping both casts dry over the next few weeks."

Talya's face fell. She hadn't thought about that. "Do you have any of those waterproof casts? I've heard about those," she said hopefully.

"I don't typically need a lot of casts in my line of work," Paul said vaguely. "So, we don't have any of those," he said, looking at Liam. "I can find something to wrap around both casts, but you will have to take a bath, not a shower so you can keep both dry."

"Okay, I can do that," Talya said. She was already thinking through how she could make it work.

"Well, then comes the getting in and getting out. You won't be able to do that on your own," he said. "You're going to have to have someone help you and probably help you wash your body and your hair since you only have one arm."

"I can do it," Liam offered..

"Um, no, you can't," Talya said.

"Well, Paul's certainly not doing it," Liam said quickly.

Talya rolled her eyes. "Neither of you are. I can do it on my own."

"I'm not sure that's a good idea," Paul said, hesitatingly.

"Can you please get me something to cover my casts?" she asked him. Paul nodded and slipped out of the room.

"Talya, you're not strong enough to do this by yourself. I can't let you," Liam said.

Talya scoffed. "You can't let me?" She shook her head. "I'm doing it. I feel so gross."

Liam didn't argue with her. Paul came back with plastic wraps for her casts. He wrapped her leg cast and her arm cast. "Do you need any more help?" Paul asked, glancing at Liam.

"I've got her," Liam said. Paul nodded and left the room. "Let me go start the bath," Liam said before disappearing into the bathroom connected to the room. He came back and looked down at her. "Are you sure you're up for this?" he asked.

Talya nodded. "Please," she said again. "Is there another hospital gown I can put on?" she asked.

"I brought clothes for you," he said.

Talya was surprised at this but really grateful. "Thank you."

He just nodded. "I know I'm going to regret this," he said as he bent over her. He reached around her and gently picked her up.

"I can walk," Talya said, embarrassed.

"No, you can't," Liam said without looking down at her. "You don't have any crutches, and you can't put weight on your foot." Talya frowned. Liam carried her into the bathroom. He stopped next to the tub and looked down at her with a frown. "Are you sure about this?" he asked.

"Yes," Talya said. She looked longingly at the sudsy water. Liam gently lowered her to her feet, well her good foot. He kept his arms around her until she was steady on her one good foot. "Thanks," Talya said, a little breathlessly.

"Call me when you get your clothes off, and I'll lower you into the water," Liam said.

Talya's eyes shot to his. "You're not coming back in here once I take my clothes off," she said indignantly.

"Talya, you won't be able to get into the bathtub if I don't help you," Liam said gently.

"I'll be fine. Please promise me you won't come back in?" Talya asked.

"Just wrap a towel around yourself or something," he said.

"No. You're not coming in. I'll be fine," she said stubbornly.

Liam ran a hand through his hair in frustration. Without a word, he turned and strode out of the bathroom, closing the door none-too-gently behind him.

Talya let out a sigh of relief. Then she got to work trying to take off the hospital gown. It was awkward but she finally got it off. Then she peeled off her underwear. Finally, she was free. Now she just had to maneuver herself into the tub. She sat down on the edge first, straddling the side of the tub with her good foot in the tub and her cast on the outside. She put her good arm on the other side of the tub and tried lowering herself in. She landed with a splash. "Are you okay?" she heard Liam ask outside the door.

"Yeah, but I got water all over the floor," she said with a grimace.

"Don't worry about it. I'll clean it up when you're done," Liam said easily.

Talya put her head back and closed her eyes for a moment. The hot water soothed her aching body. After a few minutes, she knew she needed to get started with her hair and body or she would fall asleep. Her eyes popped open. She had totally forgotten to ask about soap and shampoo. She glanced at the side of the tub and saw shampoo, conditioner, shower gel, a razor, and a fresh buff puff. She awkwardly wet her hair; then got to work. It took her a lot longer with one arm than she thought it would, but finally she was clean and freshly shaven, well at least on her good leg. Now came the hard part. Somehow, she was going to have to stand up. She tried a few different things, but nothing worked. She was starting to get frustrated when she heard a knock.

"Talya, how are you doing in there?" Liam asked.

Talya put her head against the tub wall. "I can't get out," she admitted in defeat.

Chapter Nineteen

"I'll get you," he said easily. "Just grab the towel I left next to you and put it over you. I'll do the rest."

Talya leaned forward and let the water out of the tub. Then she took the fluffy white towel and wrapped it around her, securing it the best she could. She took the other towel and wrapped it around her hair. "Okay," she said weakly. The door opened not a second later, and Liam strode in. He bent over and lifted her with ease. He didn't look down at her as he carried her out of the bathroom and to the bed. He gently set her down and went back into the bathroom. He returned a moment later with a pile of clothes that he handed to her.

"Are you okay to get yourself dressed?" he asked. Talya nodded. "Okay, I'll go clean up the water in the bathroom; call me if you need me, okay?"

Talya nodded, but there was no way she was calling him to help her get dressed. She would just have to figure it out. Once Liam left the room, she took the pile of clothes. On top was a soft v-neck t-shirt—the kind you could sleep in. Next was a pair of pink underwear and a matching bra. Talya didn't want to know how he got those, nor did she want to know how come they were her size. Last was a pair of soft pajama shorts that matched the t-shirt. She finally got the underwear on over her cast. That was a feat. The shorts slipped over her cast easily. Trying to clasp the bra with one hand was a feat, but she finally got it. She slipped the t-shirt on; then collapsed on the bed. "Liam," she called out weakly.

He opened the door and came out of the bathroom. "You okay?" he asked. Talya nodded. He held out a brush. "Want me to brush your hair for you?" he asked.

Talya nodded. She had no strength left. She sat up and leaned forward while Liam worked the tangles out of her hair. When he was done, he put the brush down and helped her onto her pillows. Talya closed her eyes as soon as her head was on the pillows. "Thank you," she whispered. She fell asleep before he even responded.

When Talya woke sometime later, Liam was in his chair working again. He looked up and saw that she was awake. "Hey," he said with a smile. "How are you feeling?"

Talya's stomach let out a rumble. "Hungry," she said.

He laughed. "I'll bet. What are you hungry for?" he asked.

Talya shrugged. "I don't know. Are you hungry at all?"

"I'm always hungry," he said with a grin. "I'll call in something; I'll be right back." He came back a few minutes later with Paul following.

"Talya, how are you feeling?" he asked.

"A lot better," she said.

"How would you like to get out of here?" Paul asked.

Talya looked up at him. "Really?"

He smiled. "Really. I just want to check a few more things, but I think you can get out of here."

Paul checked her head, her ribs, asked a bunch of questions, and talked her through pain killers for the next few days. Then he gave her the okay to leave. "I'll go get some medicine to send home with you." He disappeared a moment later.

Talya watched him; then turned back to Liam. "What is it, Talya?" Liam asked gently.

"Where am I going to go?" she asked, looking at him.

"My house," he responded right away. "You get to have me as your own personal nurse," he said with a grin as he waggled his eyebrows.

"For how long?" She asked uncertainly.

"I don't know," Liam said honestly.

Talya sighed. "I don't want to put you out," Talya said.

"You're not," he said simply. He moved around the room, packing up stuff in a bag she hadn't seen before. Liam walked into the bathroom and packed the bath supplies. Paul came in with medicine for her.

"Okay, don't get your casts wet. No putting your weight on your foot for at least the next four weeks, and then we'll go from there," Paul said.

"Four weeks! How am I going to get around? I can't do crutches because of my broken arm. What am I supposed to do?" she asked.

"That's what this man is for?" Paul said slapping Liam on the back.

Liam smiled down at her. "It will be okay, Talya. I'll take care of you."

Talya shook her head. "Four weeks," she muttered.

"Don't think about it right now. Think about the fact that you get to get out of here," Liam said.

"Want help?" Paul asked.

"I'll get Talya and you can get the doors," Liam said. Liam came and stood in front of her with the bag on his shoulder.

"Are we getting a wheelchair or something?" Talya asked.

"I'm your wheelchair," Liam said with a grin. Then he bent and easily picked her up. Talya hooked her good arm around his neck. He maneuvered her out of the room and towards the front of the building, being careful not to hit her arm or leg on the doorways. They walked outside to a blue truck that didn't look very old. Paul opened the door and Liam carefully placed her in the front seat. He dropped the bag in the back seat and closed her door. He talked to Paul for a moment before he slid into the driver's seat and started the truck.

"You ready?" he asked.

Talya nodded. "Whose truck is this?" she asked curiously.

"Mine," Liam said, glancing at her.

"I'm so sorry about your car, Liam," Talya said, feeling the need to apologize again.

"I've already told you; there's nothing to apologize for," he said. Talya was expecting a long ride, but after only about five minutes, Liam pulled into a driveway. Talya looked up and stared.

"You live in a log cabin?" she asked.

He turned to look at her. "I do," he said slowly. "Is that a good thing or a bad thing?" he asked.

"That's amazing!" Talya said. "I've always wanted to look inside a log cabin."

Liam chuckled. "Well, let's go check it out." He climbed out of the truck and came around to her side. She opened the door for him.

"Do you want me to try walking, so you don't have to carry me?" Talya asked.

He frowned at her. "Absolutely not. You heard Paul. You can't put weight on your leg."

"Well, I could hop on one leg or something," Talya mumbled.

"Come on," Liam said, ignoring her. He reached into the truck and pulled her up against his chest and began walking towards the house. The log cabin wasn't huge, but it was modest and really cute. Three steps led to a porch that held a porch swing. "Can you grab the door?" Liam asked. He bent over, so Talya could turn the door handle. They walked down a small hallway and the house opened up. There was a large living room to the right with furniture centered around a large fireplace. A large kitchen sat to the left with a round table.

She saw a loft with stairs leading to it. She couldn't wait to see what that looked like. "Liam, this is beautiful," she said in awe.

He glanced down at her. "Yeah? I'm glad you like it."

Liam turned left and walked down a hallway where they

passed a bathroom and two doors. He opened one and walked in. "I was thinking you could stay in this room. It's got an en suite bathroom. My room is usually upstairs in the loft, but I'll move next to you for now in case you need something during the night."

"Oh, you don't have to do that," Talya started.

Liam just ignored her. "You'll find clothes in the drawers. Kyle's wife, Madison, did the shopping for you. You haven't met her yet, but I'm sure you will soon. There's cosmetics in the bathroom. If there's anything else you need, please let me know. I want you to be comfortable here."

"You didn't have to do all that," she said, feeling badly.

Liam lifted her chin. "I wanted to."

"Well, thank you," Talya said.

"Food should be here any minute. Do you want to get settled out on the couch?" Liam asked.

Talya nodded. "Sure." Liam carried her out to the couch and helped her get situated. The doorbell rang, and he went to answer it. He came back a few minutes later with a bag of food. He set the bag down on the coffee table; then went to the kitchen to grab plates, napkins, and forks. "Hope you like Chinese," he said.

"I love Chinese," Talya said with a smile. He pulled out several containers of food. Talya laughed. "How much did you get?"

He grinned at her. "You said you were hungry."

"How much do you think I eat?" Talya asked.

"Not enough," Liam said seriously. Talya frowned at him, but he moved on quickly. "But I'm starved, so I'll eat whatever you don't."

"I don't know how you don't gain weight eating the way you do. I just look at food and gain weight," Talya said in disgust.

Liam looked down at her like he was going to say something but chose not to. "All right. I've got beef and broccoli, cashew chicken, sesame chicken..."

"Sesame chicken," Talya said, interrupting him.

He chuckled. "Okay, sesame chicken for the lady." He handed her the carton.

She opened it and held it up to her nose, sniffing it. She sighed. "I love sesame chicken. Thank you." It took a minute to get settled but soon she had the Chinese food settled in the crook of her arm next to her cast and was eating with her left hand. She wasn't as coordinated with her left hand, but she made it work. Liam popped open a water bottle and handed it to her.

"What do you like to drink? I wasn't sure. I can get whatever you like to have here in the house," Liam said.

"Water's fine," Talya said.

"What else do you like to drink, though? Soda? Juice? Tea? Sparkling water?" he asked.

"I like sparkling water. This is really good Chinese; I mean like the best I've had," she said. She was so hungry, but she was trying not to shovel it in too fast.

"You're also really hungry after not eating anything for five days," Liam said. "Just whatever Paul had you hooked up to."

Talya nodded and kept eating. Soon, she was so full she couldn't take another bite. "I'm full. Do you want the rest of mine?" she offered to Liam. He took it from her. "Thank you for lunch. I really appreciate it. You can just start a tab for what I owe you," Talya said.

Liam frowned. "You don't owe me anything. It's my job to take care of you." Talya looked up at him. "I mean—you're staying in my home after all," he finished smoothly and looked down to take a bite of food. Talya figured he didn't mean anything by his weird choice of words.

Chapter Twenty

Liam picked up their lunch. "I've got to leave for a few hours. Where do you want to get settled?"

"I guess right here is fine," Talya said.

"Here's the controls for the TV. I've got everything." He handed her the controls. "I'll lock the door behind me. Do you need anything before I go?" he asked.

"I'm good; thanks," Talya said. He looked uncertain, like he didn't want to leave her. "I'll be fine," she said, reassuring him.

"There's men outside the door on security; so you will be safe." He handed her his phone. "I'm going to leave this with you. If you need me for any reason, call Garrett. I'll be working with him. I'll get you a phone today."

"Oh, no, you don't need to do that," Talya said.

"See you," he said. He bent and kissed her quickly on her forehead. Talya stared at his retreating back. He had surprised her. At the door, he turned back and winked at her. Then he was gone a moment later, locking the door after him.

Liam had barely been gone for ten minutes when the phone rang. Talya glanced down and saw Garrett's number. She really hoped it was Liam. "Hello," she answered.

"Miss me?" Liam's voice sounded.

Talya laughed, despite herself. "You haven't even been gone ten minutes."

"I know," he said. "Listen, Emma and Madison, Garrett's wife and Kyle's wife, are driving me crazy. They want to come over and meet you. I told them you weren't up for it, but they won't let it go until I call and ask."

Talya smiled. "That's fine. They can come over. Will they be able to get in or do I need to get up and let them in?"

"The guys will let them in. Don't you dare get up unless I'm there to help you," Liam ordered. Talya laughed. "Why did you laugh?" he asked.

"Because I'm going to have to learn how to get around without you," she said.

"No, you're not," he said. "You can't put weight on that leg. Paul said."

"I understand that, but I'm going to have to learn to get around somehow. I have to be able to go to the bathroom," Talya said, rolling her eyes.

"Talya, if you have to get off that couch for any reason, you call me. I can be home within minutes," Liam said seriously.

"Liam, it's fine. You have a job to do. I'm fine," Talya said.

"My number one priority is you, Talya. Now the girls should be there soon. Let me know if you need me. I'll talk to you soon," Liam said before saying goodbye. It wasn't but five minutes later there was a knock at the front door.

"Come in," Talya called out. The door opened and two girls who looked around Talya's age, maybe a little older came in. Talya blinked. They were both gorgeous.

The petite redhead stepped forward first. "Hi, I'm Emma."

"I'm Madison," the other girl with long dark hair and tan skin said.

"I'm Talya. I'd get up, but I can't really," she said.

"Liam told us what happened. It's so awful. I'm so sorry for what you've been through. We just wanted to meet you. Do you need anything?" Emma asked.

"No, I just ate with Liam. Thank you. You're welcome to sit," she said gesturing to the reclining chairs.

"Thanks," Madison said. They both claimed a chair.

"So, tell us a little about yourself," Madison said. "Where are you from?"

"I'm from North Carolina. I'm currently a senior in high school." She saw the two girls glance at each other from that, but she ignored it and kept going. "I worked at a diner before coming here and live with my grandparents. How about you two?"

"Well, I grew up here in Hopewell, Wisconsin. I met my husband at a young age and knew we would get married some day," Madison said with a grin. "I do security for a living, and I love shopping."

"I did not grow up here. I'm originally from Atlanta," Emma started. "I escaped my family and ran away when I turned eighteen and ended up in Hopewell where I met Garrett. We've been married for almost four months," she said with a sparkle in her eye.

"Aw, congratulations," Talya said. "I'm sorry that you had to run away from your family though. That sounds awful."

"It was, but it brought me here. I can't complain. I got an amazing man out of the deal," she said.

"Is he nice?" Talya asked. "He seems kind of scary." Madison and Emma both cracked up at that.

"He's amazing," Emma said lightly. "He's so good to me, but he can be intimidating when you first meet him. He's definitely different when we're alone, softer and more gentle. But don't tell him I said that," she said with a laugh.

"Don't listen to Emma," Madison said. "He's crazy scary. I've known him a long time. She sees a side of him that nobody else sees. But with all that said, he's a good leader."

"Hmmm," Talya said, not convinced.

"So, what has Liam told you about us?" Emma asked, curiously.

"Nothing," Talya said. "I didn't even know he lived here. I thought he lived in North Carolina. Everything happened so fast that we haven't had a chance to really talk."

"Oh boy, here we go again," Madison mumbled, and Emma frowned.

"What's that supposed to mean?" Talya asked.

"It just means that Liam is going to be in trouble for dragging you up here without telling you anything," Emma said with a frown.

"Yeah, he totally should have told you more," Madison said. She really liked both of them and hoped they could be friends. They made her think of Sage and miss her. She would have to call her friend as soon as she got a phone. Weariness tugged at her, and she fell asleep before she even realized what was happening.

Talya found herself in her dream place. She took a deep breath. She had missed it here. It was so peaceful, so different from real life. She spent time wandering around, taking in the beauty of this place before she sat down in her favorite place—the base of the big tree. It wasn't long before her wolf friend appeared.

"I missed you," she said. "Life's been so crazy. It's so good to be back here. What is this place anyway?"

The wolf didn't respond for a moment. "It's called the dream state or a dream stasis... It's a place that only exists in your mind, Talya."

Talya frowned. "Did I make it up?"

"No, this is a real experience; but it doesn't exist outside of your head," the wolf said, not really clearing things up.

"Well, I love coming here. It's so relaxing and rejuvenating," Talya said.

"It is, but I will warn you, Talya. It won't always be this way," he said ominously.

"Why not?" Talya asked.

"Because the darkness of your world reaches even into a place like this. It wasn't how it was supposed to be, but evil has a way of tinting everything that was once good and making it no longer good," the wolf said.

Talya stared at the wolf. "Are you saying that this place won't always be peaceful? It could become a place of my nightmares?"

The wolf didn't respond for a moment, taking his time as usual to answer her. "It will," he finally said. "But Talya, you need to remember something. No matter how dark things may seem, I am always here just a call away. I will always hear you; I will always know when you are in trouble. Sometimes, when it seems I'm the furthest away, know that I am right beside you. You may not see me or at times even be able to feel me, but it's during those times that I will be the closest to you."

Talya listened to what he was saying. She felt a shiver of fear run down her spine. His words felt ominous. "Why can't it just be peaceful all the time?" she asked, not really even knowing if she was talking about this place or real life. She was kind of lost in the middle of both.

"Because just as good exists, so does evil. There will always be a battle between evil and good, between light and dark. The only way to banish the darkness is for good to rise up, to conquer evil. That's been the ongoing struggle since the beginning of time," the wolf explained in his ancient-sounding voice. "The battle has already started. There will be death and loss. In the end, good will triumph, but there is always a cost. Come, child. I want to show you something."

Talya stood and walked towards the wolf. He began walking, and she walked beside him. He walked towards the edge of her dream world, where she always thought it came to an end. He walked ahead, and Talya followed him feeling like they were walking through fog. It got so thick, Talya felt like she couldn't breathe, nor could she see where she was going. Just when she thought she needed to turn around and go back, it cleared up. She blinked and looked around. They stood on the side of a road. Everything looked so real. She could hear the cars driving past. "Is this real?" she asked the wolf.

"It's real in that this is a real point and time, but it's in the past. Watch," he said. Talya took this as her cue to be quiet. She looked around but didn't recognize anything. Suddenly, her eyes snagged on a big barn. Her breath caught as she recognized the barn. Her breathing started speeding up.

"No," she said shakily. Then her eyes turned, and she saw a car she recognized. "No, no, no," she said. She wanted to look away, but she couldn't. She watched silently as the car came flying down the road towards where she and the wolf sat. She watched as the brake lights came on; she desperately wanted to close her eyes. She didn't want to see what came next. But she couldn't. It was as if her eyes refused to obey her brain's command. She watched as the car behind slammed into the car in front of it.

Talya watched in horror as the car went airborne, glass exploding from the windows, the car flipping several times before landing with a sickening sound. Talya couldn't hold back the sound of anguish that escaped her throat. "Talya! Talya!" she heard Liam screaming, but she couldn't look away from the scene in front of her. She watched as one of the men climbed out of the car and ran over to where she lay upside down inside the destroyed car. From this angle, she could see the deep red of the man's eyes. She gasped in fear. She watched as he sped towards her helpless self, trapped in the car. She couldn't breathe. She could feel the evil coming off this man. Somehow, she knew he was going to kill her. She glanced to where Liam was running towards her. He was running fast, faster than a human should, but she knew in her heart that he wouldn't get there in time.

Suddenly, a wolf appeared and stood in front of her. The vampire stumbled and stepped backwards before turning and leaving. Talya stared, absolutely stunned. The wolf turned back to the car and sat in front of it. Just before Liam reached the car, the wolf vanished.

Talya stared at the scene. Then she slowly turned her eyes to the wolf at her side. "That was you, wasn't it? He was going to kill me, and you protected me," she said, astonished.

The wolf was quiet for a few moments. "I do not always directly step in, but sometimes it is a necessity. You have a vital role in this world, Talya. I couldn't allow for you to be taken out."

"Th-thank you," Talya said in a shaky voice.

The wolf nodded. "You have a new protector—one of my own. He will protect you with his very life. I have created him to do so. There are hard times ahead, Talya. You must let your protector do his job. Your life is too valuable."

When he didn't say anything more, Talya turned towards him. "I don't understand. What's coming? Who's my protector?"

"You already know who he is," the wolf said.

Then everything faded. Talya opened her eyes and pandemonium ensued.

Chapter Twenty-One

Talya blinked at the level of noise. Liam was yelling at some-body; she couldn't see who. Madison and Emma were stand-ing in the corner looking worried. She saw Garrett and Max and another guy she didn't know. Everybody was talking over each other, and Talya blinked at the insanity of it. She finally saw who Liam was yelling at. It was the doctor, Paul. Liam looked like he was about to come to blows with him. Talya had no idea what was going on, but she decided she needed to try to get control of the situation fast.

"Liam," she called out hoarsely. Everything went deathly still in an instant. Liam's eyes shot to hers; she was startled to see the color of his eyes. He was in front of her a moment later. He blinked, and his eyes were a brilliant blue once again.

"Talya," he breathed. He pushed her hair behind her ear. "Are you okay? What happened?"

Talya frowned. "I just fell asleep."

"No, you didn't," Liam said, his voice rough. Talya stared at him, confused.

"You fell asleep while we were talking," Emma began gently. She walked towards Talya, but when she got close to Liam, Garrett put his arm around her waist and pulled her close to him. "Sometime later, you started mumbling. Then you started crying out in your sleep. We thought maybe it was a nightmare. I've had experience with nightmares. We didn't want you to have to suffer through that, so we tried to wake you up but we couldn't. After trying, we got worried and called Liam."

"I couldn't wake you up," Liam said, his tone of voice rough. "I called Paul, but he couldn't figure out what was wrong with you." Talya could feel his desperation. She put a hand on his chest. He put his bigger hand over hers, trapping it against his chest. "Are you okay? Are you in pain?" he asked.

"I had another one of my dreams," she said softly. "You know, with the wolf." She whispered the words, but as if she had shouted them, everyone in the room stilled.

"What dream? What wolf?" Garrett asked in a deep voice.

"Garrett, let her be," Liam said in an angry voice.

"If it involves a wolf, then it involves me," Garrett said, not backing down.

Talya had no idea what he meant by that, but she felt Liam's muscles stiffen under her hand. She could see what was going to happen in literally the next moment. She watched as Liam's eyes flashed with color again. She looked up at him. "Liam," she said, touching his face. "Stop." He closed his eyes and leaned forward before taking a deep breath. He seemed to calm down for the moment at least. He pulled back and looked down at her.

"Can I tell them?" she whispered.

Liam blew out a frustrated breath. "Yeah, but let me get you settled first." Without a word, he bent down and picked her up, surprising her. He sat down and positioned her on his lap so that she was sideways. Her leg was out in front of her on the couch and her good arm was trapped between her body and Liam's. Talya could feel her face burning, but when she looked up, she saw smiles on Emma and Madison's faces. Even the guy with his arm around Madison, who she was assuming was her husband, was smiling. Liam buried his nose in her hair for just a moment before muttering, "Okay."

Talya tried to tap down the nerves she felt being held by Liam like this and focus on everybody in the room. "You might want to get comfortable; this might take a little bit." The guy she knew as Max didn't move from his position against the wall. Paul stayed where he was. Garret sat and pulled Emma into his lap, and Madison and her husband sat on the love seat.

Talya suddenly felt nervous. Would they think she was crazy? "So, I uh, have dreams about a talking wolf," she said with a slight laugh. "Crazy right?" Not one person smiled or laughed. Taking this as encouragement that they didn't think she was crazy, Talya began to tell them about the dreams, starting with the first time she saw the wolf and finishing with the dream she just had. When she told them about walking through the thick fog and seeing herself driving the car, she felt Liam stiffen underneath her. When she talked about seeing the car flying through the car, he let out a loud, angry sound that sounded like a growl. Talya jumped in surprise. But that was nothing compared to what happened when she told them about the vampire who had climbed out of the car and made his way to her car. Liam let loose an expletive with a roar and stood up. He practically threw her on the couch and was gone a second later, slamming the front door behind him.

Talya stared in stunned silence after him. Nobody made a sound. Then Emma stood up and came and sat next to her. "It's okay. Garrett used to do that to me when we first started dating. I thought he was mad at me, but then I began to understand that he was mad for me."

"Liam and I aren't dating," Talya said absently, still looking at the door. Nobody said anything.

Madison stood up from the couch. "I'm glad you're okay, Talya. I'm going to go see what Liam has in his kitchen for dinner."

"If it's anything like his last house, nothing," Talya said. "But I'll come help you," she said, taking off her blanket.

"Talya, you can't put weight on that foot," Paul admonished.

"But I need to get to the kitchen," Talya argued. Paul looked at Garrett.

"I called him back, but he's not here yet," Garrett said. He nodded his head at Talya. Talya had no idea what that exchange was about, but Paul came towards her a moment later. "I'll carry you," he said bending down. Before she could protest, Paul picked her up and held her against his chest. He was walking her towards the kitchen when the front door opened.

Paul cursed. Liam's eyes locked on them. He let out a legitimate growl and lunged at them. Garrett intercepted him and threw him against the wall. Talya screamed. That just infuriated Liam more. He threw Garrett off of him and started towards them again. This time when Garrett grabbed him, Max, and Madison's husband did as well. Soon they had him pinned to the floor, though Liam was still moving around. "Don't hurt him," she yelled out. She couldn't help it.

"Paul, put her down and get out of here!" Garrett yelled at him. That got Paul moving. He walked into the kitchen and set her on the counter.

"Don't put weight on that leg," he admonished one last time. Then he disappeared. Madison came and stood next to Talya.

"You okay?" she asked sympathetically. She heard another snarl and a loud thud, like they were slamming Liam back into the ground. "They're not hurting him, if that helps," Madison said. It didn't at all. When she heard another sound that sounded like they were hurting him, Talya was done. She hopped off the counter, landing on her good foot and began hopping around the corner to where she could see him. Horror flooded her when she saw all three men holding Liam down.

She snapped. "Get off him, you brutes!" she yelled. Everybody froze for a moment. "I'm not kidding. Get off him!"

"Are you in control?" Garrett asked in a low voice. She couldn't hear Liam's response, but a moment later, the guys stood up. Garrett was the last to stand. As soon as he stood up, Liam jumped to his feet. He came towards Talya. Without stopping, he swung her up and into his arms and strode down the hallway. He carried her into his bedroom and slammed the door shut behind them.

"Are you okay?" he asked in a low angry voice.

"Yes, are you?" Talya asked almost hysterically. He had a split lip, a bruised eye, and a torn shirt. But more than any of that, she could feel the fury coming off of him. His body was quivering with restrained anger. Talya didn't know what to do to get him to calm down. She put her hand on his chest. He pulled her close to him and just breathed her in. She could feel the anger draining out of him. Talya touched his split lip carefully. "Why did they hurt you?" she asked, confused. "I thought they were your friends."

Liam sighed. "They restrained me, or I would have killed Paul," he said, totally serious.

Talya gasped. "Why?" she asked incredulously.

"Because he touched you; more than that, he carried you," he said in anger.

"But you carry me all the time," Talya said in confusion. "He was just carrying me to the kitchen because of my leg." she said. Liam started breathing heavy again. Talya's words didn't have the calming effect on him that she thought they would. "I'm confused," she whispered.

"I know; I'm sorry. I want to explain everything to you, I just..." he paused.

"What?" she whispered.

Liam ran a hand through his hair. "Will you go outside with me? I want to show you something." Talya nodded.

"You'll have to carry me, though," she said with a smile.

"That I can do," he said with a gentle smile. He stood up and grabbed something from his drawer, putting it under his arm.

"Do you think anybody's still here?" she asked quietly.

"No, they all left," Liam said in a voice that reflected that he was glad that was the case. Liam carried her outside towards the woods that surrounded his house. Talya wanted to say something, but she was nervous. She didn't know what he wanted to show her, but she had a feeling it was huge.

Liam finally stopped when they had walked a little ways into the woods. He carefully set her down on a tree log. He knelt in front of her and put a hand on her knee. "I want to reveal my true self to you. Don't be scared. I would never hurt you," he said. Then he stepped back from her.

Talya felt like she couldn't breathe. She didn't know what to expect, but nothing could have prepared her for what happened next. One minute Liam was standing in front of her, the next, a large brown-colored wolf stood before her. Talya's breathing sped up. She didn't feel fear necessarily, just shock.

Suddenly, the words from the wolf in her dream came back to her mind. *Now you have a new protector. One of my own. He will protect you with his very life. I have created him to do so. There are hard times ahead, Talya. You must let your protector do his job. Your life is too valuable."*

Talya remembered asking, "Who's coming? Who's my protector?"

And she remembered his words, "You already know who he is."

Talya stared at the wolf in front of her as tears came to her eyes. Yes, she already did know who he was.

Chapter Twenty-Two

"It's you," she said softly. The wolf watched her carefully. Talya put out her hand, and he stepped closer. She ran her good hand over his fur. For as deadly as he looked, she should be terrified. Yet she wasn't. It was as if some part of her knew that this wolf would never hurt her. She was still trying to get used to the idea that Liam was inside this magnificent creature. "You're beautiful," she said. The wolf snorted, and Talya looked at it. Then she smiled. "Correction. You don't look beautiful; you look handsome and fierce and terrifying," she said. The wolf nudged against her. Talya ran her hand through his fur again.

Suddenly, Talya felt her energy fade; she was absolutely depleted. She had been running on adrenaline, and now the enormous day was catching up with her. The wolf backed away slowly, and Talya lifted her head. A moment later, a very naked Liam stood in front of her with his back to her. He quickly threw on a pair of black sweat pants, then turned back to her. He picked her up and pulled her against his chest, kissing her lightly on the cheek. "Thank you," he breathed out.

"Thank you," Talya replied. "Thank you for showing me."

"Why did you cry?" Liam asked in concern, looking down at her as they walked.

Talya smiled. "The wolf from my dreams told me that I have a protector now. He was talking about you."

Liam pulled her close to his chest. "I will always protect you, Talya."

Talya looked up at him. "Why?" she asked simply.

Liam looked down at her and took a deep breath. "Because you're my mate, Talya. Wolves wait their entire lives for their mate. For the one person created specifically for us, the other half of our soul, our perfect completer. I knew the minute I saw you and smelled you that you were mine," he said with a smile.

Talya frowned. "You smelled me? That doesn't sound good?" she said.

Liam laughed "It's a good thing. You always smell like fresh strawberries to me," he said. "The first time I smelled it, it was enough to almost bring me to my knees. Then when I saw you, I knew my life had changed forever. Everything shifted in that moment. You became the most important thing to me in the world. My sole job now is to protect you, love you, care for you, and make you happy."

"Is that why you freaked when Paul carried me?" she asked, genuinely wanting to know.

Liam shuddered. "Yes," he said, his voice dropping. "Wolves are very territorial creatures and extremely possessive of our mates, especially when they are in danger, in pain, or emotional.

My wolf went crazy when we heard we almost lost you. I had to leave the house or I would have shifted right there. I would have stayed out longer, but Garrett called me back through our pack link."

"That's how you always communicate with them!" Talya said. Liam smiled. "People always show up whenever you need them, and I could never figure out how."

"Yeah, we can communicate through our pack link," Liam explained. "Anyway, when I came back and saw you in Paul's arms, my wolf lost it and I almost shifted again. That's why Garrett caught me and the guys held me down. If they hadn't, I would have shifted and hurt Paul."

"But he's your friend," Talya said, not understanding.

"Wolves don't think on an emotional level. My wolf thinks on an instinctual level. He saw another man's arms around our mate, so to him, that man must die," Liam said easily.

"Wait, die?" Talya questioned. "That's crazy!"

"Not to my wolf," Liam said. "And at the moment, not really to me either," Liam said with absolutely no emotion.

Talya's eyes widened. "Liam, he's your friend."

"He touched you, Talya. He held your body against his," Liam said in anger.

"Because I couldn't walk," Talya said slowly and distinctly.

Liam shrugged. "Agree to disagree."

Talya blew out a breath. This was exhausting and more than she could handle tonight. She lay her head on Liam's shoulder as he carried her inside to her room. He set her down gently on the bed. He walked over to the dresser and pulled out a pair of sleep shorts and a tank top. He came back and handed them to her. He knelt before her. "Do you need help getting changed?" he asked. Talya shook her head. "Are you hungry?" he asked.

Talya yawned a huge yawn. "I'm not. I'm just ready for bed."

Liam stood up. "Okay. I'll let you get changed and then come back to help you get settled for the night." After he left, Talya began the painfully slow process of getting changed for bed. Finally, she had her pajamas on.

"Okay," she called out. The door opened and Liam came back in. Without a word, he picked her up and carried her into the bathroom. He set her on the floor in front of the sink. While she brushed her teeth and washed her face, he got her bed ready for her. When she was done, he picked her up and carried her back to her bed. Once she was settled, he sat next to her on the bed.

"Are you okay with everything I shared?" he asked as he gently tucked her hair behind her ear.

"I should be shocked or terrified, but I'm not. I guess my dreams sort of prepared me for you," she said with a smile.

Liam gave her a brilliant smile. Then he slowly bent and kissed her on the lips. It didn't last long. He pulled back and pulled her blankets up and over her shoulders. "Good night, beautiful," he said softly.

Talya smiled. "Good night, wolf man." He chuckled softly before leaving her room. Talya lay still, thinking through all the events of the day. It had been quite the day. She fell asleep before she even realized she had done so.

The next morning, Talya woke up to pain in both her arm and her leg. She lay there trying to catch her breath. She must have gone too long without pain relievers. She tried to sit up, so she could try to get some medicine, but pain radiated down her leg, causing her to whimper in pain.

"Talya?" Liam asked, appearing in her room. He must have come right from bed because his hair was messy, and he didn't have a shirt on. He knelt in front of her. "Are you in pain?" he asked.

Talya just shook her head miserably. He opened the drawer next to her and pulled out pills. He disappeared a moment and came back with a bottle of water. "Here," he handed her the pills and water. She quickly threw the pills back and chased them with water. "I'm sorry you're in pain," he said, his voice ragged. Talya could tell he didn't handle her being in pain well.

"I'm okay," she whispered.

"No, you're not," he said quietly but let the matter drop. "Let's get you settled, so when they kick in, you can sleep." He helped straighten her covers and get her tucked in again. He sat next to her and held her good hand while she waited for the pills to kick in. She didn't have to wait long for them to take effect. The pain started reducing to a manageable level, and she started getting sleepy. "Don't fight it; just rest, Talya," Liam said. He continued to hold her hand, stroking the back of it until she fell asleep once again.

Talya wasn't sure how long she slept, but when she woke up later, it was really bright in her room. She turned her head and saw a purple phone sitting on the nightstand. She picked it up and saw it was after eleven. She shook her head. She couldn't wait until she was healed and didn't have to sleep all the time.

She noticed she had a text on the phone. She swiped it. She smiled when she saw it was from Liam. He had put his name in the phone as Wolf Man.

In all the craziness last night, I never gave you this. Everything should be programmed and ready to go. I had to leave to go to work. Text me when you're awake, beautiful, and I'll come help you.

Talya smiled. He was so sweet, but she really needed to learn how to get around without him. She used her new phone and pulled up her favorite online retailer—Amazon. After a quick search, she was able to find exactly what she was looking for. She added a leg scooter to her cart. She had seen other people use them when they had a broken leg. She hoped it would work with one good hand. She just needed Liam's address. She pulled up her contacts and opened Wolf Man's name. Perfect. He had put his address in under his name. She added that to Amazon and checked out. Luckily her card was still stored on there from all her other purchases. She didn't have a lot of money, but she had a few hundred dollars in her bank account still. She had been saving it to buy medicine for her grandma. Guilt swamped her. She was going to have to figure out how to work and make money while she was here healing, so she could send money to her grandparents.

She pushed those thoughts away for now. She needed to deal with one problem at a time. First problem to deal with was getting mobile again. She was happy to see they had next day delivery. She ordered it, excited. Once that was done, she moved on to the next order of business—getting groceries. She pulled up the map on her phone to see what grocery stores were nearby and which ones delivered. Once she figured that out, she started making a grocery list. She thought of a few meals she would like to make and started adding those ingredients to the list. She was suddenly grateful her grandma had made sure she learned how to cook. After ordering groceries, she called her grandparents.

"Hey Grandpop," she said.

"Tallybear," he said with affection. "Just a second, let me get your grandma." Talya waited until they were both on the phone.

"How are you, dear?" Grandma asked.

"I'm good," Talya said. "Each day is a little better. How are you both doing?"

They talked for a little while and ended the conversation with Talya promising to check in again soon. Then it was time to face Sage. She called and left a message telling Sage that this was her new number. Not thirty seconds later, Sage called her.

"Hey Sage," Talya said. "Aren't you supposed to be in class?"

"You are in so much trouble," Sage said.

Talya cringed. Those were not the words she wanted to hear from her gentle, sweet friend. "I know. Sage, I'm so sorry. If you promise to not hang up on me, I will tell you the entire story." It was quiet for a moment, and Talya held her breath.

"I'm waiting," Sage said. "And I'm hiding in the bathroom, skipping my next class. This was more important."

Talya blew out a breath and smiled. "Okay. You're never going to believe all that's been going on."

Chapter Twenty-Three

Talya brought Sage up to speed as much as she could without telling her about the wolves and vampires. There was no way Sage was ready to hear that; besides she would have to ask Liam if she was even allowed to talk about it. She'd lived her entire life without knowing they existed, so they must guard their secret carefully.

"I can't believe you have a broken arm and a broken leg. How do you even get around?" Sage asked.

"Well, um, I manage," Talya said awkwardly.

"Wait, does Liam carry you? I bet he totally does, doesn't he?" Sage asked.

Talya tried to find a way around it but gave in. "Yes, he does," she said with a smile.

Sage squealed. "He has it so bad for you." Talya smiled, thankful Liam wasn't here right now to ask what she was blushing about. "When are you coming home?" Sage asked.

"I have no idea," Talya said. "I don't think it's going to be anytime soon."

"It stinks without you here. I wish I was there with you," Sage complained.

"I know. Me too," Talya said. "Maybe once school is done, if I'm still here, you can visit."

"That would be awesome," Sage said. She groaned. "Well, I'd better get back to class. One of us has to graduate," she said snarkily.

Talya laughed. "Well, hopefully both of us will graduate; but I'll let you go. I promise to stay in touch now that I have a phone again."

"See that you do, or I will show up there," Sage threatened.

"Okay," Talya said with a smile. They said their goodbyes and Talya hung up. Now she just had to figure out how to get around so she could take a shower. She managed to get upright on her good leg, but she didn't know how to move from there. She hopped over to her dresser and closet and grabbed clothes, but that was as far as she got. She was still standing there when a soft knock sounded at her door.

"Come in," Talya called out.

The door opened and Liam walked in. Talya couldn't help but stare at him. He was wearing a designer suit with a blue button-up dress shirt. He looked dangerously sexy. She finally managed to look back up at his eyes again which looked even more brilliant against his blue shirt. A huge grin was on his face, and his eyes were dancing. "Like what you see?" he asked. "I told you I rocked a suit."

Talya felt her face light up. "Well, it's not fair for you to waltz in here looking like that, while I look like this," she said motioning to her body.

His eyes flicked down her body then back to her eyes. "Yeah, it's not really fair." Talya didn't think they were talking about the same thing, but he moved on quickly. "What are you doing out of bed? You should have waited for me," he scolded gently.

"Well, I felt like a loser sleeping in so long," Talya said.

Liam frowned. "Talya, you're recovering. You could sleep all day."

"Well, I'm up now. I need a shower. Do you mind..." She didn't even get the question out before he swept her into his arms. He carried her into the bathroom and set her carefully on the bathroom counter. He walked over and started the shower; then came back to her. "Do you have any of those plastic covers Paul gave you?"

Talya nodded. "They're in that drawer," she said. Liam opened the drawer and pulled them out. He helped her cover each of the casts. Then he picked her up and carried her over to the shower. He frowned down at her. "Are you sure you're okay to take a shower?"

"I'll be fine," Talya said. "At least I won't get stuck in there like I did the bath," she said. "Go on out," she said. "I'll call you if I need you."

He looked uncertain, but he left a moment later. "I'll hear you if you call, Talya," he said over his shoulder.

Once he was gone, Talya got undressed and slowly made her way into the shower. She was slow with one hand, but finally she got her hair and body washed. Then it was a practice in patience to get out of the shower, dried off, and dressed. She pulled on a pair of white shorts, thankful it was getting warmer. There was no way she could get pants over her cast. She pulled on a light blue t-shirt after that. Then she hopped over to the sink to do her teeth and brush her hair. She pulled her long, wet hair into a braid; then hopped out of the bathroom into her room. She put in a pair of silver hoop earrings. Then she hopped over and made her bed. Finally, she made her way to the door. She opened it and hopped out into the hallway. Liam came towards her, a scowl on his face. "You were supposed to call me."

Talya didn't even argue with him. She was depleted after all that. He swept her up into his arms, and she rested against his chest. He carried her to the kitchen and set her in a chair. He opened a bag and gave her a sub sandwich. "It's chicken salad," he said.

"Yummy. Thank you," Talya said.

He pulled out three more sandwiches and a few bags of chips. "Two of the guys guarding the house are joining us for lunch if that's okay."

Talya nodded. "Of course. I forgot there were guys outside."

"Good. Then they did their job," Liam said.

"They can come inside," Talya offered. "They don't have to stay outside the whole time."

"Yes, they do," Liam said. The front door opened and two guys came in.

"Talya, this is Wyatt and Steven." Talya looked up and saw two good-looking, muscular men walk into the kitchen.

"Good night, is it a wolf thing that you all look handsome

and are built like tank trucks?" Talya asked.

Wyatt and Steven grinned, and Liam scowled. "Talya," he growled.

"What? I'm just sayin'," Talya said with a grin.

"Well, don't," Liam said. He moved towards her. "You're only supposed to notice one man in this room," he said in a low growl.

"Oh, right," Talya said. "Which man is that supposed to be again?" she asked teasingly.

Liam sat next to her and scowled at her. "Eat your sandwich, woman." Talya laughed out loud; he gave her a begrudging smile.

Talya looked towards Wyatt and Steven. "Thanks for doing security," she said.

They both nodded. It was quiet as everybody started eating. Talya picked up her sandwich and took a bite. "Mmm," she said. After she swallowed, she looked at Liam. "It's really good. Thank you."

Liam smiled at her. "You're welcome." Liam kept the conversation flowing during lunch. After lunch, the guys went back outside to doing whatever it was they did. Liam picked her up. "Where do you want to settle?" he asked.

"Um, I guess the couch," Talya said. He bent down and picked her up. He helped her get settled on the couch.

"Do you need anything else?" he asked.

"No, thank you. Thanks for lunch, too," she said again.

"You're welcome. Get some rest. I'll be home after five," he said. He bent and kissed the top of her head. "Call me if you need me." Then he was gone.

Talya waited a few minutes until she was sure he was gone before she began the arduous process of getting up and across the room. She finally made it to the front door. She opened the door, and Wyatt looked up at her and began coming towards her. "Talya, do you need something?"

"Hey, I'm getting groceries delivered sometime in the next hour or two. I just wanted to give you a heads up," she said.

"Okay, thanks. We will bring them in when they arrive," Wyatt said.

"Oh, you don't have to do that. I can get them," she said. He looked down at the cast on her leg and back at her with a cocked eyebrow. "Okay, yes. I could use the help. Thank you."

He smiled. "No problem. Do you need help getting back into the house?" he asked in concern.

Remembering what went down when Paul had carried her, Talya shook her head no. "No, I'm good. Thanks." Talya hopped back inside, closing the door behind her. She made her way to the kitchen and sat in one of the chairs, catching her breath for a moment. She looked at the list of meals she had made, so she could decide what to make for supper tonight. She decided to make Chicken Alfredo. It wouldn't be too hard for her and wouldn't take too long standing at the stove.

A quick knock sounded at the front door; then the door opened. "Talya," Wyatt called out. "Your groceries are here."

"Oh, great. Come on in." She stood up and hopped out of the way as Wyatt and Steven carried in all the groceries. They set everything down on the counters. "Thank you so much."

"We'll help put them away," Wyatt said. He started pulling stuff out of bags. Together, he and Steven put everything away. Talya tried to help, but she ended up being in the way more than anything. She finally just moved to the side and let them do the work. When they finished, they checked with her to see if she needed anything else then disappeared again.

Talya decided to start with the dessert first and get that out of the way. She wanted to make cream cheese brownies. She figured most people liked those. She needed to find out what kind of desserts Liam liked. After the brownies finished, she started on the sauce and chicken.

The afternoon passed quickly. Talya definitely worked much slower with one arm, but by the time five rolled around, she was feeling pretty good. The salad was ready to go; she just needed to add the dressing. The pasta, chicken, corn, and sauce were all ready. The garlic bread would finish baking in the next few minutes. She heard the front door open, and she turned around ready to face Liam.

He came around the corner and stared at her. Talya smiled at him. "Hey."

"I can't decide whether I should hug you for making what smells like an amazing dinner or scold you for doing all this when you're supposed to be resting," he said with a frown.

Chapter Twenty-Four

Talya laughed. "How about a hug?" she asked. She took a hop towards him before he cleared the distance between them in two steps. He pulled her into his arms, being careful of her injured arm.

"Thank you for doing all this. I can't remember the last time I came home to a home-cooked meal," he said. That made Talya even happier that she had been able to pull it off. He leaned forward and kissed her on the forehead. "So, is it ready?" he asked.

Talya smiled. "Yes. I just have to grab the garlic bread out of the oven."

"There's garlic bread?" he asked.

"Yes," Talya laughed. He was like a little kid.

"I'll grab it." He grabbed a hot pad and grabbed the bread from the oven. Talya watched him for a moment, before turning away. She wasn't going to lie; it was a nice look—him in a suit pulling food from the oven for their dinner.

"Do you mind calling the guys in?" Talya asked.

"Do I have to?" Liam asked with a frown. "I don't want to share."

"Yes, you do. And there's plenty of food, I promise," Talya said.

"I wasn't talking about the food," Liam grumbled.

Talya put her hands on her hips. "Are you going to get them?"

"I already let them know," he said, none too happy about it. The front door opened a moment later, and the guys came in.

"That smells good," Steven said with a smile.

"I'm glad. Come on in and grab a plate," Talya said with a smile.

Wyatt and Steven both filled their plates with food. Liam went next. He grabbed two plates and filled them. He walked over to the fridge and opened it. His eyes widened at all the stuff. He grabbed water bottles for everybody and brought them to the table. He gave Talya a plate of food.

It was quiet after that. Hopefully that meant they like it. Liam took a big bite and groaned. "This is so good. If I'd known you could cook, I would have kidnapped you a lot sooner," he said dramatically. The guys laughed and Talya hit him on the knee. He snagged her hand and squeezed it before releasing it. Talya smiled.

Conversation flowed easily around the table. "Are either of you men married?" Talya asked.

Steven's smile nearly stretched off his face. "I am. Well, technically I'm not married, but I am mated," he said.

"What about you, Wyatt?"

"Nothing yet." Talya could hear the underlying frustration in his voice. The conversation continued on around her.

"Are you going to fight night?" Wyatt asked Liam at one point.

Liam glanced at Talya and scowled. "I didn't want to, but Garrett's making me."

Wyatt and Steven both grinned. "What's fight night?" Talya asked.

"It's a monthly gathering of our pack where anybody that wants to signs up to fight. It's single-round elimination. Whoever makes it to the end gets to face the Alpha," Steven said with a grin.

Talya thought of Garrett for a moment. "That sounds terrifying." Steven and Wyatt laughed, and Liam smiled at her.

"Have you ever done that?" she asked Liam. Steven and Wyatt both smirked. "What?" Talya asked them.

"Liam's the Beta," Steven said.

"I know. He told me, but what's that got to do with anything?" Talya asked.

"It means that he can beat anyone in the pack, if he chooses to," Wyatt said.

Talya turned and looked at Liam. He was so easy-going that it was hard to think of him as a fighter, but she had seen a glimpse of it when Paul picked her up. "Has he faced off with Garrett?" she asked the guys, absolutely fascinated with all this wolf stuff. Out of the corner of her eye, she saw Liam cross his arms and sit back against his seat.

Steven nodded. "Liam's never won against the Alpha; neither has Max."

"And that's the way it will always be," Liam said, standing up. He began picking up the dishes. Steven and Wyatt stood and started doing the same. Talya stood and hopped over to the counter. "I can get whatever you need," Liam scolded.

"I need dessert," she said with a grin.

Liam looked down at her. "There's dessert too?" Talya laughed. "You need to marry me, woman," he said wrapping her in a hug.

"Do we need to leave?" Wyatt asked with a smirk.

Talya said no just as Liam said yes. Talya smacked him as the two guys chuckled. Liam guided Talya back to her seat before grabbing the brownies and bringing them to the table along with dessert plates and forks. Talya cut three large brownies and passed them to the guys and cut a smaller one for herself. "What are these?" Steven asked.

"They're cheesecake brownies," Talya said. She sat back in her chair and enjoyed watching the guys enjoy their dessert while she ate her piece. When Wyatt and Stephen left to go back outside, Talya asked Liam, "When do you have to leave tonight?"

"In a little bit. Will you go with me?" he asked.

"Do you want me to? I'm going to slow you down with my cast," she said, pointing to her foot.

Liam frowned. "Yes, I want you there. You shouldn't have to even ask, and you won't slow me down. I usually emcee the fights. The only time I don't is when I'm fighting. You can sit with me for the night."

Talya shrugged. "Okay, if you're sure I won't be a bother."

"Not possible," Liam said.

"What do I wear?" Talya asked.

Liam glanced at her outfit. "What you have on is totally fine." He stood up. "I have to do a few things. We need to leave in about thirty minutes. Does that work for you?" Talya nodded. "Okay, I'll be back. Thanks for supper," he said, dropping a kiss on her forehead. "Don't worry about the dishes. I'll get them later," he said before leaving the kitchen.

Talya ignored him and started on the dishes. She was almost done when she heard a knock on the front door. Knowing the guys were keeping watch, she figured it was somebody they knew. "Come in," she called out. The door opened and Emma and Madison came in. "Hey," Talya said in surprise.

"Hey," Emma said. She came over and gave Talya a hug. Madison did as well.

"What are you two doing here?" Talya asked.

"Are you going to fight night with Liam?" Emma asked.

Talya nodded. "Yeah, he just told me about it."

"Is that what you're wearing?" Emma asked.

Talya looked down at her outfit and frowned. "I asked Liam if this was okay, and he said it was. Is it not?"

Madison and Emma gave each other a knowing look. "Not at all, girl," Madison said. "We need to get you ready or you will get chewed up and spit out tonight."

"I don't understand," Talya said.

"You're the mate of the Beta, Talya," Madison explained. "He's the most sought-after guy now that Garrett is married. Every woman in this pack wants Liam. This is your first night meeting the pack. You need to dress the part, so that everybody knows he's yours and they can't mess with you," Madison said fiercely.

"Yeah, take it from me. You need to be strong," Emma said with a frown. "My first fight night was a disaster."

"What happened?" Talya asked.

"Well, let's just say that these two evil girls were trying to take Garrett away from me," Emma said.

"That's terrible," Talya said.

"Yeah, but I showed them who was boss," Emma said with a huge grin.

Talya was sucked in now. "What did you do?" she asked.

"I fought Garrett," Emma said with a shrug.

Talya's mouth dropped open. Madison and Emma both laughed. "Do I have to fight Garrett?" Talya asked.

"Absolutely not," Liam's voice came from behind her, causing her to jump. "Leave my girl alone," Liam said to Emma and Madison.

"We're taking your girl to get her ready for tonight," Emma said.

Liam frowned. "I told her she was fine in that."

"Yeah, well we don't want *fine* tonight, Liam," Madison said. Liam frowned again, but Emma and Madison ignored him. Liam came towards Talya and lifted her into his arms.

Madison grabbed a bag and followed them with Emma right behind her. Liam put her down on her bed. "I can send them away," he said in a soft voice, looking at Talya.

"No, you can't," Madison said. "Now shoo." With one more look at Talya, Liam left the room.

"Okay, the first step is to figure out what she can wear that will work around that leg cast," Emma said.

"I'm thinking short skirt," Madison said. Emma nodded. Madison began looking through her closet. Talya didn't say anything. Madison bought all this stuff; she knew what Talya had better than Talya did.

"I've got it!" Madison said. She pulled something out of Talya's closet and handed it to Emma.

"Oh, that's perfect!" Emma said.

Then Madison grabbed a short sleeved-leopard print blouse off its hanger and brought it over to the bed. She laid the blouse on the bed and grabbed the item from Emma. It was a short leather skirt with a zipper on the front. Madison grabbed one tall black boot and large hoop earrings.

"Okay, Talya go ahead and get dressed in this outfit. Do you need help?" Madison asked.

"Probably," Talya said. Between the three of them, they finally managed to get Talya dressed. She hopped to the bathroom where Madison did her makeup. They decided to just leave her hair down. When they finished and Talya hopped back into her room, she looked in the mirror and grinned. "You two are amazing."

"Nope, that's all you," Emma said.

"You're gonna drive Liam crazy," Madison said with a grin. Talya looked at her uncertainly. "He deserves it, believe me," she said. "For all he put Garrett through with Emma."

"All right. Are you ready, Talya?" Emma asked.

Talya glanced in the mirror one more time. She really liked

the leopard print blouse paired with the leather skirt and the tall black boot with a heel. The whole thing looked really sexy if you ignored her two casts.

"All right, we're going to tell Liam you're ready, so he can come get you," Emma said. They left her room and closed the door behind them. Talya waited nervously.

A tap sounded at her door. "Come in," she called out nervously.

The door opened and Liam came in with a grin that immediately dropped from his face. He started at her for a moment. Emma did some staring of her own. He was dressed in the same hoodie he had worn to her gym class—the gray one with the cut-off sleeves. She could see his powerful biceps. He was wearing black athletic pants and sneakers. He looked hot. Liam shook his head. "I'm going to kill them," he muttered. Talya grinned. Liam took two large steps and was suddenly in front of her. "You look incredibly sexy," he said in a low voice. "But I can't take you wearing *that*," he said. "You are literally going to attract every available male in there tonight, and I'm not even fighting so I can't beat them to a pulp."

"That's a little overkill, don't you think?" Talya asked.

Liam shook his head. "You have no idea. Now, go change," he said.

"She's not changing, Liam," Emma's voice sounded from the hall. A moment later, she and Madison were standing in the room. Liam turned and scowled at both of them. "She's going to be facing the pack for the first time and in an arm cast and a leg cast. She's going to need all the help she can get. This is her power outfit. It shows that she's not afraid of anybody."

"It shows *something*," Liam muttered.

"Besides, you deserve this after all that you put Garrett and I through," Emma said as she crossed her arms.

Liam glanced at Emma then back at Talya. "Fine, but you don't leave my side for the night," he said.

Talya huffed. "I can't even walk. Where am I going to go?" Before she could say anything else, Liam picked her up.

"I need my phone," Talya said. Emma grabbed it and handed it to her. "Thanks," Talya said to her.

Liam carried her through the house and out the front door. Talya squirmed in his arms trying to pull her skirt down as Liam carried her. "Should have maybe rethought the skirt since I'm going to be carried around," she muttered.

"You think?" Liam asked sarcastically. She watched as his eyes darted down to her blouse then to her legs before he closed his eyes and shook his head. Talya smiled; this was the perfect outfit after all.

Chapter Twenty-Five

Wyatt and Steven came towards them. "Don't look at her," Liam practically snarled at them. Both men immediately dropped their eyes. She heard Madison and Emma laugh behind her. A black Land Rover pulled into the driveway. Talya looked up to see Garrett and Madison's husband climb out of the car and make their way to their wives.

Liam stopped for a moment. After hugging and kissing his wife, Garrett turned towards them with his arm around Emma. "How are you feeling, Talya?" he asked.

"Much better. Thank you," Talya said respectfully. He made her really nervous.

Garrett's eyes shifted to Liam. He smirked, but Liam cut him off. "Not a word. This is your wife's fault and his wife," he said pointing to Madison's husband. Her husband grinned and tugged Madison closer to him.

"You deserve every ounce of it," Garrett said as he pulled Emma tighter against him.

"That's what I told him," Emma said.

Talya looked up at Liam. "I don't think anybody likes you," she said.

"I know," he grumbled. Everybody laughed.

"Talya, I don't think you've ever officially met my husband," Madison said. "This is Kyle."

"Oh my goodness. You're the one who helped me on the phone," Talya said. "I didn't make the connection before. Thank you," she said sincerely.

Kyle smiled. "I'm glad it all worked out."

After that, they drove to the building where the fighting was taking place. Talya stared out the window. "How many of you are there?" she asked.

Liam glanced at her "We have over four hundred in our pack."

Talya swallowed. It was time to put her game face on. Liam climbed out and came around to her door. He reached in and picked her up.

"You guys go head on in. I'll be in a moment," Liam said to Steven and Wyatt. The guys nodded and took off. Liam looked down at Talya. "I know everybody is teasing me, but I really am serious that I really don't want you in there with all those un-mated males tonight." He took a deep breath. "Please stay near me tonight."

Talya took compassion on him. "I will, Liam. Besides, remember, I can't go anywhere? And, nobody's going to be looking at me. I have two casts on, remember?"

Liam shook his head. "You literally have no idea," he said

cryptically. But he started walking again. By the time they reached the gym, he was the Liam that she was coming to expect. He smiled at everybody as they walked. Talya was totally overwhelmed at all the people and the noise. Liam made his way through the crowd, being careful not to bang her foot or bump into anybody. When they got to where the fight rings were set up, Liam bounded up the steps to the small stage.

He set her down in a chair gently. He stood right next to her as he and Garrett looked over an open book on the table. Emma came over and sat next to her. "You overwhelmed yet?" she asked sympathetically.

Talya shook her head. "It's a lot."

"Yeah, but you get used to it," she said. "They're good people."

Talya smiled. "Not fighting tonight?" she asked Emma with a grin.

Emma laughed. "Not tonight."

When Liam and Garrett finished whatever it was they were working on, Garrett took Emma's hand and they left the stage. Liam winked down at her before grabbing the microphone. "Welcome to Fight Night," he yelled into the mic. The music increased, and the crowd cheered. Talya couldn't help but get caught up in the excitement. After Liam got the night started, he came back over to her and picked her up and positioned her on his lap. He put his hand on her leg above her knee and stroked the skin there. He was watching the fights taking place. She didn't even think he was aware of what he was doing, but she was more than aware. They stayed that way most of the night.

He would stand every time a fight was over, so he could announce the winner and tell everybody who was in the next fight.

All throughout the night, people walked past and called out congratulations to Liam and nodded at Talya. The night stretched on, and Talya started getting tired. She didn't say anything to Liam because she didn't want him to worry about her. By the time the last fight of the night came, Talya could barely keep her eyes open.

"This is the last fight; then I'll get you home to bed," Liam said quietly in her ear. He kissed her cheek before standing and putting her in the chair while he stood to emcee the last fight. The fight was between Garrett and one of the enforcers. Liam had told her that he just became an enforcer, and this was sort of a right of passage for him. Whoever had actually won the chance to fight Garrett had given his spot to this guy.

Talya watched the fight. It seemed that Garrett was letting the fight continue, but she wasn't sure. She wasn't really into the fight scene. Her suspicions were confirmed a moment later when Garrett moved quickly and pinned the guy. Liam yelled into the microphone and everybody screamed and cheered. Garrett stood up and made his way over to Emma. She grinned up at him, and he pulled her in for a passionate kiss. The place erupted, and Talya smiled.

A few minutes later, Liam picked Talya up, and they began making their way through the crowd of people. They finally made it to the car; she was pleased to see Wyatt and Steven had already made it ahead of them. The ride home was quick and quiet. Liam dropped her off in her room. "I need to talk to the guys really quick. I'll be back in a minute," he said.

As soon as he was gone, Talya began the task of trying to get dressed for bed. A knock sounded at her door a few minutes later. "Come in."

Liam came in and helped her get to the bathroom. He waited in her room while she went to the bathroom and finished getting ready for bed. "I'm done," she called out to him. He opened the door and came in a moment later. He picked her up and carried her to her bed, placing her carefully on the bed and pulling the covers over her.

"Do you need anything?" he asked. Talya shook her head. He bent down and kissed her on the forehead. "Get some sleep, sweetheart." With that, he was gone. Talya closed her eyes and went immediately to sleep. She was exhausted.

Sometime later, Talya opened her eyes and cried out in pain. She tried to sit up, but that just made it worse. "Liam," she gasped out.

Liam was in her room moments later. "Talya, what's wrong?" he asked. He crouched down beside her.

"My leg," she cried out. She reached for her leg, but she couldn't get to it through the cast. The muscle was cramping horribly in her cast, and the pain was agonizing. She couldn't move her leg to undo the cramp. Tears rolled down her cheeks at the agony.

Liam ran out of the room, and came back a few moments later with a tool in his hand. He leaned over her leg. She wasn't sure what he was doing; she couldn't sit up to see. She was just trying to survive the agony. Miraculously, Liam removed her cast gently. "Where is the cramp?" he asked. Talya directed him and he touched the spasming muscle. She cried out in pain, but soon the pain began to diminish as he continued to rub the muscle.

Talya was finally able to take a deep breath and relax. "It stopped," she said weakly. She collapsed back down on the pillows. A few minutes later, the door to her room opened and Paul came in.

He came right over to the bed and knelt next to Liam. He felt around Talya's leg. He stood up and looked at Talya. "I'm sorry you had to endure that. Are you okay, now?" he asked.

Talya nodded, completely spent. Liam came and stood next to her. He picked up her hand and held it. "It should be okay tonight, but you need to come over first thing in the morning to get a new cast, Talya. Okay? No showering, no trying to get around, nothing. You could seriously injure your leg in this state without a cast on. You let Liam do everything for you, do you understand?" Paul asked seriously. Talya nodded, too exhausted to say anything else. "Where are your pain pills?"

Liam grabbed them from the drawer next to her bed. He popped the lid and gave her two. Paul handed her another pill. "I want you to take a muscle relaxant as well." Talya added it to the other two pills and threw them all back. "What happened today to cause your muscles to spasm?" Paul asked.

"She did too much," Liam said unhappily.

Paul nodded. "I know it's hard, but you really have to take it easy, okay?" Paul moved a pillow and put it gently under her leg to stabilize it and keep it still until morning.

Talya nodded again, feeling like a little kid getting in trouble.

She didn't say anything. Liam and Paul walked out of her room. Talya could hear them talking in low tones. She picked up her phone next to her bed and cringed when she saw it was two in the morning. Now, she really felt bad.

Liam came into her room a few minutes later and crouched next to her. "I'm sorry," she said softly.

His hand came out and gently palmed her face. "There's nothing to be sorry for. I'm sorry that you were in pain. Do you think you can sleep now?" Talya nodded. "Call me if you need me." Talya's pills were already kicking in. She fell asleep moments later.

Talya found herself in her dream land. She looked down and noticed she didn't have a broken foot or arm in her dreams. It was so nice to walk around regularly. She walked around for a while before her wolf friend eventually joined her. "I met my guardian," she told him. "It's Liam, isn't it?" The wolf nodded.

"Why do I need a guardian?" she asked.

The wolf was silent for a few minutes. Talya was used to that. She just continued walking, and he stayed at her side. "Because you are a precious gift, and a precious gift as such needs to be guarded and protected from those who would try to steal the gift or try to devalue the gift."

"Why me? I'm really nothing special. Why am I a gift?" she asked, clearly not understanding.

"You are one of four gifts that have been gifted to the Northwoods pack," the wolf said.

"One of four?" Talya asked. "What are the other gifts?"

"Not what, who?" the wolf said.

"Who are the other gifts?" Talya asked.

"One is already among the Northwoods Pack." The wolf was silent for a few minutes. "As for why..." he was silent again and Talya patiently waited. "Do you know why the werewolf race was created?" Talya shook her head.

"Since the world began, there has always been imbalance in the world. For just as good exists, evil exists. Good and evil have always warred against each other. Thousands of years ago, evil triumphed in that the first vampires were created. Without a counter action, evil would have prevailed. With the new race of evil, a new race for good needed to be created to keep evil in check. That was the werewolf race."

"So, the wolves were created to keep the vampires in check? Who created the wolf race?" Talya asked. The wolf turned its head towards her; somehow, he didn't need to say anything. Talya just knew. "You did," she said, knowing in her heart it was the truth.

Chapter Twenty-Six

"My wolves have lost their way. They have forgotten why they were created. Their race has been in decline; and in fear, they have closed themselves off. They no longer fight the evil; they no longer protect the balance of good in this world. It's time for them to wake up and remember why it was they were created. The gifts I am gifting them will help them in their cause," the wolf said.

Talya took a deep breath. "I'm going to be honest. That doesn't sound very good."

The wolf was quiet for a long time. "I didn't create this race so that they could just enjoy life and live it for themselves. I created them for a specific purpose. They will be most fulfilled when they begin to live out that purpose, no matter how hard it may seem. Talya, the road ahead is a difficult one. It's not going to be easy, but anything accomplished for good seldom is." He was silent again, and though Talya wanted to ask questions, she kept her mouth shut and waited. Eventually, he started talking again. "I have already gifted the Northwoods Pack with the Finder. She will find the humans with special gifts and abilities that I have created and begin to bring them into the Northwoods Pack. She's already found you—the Dreamer, and you need to encourage her to keep going. The Alpha is fearful for her protection, but he needn't be. She is under my protection. As the Dreamer, your gift lies in your connection to me. You are my voice to my wolves, wolves that have forgotten why it was they were created. Your job is to point them back in the right direction."

"Who are the other two gifts?" Talya asked bravely.

"They will be revealed in time. Your task now is to relay my messages to my wolves. The Northwoods Pack is the largest of all the packs. As such, they will take the lead in returning the wolves to their purpose."

"I don't know if they will believe me. I'm new to this pack. I'm not even a wolf," Talya said.

"They will believe you," he said simply. Then he turned his head away. Talya recognized the action. That would be all she would get out of him for now.

"I will do my best," she said simply.

Talya opened her eyes. It was morning. She took a deep breath and thought through her dream. She sighed. She had no idea if anybody would believe her, but she had to believe the wolf's assurance that they would. Her eyes drifted to her foot. First business of the day was to get a new cast.

She grabbed her phone and texted Liam.

Are you up?

He appeared in her room a moment later. "Hey, how are you feeling?" he asked.

"I'm good. I want to get this over and done with so I can get back to my life," she said. "I feel like I can't move it at all or I'm going to hurt it."

Liam nodded. "Yeah, let's get it done." He moved towards her and carefully picked her up.

"Can you take me to the bathroom first?" she asked. He took her there and carefully put her down.

"Be careful," he warned. Then he disappeared.

Talya managed to go to the bathroom, get her teeth brushed and brush her hair and put it into a ponytail. "Liam," she called out. He came right in.

"Here," he said. He handed her a black sweatshirt. "Just put this over your pajama top, and you'll be good."

"We're just going there and right back, right?" Talya asked. He nodded and helped her pull the sweatshirt over her head. He smiled when she had it on and picked her up again. Then he carried her through the house and out to the car. Wyatt and Steven were already in the car waiting when Liam settled her into the car. Talya stared out the window during the short ride. When they arrived, Liam carried her inside.

"You okay?" he asked, looking down at her in concern. "You're really quiet."

Talya looked into his eyes. "I need to talk to you," she said.

His steps slowed. "What's wrong?" he asked.

Talya sighed. "I had another dream last night," she said quietly. "I just need to fill you in and Garrett too. And probably some of the others as well."

"What aren't you telling me?" Liam asked.

"Nothing. It's just a lot. Everything's fine. I just need to tell you about my dream, okay?" she looked into his serious eyes. "I mean I'm not called the Dreamer for no reason," she said trying to get him back to his easy-going self. He just continued to stare at her. "It's okay, Liam."

"Let's get this over and done with and then get home so we can talk," Liam said.

"Okay," Talya said with a small smile. She hated the worry she saw on his face. Without thinking, she moved forward and kissed his cheek.

He looked down at her. She was happy to see a smile on his face. "What was that for?"

"Because you're so good to me," Talya said.

He squeezed her against his chest and brushed her forehead with a kiss. Then he took her inside. "Hey Talya, how are you feeling this morning?" Paul asked kindly.

"Horrible that I made you come to the house at two in the morning," Talya grimaced.

Paul just smiled. "That's what I do. Don't worry about it. Now let's get this leg in a cast again." Liam didn't say anything the entire time Paul worked. He just held her hand and stood next to her.

"You two okay? You're both quiet today. Liam, you're never quiet," Paul said in concern.

Talya let a laugh slip out. She looked up at Liam. He only gave her a small smile. "He's just worried about me," Talya said, giving his hand a squeeze.

"Okay, Talya, you are good to go. Call me if you have any more problems. Here's a bottle of muscle relaxants too in case you continue to have problems," Paul said.

"Oh, I ordered one of those leg scooters for getting around. Do you think that's okay?" she asked. Liam frowned at her but didn't say anything.

"That's a good idea, Talya. It should be less strain on your leg than hopping around," he said. "As long as you can manage it with one arm."

"We'll see," Talya said with a smile. "You ready?" she asked Liam. He nodded. "Thank you, Paul," Talya said.

"You're welcome," Paul said with a smile. He put his hand on Liam's shoulder. "You good?" he asked in a quiet voice.

"Yeah, just thinking," Liam said. Liam picked Talya up. "Thanks, Paul." Then he walked out towards the car. The ride back home was just as quiet as the ride there. Liam carried her inside and set her on the couch. "Do you need anything?"

"No, I'm good," Talya said.

He crouched in front of her. "How did you get the groceries and the scooter?" he asked.

Talya looked up at him in confusion. "Online."

"I mean, how did you pay for them?" he asked.

"I can order stuff online because my debit card numbers are available on my banking app that I have on my phone," Talya explained.

Liam ran a hand through his hair. "I'm doing such a bad job of this," he muttered to himself.

"Of what?" Talya asked.

"Of taking care of you," Liam said in frustration. "I should have given you a debit card right away, and I didn't. I'm sorry, Talya."

"Liam, it's fine," Talya said.

"It's not fine. I'll get you a card first thing tomorrow. I'll add you to my bank account; that way you can have access to funds whenever you need," he said.

Talya laughed. "I'm not using your money, Liam."

"Yes, you are," he said. "It's my job to provide for my mate. Speaking of which, are you hungry?"

Talya blinked at the sudden change in conversation. "Um, I guess."

"Oh wait, I think Emma said she's bringing food when she comes over," Liam said.

Talya looked up at him. "Emma's coming over?"

Liam nodded. "For the meeting."

"What meeting?" Talya asked.

"I told Garrett that you needed to talk to us. He's coming over in about five minutes with Emma, Kyle and Madison, and a few of the other enforcers, and I think Paul too.

Talya blinked. "Well, I guess I should probably get out of my jammies then," she said pointedly.

Liam looked down at her. "You're fine. Besides you're wearing my sweatshirt."

Talya shook her head. When she looked up at him, she saw him looking at her in concern. "What's wrong?"

"It scares me," he began. "I can't be in your dreams with you. I can't protect you there. I don't know what any of this means— the fact that you're having these dreams. It terrifies me," he said vulnerably.

Talya nodded. "I get that. That's why I'm going to start sharing with you and the others what my dreams are about. I think it will clear things up. I'm not going to lie, though, Liam. I think harder times are coming."

His jaw tightened. "That's what I'm afraid of."

"But we'll face it together. Right, Wolf Man?" she asked with a smile.

He smiled a small smile at her endearment. He slowly leaned closer, giving her a chance to pull away. Then his lips were on hers in a gentle kiss. He pulled back and put his head in the crook of her neck, and she turned her head giving him access. "Someday," he whispered. "That's where my mark is going to be." He kissed her one more time; then pulled back. "They're here," he said.

"Oh shoot," Talya said. She smoothed her hair. She looked up at him. "Does it look like..."

"Like you were just kissed?" he asked, cutting her off. "Yes, and I love it."

Talya rolled her eyes. "Can I at least go change really quickly?"

"No time. They're here," Liam said as he strolled towards the door.

"Wait," Talya said. "What about the sweatshirt? It's huge on me. Everybody's going to know it's yours."

"That's the point, sweetheart. So, they know you're mine. I'm marking my territory," he said confidently.

Talya wrinkled her nose. "Why do I feel like I just got peed on?" Liam let out a loud laugh before opening the door. Talya smiled to herself. At least she got him laughing again. The smiled faded from her face as she thought about the conversation she was going to have with him and Garrett and the others in just a few minutes. She stood to her feet, so she didn't feel so awkward as everybody came in. Nerves filled her; she hoped she was up for this.

Chapter Twenty-Seven

Talya forced a smile to her face. Garrett and Emma were the first in the door. Garrett was carrying several paper bags, and Emma had a tray of coffee drinks. Madison and Kyle came next, carrying more trays of coffee drinks. Emma put her stuff down and came towards Talya for a hug. "How are you doing? I heard about your awful episode last night. I'm so sorry."

"It's okay. Paul got me all fixed up again, good as new," Talya said.

"Good," Emma said. "I hope you like coffee. I brought you a drink. I took a guess at what you would like. I made you a salted caramel white mocha."

"Ooo, that sounds so good," Talya said. Emma smiled. She walked over and grabbed a cup and brought it back to Talya.

"Give it a try," Emma encouraged.

Talya tipped it back and took a sip. "Oh, my goodness. That's orgasmic," she said. Liam's head whipped around to look at her. Talya swore it got totally silent for a moment before Madison broke the silence by cracking up; Emma was right behind her. Liam moved towards her and wrapped an arm around her stomach, pulling her back flush against his chest. "I'm sorry," she whispered. "Sometimes I just open my mouth and say stupid stuff."

Liam's chest shook with his laughter. He dropped his head and kissed her neck. "That coffee has nothing on me," he said in a low rumble right in her ear. Talya could feel her face heat up.

Madison caught her eye. "You okay, Talya? Your face is a little red," she said with a grin.

Liam laughed again before releasing her. Emma made the rounds passing out coffees to everybody. Then she told everybody that she had cinnamon rolls and an egg bake. "Cinnamon rolls?" Talya asked nearly squealing.

Liam turned and grinned at her. "And they're amazing," he said. "I'll bring you a few," he said before disappearing into the kitchen.

"Just one," she called out after him. Liam brought her a plate with three cinnamon rolls. "I said one," she said, shaking her head at him.

"I'll eat whatever you don't eat," he said. He sat down on the couch and pulled her carefully down next to him. Soon, everybody was settled around the room. Garret stood with Emma near him in a chair. Max stood against the wall in the back along with Steven, Wyatt, and several other men and women she didn't know yet. Kyle and Madison sat on the love seat.

"All right," Garrett began. "Talya has some stuff she wants to tell us."

Talya choked on her bite. "Well, that was direct," she said without thinking. "Oh sorry, sir, uh Alpha sir." Talya felt mortified. It was deathly quiet in the room, but a quick glance showed her that everybody was holding back smiles. Liam looked like he was about to bust a gut, holding in his laugh.

"Just Garrett's fine," Garrett said unemotionally.

Liam smirked before turning to everybody. "Let me set it up a little better than Garrett so eloquently did," he said and grinned. Turning serious, he said, "Well, all of you remember Talya's last dream, I'm sure. If you haven't heard about it, then ask somebody later because I'm not repeating it and going through that again. Anyway, Talya had another dream last night. She told me this time that she needed to share it with me and Garrett and she wasn't sure who else. So, here we are. Talya," he said, turning to her. "You have the floor."

Talya took a deep breath, and Liam squeezed her hand encouragingly. "So, what I'm about to tell you is going to be difficult. I want everybody to keep in mind that these aren't my words; they're the wolf's." She paused and took another deep breath. "So, the wolf that keeps appearing in my dreams," she paused. "He's the one that created your race," she said quietly. Nobody made a sound. "He told me that he created the wolf race to keep the balance of evil and good in the world and that your race was created after the greatest of evils was created thousands of years ago."

"Vampires," Garrett said in a low voice.

Talya nodded. "He talked about how good and evil are always battling each other. He said that wolves were created to protect and to keep evil in check. But along the way, their numbers started to decline and wolves got scared. So, they stopped being the protectors they were created to be and started pulling inwardly. They worried about their survival; they forgot what their purpose was," she continued telling the indictment in a quiet voice. She took a fortifying breath. "He said that it's time for the wolves to remember their purpose, why they were created. If that doesn't happen, evil will triumph more and more. Because you are the biggest pack, he is gifting the Northwoods Pack with four gifts. The first, he said he already gifted to the Alpha." Talya smiled at Emma. "That's you." She looked at Garrett and tried to find the courage to say what needed to be said. "He said that you need to stop being afraid and let her use her gift more freely. She is the Finder, a gift to the Northwoods Pack." She could tell that Garrett was about to lose his cool, so she spoke swiftly but calmly. "He also said not to worry about her; she is under his protection," Talya said softly. She watched as the fight went out of Garrett. "I am the second gift to this pack. Nothing like praising yourself, right?" Talya said with a nervous laugh. She saw a few smiles on faces. Liam's hand tightened on hers. "I am the Dreamer. My job is to relay messages to you from the Wolf, your Creator," Talya said gently. "I am to remind you of your purpose and to point you in the right direction once again and to remind you that your Creator didn't design you to simply sit back and enjoy life. Your purpose was to bring justice and light into the world and keep the balance between good and evil." Talya finished quietly.

"Who or what are the other two gifts?" Kyle asked, breaking

the silence.

Talya shook her head. "I don't know. He wouldn't tell me when I asked. He simply said they would be revealed in time." She looked at Garrett. "He said that as the largest of all packs, it is your responsibility to lead the wolves back to their intended purpose."

When she finally got it all out, she leaned against Liam, feeling depleted. He dropped his hold on her hand and put his arm around her shoulder, drawing her close to him. "Well, now that the entire wolf race has been put in its place by my girl, let's get some food," Liam said, making everybody smile.

Talya looked up at Liam. "If I'd known everybody was coming over, I would have made food," she whispered.

"I know. That's why I didn't tell you, my Dreamer," he said quietly. He leaned forward and placed a kiss on her forehead.

It took about two hours for everybody to clear out. Garrett and Emma were the last to leave. "Thank you for sharing all that," Garrett said to Talya. "That couldn't have been easy." He looked at Liam. "We're going to have to figure out what the next step is."

Liam nodded. "And you're going to have to let me do more finding," Emma said to Garrett. He didn't look happy, but he didn't argue with her. After they left, Liam picked up. Talya tried to help as much as she could. Then he helped her get settled on the couch to rest while he went to work for a few hours.

"Do you need anything before I go?" Liam asked.

"No, I'm good. I think I'm just going to take a nap. I'm really tired," she said as a yawn escaped her.

"Sounds good, beautiful. Call me if you need anything. I'll try to be home around five." He kissed her on the top of her head and left a moment later.

Talya hadn't been lying. Between getting a new cast and sharing everything from her dream with everybody, she was tanked. She fell asleep quickly but awoke sometime later to a knock on the front door. She felt disoriented and sluggish, but she managed to sit up. She figured it must be Steven or Wyatt.

"Come in," she called out. The door opened, and Talya couldn't have been more shocked.

"Hey Talya, miss me?"

Talya stared at Brandon in shock. "Talya, he said he was a friend of yours but..." Steven's voice trailed off. She could see the uncertainty in his face.

"It's okay, Steven," she said. She managed to get to her feet awkwardly.

"Looks like you're doing quite well here," Brandon said with a sneer, nodding at her two casts.

"Why are you here?" Talya asked, heart pounding.

Brandon grinned. "I missed you. Can't a guy miss his girlfriend?" he asked.

"Ex-girlfriend, Brandon. We are no longer together," she reminded him. "You dumped me, broke my heart, remember?"

"Well, I'm not with her anymore. I want you back," Brandon said with a smile.

"Well, guess what? I don't want you back," Talya said, crossing her arms.

"Yes, you do," Brandon said confidently.

217

"No, I don't, Brandon. I have moved on," Talya said.

Brandon nodded his head. "I can see that," he said looking around the house. "Do you have any idea what kind of guy you're even with?" Before she could say anything, he continued. "He put me in a coma, Talya. He broke every one of my fingers. He broke Trevor's hand so badly, he can never play football again! Is that the kind of man you want to be with?" Talya swallowed hard; she hadn't known that. He continued. "How old are you, Talya?" he asked, looking back at her.

"You know how old I am," Talya said, frowning.

"Humor me."

"I'm seventeen," Talya said, exasperated.

"Oh, right. You don't turn eighteen for, hmmm, a few more weeks yet, right?" Brandon asked.

"What are you getting at?" Talya asked.

"Oh, just that you're a minor, and your new boyfriend...Well, let's just say. Keeping a minor here? He could go away for a long time. One call to the please, and bye-bye Liam," Brandon said with a chuckle. Talya felt the blood drain from her face. Brandon stepped closer to her. "Struck a nerve, did I?" he asked softly. "What do you say, Talya? How about you come home with me before it gets messy, okay baby?" he said. He reached out and stroked her cheek softly.

"You touch her again, and I will rip your arm from your body," Liam said as he strode into the house. She tried to take a breath, but it got caught. Liam put his arm around her waist and pulled her against him. "I suggest you leave, *now*," Liam's deadly voice sounded behind her. She shuddered at the tone of his voice.

Brandon had the audacity to grin at him. "Talya will be going with us," he said, crossing his arms.

Liam's arms tightened around her. "Yeah, I don't think so," Liam said.

"She will," Brandon said. "Because Talya understands what will happen if she doesn't, right Talya?" he asked.

"Are you kidding me right now? You're seriously threatening her in front of me?" Liam asked incredulously. Talya could feel his muscles tighten; he was amped up and ready for a fight. She knew just how deadly it would be if he truly let loose, or if he let his wolf loose. She needed to protect him, to get him to calm down. She turned around in his arms.

"Liam, look at me," she said in a low voice. He didn't take his eyes off Brandon. "Liam!" she said again. Nothing. She needed to figure a way to de-escalate the situation before it got out of hand.

Chapter Twenty-Eight

"Brandon, you need to leave," Talya said calmly, turning back to face him.

"Oh, we will be, very soon," he said with a cocky smile. Talya was just about to ask what he was smiling at when she saw red and blue lights flash outside. She felt Liam's body stiffen behind her. "Huh, looks like the police are here," Brandon said with a smug look on his face. "Let's go see what they want."

Talya felt fear flood her system. Would they arrest Liam? Liam pulled her tight against him. "Don't be afraid, Talya. I won't let anything happen to you," he said in a low, angry voice. Talya didn't have a chance to tell him she wasn't afraid for herself before Wyatt came inside.

"We've got a problem," he said to Liam, his face grim.

"I'm coming," Liam said. He turned Talya around carefully to face him. "Stay inside. I will go deal with this mess." He didn't give her a chance to argue with him. He turned and strode out the door. Wyatt turned to look at her; she could tell he was unsure whether to stay with her or go with Liam.

"Go with him, please. Don't let him do anything stupid," she said, worried.

Wyatt nodded and went out the front door. Talya hopped towards the window and looked out. Her stomach sank when she saw two police cars and four officers. She was shocked to see Brandon's dad as well. She always tried to keep her distance from him because he was terrifying.

The door opened, and Talya turned to face the officer. He looked down at her two casts and frowned. Talya felt her stomach drop; this didn't look good. "Miss, we are here to take you home. Please come outside with me."

"But I'm not being held here," Talya tried.

"Please come with me," he said in an authoritative voice. Talya had no choice but to hop towards him. He frowned. "Do you need some assistance?" he asked.

"I'll carry her," Brandon said coming into the room. Before Talya could do anything, he held her in his arms, tighter than was necessary. Talya bit her lip, so she wouldn't lash out in anger at him. The officer went ahead of them and opened the door. Talya's eyes immediately sought out Liam's. She saw the fury in his eyes when he saw her in Brandon's arms. He took a step towards her before Wyatt and Steven stepped in front of him.

"There she is," Brandon's dad said in his booming voice. "We were so worried, Talya." Talya tried to dislodge herself from Brandon's arms, but he wouldn't let her go.

A black Land Rover pulled into the driveway, and a moment later, Max, Garrett, Kyle, and Madison stepped out. "What's going on here?" Garrett's deep voice sounded.

"Oh, good. Everybody's here," Brandon's dad said sarcastically. Garrett ignored him and strode over to stand beside Liam. Max came and stood next to Brandon; so did Kyle and Madison.

"Officers, what's the problem?" Garrett asked.

The officer who seemed to be in charge stepped towards Garrett. "We have a missing minor. We were called out to check into it."

"I'm not missing," Talya said.

Everybody's head turned towards Talya. "Put me down," she said loudly to Brandon. This time he did as she said. Talya limped forward, tripping slightly on the uneven ground. Liam tried to get to her, but a sharp word from Garrett kept him where he was.

"I think there's been some confusion here," Garrett said.

"There's no confusion," Brandon's dad said. "My son's girlfriend was taken from her home."

"That's not true," Talya said. Everybody's head turned in her direction. Talya swallowed.

Two of the officers approached her. "Is this where you live?" one of them asked.

"Well, no, but-"

"How old are you?" the other officer asked immediately.

"Seventeen," Talya said quietly.

"Did these men take you from your home?" one of them asked.

"Did they hurt you?" another one asked before she could answer the first one.

"No," Talya responded but nobody was listening to her.

"Do you live nearby?" one asked.

"No," Talya said softly.

Finally, one of the officers had had enough. "You're going with us," he said. He grabbed Talya's arm and began to pull her towards the car, and everything turned to chaos. Liam shouted and tried to get to her, but Garrett and the other enforcers held him back.

"Stop, you can't take her away!" Madison yelled and stepped forward before Kyle grabbed her and yanked her back.

Brandon's dad was in a yelling match with Garrett. In the midst of the chaos, the officer tried to push Talya into the car. "But I don't have my stuff," she said, trying to get him to listen. She was starting to panic. "Liam," she cried out right before the officer shoved her head down and into the car. She gained her balance and looked out the window. "NO!" she yelled. Liam was on the ground, and no less than four men were on top of him trying to keep him there. She saw when he still managed to sit up right before Garrett punched him hard. She reached out and tried to open the door handle, but it wouldn't open. "No," she cried, softer this time. A smug Brandon slid into the backseat next to her. Talya turned her head away from him. She was furious with him. She didn't look back as they left; she couldn't bear to.

Thankfully, the officers were quiet during the ride. Brandon tried talking to her several times, but she simply ignored him. At the police station, Talya sat in a chair and tried to ignore everything going on around her. She heard Brandon's dad yelling at the officers, but she just tuned it out. A female officer sat with her and took her statement. She told her again and again that nothing had happened, that Liam was a good guy; but she could tell the officers didn't believe her.

The next twelve hours blurred together. She found herself being driven to the airport and flying home with an officer at her side at all times. Finally, Talya was dropped off at her grandparent's home, where her grandparents were outside waiting for her. She fell into their embrace. They helped her inside and to her room. Talya fell on her bed in exhaustion. She could hear the officer that had brought her home talking to her grandparents, but she tuned it out.

Eventually, it was quiet. Talya heard the door to her room open. She turned her head to see her grandma come towards her. "Talya, are you okay, honey?" she asked. Talya just shook her head; she felt so overwhelmed and exhausted. She had no idea what to even say. Thankfully, her grandma didn't demand answers from her. She just held Talya's hand until she went to sleep.

When Talya woke up the next morning, she felt terrible. She had no desire to get out of bed and face the day. She was planning on staying in bed the entire day. That was until Sage showed up.

Chapter Twenty-Nine

"Hey Talya," Sage said quietly. She walked over and sat on the side of the bed. "What happened?"

Talya just shook her head. "Everything is such a mess," she said. "Brandon showed up with the police."

"Why?" Sage asked in confusion. Talya told her everything that had gone down. By the time she was finished, she was exhausted again. "I'm so sorry, Talya," Sage said when Talya finished. She hugged Talya and sat with her until Talya fell back into an exhausted sleep.

The next two days dragged by, and Talya didn't get out of bed. She couldn't figure out why she was such a mess. She missed Liam, definitely, but it shouldn't feel as terrible as it did. She felt like her heart was splintering. She couldn't face life; she couldn't function. She didn't feel like eating or doing anything; she just felt miserable. Her grandparents tried to talk to her. She knew they were worried about her, but she didn't know what to do to snap out of it.

On the third day, Sage showed up. "Okay, Talya. Out of bed. You are going to shower and get dressed and come out of your room and eat something." Talya tried ignoring her. "I will pull you out of this bed and onto the floor if you don't get out of bed. I don't care that you have two casts on," Talya said.

"Fine," Talya huffed when Sage wouldn't leave her alone. With Sage's help, she finally made her way to the shower. After showering and getting dressed, she didn't want to admit it, but she did feel a little better.

"Listen to me, Talya," Sage began when Talya finished brushing and braiding her hair. "We're not going to let Brandon win. Tomorrow, you are going to get up and go to school. You've got eight weeks until you graduate. You are going to finish, and then you can do whatever you want because you will be eighteen the day after graduation," Sage said.

Talya groaned and sat down on the bed. "I don't want to go to school."

"I know," Talya said as she reached down and put her arm through Talya's good arm and pulled her to her feet. "But you have to. I'll be with you every step of the way. It's only eight weeks."

Talya closed her eyes. "Okay," she whispered.

She helped Talya out to the kitchen where her grandparents were waiting for her for lunch. "I'll be here tomorrow morning to help you get ready for school," Sage said. Talya just groaned.

―――――――

True to her word, Sage showed up the next morning to help Talya get ready for school. She showed up bright and early with a leg scooter. "Why are you frowning?" Sage asked.

"I was just remembering that I ordered one of these and never got it. It's probably at Liam's house," Talya said.

"No, it's not. This is it. Liam sent it to my house," Sage said.

"What? Why?" Talya asked.

"Because you need it and it's yours," Sage said, looking at her funny.

"Why didn't he send it to me?" Talya asked.

"He wanted me to put it together for you so you wouldn't have to," Sage said, rolling her eyes.

"He told you that?" Talya asked.

"Yeah, he was worried about you. He thought it might help you to get motivated to get out of bed if you had this," Sage said.

Talya stared at her. "Have you been talking to him?" Talya asked in outrage.

Sage cringed. "Just a few times."

Talya couldn't even form words. "Why is he talking to you?" she exploded. "Why isn't he talking to me?" Talya asked, hating that her voice cracked on the last word.

Sage looked at her sadly. "I don't know, Talya. I don't know what happened. But if it helps, he's really worried about you, and he sounds terrible. He actually sounds worse than you."

Talya tried to push the tears back that threatened to spill. "Well, he obviously doesn't care enough to call and check on me," she said, and the pain came surging back. She hated her weakness. She pushed aside her feelings. "I need to move on. He obviously has." With that, she pushed Liam from her mind. "I need to get my life back on track, and that starts with finishing school."

"That's the spirit!" Sage said triumphantly.

A few hours later, Talya's tune had changed. She couldn't believe how much she hated school. Sage helped her maneuver her leg scooter. It took some getting used to, but she made it through her first day. One day became two days and two dragged into three. It wasn't until almost two weeks had passed from when she had last seen Liam that she had another dream.

Talya opened her eyes and let out a sigh. She walked around for a while, just enjoying being back here. She felt the wolf's presence before she ever saw him. When he appeared, she studied him. "I thought maybe you had forsaken me too," she said. The wolf didn't say anything right away; no surprise there. "I'm no longer with the Northwoods Pack," she said. She figured he knew, but she threw it out there anyway.

"I know. That's why it's harder for me to reach you in this state," the wolf said.

Talya looked at him in surprise. "It is?"

He nodded. "My connection to you is through my wolves. It's strongest when you are with them. Normally, I wouldn't even try to communicate with you until you are with them again, but this can't wait."

"What can't wait?" Talya asked.

"I need to prepare you for your job," he said.

"I thought this was my job. I'm the Dreamer," Talya said.

"Yes, but there is more to it than just me communicating to you. You have the power to dream walk," he said.

"Say what now?" Talya asked.

"You can dream walk when you're in this state, but it's not easy. It's going to take training and discipline for you to pull it off. I wanted to wait until you were with my wolves again for an easier connection and for protection for you, but it's imperative that we get you ready now."

Talya watched him carefully. "Why the urgency? There must be some reason you're pushing for it."

"There is," the wolf said in an angry voice. "The vampires are taking their evil to new levels."

"What are they doing?" Talya asked, cautiously.

"They are trying to turn human females," he said. Talya could hear the anger in his voice.

"Turning them into vampires?" Talya breathed. The wolf nodded. Talya put her hand to her mouth.

"You are going to have to dream walk in the vampire's dreams to find out where," the wolf said. "We have to put a stop to it."

Talya stared at him, trying to understand what he was saying. "I have to do what I do with you with a vampire?" she asked.

"Similar," the wolf said.

"Why can't you just tell me where they're doing it?" Talya asked.

"I do not know," the wolf said.

"I thought you knew everything. Aren't you like a god or something?" Talya asked.

"I know everything about my wolves and can see everything in the shifter world, but only the shifter world. In the human world and the vampire world, I am just as lost as anybody else," he said.

Talya took in that information. "Wow," she said. "How do you know the vampires are turning humans?" she asked.

"One of my wolves in Boston discovered a newly turned girl. She was drained of blood; that is a vampire trait. She was found dead in a dumpster," the wolf said in anger.

Talya felt her stomach roll. "That's terrible."

"She was only sixteen," the wolf said.

Talya sucked in a breath. "That's awful," she breathed out.

The wolf nodded. "She's not the only one." Talya nodded but didn't ask for any more information. She didn't want to know.

"So, what do I do?" she asked simply.

"It starts with entering the vampire realm within the dream stasis. You've probably never noticed, because you haven't wandered far from here, but human and vampire dream realms are located in this same dream stasis," the wolf said.

"Really?" Talya asked.

The wolf nodded. "Follow me." He started walking, and she followed. "Wolves love nature, so the wolf stasis is made of rolling hills, woods, creeks, and grass. Humans love heavenly things, so their realm is entirely made of clouds."

"What about the vampire realm?" Talya asked.

"Their realm is made of the two things they love most—blood and darkness." Talya shuddered. She was not looking forward to going to that realm. They walked a little ways longer before the landscape suddenly changed. One minute they were walking on grass, the next they were literally on clouds. Talya panicked for a moment.

"You're completely safe. You can't fall," the wolf said. "Remember, it's just a dream state."

Once Talya realized she was not going to plummet to her death, she was able to relax some. She looked around. "This really is beautiful."

The wolf didn't say anything for a moment. "Are you ready to check out the last realm?" he asked.

Talya grimaced. "I guess." The wolf turned and began leading her back the way they had come. It took a fairly long time to reach the vampire realm.

"Once you get used to dream walking, you will be able to jump realms quickly," the wolf said.

Talya nodded. That was a nifty trick. The smell greeted Talya first before she ever stepped foot onto the vampire dream realm. She gagged and plugged her nose.

"Blood," the wolf answered her unspoken question. Talya took a few steps into the darkness. Her eyes adjusted. It was still dark, but at least she could see enough to see where she was going. She looked behind her and noticed the wolf wasn't with her. She took a few steps backwards, blinking when sunlight hit her. She was back on the wolf side. After her eyes adjusted, she looked at the wolf. "Aren't you coming?"

The wolf shook his head. "I cannot cross over to the vampire side."

"What? Why?" Realization dawned on Talya. "Because you're enemies?" she asked.

The wolf nodded. "Come. We have much work to do." The wolf led her through the wolf realm once again. They continued walking into an area she had never been before. He stopped in front of a large body of water. "This is what we call the melding. Each realm has one. This is where you find the individual strands that make up dreams. Each realm has a gathering place like this. I can only imagine that the vampires' melding is in a river of blood." Talya tried to keep the grimace off her face. She wasn't sure she had been very successful at it, but the wolf continued on.

"Each strand is a dream being woven for one creature. Your job is to find the strands that connect to the vampires that know about the locations and follow the strands until they give you a location," the wolf said.

Talya stared at the wolf. "Um, not to question you or anything, but that sounds like an incredibly difficult job. Is that even possible?" she asked.

"It's the only option we have," the wolf said.

"Oh boy," Talya muttered. "Well, okay then. Train me how to do it."

Chapter Thirty

"We wade in and begin to examine the strands. Follow my lead." The wolf turned and walked into the water.

Talya followed him and was shocked to find it wasn't really water after all. It was a substance similar to water but thicker with more viscosity to it. She ran her hand through it and was amazed to see her hand wasn't wet at all. When they had walked out a little way, the wolf stopped. "Now, notice the lines," he said. Talya looked down. She was surprised to see colors. "The thicker the line, the closer connection to the creator. My alphas have the thickest lines here. The colors represent emotions. The more you dream walk, the more you will be able to isolate the colors. I don't know about the other realms, but I know about colors in this realm. Blue is calm, red is anger, pink is passion, yellow is stress, black is shame, purple is lust, green is guilt, and on the colors go. You don't need to worry about memorizing those because I have a feeling the vampire realm colors will be completely different. For now, let's practice. Find a line." He waited for her. "Isolate it, but don't touch it."

Talya looked down at the thousands of intersecting lines. They looked kind of like blood veins in drawings of the human body. She found a thick yellow line. "That one," she said pointing to it.

"Okay," the wolf said. "Yellow here represents stress. So, this wolf's dream is going to be related to the stress he is experiencing in his own life. Now, remember, this is a dream. Dreams do not work in a one-to-one ratio with our hold on the reality of life. They are more abstract. The dream may not have anything directly to do with what the wolf is stressed about, but there will be glimpses of it. You have to find those glimpses and piece them together to put the picture together of what this wolf is stressed about. It may not happen in one dream. It may take several nights and several dreams to get a full picture."

Talya looked at the wolf. "This seems like an impossible task."

"It won't be easy," the wolf agreed. "Sometimes, you may catch an actual memory mixed into the dream. You have to just watch carefully. But you will get better each time you dream walk. Okay, let's begin your practice. Stand firmly on either side of the line. You can walk through any of the lines, but as soon as you touch one, it will suck you in. You need to be ready for it. Don't ever touch one accidentally if you're not ready for it," the wolf explained.

Talya stepped so that the yellow line lay between her legs. She planted her feet widely so she didn't fall over. "Now, when you're ready," the wolf said. "Grab hold of the line with both hands. You will get sucked in immediately. Once there, take note of details. See if you can piece together why this wolf is stressed."

"How do I get back out?" Talya asked.

"Simply let go of the line."

Talya looked at the wolf. "That's it?" she asked.

"That's it," he said.

Talya took a deep breath. "Okay, I'm ready."

"Begin when you're ready. Remember, nothing bad can happen to you. It's only a dream," the wolf said. Talya tried to not think about his ominous words. Before she could talk herself out of it, she reached down and grabbed the line firmly in both hands.

Immediately, she was sucked into a dream. She saw a man, probably in his late twenties, in a nice suit running behind a taxi. Every time the taxi stopped, the man would catch up to it. But before he could get in, the taxi would pull away. The man glanced down at his watch. It was eight o'clock. Suddenly, the taxi was no longer a taxi. It turned into a white screen. The man stood in front of a group of people; it looked like a table full of board members. The same man stood at the front speaking. But every time he tried to make a point, a man at the head of the table cut him off. The man was so frustrated and angry, he was visibly shaking. Suddenly, Talya felt a hand on her arm. It startled her and she jerked, losing her hold on the line.

Instantly, she was out of the dream and standing next to the wolf. "What did you see?" the wolf asked. Talya relayed everything she had seen. "Interpret it for me," he said. Talya tried to think through what she had seen.

"I have no idea," she finally said.

"Let me do the first one for you," he said. "The man was chasing the taxi and never catching it right?" Talya nodded. "What time was on his watch?"

"Eight o'clock," Talya said.

The wolf nodded. "We're picking up on his stress that he's not home on time."

Talya thought about it. "That makes sense. And the boardroom..."

she thought for a moment before the pieces clicked into place. "His boss is not happy with him?" she asked.

The wolf nodded. "Very good. He can't please anybody. His wife is mad that he's not home on time for dinner and to spend time with the kids; his boss is mad that he won't stay late to put in the extra time needed to fulfill his duties."

"Wow, you got all that from that?" Talya asked.

"I've been doing this a long time. You'll get better at it," the wolf said in a comforting manner.

"Should I try it again?" Talya asked.

"That's enough for tonight. It's time for school for you," he said.

Talya's eyes widened. "Already?" She felt like it had only been a few minutes.

The wolf nodded. "We will meet each night and continue to train until it's safe to send you into the vampire realm where you can find the answers we need."

"Okay," Talya said.

Talya opened her eyes and blinked. "Guess he wasn't kidding," she said with a smile to herself. Talya let herself lay there a few minutes longer before she got began the arduous process of getting ready. The leg scooter helped a lot.

When Sage got there to pick her up for school, she was ready. "What happened to you between today and yesterday?" Sage asked once they were in the car.

"What do you mean?" Talya asked.

"You just seem so much more at peace today and happier. Did you talk to Liam?" she asked.

Talya felt a tug on her heart at his name. "No," she said, pushing the emotion away. "I just feel good today," she said. Sage looked at her skeptically but didn't say anything more.

The day seemed to drag on and on. Talya couldn't keep her mind on her subjects; all she could think about was her dream last night. She made it through the day, including study time with Sage, dinner with her grandparents, and her homework. Finally, it was time for bed. It took Talya a little longer to fall asleep than usual; she was too anxious. She made herself relax and do breathing exercises. Finally, she fell asleep.

The wolf wasted no time leading her to the wolf melding. She worked through four dreams, practicing isolating details about the wolf. Who was the wolf? Where did it live? What was it feeling and why? There were so many questions. Talya felt like she knew less each time she came out of a dream than she had before she went into one. The night ended the same as the night before. She blinked, and it was over. She was once again back in her bed, and it was morning.

The days passed in similar fashion. She couldn't work at the diner because of her broken arm and foot, so she threw herself into her studies during the day. She had to because of all the time she had missed. At night, she threw herself into learning how to use her dream walking skills.

Life seemed to be settling into a predictable pattern, except for Brandon. She couldn't figure him out. He seemed to think that she was his now. He always acted like they were a couple, even though Talya wanted nothing to do with him. She didn't know why he bothered. She had made it abundantly clear she wasn't interested in him.

Eventually, six weeks passed. She was able to get her arm cast removed and move to a walking boot for her foot. Talya hugged the doctor when he finished. "Thank you so much," she said to him.

"How does it feel?" Sage asked as they walked out of the doctor's office.

"It feels a little funny, but it's so nice to be able to walk again. So, I'll take it," Talya said with a smile.

"Let's celebrate," Sage said.

"Ice cream," they both said at the same time. "I'll pull the car up," Sage said. Talya climbed into the car Sage's parents had given her for her birthday, and Sage drove them to their favorite ice cream shop.

"What are you wearing to the graduation ceremony?" Sage asked.

"I don't know," Talya replied. "I haven't even thought about it."

"Well, now that you are free from your casts, let's go shopping. Let's each get a dress for graduation—something we feel really good in. My treat," Sage said.

"You don't need to do that," Talya said.

"I want to," Sage said. "This is a big deal. We're graduating high school. That only happens one time, you know," she said with a grin.

"It does kind of sound fun, but I don't want you to pay for it," Talya said.

"Talya, let me. I want to do this," Sage said. Talya finally agreed. Sage's parents had lots of money, so she always had access to spending money.

They spent the rest of the afternoon trying on dresses. Sage chose a beautiful dark green dress that was knee length that she looked beautiful in. Talya chose a soft pink dress with a v-neck that was fitted around the waist and then flared out, landing just above her knees.

"Thank you for an amazing day," Talya said to Sage.

"You're welcome. I had an awesome time too," Sage said.

Talya disappeared inside and got right to work. She had two more weeks to finish all her assignments and get them turned in.

That night, when Talya reported for training, the wolf surprised her. "You're going into the vampire realm tonight," he said.

"Really?" Talya asked, slightly terrified. "I mean I'm glad that I've progressed that much, but I'm scared it's not enough."

"You're ready," the wolf said.

Those two words gave Talya the boost of confidence she needed. The wolf spent the entire time walking their talking through last-minute instructions. "After you've traveled here enough times, you will be able to dream walk yourself here without having to walk here," he said.

"That's cool," Talya said absently.

"All right. Now the first tries are just going to be about acclimating yourself to this world. You need to figure out the colors, the sizes, see if they work similarly to the wolf realm or if they have their own system. Only do three dreams tonight, Talya. Okay? I can't come across, so it's up to you to come back."

"Three dreams. Got it," Talya said.

"Just remember, Talya. Nothing can happen to you. It's only dreams," the wolf said.

Talya wasn't really sure if that thought was very comforting.

"Okay. I'll be back." Talya made herself step over the line dividing the wolf realm from the vampire realm before she could talk herself out of it. She began walking. She and the wolf had figured that the melding was probably in the middle, just like it was in the wolf realm. There was no guarantee of that, but that's what she was hoping for. Talya had once asked the wolf why he didn't know any of this. He said he'd never had a dream walker before. He'd never needed one.

"This is all new to me too, Talya," he had said. "You, my dreamer, are my newest creation."

Chapter Thirty-One

"I had to do something. The tide has been turning in favor of the vampires for the last few generations. I can no longer sit back and hope that my wolves will do what they were created to do. They need a push in the right direction. That's why I created you and Emma too," the wolf explained.

"What are we exactly?" Talya asked.

The wolf looked at her. "You are made of my wolf energy, but you are not wolves because you don't have a wolf inside of you. That's why the wolves are curious about you and why the vampires seek you to destroy you. They recognize my essence, and I am their mortal enemy."

"Well, when you put it that way..." Talya said as she shook her head. That was all he said about it, but it was enough for Talya to think about for a long time. Talya pushed those thoughts from her mind for now and focused on finding the melding. She wandered for a long time, too long it felt.

"What are you doing in my realm?" a voice said from behind her and Talya jumped and let out a shriek. With heart pounding, she turned around. She took in the tall man with incredibly pale skin standing before her. She knew without hesitation that he was a vampire, and not just any vampire. She knew he was the leader of the vampires. He exuded the same power that the wolf in the wolf realm did.

Talya had no idea what to say. Why in the world she hadn't thought through the fact that the vampire leader would be here, she had no idea. She mentally prepared the attack she was going to launch on the wolf when she made it back to the wolf realm...if she made it back.

The vampire took a deep breath. "I know what you are. I've heard about you," he said, drawing closer to her. Talya took a step backwards, wishing she was closer to the dividing line so she could step back into the wolf realm. Talya made the mistake of looking into his eyes. They were the darkest red she had ever seen, almost black; she had never seen such lifeless, dead-looking eyes. She glanced away quickly. "I am curious to know what you're doing here," he said. "So curious in fact that I have no plans to stop you. Continue on with what you have planned," he said, putting his hand out like he was directing her forward.

Talya had no idea what to do. Stay here? Go back? As much as she wanted to go back, she decided to go forward. This might be the only chance she got to ever do this again. The vampire was giving her one chance; he probably wouldn't be nearly as gracious when he saw what she was trying to do. Talya determinedly stepped forward, intent on her mission. She did her best to ignore the creature behind her. The further Talya walked, the stronger the smell got. She figured that was a good sign. It got so bad that she had to pull her shirt up and over her nose, not that it helped much.

Finally, Talya came upon the melding. She stared at it for a moment, trying not to feel nauseated. Sure, send the person who's queasy about all things blood-related to the actual river of blood, *she thought to herself as she he tried not to gag. She closed her eyes and took a few deep breaths.* Not the time to be weak, Talya, with the vampire god standing right behind you, *she mentally tried to pep talk herself. Talya took another deep breath; then plunged in before she could talk herself out of it.*

"Just pretend it's water. Just pretend it's water," she whispered to herself over and over again. She looked down and began studying the lines. They were a variety of colors, and different colors than in the wolf realm. While the wolf realm had bright colors, the colors here were all muted shades of black, gray, browns, and creams. It was much harder to determine the different colors and hues. Talya sighed. This would be harder than it had been in the wolf realm, and she had weeks to learn those colors. She took a deep breath and tried to think through what some of the colors could possibly represent. She and the wolf had talked about the possibilities of emotions the vampires would have, all of them on the spectrum of evil—hatred, lust, envy, anger, disgust, pride, indulgence, and more. After trying and failing to figure out what the colors could represent, she decided to just go for it. She located a thick cream line. She figured she didn't want to start with black; she had a feeling it would be awful.

She planted her feet, took a deep breath, and bent down to grasp the cord in her hands. Immediately she was in a dream. The dream was confusing, but Talya believed she was able to get what she was going to get from it. It was pride. She quickly followed that first dream with two more. Those dreams were no less confusing, but she tried to gather as many details as possible. None of the dreams gave her anything remotely helpful in her task.

"Did you find what you were looking for?" the vampire asked in a cold voice behind her. Talya ignored him and began walking back towards the wolf realm. She felt the vampire behind her every step of the way. He didn't say anything else. Talya just kept putting one foot in front of the other, hoping she would reach the wolf realm soon. It was sudden. One step she was in the vampire realm; the next, she was in the wolf realm. She glanced behind her, but she couldn't see the vampire realm. Not taking any chances, she continued walking away from the dividing line. The wolf moved alongside her gracefully without saying a word.

When she thought they were far enough, she spun around to face the wolf. "Why did you do that? You had to have known he would be there!" she said angrily.

"I did," the wolf said calmly.

"Why didn't you say anything? Why didn't I think about it?" she asked, as mad at herself as she was at the wolf.

"If I had breathed one word about him being there, you would have never crossed over and gone far enough in," the wolf said.

Talya suddenly felt depleted of energy. She sank down to her knees.

Talya opened her eyes and groaned. "Are you kidding me?" she shouted to her empty room. She heard a knock on her door.

"Talya, are you okay, honey?" her grandma asked as she opened the door.

"Yeah, I just remembered something for, uh, a class today that I forgot about," she said lamely.

"Okay, sweetie," her grandma said. "Is there anything I can do to help?"

Talya smiled at her grandma. "No. Thank you, though."

When she left the room, Talya's smile faded. She was so frustrated, and now she had to wait until tonight to get the answers she needed. With a groan, she dragged herself out of bed.

Talya had to put thoughts of her dream walking aside as she was facing down exams. She couldn't afford to be distracted these last few days of classes before her exams. After a long afternoon and evening of studying with Sage, she said goodbye to Sage and prepared for bed. She fell asleep quickly and landed in her dream state.

The wolf met her right away. "Are you ready?" he asked.

Talya crossed her arms. "Nice ending last night," she said sarcastically.

The wolf ignored her comment. "Let's get you to the vampire realm."

Talya didn't move. "What about the vampire?"

"I don't think he can hurt you," the wolf said.

Talya cocked an eyebrow. "You don't think?" she asked incredulously.

"You are his opposite. A being made of shifter energy. I think you will repel him," the wolf said.

"Well, what if I don't?" she asked.

"I'm sure you will," the wolf said and continued walking.

Talya hurried after him. "Not to be the negative one here, but I don't think this is going to work."

"It will be fine," the wolf said.

Talya closed her eyes, willing patience to come to her. When they got close to the vampire realm, Talya slowed her steps down. "Are you sure about this?" she asked, starting to breathe heavily.

"You will be fine. If you feel threatened for any reason, simply step

back into the wolf realm. He cannot touch you here," the wolf said.

"But what if I'm not close?" Talya asked, panicking now.

"Just imagine yourself in here. Your abilities as the dreamer have increased enough that you should be able to dream walk yourself right back, should you need to," the wolf said.

"Should?" Talya asked, her voice high. "You're not helping my confidence here."

"You won't know unless you do it," the wolf said. "Don't overthink it."

Talya was busy doing just that; otherwise, she would have noticed when the wolf darted behind her. Suddenly, Talya felt herself falling forward. She tried to catch herself, but she landed on her knees...in the vampire realm. Panic seized her for a moment. She quickly jumped to her feet and was about to make her way back, but she paused. She glanced around and didn't see the vampire. Maybe he was busy with something and not around. She decided to just go for it and started walking quickly towards the melding.

Without any warning, the vampire appeared in front of her. Talya shrieked and stumbled backwards. "You are not welcome here, Dreamer," he said. With that, he pushed her backwards. His power was so strong that Talya flew backwards. He came at her again, but Talya was already on her feet. She had no time to think. She just envisioned the wolf realm.

Talya blinked. She was back in the wolf realm. She sank to her feet shakily. "What happened?" the wolf asked.

Talya shook her head. "He wouldn't let me near the melding. He shoved me out of his realm."

The wolf shook its head in frustration. "We will have to come up with another plan."

Talya opened her eyes. "Oh, come on!" she said in frustration as she looked up at her ceiling again. "That wolf is going to be the death of me," she muttered. After a long night of no sleep, she finally decided to get up and get going. She had a big day ahead of her. As important as her job as the dreamer was, so was graduating high school. "Time to face the music," she said to herself.

That night, Talya didn't make a trip to her dreamland. Neither did she the next night or the night after that. After a week, Talya had gone through every emotion from relief, to worry, to frustration, to fear, to anger, and finally numbness. She didn't know what was going on, but she couldn't waste any more mental energy on it. There was nothing she could do about the situation until the wolf brought her back. She managed to put that part of her life aside for the time being and focus on finishing school.

The next two weeks flew by. Her birthday came and went. She celebrated at home with her grandparents and Sage. Suddenly, it was graduation day. Sage showed up at Talya's house first thing in the morning. Talya was walking carefully around the room without her boot on.

"How does it feel?" Sage asked.

Talya shook her head. "It feels weird but good. I'm so glad my doctor let me get it off a few days early."

"I know. That's so great, so all your graduation pictures won't be of you in your boot," Sage said with a smile.

"Yeah. Are you ready to get started?" Talya asked. "I was thinking that we could do hair first, then make-up, then get dressed."

"You're the expert," Sage said.

"Okay, let's do your hair first," Talya said. She spent the next hour curling Sage's hair and styling it for her. Then Sage started doing the basics for makeup on her face while Talya started doing her own hair. Talya had finally gotten it cut, so it wasn't so long and heavy anymore. It was still halfway down her back but not nearly as long as it had been. She decided to just straighten it and leave it down for the day.

She tackled Sage's makeup next. When she was finished, she stepped back and smiled. "What do you think?"

Chapter Thirty-Two

"Wow, I don't even look like me," Sage said, staring at herself in the mirror.

"Yes, you do," Talya said with a smile. "You're beautiful, Sage."

After that, Talya got to work on her own makeup. Soon it was time to put their dresses on. Talya sat on the bed to put her shoes on. She had chosen a pair of flats because she knew there was no way she could do heels because of her foot. She stood up and tested them out. "This feels so weird," she told Sage.

"I'm sure," Sage said sympathetically. "You look beautiful, Talya."

"Thanks, so do you. Are you ready to do this?" Talya asked.

"So ready," Sage responded. They walked out into the living room where Talya's grandparents oohed and aahed over them.

"Are you sure you will be okay coming over by yourselves?" Talya asked them.

"We're fine. You two girls go on and enjoy your day. We'll be over later for the ceremony.

After hugs and kisses, Sage and Talya left to drive to the school. They had several things they were required to do before the actual ceremony.

"Are your parents coming today?" Talya asked Sage.

Sage shrugged. "I told them about it, but who knows."

"I'm sorry, Sage," Talya said. She hated that Sage's parents were too busy for her. Sage didn't say anything else, and Talya let it go. She didn't want to ruin Sage's day.

After parking, they made their way inside. Talya walked slowly and carefully so she didn't hurt her foot. They soon joined their classmates in all the festivities of graduation day. Talya was determined to enjoy the day. Even Brandon didn't bother as much as he usually did. Mostly, that was due to the fact that he was busy with his friends

Finally, it was time for the actual ceremony. She had made sure her grandparents got inside and seated okay. Now, she just had to endure the long ceremony. Talya glanced around the room again. It was a huge crowd, but that was to be expected for such a large graduating class.

The ceremony dragged by. Finally, it was Talya's turn to walk across the stage. She waited at the edge of the stage until her name was called. Talya focused on walking slowly and carefully. She was able to make it successfully across the stage without any mishaps. She paused for her picture and then soon made her way off the stage. Only when she was seated did she finally relax.

When the ceremony was finally over, Sage found her. "We

did it!" she said as she wrapped her arms around Talya.

"I need to find my grandparents. Come with me?" Talya asked. Sage nodded, and they began making their way through the crowd. Before she could find them, somebody grabbed her from behind and swung her around.

"We did it!" Brandon shouted.

"Put me down, Brandon," Talya told him.

He put her down roughly and pulled her into his arms. Talya turned away when he tried to kiss her, but he grabbed her chin in a bruising hold and forced her to kiss him.

"I think it would be in your best interest to release her," Talya heard from behind her, and Talya stiffened at the voice.

Brandon tightened his hold on her temporarily before finally releasing her. Talya shoved him away from her and turned around. Shocked didn't begin to describe what she felt when she saw who was standing there. Garrett stood with his arms crossed, staring down Brandon. Emma, Madison, Kyle, Max, Steven, Wyatt, and a few other wolves she didn't know stood around him.

"Leave Talya alone," Garrett said to Brandon. "She's not yours."

Brandon laughed and crossed his arms. Mitch and Trevor came and stood next to him. "You sure about that?" Brandon asked. "You have no authority in this territory," Brandon said arrogantly. "Are you really going to fight me for her?" he sneered.

"I won't have to," Garrett's calm reply came.

"And why is that?" Brandon asked.

"Because I will." Talya closed her eyes, fighting the instant

response she had to his voice. When she opened them, her eyes met startling blue eyes. But they weren't the eyes she remembered. They were cold and had no life in them.

"Talya's mine," Liam said in a guttural voice, and Talya saw his eyes flash yellow. Talya took a step backwards, but that was a mistake. Liam's head jerked in her direction. She was caught in his yellow gaze. His eyes were glowing, and Talya knew his wolf was close to the surface.

"Liam," Garrett said in a calm yet authoritative voice.

"This is enough," Talya finally said. "I am not a possession to be fought over, and I am certainly not yours, Brandon." She heard a low growl and knew it had come from Liam. She turned towards him and all the hurt and anger at him for just disappearing from of her life came flooding to the surface. "I'm not yours either," she said angrily.

A savage growl ripped from Liam's lips, and Garrett and Max both snapped at him. Liam jerked forward, and Garett and Max both grabbed ahold of him. Kyle joined them, trying to hold him back. The others stood around them trying to shield them from curious eyes.

Talya didn't think things could get any worse, but she was wrong. Brandon grabbed Talya and pulled her against him with bruising force. Talya stumbled as she was yanked backwards. "Don't touch her again," a furious Kyle said as he pushed Brandon away from her. Madison put her arm around Talya and started walking.

"Come on, Talya; let's get of here," Madison said. Sage came and stood beside Talya.

252

"What is the meaning of this?" a new voice joined the fray. Talya knew that voice. It was Brandon's dad.

Are you kidding me? Could this day get any worse? Just as Talya had those thoughts, she heard yet another set of voices.

"Talya? Are you okay?"

"What's going on?"

Talya spun out of Madison's hold and saw her grandparents standing nearby with worried expressions on their faces. Talya took in the guys still holding back a seething Liam, an angry Brandon, his furious dad, and her confused grandparents and wanted to cry. This was supposed to be her special day and it was going up in flames.

It was absolutely silent with the arrival of her grandparents. It was as if everybody had frozen; well, everybody that is, except for Liam. He was still fuming. She didn't have to look at him to know that; she just knew somehow.

"Good afternoon and congratulations to you on Talya's graduation," Brandon's father said in his booming voice, instantly changing his demeanor. "Wasn't that a great ceremony?"

"It was," Talya's grandma said. "Congratulations to you to, Brandon," she said stiffly.

Brandon grinned at them with a smug smile like he was so much better than they were; Talya hated it. "Thank you."

"Well, why don't we all head over to the reception," Brandon's dad said merrily.

Talya didn't want to; her desire to party had evaporated, but she didn't know how to get out of it. The school held a reception for the graduates and their families every year right after graduation. "Yes, let's go, Talya," her grandma said, putting out her hand to her. Talya forced a smile to her face and took her grandma's hand. "You too, Sage dear." Sage smiled and took Talya's grandma's other hand. Without a word to anybody, Grandma started leading them away from the group. Grandpop fell into step beside them.

Talya took a deep breath, happy to be leaving the chaos behind. She had no idea what was going to happen, but she left them to figure it out. "You okay, Talya?" Grandma asked.

Talya sighed. "Yeah, let's just put all that behind us and go celebrate."

"Sounds good to me," Sage said.

"Me too," Grandma said.

Talya glanced at her grandpop. He hadn't said anything, but he didn't look too upset. Talya thought back to the pack. Why were they here? Why now after all this time? And what about Liam? Her heart hurt thinking about him, so she didn't. It was time to celebrate.

Talya enjoyed the amazing dinner with Sage and her grandparents. Before too long, they were out on the dance floor with the rest of their classmates, dancing and being crazy. Talya was careful not to get too carried away because of her foot. The evening was going really well until Brandon came up behind her and slid his arms around her waist. Talya turned around. "Brandon, stop."

"I need to talk to you," he said.

Talya was already shaking her head. "No."

"It's serious. I need to talk to you," Brandon said with a serious expression.

Talya huffed. "Five minutes," she reluctantly agreed to.

"I'll take it," he said. He grabbed her wrist and pulled her away from the dance floor before she could say anything to Sage. She tried to yank her wrist back, but he tightened his grip on her hand. He led her out of the huge banquet room and into another empty room. He shut the door behind him.

"What do you want, Brandon?" Talya asked. "I just want to get back to the party."

"I need you to tell the pack that you're my mate," he said.

Talya blinked. "What?"

"You need to tell the Northwoods Pack, specifically their Alpha, that you're my mate," he said.

Shock coursed through her. "You know about them?" she asked incredulously.

Brandon looked at her with disdain. "Of course," he said.

"How did you know what they are?" she asked.

"Talya, they're wolves," he said, like she was stupid.

'I know that. How did you know?" she asked.

A smirk appeared on his face. "I'm a wolf," he said. Talya took a step backwards and stumbled.

"You, you're a, a," she stuttered.

"I'm a wolf. So are Trevor and Mitch," he said. "My dad is the Alpha." Talya was shocked. How had she not known? "You need to tell them that you're my mate, so they will leave."

"But I'm not your mate," Talya said.

The blow came so fast, Talya never even saw it. Her eyes watered and she put a hand up to her cheek where he had hit her.

"You are my mate; don't deny it," he said in fury. Then he did a complete one-eighty. "Now I need you to go out there and tell them that."

Talya stared at him. "Why in the world would I tell them that?" she asked, still holding her cheek.

"Because if you don't, Talya..." Brandon said, taking a step closer. "I will be forced to do something I don't want to do." He looked towards the door. "Bring her in," he commanded.

Talya gasped when the door opened and Trevor and Mitch dragged Sage into the room. Her eyes met Talya's, and Talya could see the fear in her eyes. "What are you doing? Let her go!" she yelled at them.

"Just as soon as you tell them that you're my mate," he said.

Talya spun around. "I will never be your mate," she said in disgust.

"Fine. Don't say I didn't warn you," he said. He nodded at Mitch and Trevor. Before Talya could stop them, Trevor hit Sage hard across the face. Talya screamed and tried to run towards her, but Brandon grabbed her arms and held her back. Mitch kicked Sage in the ribs.

"Stop!" Talya screamed. Mitch crouched next to Sage and grabbed her hair, yanking her head back at an awkward angle. Sage's eyes met Talya's, and Talya couldn't bear to see the pain in her eyes. "Leave her alone," she screamed as she fought against Brandon. But it was like fighting a brick wall. She watched as Trevor crouched next to Sage. Talya couldn't see what happened, but she heard Sage scream.

"Stop!" Talya screamed. "I'll do it. Just stop," she pleaded.

Brandon motioned for the guys to stand Sage up. Sage slumped against Mitch. Talya couldn't stop the tears pouring down her face. "I'm so sorry, Sage," Talya said.

Sage met her eyes. "Don't do it, Talya," she said weakly.

"Shut up," Brandon growled at her as he yanked Talya forward. Talya tried to stop to check on Sage, but Brandon pulled her with him. He stopped when they were in the hall. "Now dry it up and pull yourself together. You need to convince them that you're my mate. If you don't," he shook his head. "Well, you already know what will happen."

"I hate you," Talya said putting every ounce of her hate into her gaze.

"You won't," he said simply. "Not once we're mated. You will love me."

"Never," Talya hissed at him.

He jerked her arm hard. "You'd better start acting like it, *Mate*; or Sage will reap the consequences." Talya bit back a sob. Why was her life so messed up? "Are you ready?" he asked with a gleam in his eye. Talya simply nodded; she had no other choice. She took a deep breath. She wouldn't allow Sage to get hurt any more than she already was. She wiped her eyes and nodded.

"Let's go," Brandon said with a smile. He grabbed her arm roughly and began pulling her along with him. He led her through the building before they came to a room. When he opened the door, Talya saw Liam's pack as well as Brandon's dad and several men she didn't know. She assumed they were from Brandon's pack because they were standing with his dad.

Brandon wrapped his arm around her and pulled her tightly

against him. "Talya has an announcement," he said smugly. Talya didn't lift her eyes off the floor; she couldn't bear to look at anybody.

Talya took a deep breath. "I'm Brandon's mate," she said softly. Harsh words and curses followed her words.

"Well, gentlemen. The little lady has spoken. I believe that's all there is to say. I suggest you take your pack and leave," Brandon's dad said.

"I don't think so," Garrett said in anger. "It's obvious she's under duress. I don't know what your boy did to her, but she's not saying that willingly."

Brandon's grip tightened painfully on her arm. Talya closed her eyes for a moment. She opened them and looked right at Garrett. She didn't know where Liam was, but she focused on the Alpha. "I'm. Brandon's. Mate." Talya said the words distinctly and void of emotion. She pushed all her own feelings aside and focused on keeping Sage safe.

"Now that was beyond clear," Brandon's dad said. "So why don't we..."

"Then I challenge you for her." It was suddenly quiet. Talya looked up as Liam stalked towards Brandon. She didn't know where he had come from, but he was far from the angry man she had seen earlier. He was completely emotionless and cold. He never looked at her. He kept his eyes locked on Brandon.

"Do you accept the challenge?" Garrett's deep voice sounded.

Talya looked at Brandon, wondering what he would do. A cocky smile flashed across his face. "I accept."

Talya didn't know what any of that meant, but from the silence in the room, she had a feeling it was going to be bad—really, really bad.

Chapter Thirty-Three

"Well, at least we will finally settle this once and for all. We will reconvene on our property in one hour. Talya will be going with us," Brandon's dad said. Angry protests sounded from Liam's pack. "She was with my son when the challenge was made. She will stay with him until the fight. That's standard procedure."

Garrett looked angry but nodded. "Fine, but Max stays with her at all times as a representative from our pack." Brandon's dad nodded. With that, Garrett walked out of the room with Emma at his side. His pack followed. Talya kept her eyes on the floor, but she knew when Liam passed her. He didn't stop or say anything, but he slowed as he walked past her.

She felt Max come and stand beside her. He was silent, but somehow just knowing he was there made her feel safer. Brandon's dad led the way out of the room. Brandon pulled her along with him, and Max followed behind her.

They left the banquet and loaded into several cars and began driving towards Brandon's dad's house. As Talya sat in the car, she wondered why she had never thought it was weird that she hadn't been to Brandon's home. They'd dated for nearly three years. Clearly, she had been clueless about Brandon, his family, and his friends' true nature.

They drove about twenty minutes before stopping in what looked like the middle of nowhere. Everybody climbed out of the vehicles. Brandon pulled her out of the vehicle, and she stumbled on her bad foot. Max caught her arm and steadied her.

Wordlessly, the group walked towards a large field. When they got closer, Talya could see a big circle in the middle of the field. Brandon dropped her arm and went to talk to his father. They walked a little ways away from everybody else.

Max stood next to Talya. "You okay?" he asked in a quiet, gruff voice.

She saw Brandon and his dad making their way back towards them. "Max," she whispered. "They have my friend, Sage," she said in a broken voice. Max didn't move a muscle. She had no idea if he heard her or not, but she couldn't say anything more because Brandon and his dad were almost to them.

Brandon grabbed her arm and pulled her away from Max. "What is this challenge?" Talya asked.

Brandon smirked down at her. "It's a fight to the death. Winner gets you," he said easily.

"What?!" Talya exploded. Nobody had told her that! "That's ridiculous. Why in the world would you do that?"

Brandon shrugged. "It's how we do things as wolves."

Talya stared at him. How had it come to this? Before she could say anything else, the Northwoods Pack arrived. Talya watched them climb out of their vehicles and begin heading their way. Talya glanced at the group and noticed that Madison, Kyle, and Wyatt weren't with them. She wondered absently where they were. She looked back at Liam. As if he felt her gaze, his head turned towards hers. They locked eyes for a moment before Brandon grabbed her arm and jerked her towards him. Garrett's pack gathered on their side of the circle.

Brandon's dad came and stood next to Talya and Brandon. "Get in there, Brandon," he said. Brandon took off his shirt and shoes. Talya looked across the circle to see that Liam had done the same. Brandon grabbed Talya and kissed her hard on the lips. She heard a vicious growl from Liam. When Brandon let her go, she saw Garrett and Steven both had a hand on Liam's shoulders and were holding him back.

"Both men step into the circle," Brandon's dad called out. Talya felt a hand reach out and squeeze hers. She turned her head and saw Emma standing next to her. Talya clung to her hand, trying to find grounding. When both Liam and Brandon were inside the circle, his dad yelled, "Begin." She watched Garrett step up next to the circle on his side, and Max did the same on her side. So did Brandon's dad and another guy.

Talya wasn't prepared in the least for what happened next. Liam ran and jumped. In the air, he shifted. When he landed, he was a magnificent brown wolf. He was at Brandon's throat before Brandon had barely finished shifting into a gray wolf. Liam's wolf was aggressive and powerful. He had Brandon pinned instantly. Talya had no idea what was going to happen next. Suddenly, the Brandon's gray wolf swiped a paw across the brown wolf's back. The brown wolf stumbled backwards. The gray wolf stood to its feet and followed it. The brown wolf attacked again, and the gray wolf fought back. It was only moments before the gray wolf was pinned again. The moment the brown wolf was ready to close his teeth around the gray wolf's throat, the gray wolf swiped it again and the brown wolf went teetering backwards again.

Talya held her breath as Liam's wolf got back up again, shakily. Then it charged at Brandon's wolf. But the gray wolf gave it another hard swipe and Liam was down again. Talya watched Liam's wolf struggle to get back up. "No," she whispered. She was mad at him; that was a given. But she didn't want him to die. She clenched her hands tightly as the gray wolf circled the brown wolf. Then he lunged at the brown wolf. "No!" Talya cried out. That seemed to get the brown wolf's attention. He staggered to his feet once again. The gray wolf came at him, and they fought viciously. But Talya could see the brown wolf was getting weaker as the fight dragged on.

Time seemed to slow down. The gray wolf attacked again, and the brown wolf went down. The gray wolf pounced on him and went for his throat. Talya screamed, waiting for the killing blow. Instead, a huge black wolf burst into the circle and plowed into the gray wolf. A second later, a gray wolf similar to Brandon's but larger charged into the circle. But he was a moment too late. The smaller gray wolf had been seriously injured by the black wolf.

A quick glance at both sides of the circle showed that the large black wolf was Garrett and the large gray wolf was Brandon's dad. Emma squeezed her hand tightly as the two alphas fought viciously. Movement caught Talya's eye, pulling her eyes away from the fight. She watched the brown wolf stagger to its feet. It steadied itself before it lunged forward. A moment later, Talya gagged as she watched the brown wolf rip the throat out of the smaller gray wolf.

Talya cried out in horror and put her hand over her mouth to keep from throwing up. She watched the brown wolf drop to the ground. Without thinking, she ran towards the wolf. Strong arms caught her around the waist and held her back. "You can't go in there. It's too dangerous," Max said gruffly.

"Let me go," Talya yelled at him; but he held her tightly. Talya's eyes were yanked back to the fight when she heard a vicious growl. She watched as the black wolf pinned the large gray wolf. She looked away this time, knowing what was coming. An awful sound made Talya's knees go weak. When she looked up, the gray wolf was dead. Talya leaned over Max's arm and threw up. She gagged until nothing else came up.

"Who's the Beta of this pack?" she heard Garrett's powerful voice call out.

"I am." Talya looked over and saw a man she always saw with Brandon's dad.

"Your wolf cheated; he used silver," Garrett said in fierce anger. "In doing so, he forfeited the challenge. That's why I stepped in. Check him, and you will find it on his paws. Will you challenge me, Beta?" Garrett asked.

The man dropped his head. "No, Alpha. What he did was wrong."

"Then you are now the leader of this pack." Garrett paused for a moment. "If I ever hear of a wolf in your pack using silver in a challenge or for anything else, I will be back," he said ominously. Then he strode towards Liam. He picked Liam's wolf up as if it weighed nothing and began jogging back towards the car.

"Let's go," Max said to Talya. He stayed next to her as they followed Garrett and his pack members.

Steven folded the chairs down in the wheel well in the Land Rover, so they could lay Liam down on the floor. "Will he be okay?" Talya asked Emma who stood next to her.

"He won't be if we don't get that silver out of him," Garrett said grimly. "We have to get him to Paul." He placed Liam down and pulled on a pair of sweatpants.

"Why can't you take him to the hospital?" Talya asked.

"Can't take a wolf to the hospital," Garrett responded gruffly. "Are you going with or going home?"

"They have my friend Sage," Talya said worriedly.

"Not anymore. Kyle, Madison, and Wyatt rescued her and took her to the hospital. She's okay. We have to roll out now. I need to know if you're coming or staying," Garrett said brusquely.

Talya tried to think quickly what to do. Did she stay with Sage? Or did she go with Liam? She glanced at the wolf lying in the back of the car. They said Sage was going to be okay. They couldn't say the same yet for Liam. "I'm going," she said.

"Are you sure, Talya?" Emma asked gently.

"No," Talya said honestly. "But he fought for me; he was willing to die for me. I can't just let him go, not knowing if he's going to be okay."

Emma nodded. "What about your grandparents?"

"I'll call and explain everything. I'm eighteen now, so the police can't get involved this time around. I don't have anything, though," Talya said.

Emma nodded. "We'll take care of everything you need."

"We have to go, now." Garrett said urgently.

Talya hopped in the back and sat on the floor next to Liam. Garrett closed the doors. Max slid into the driver's seat, and Steven climbed into the passenger seat. They took off a moment later. Talya looked down at the still wolf in front of her. He was huge; she had forgotten just how big he was. She barely fit in the back with him. She wondered if he was in pain; that thought gutted her.

"Is there anything I can do to help him?" Talya asked Max.

He met her eyes in the rearview mirror. "Just being near him will do him a world of good and help to keep his wolf calm. We have to get him to Paul. Paul can help drain the silver from him."

"Will he be okay?" Talya asked, worried. Max didn't say anything for a moment. "Max?" she questioned. "Tell me the truth."

"If the silver reaches his heart, he will die," Max said unemotionally.

Talya's breath left her in a whoosh. "Well, we can't let that happen then," she said stoically. She took her phone out of her pocket and dialed her grandparents' house.

"Hello," Grandpop answered.

"Hey Grandpop," Talya said resignedly. She wasn't sure how this was going to go. "Can you put Grandma on the line too?"

she asked.

"You okay, Tally Bear?" Grandpop asked in concern.

"Yeah, I just need to talk to you both," Talya said. Thankfully, he didn't ask any more questions. Talya waited until they were both on the line.

"Talya, what's going on? Are you okay?" her grandma asked.

Talya closed her eyes trying to think of what to say. "You know how I went with Liam before when I was hurt?" Neither of them responded. "Well, I need to do the same for him now. Liam's been hurt, really badly. They're not sure if he's going to make it. We're enroute to the same place that cared for me." She held her breath as she waited for them to respond.

"What's happened to him?" Grandpop asked.

Chapter Thirty-Four

Talya didn't respond for a moment. She decided to stick as close to the truth as possible. "He fought Brandon over me, and well, Brandon didn't fight fairly. He really hurt Liam badly," she said, her voice cracking.

"Are you safe?" Grandpop asked in a rough voice.

"Yes, I'm with Liam and his friends. They take really good care of me," Talya said.

"You're sure, Talya?" Grandma asked. "I thought he broke your heart."

"He did," Talya said honestly. "But he fought Brandon when Brandon was trying to hurt me. I owe it to him to stay with him and make sure he makes it."

It was quiet for a minute. "Well, I don't like it; but you have to do what you have to do," Grandpop said.

"Keep in touch this time, Talya," Grandma said.

"I will, I promise. I love you both," she said with emotion.

"We love you, too. You be safe and take care of Liam," Grandma said.

Talya agreed, and they talked for a few more minutes before hanging up. She called Sage next.

"Hey Talya," Sage said in a quiet voice.

"Sage! Are you okay? I've been so worried about you!"

"I'm okay. I got checked out at the hospital. They're keeping me overnight, but I'm okay. The painkillers are working wonders." Talya could hear the smile in her voice.

"I'm sorry, Sage," Talya said.

"It's not your fault," Sage protested.

"I'm pretty sure it is, but I'm glad you're okay. Did your parents come to the hospital?" Talya asked.

"I didn't even tell them, but I told my Aunt Beth. She's here with me now, and she said I can go home with her tomorrow."

"Oh good," Talya said, relieved. "Listen, I've got bad news."

"What now?" Sage asked, worried.

"Brandon and Liam got into a fight. Brandon didn't fight fairly and hurt Liam really badly. They're not even sure if he's going to make it. We're on our way back to Wisconsin," she explained.

"Oh, Talya! I'm so sorry. I didn't know. What can I do?" Sage asked.

"Well, you can heal for one thing. Can you also check on my grandparents for me while I'm gone? I'm not sure how long I'll be gone. I'll stay in touch, though."

"Of course, I'll check on them. And do your best to stay in touch. Call me if I can do anything at all," Sage said.

"I will," Talya said. They said their goodbyes and hung up. Talya slumped against the door. Those calls had exhausted her emotionally.

The next twenty-four hours were grueling. They only stopped when they needed gas. Talya was exhausted. She hadn't let herself fall asleep for fear that Liam would get worse while she was sleeping. But she finally gave in when she just couldn't stay awake anymore. She snuggled up next to Liam's wolf. She stroked him affectionately as she had been doing since they started the trip. It took her only moments to fall fast asleep beside him.

Talya opened her eyes, surprised to see she was back in her dream state. She instantly sought out the wolf.

"Liam's hurt," Talya blurted out when she saw him. "He's got silver inside of him. Can you save him?" she asked.

"I cannot," he said sadly.

"But why? You're their creator?" she asked, frustrated.

"That's not how it works," he said vaguely.

"Why?" Talya asked bluntly. "You're their creator; shouldn't you help them?' she asked, anger kindling inside her. "Or better yet, shouldn't you have kept him from fighting in the first place?" she asked again as her anger continued to build.

The wolf looked off into the distance; then back at her. "How did Liam get hurt?"

Talya looked at him in surprise. "You don't know? I thought you knew everything. I thought you could see everything."

The wolf watched her, his head still. "How did Liam get hurt?" he asked again, calmly.

"In a challenge. He was fighting for me," Talya said with emotion.

"Who was he fighting?" the wolf asked calmly.

 270

Talya snorted. "This jerk who I used to date. He was horrible to me."

The wolf nodded. "Is he still alive?"

"Brandon or Liam?" she asked in confusion.

"The one who hurt you," he said calmly.

"He's dead," Talya said emotionlessly.

"Then would you say justice has been served?" the wolf asked. Talya opened her mouth but snapped it shut as she thought about it for a moment. Finally, she nodded. "Then why would I have stepped in?" the wolf asked.

"But he's hurt," Talya said. "What if he dies?" she asked fearfully.

"Then he will have accomplished what it was he was supposed to accomplish, and his journey will be complete," the wolf said.

Talya stared at him. "Is that what's going to happen?" she asked, feeling like she had lead in her stomach.

The wolf was quiet again before answering. "Talya, you cannot plan out every moment and detail of this life ahead of time. You have to live it. You can't be so afraid of what might happen that you don't embrace the life in front of you completely. You have to trust that I have a firm grasp on what is going on. I can see the full picture; you cannot. The wolves are my creation. I love them more than you possibly could. Do you not think it hurts me when one of my own is hurt?" he asked solemnly.

"Then why allow it to happen in the first place?" Talya asked, trying and failing to understand.

"Because that is what makes my wolves the extraordinary creatures that they are. The challenges of this life develop them into the fierce warriors that they are. If I took away every pain and trial from their lives, they would never grow into who I need them to be. How do you think Liam got to be the incredible Beta that he is today? Do you think it was because he had an easy life of no pain? That I just dealt with everything for him and kept him wrapped up protectively so nothing bad could happen to him?"

Talya felt her shoulders drop. "No," she said softly.

"My wolves were not designed for an easy life. I created them to combat the evils of the vampires. Their very existence is to fight and win against evil. To do that, I need warriors. My wolves need to be strong, battle-tested, dependable, and resilient. They would never become that if I stepped in and handled life for them every time it got difficult," the wolf said sternly.

Talya plopped down into the grass feeling thoroughly rebuked. "I get it," she said tiredly. "What am I supposed to do in the middle of all this?"

"You need to focus on the task at hand. I believe that you will be able to get through to the melding now. I think you will be stronger now that you are with Liam once again. The goodness of the wolf is the exact opposite to the vampire's evil. I believe he won't be able to stop you."

"Okay, I'll try." She didn't want to have to think about Liam, about the fact he could be dying. She needed to focus on her task.

"Imagine yourself right at the melding this time. Hopefully that will buy you some time," the wolf said.

Talya nodded. She closed her eyes and pictured herself in the midst of the bloody melding. When she opened her eyes, she was in the right spot. Without thinking about it, she grabbed the largest black line she could find. She immediately fell into the dream. She opened her eyes and saw blood everywhere. She wanted to release the line immediately, but she knew she couldn't. She saw a bed with a pillow and blanket. It looked so relaxing and inviting. She watched as the vampire tried to lay down, but every time he tried, the bed filled with blood.

Talya released that cord. She quickly searched for the next largest black cord. She immediately grabbed it and fell into the next dream. It was a party. She saw several vampires standing around laughing and talking. She was confused for a moment because she wasn't sure whose dream it was. That is until one of the vampires turned and looked right at Talya. He stared, and Talya felt a shiver run through her until she remembered they couldn't see her. She turned and saw a young girl standing in the hallway with blood on her nightgown. Talya shivered and dropped the line.

Without looking around to see if the vampire was near her or not, she searched for the next black line. She knew she was onto something. She just needed to find a location. It took four more dreams before she finally saw something. There!

She dropped the line and pictured herself back in the wolf realm. She opened her eyes and blew out a breath when she saw she was back in the wolf realm. "I've got it!" she said triumphantly. "Chicago."

"Good work, Talya. Did he bother you?" he asked.

"I never even saw him," she said.

The wolf was quiet for a moment. She knew by now he was thinking. "He may have been absent, busy helping his vampires. You may not get so lucky again."

"Well, I'll take it for now. I saw blood and a young girl. Eventually I saw the bean in Chicago. I'm convinced that it's Chicago. It has to be," she said excitedly.

The wolf took a few steps towards her and stopped. He sat on his *hunches and watched her intensely. "You need to convince the Alpha to stop."*

Talya stared at him. "You want us to stop before we get Liam to Paul?" she asked incredulously. "But he could die!"

The wolf nodded once. "He could. But if the vampires aren't stopped, many will die."

"I-I can't," Talya began.

The wolf stood to its feet. "It is your choice." He turned as if he was about to walk away.

Panic exploded in Talya. "Wait! Will Liam be okay?" The wolf continued to walk away, fading from view. Before she could process the extent of her frustration and anger, the world around her began to fade.

Talya opened her eyes and sat up. They had stopped. A quick glance down at Liam assured her he was still unconscious. She put her hands over her face and groaned. She shook her head as she ran her hand through Liam's fur one more time before she scooted to the back of the car. Steven climbed out of the car without a word and came around to the back and opened the door for her.

Talya climbed out and stretched; then glanced back at Liam. "I'll keep a watch over him," Steven said.

Talya managed a small smile. "Thank you." She began walking towards the gas station. She needed to go to the bathroom desperately; then she needed to find a certain Alpha and convince him not to take his good friend who was dying to the only person who could save him and instead go hunt down some vampires in an unknown location somewhere in Chicago. "Yep, seems like a solid plan to me," Talya muttered to herself, then groaned. "Why me?" she asked out loud.

She stepped into the gas station and walked towards the bathroom. When she came back out, she saw Max waiting for her. He followed her as she walked through the store and out the front door. She looked up at the big man next to her. She swallowed hard. "I need to talk to Garrett," she said in a shaky voice.

Max looked down at her and nodded. He led her towards another Land Rover parked a few spaces away from them. Garrett was just about to climb into the driver's seat when Max stopped him. "Boss," he called out. Garrett turned to face them. Talya felt her breathing pick up. Too soon, she was standing in front of the man. Max nodded at her, and Garrett turned his attention to her.

Talya tried to draw in air but felt like she couldn't get a full breath. "Um, so I had a dream," she started lamely. She took a quick peek up at Garrett. His sunglasses hid his eyes, and his face was expressionless. "I don't really know how to say this, so I'm just going to say it. We have to stop. There's a," she paused and continued in a whisper for a moment, "vampire site." She didn't say anything more. She peeked up at Garrett's face again and still saw no expression.

"Where?" came his clipped question.

Talya sighed. *Here we go,* she thought to herself. "Somewhere in Chicago. That's all I know."

"Somewhere in Chicago?" Garrett repeated. Talya nodded.

"How many vampires?" he asked.

"I don't know," Talya responded.

"What kind of facility?" Garrett tried again.

"I don't know," Talya said even softer this time.

Garrett was silent for a moment. "So, you want me to risk my Beta's life to find a site that's located somewhere in the huge city of Chicago and you don't know anything more than that?" he asked, his anger permeating his words.

"Garrett?" Talya turned to see Emma making her way towards them. She moved close to Garrett and put her hand on his stomach; he wrapped an arm around her and pulled her tightly against his chest. "What's going on?" she asked calmly.

"She's trying to keep us from getting Liam to Paul by suggesting we stop and try to find a vampire site that she knows absolutely nothing about!" He bellowed the last part out.

Talya had had enough. She got right in Garrett's face. "You think this is my idea? That man in there risked his life for mine, and now he's dying. You think I want to stop instead of getting him the help he needs? You don't think I hate this? I know what it sounds like. It sounds like I don't have a clue what we're supposed to do; that's because I don't!" she was yelling at him now. "All of this is one giant experiment! I'm trying to find out the information as fast as I can, but it's next to impossible!"

Chapter Thirty-Five

It was utterly silent after her outburst. Talya startled when she felt a hand on her arm. She looked away from the Alpha and saw Emma's hand on her arm. "It's okay, Talya. You're doing the best you can," she said gently. "Garrett, what are we going to do?" Emma asked.

Madison came and stood beside her with Kyle and Wyatt right behind her. Talya hadn't realized they had rejoined their group. It was absolutely silent for an excruciatingly long minute before Garrett pushed his sunglasses to the top of his head. His eyes locked on Talya. Talya could see the war in his eyes. She knew what he was struggling with; it was the same thing she was struggling with. Did they take a chance on Liam's life to try to stop vampires at a site they knew nothing about? Garrett looked away from Talya, and Talya finally felt like she could take a breath.

"It's young girls," she said softly.

She watched the fight leave Garrett. He looked at the other

members of his pack surrounding them. "If we do this, we have to all unanimously decide to pursue the vampires," he said in a low voice. "We are risking the life of our Beta and our friend. We have to be absolutely sure that this is the right path." He took a deep breath. "As your leader..." he paused. Talya could see he was at war with himself, and she saw when he made his decision. He straightened. "As your leader, I believe we have no choice but to follow Talya's leading, but I am willing to listen to anyone that believes otherwise."

It was quiet. After a moment, Emma spoke softly. "I don't think we can afford not to."

"I agree," Kyle's voice came from behind Talya.

"Me too," Wyatt said.

"I'm in," Steven said.

"Madison?" Garrett asked. Madison looked down for a moment before meeting Garrett's eye and nodding. "Max?" A heavy silence came over the group as they waited to hear Max's response. He finally nodded. "All right. The decision's been made." Garrett looked at Talya. "Now what?"

Talya felt everybody's eyes on her. A sick feeling came over her; she had no idea what she was supposed to do. *A little help please*? She mentally called out to the wolf. Talya tried not to panic as she thought through their options. "We drive to Chicago," she said simply. She didn't know anything more than that. Did they drive around until they saw something? Did she lay next to Liam and go to sleep again, so she could dream and get more instructions? She really didn't know. She hoped something would come to her when they got to Chicago.

Garrett studied her a moment before nodding. "We continue heading north for now," he said. "Load up." Everyone turned to get into their respective vehicles. "Talya," Garrett said before she could turn away. "I'm putting a lot of faith in you. Don't let me down," he said in a commanding voice before climbing in the car.

Talya blew out a breath of air. She could only hope that she wasn't going to do exactly that.

Talya climbed back into her spot next to Liam's wolf. "I wish you were awake to help me figure out what to do," she said softly. She fell silent when Max and Steven climbed in. Before they could pull out, the back door opened.

"You're in our car," Garrett ordered. Talya touched Liam's wolf one last time and climbed out, following Garrett to his car. He opened the door for her, and she slid into the seat next to Madison. Madison sat in the middle with Kyle on her other side.

"Welcome to the cool car," Madison said with a grin. Talya gave her a small smile before looking out the window towards where Liam was. "He'll be okay," Madison said softly, putting her hand on Talya's knee. "He's strong, and he's got something to live for now."

Talya didn't respond. She really hoped Madison was right. Nobody said anything more as they pulled out. *Please help me,* Talya thought out loud, hoping the wolf from her dreams was listening. *I really don't know what I'm supposed to do.* Talya looked out the window and watched as they drove. You could feel the tense silence in the car. She felt like Garrett was moments away from blowing his top. She could feel the tension and power radiating from him as they turned onto the highway.

They drove for an hour, an hour of excruciating silence and tension. Talya felt like she was going to scream; she couldn't take one more moment of it. Suddenly, she felt a tugging sensation inside of her. She reached down and rubbed her chest, trying to ease the sensation. That didn't help, though. The feeling continued to build. She sat up and leaned forward, looking at the road. She saw signs for the exit up ahead. As soon as her eyes locked on the sign, she knew that was where they were supposed to go. "Take the next exit," she said.

Nobody said anything at first. Emma turned to look at her. "Are you sure?" Talya nodded. She knew it with every fiber of her being. Garrett took the exit. Talya looked behind her to see the other two cars following them. When they came to the end of the exit, Talya looked at both signs. She got the feeling strongly in her chest when she looked to the sign on the right. "Right," she said.

The next few minutes were the same thing. Talya continued to give directions until they found themselves in the parking lot of an old run-down shopping center. Talya put her hand on her chest, trying to ease the sensation there. It was the strongest it had been up to this point, almost painful. Without a word to anybody, she climbed out of the car. A moment later, she was flanked by no less than three wolves. Garrett stopped her. "Wait." Talya paused for a moment, but it was difficult. The sensation worsened when she wasn't moving.

"Hurry," she said, rubbing at her chest.

Madison and Emma stepped close to her. "Are you okay?"

Madison asked.

Talya shook her head. "There's this painful sensation in my chest. I think we need to hurry," Talya said.

"We have no idea what to expect. We're not going in until we have a plan," Garrett said firmly. The others gathered around them. Garrett started talking to them, making a plan.

While he talked, Talya turned and looked at the building. She let her eyes scan each of the shops. The sensation in her chest worsened when she looked at the large shop on the end. Without conscious thought, she started moving in that direction, urgency tugging her forward. Soon she was running. Each step she took increased the sensation in her chest. She only got a few steps before she was grabbed from behind. It startled her so much, she screamed. A hand clamped down over her mouth. "Talya," she heard the gruff words and knew instinctively it was Max. He let go of her.

"Were you trying to get yourself killed?" Garrett asked, his eyes flashing.

"We have to get in there," Talya said with urgency.

"We will," Garrett said. "But on *my* terms. Liam will kill me if I let something happen to you," he said more to himself than anybody else. "Emma and Talya, you will wait in the car. Wyatt, you're with them." Wyatt nodded while Emma and Talya both protested. He turned to Emma. "Absolutely not," he said. He turned towards Talya.

"I'm going," Talya said, crossing her arms.

"No," he said right away.

"You need me in there to direct you," she said defiantly.

"No," he said again, and this time she could feel the power behind his words. She opened her mouth to argue but before she could say anything he spoke again. "I know you're not part of my pack, so you don't feel my orders the way others do. But I am ordering you to stay out here. We have no idea what we are up against in there. I'm not taking a human female in with me. Besides, Liam would legitimately end our friendship and probably start his own pack if he found out I take you anywhere near vampires; and that's a risk I'm not going to take. So go to the car with Emma and Wyatt," he ordered.

Talya was about ready to argue when Emma put her hand on her arm. "Come on, Talya," she said softly. Talya was about to argue, but the look in Emma's eyes stopped her.

"Fine," she said with bite in her voice. They started towards the car, but they never got there. She heard Emma's scream a split second before she saw them. Two guys appeared out of nowhere and grabbed Talya and Emma. Talya tried to pull away, but the hold on her was too strong. She saw a dark blur fly past her. At the same time, two wolves launched themselves towards the man holding her. He dropped his hold on her, and she fell to the ground. She scooted backwards, trying to get out of the way.

She watched as the wolves made quick work of the men or vampires as she assumed in this case. When it was done, Talya urged them to hurry. The odd sensation was back in her chest again. "We need to get in there," she said.

She expected Garrett to argue with her, but he shocked her when he nodded. "We stay together," he said in a rough voice. His arm was tight around Emma. Talya could tell the Alpha was worked up. Emma's scream had scared Talya; she couldn't imagine what it had done to her mate. "Steven, you stay behind to protect Liam." Steven nodded. "We go in wolf form. Stay in groups of two at all times. We will do a systematic search of the building. We don't really know what we're looking for. Stay alert and stay in touch through the pack line. Emma's with me. Talya, you're with Max. We need to get in, assess, and get out. We have to keep moving for Liam's sake." Everybody agreed.

Chapter Thirty-Six

Once they were close, Garrett motioned for them to shift. Garrett's big black wolf led them through the door Emma opened for them. Talya glanced at the formidable wolf next to her. Max's wolf wasn't as dark as Garrett's; it was more like a dark gray. But it was just as scary-looking. She tried to push aside her fear and remember it was Max, not that that was a super comforting thought. He was almost just as scary in human form as he was in wolf form.

Talya pushed those thoughts aside and focused on the feeling in her chest. They stepped inside the dark, dank building. Talya couldn't see much, but she felt the tug pulling her to the left. Wordlessly, she began walking that direction. The dark gray wolf stayed right at her side, and the others followed. A rank smell met Talya's nose as they walked. She wondered how much worse it was for the wolves, since they were so sensitive to scents. Several doors came into view. Talya stopped outside the first door. A soft growl stopped her from opening the door, and she stepped back. Garrett shifted and motioned them back as he slowly tried the handle. Nobody was surprised to find it locked. Garrett used his shifter strength and simply broke the lock and opened the door slowly. Max moved forward to stand next to Garrett. They both slipped into the room silently.

Talya felt her heart thundering in her chest while she waited for them to come back out. The door opened a moment or two later, and a grim-faced Garrett stepped out with the gray wolf at his side. "Kyle, take the women down that way just a little bit," he ordered. Even Talya felt the power coming off of him from that command. She didn't even bother trying to argue with him. She and Emma followed Kyle and Madison's wolves a short distance away. Oddly, the sensation in her chest had finally eased. It was like she had done what she was supposed to do, and now she could relax. But relaxing was not on her radar. She had no idea what was in those rooms, but she didn't think it was good.

Garrett and the other wolves checked each room. There must have been twelve rooms, maybe more. Finally, they came back towards them. Without a word, Garrett motioned everybody to follow him. Only once they were outside did anyone say anything. "Garrett?" Emma asked softly. He didn't respond. He just shook his head and kept walking, his arm tight around Emma. Talya looked at Max and Wyatt's faces. She saw the set lines in each of their faces. She had to know what they had seen.

"What was it?" she asked, no longer able to wait. "What did you see?"

Everybody froze as if what Talya asked had the potential to wreak havoc. For all she knew, maybe it did. Nobody said anything for a moment. "Experiments," Garrett grunted out. Talya wanted to ask more, but she was scared.

"What kind of experiments?" Emma asked Garrett softly.

They were almost back to the cars now. "Girls," he bit out. "Probably around fourteen or fifteen."

Talya couldn't keep the shock off her face. She heard Emma's intake of breath. "Are they..." her voice trailed off.

"Dead," Garrett said in anger. The wolves around her growled viciously. Talya felt like she'd been kicked in the stomach. "Load up now. We killed the vampires that were here. We can't do anything to help those girls now. We will head back to pack lands and make a plan. We will be back, and we will find every vampire that had a part in this and tear them limb from limb," he said in a fierce voice. The wolves howled their agreement.

Talya felt the pain explode inside of her. They had been too late. Without asking permission, Talya made her way to the car where Liam's wolf lay and crawled in beside him. She let the tears fall and the anger build. She had failed those girls; she had failed as the dreamer. Talya cried bitter, frustrated tears. When she had cried all she could, she collapsed on the floor next to Liam's wolf.

A few hours later, they finally made it to their destination. As soon as they stopped, the back door opened. Talya climbed out, and Garrett and Max carefully pulled Liam's wolf from the back of the car and carried him inside. Talya followed behind them. Nobody stopped her as she came into the room. Liam's wolf was laid out on a table. Paul was busy assessing him. Max and Garrett backed away to leave him space to work. Talya stayed in the corner of the room and leaned against the wall. She didn't want to be in the way, but she also needed to know Liam was okay.

Talya wasn't sure how long she stood there. It could have been minutes or hours. She just stared at the huge brown wolf, willing him to open his eyes. Max and Garrett had come and gone, as had Emma and Madison and Kyle and some of the other wolves. Paul stood up after working tirelessly and wiped his forehead. His gaze snagged on Talya across the room.

"Talya, have you been here this whole time?" he asked. Talya nodded. "I didn't realize."

"How is he?" she asked, scared to hear the answer.

Paul didn't say anything for a moment. "I'm not going to lie to you, Talya. He was pretty bad off when he got in here. Only time will tell if we got enough of the silver out in time."

Talya sagged against the wall. That was not what she wanted to hear. Before she could ask him anything else, one of the monitors started beeping. Paul said something under his breath and got to work. Talya watched him and saw the urgency in his movements. She moved closer to the bed; she couldn't help it. "What's happening?" she asked.

Paul didn't respond, and Talya felt her heart race. She was terrified for Liam. Without thinking about it, she put her hand out and ran it over his fur. She saw Paul set up what looked like an IV line. She saw him roll up his sleeve quickly. "What are you doing?" she asked.

"He needs blood," Paul said without looking at her.

"Take mine," she said, already pushing up her sleeve. "So, you can keep working on him."

"What blood type are you?" Paul said.

"AB negative," she said.

"Really?" he said in surprise. Talya nodded. "That's what most wolves are; I didn't think you would match. Are you sure?" he asked.

"Yes. Do it." She didn't want to think about it. She hated having her blood drawn, but she would do this for Liam.

"Hop on the bed next to his," Paul said. Talya climbed onto the second bed. Paul got right to work, getting her ready. She looked away and tried to relax. "Now, you need to tell me when you start to feel dizzy or weak. I'm used to taking wolves' blood. You have to tell me, Talya. Okay?" Talya nodded, still not looking. She hated this part. She made herself think of Liam. *I'm doing this for him. I'm doing this for him.* She said the mantra over and over in her mind. She flinched when the needle went in, but she kept her eyes closed and kept repeating the words in her mind. It didn't take long for Talya to get woozy, but that was no surprise. She usually got woozy before she even started losing blood. It was the entire process. She closed her eyes tighter and made herself focus on Liam.

Talya wasn't sure how it happened. One minute she was trying to keep the contents of her stomach down; the next, she was in her dream state.

She looked around in surprise. She felt the wolf's presence before she turned to face him. "Did you help me go to sleep?" she asked.

"You were helping one of my wolves, so I helped you," he said simply.

"Well, thank you," Talya said. "I hate giving blood. Is Liam going

to be okay?" she asked worriedly.

"There's nothing you can do for him more than you're already doing," the wolf said.

Talya really hoped that was code for, 'He's going to be okay.' She sighed and sat down. "We found the vampire site," she said without inflection.

"I know," the wolf said.

"We didn't get there in time. They were all dead," she said, her voice heavy. The wolf didn't say anything; she could feel his sorrow.

"Why do they keep trying to turn humans if they know it's not going to work?" Talya asked.

"Why do men do the things they do?" the wolf questioned in return.

Talya had no answer. "How do we stop it?" she asked.

"My wolves will have to destroy each of these facilities where they are doing this," the wolf said.

"There's more?" Talya asked.

"Yes," the wolf said tensely. "It is your job to find the other locations and guide the wolves there. They must destroy the facilities."

Talya nodded. "I'll get to work."

"There's no time," the wolf said.

Talya opened her eyes and was startled to see a pair of intense blue eyes peering at her. "Are you okay?" Liam asked roughly. Talya took a second to get her surroundings. A quick glance told her she was in the wolves' clinic. She was laying in the bed next to Liam's. Only Liam wasn't laying down now. He was standing over her with just a pair of black sweatpants on. Talya tried to sit up, but she felt dizzy. "Just take your time," Liam said.

Talya shook her head and looked up at him in confusion.

"You're all right," she said, stating the obvious. "You shouldn't be standing. You need to be back in bed. You almost died!"

Chapter Thirty-Seven

"I'm okay," he said. His eyes hardened. "But you're not. Paul said you lost too much blood. That's why you passed out. Don't do that again, Talya!"

Talya's eyes widened. "Are you serious right now? I haven't seen you in weeks and you show up and challenge and kill a guy and almost die in the process. I had to sit next to your wolf, not knowing if you were going to die or not for *days*, Liam. So don't go yelling at me!" she said as she crossed her arms over her chest. It was quiet for a moment as they both stared at each other in anger. "Why did you do it?" Talya finally asked.

Liam crossed his arms and stared down at her. "The last two months have been hell for me. I couldn't eat, couldn't sleep, couldn't even function. When I heard you were the same way, I almost defied Garrett's order and came to see you. The only reason I didn't, Talya, is because you weren't eighteen. I knew it would just create another mess. But hear me when I say this. I won't allow anybody to keep us away from each other ever again. Now that you're eighteen, you're mine. Nobody will keep us apart."

"I felt the same way," Talya said. "Why?" She was snippy with her words, but she wasn't ready to just forgive and forget. He had really hurt her by just dropping out of her life.

"It's the bond," he said. "Because we spent time together, a bond started forming between us. It will develop further when I give you my mark, and it will finalize when we fully mate. But because it started to form, we were weak away from each other." His intense eyes bore into hers. "I promise you, you will never go through that again."

"But why didn't you ever reach out? You never came to see me. You never called me or even checked in with me," Talya said, trying and failing to keep the hurt from her voice.

Liam's eyes hardened. "Garrett gave me an Alpha order. I wasn't allowed to contact you in any way. The only way I got around it was to check in with Sage to see how you were doing. Like I said, I listened and followed his order this time because of your age, but never again."

"I thought you didn't care about me anymore; I thought you were gone from my life," Talya said, trying to stay non-emotional.

Liam let out a growl and said Garrett's name in anger. "That is the furthest thing from the truth. It killed me not to come to you, but I was trying to do the right thing. It killed me to get updates from the guys when I couldn't be there myself."

"What guys?" Talya asked.

"The wolves who were assigned to your safety," Liam said.

"But I never saw them," Talya said.

"They weren't supposed to reveal themselves to you except in the case of an emergency," Liam said. "Did you think I was going to leave you without protection?" he asked incredulously.

Talya shrugged. "I thought you didn't care."

Liam ran a hand through his hair in frustration. "I'm going to kill Garrett," he muttered.

"I don't think that's the answer," Talya said dryly. "Listen, are you even supposed to be out of bed?"

Liam shrugged. "I'm fine."

"Is the silver completely out of your system now?" Talya asked.

"Paul told me he got it all out. I'm good as new now," he said with a grin, but it was forced. There was none of his usual light-heartedness in him.

Talya sat up and swung her feet around. "I've got to talk to Garrett."

Liam's eyes hardened. "Why?"

"I need to talk to him about the vampire sites," Talya said impatiently.

"I can't take you to him," he said.

The way he said it caught Talya's attention. "You need to be there too, Liam."

Liam's jaw tightened, and he looked away for a moment. "I can't. I can't be around him right now," he said in anger.

Talya stood up on shaky legs and put her hand on his arm. "Are you okay?" He didn't answer. Talya wasn't going to have any of that. She wrapped her arms around his middle, surprising him. She held him tightly. It took him a moment, but then he wrapped his arms around her and held her tightly. His hold almost hurt, but she didn't say anything. He needed this.

"I'll take you to Garrett, but I can't stay there with you," Liam said, repeating what he had already told her.

"Why?" Talya asked, tilting her head back to look up at him.

His jaw was tight. "Because I can't be in the same room as him right now."

Talya wanted to ask more, but she didn't want to push him. She tried to think of a way to get his mind off of Garrett and onto something else. "Hey, did you see—my casts are gone. We should go out and celebrate before we go see Garrett," she said.

Liam looked down at her with a small smile. "What did you have in mind?"

"I don't know, but I could go for something sweet and fattening and sinfully delicious," Talya said, trying to coax another smile out of him.

"Come on," he said. He grabbed her hand and started pulling her towards the door.

"Where are we going?" she asked.

"I've got the perfect thing in mind," he said without slowing down. Before they could go out of the room, Paul came in.

"Hey, you two, let's get you checked out really quickly before you take off," he said in a relaxed manner but in such a way that Talya knew they weren't getting out of here without him checking them both out. Liam growled softly, but Talya tugged his hand.

"Come on, Liam," she said. He allowed her to pull him towards the bed. She sat down on the bed and pulled him down next to her. She was acutely aware of the fact that he was letting her manhandle him. She sat next to him as closely as possible. A quick glance at him showed he was not going to make this easy for Paul.

Paul came towards them with an easy smile on his face. "Talya, let's start with you. Do you still feel dizzy? Nauseated?" Talya shook her head no for both. "Let's get a check on your blood pressure." He picked up her arm to put the cuff around it. Liam let out a low growl next to him. Talya glanced quickly at Paul's face, but it didn't seem to faze him. Liam put his arm around Talya and dragged her closer to him.

Paul moved to Liam. "Okay, Liam, let's get a quick check on you." He asked Liam several questions, all of which Liam just grunted a response to. Apparently, Paul understood caveman language because he didn't seem fazed by Liam's responses. Finally, Paul gave his approval for them to leave. Liam stood up and pulled her up next to him. He snagged her hand and led her towards the door.

"Talya," Paul called from behind her. Talya turned back towards Paul. Liam growled behind her, but Paul ignored him. "Liam's wolf is really on edge right now after not having you around for eight weeks and him getting hurt. The final nail in the coffin was waking up to find his mate passed out next to him." Paul talked to her as if Liam wasn't right behind her. "I'm telling you this so that you know that Liam's going to need you close over the next few days. Only you can help calm the storm raging inside of him and his wolf." Liam growled again, louder this time. He grabbed her hand and pulled her with him out the door.

"Thank you," Talya called out over her shoulder as Liam led her away from the room.

Once they were outside the building, Liam looked down at her. "How is your foot? Are you up to walking a little bit?" he asked gruffly.

"I'm good to walk," she said. He nodded and they started walking. Liam kept his hold on her hand. Talya was quiet as they walked, trying to decide what to say to him. Talya was lost in her thoughts, so she looked up in surprise when he stopped. Talya looked up and realized they were standing in front of a coffee shop. "I love coffee," she said with a smile.

Liam didn't say anything, but he did squeeze her hand. She hoped that counted for something. He led them inside. Talya stopped and stared at the shop. "This is beautiful!" Everything was bright and clean. There were huge windows letting in lots of light. The gray hardwood flooring was gorgeous and went so well with the large white serving counter up front. Scattered around the shop were hanging white pots filled with greenery. There were white lights hanging from the exposed wooden beams in the ceiling. A door opened from behind the counter, and Talya turned to see Emma walk out from the back. "Liam!" she said. She hurried forward and hugged him. "We were so worried for you," she said. "Does Garrett know you're okay?" she asked.

Talya watched Liam's face harden. "It smells so good in here!" Talya said, quickly redirecting.

Emma smiled. "I'm glad," Emma said softly. Talya knew she had picked up on Liam's response.

"We're here to get Talya one of your cinnamon rolls," Liam said gruffly

"Perfect," Emma said. She walked behind the counter. "Do you guys want coffee?"

"Yes!" Talya said quickly.

Emma laughed. "What kind?"

Talya looked at the board. "Everything looks so good. Hmm. Let's see. How about...ooo. Ooh, how about a death by chocolate, iced.

"And two cinnamon rolls," Liam said.

Talya watched her work for a few minutes, fascinated.

"Do you ever need help in here?" Talya asked.

"Yes, all the time. There's a few girls that work part-time, but it's hard with their school schedule. Why? Are you interested?" Emma asked.

"I would love to work here!" Talya said.

"If you're serious, I would take you in a heartbeat!" Emma said.

"I don't know how long I'm sticking around for-" Talya began, but Liam's growl cut her off. Talya glanced up at him and back at Emma. She wasn't sure what to say, so she just shrugged. Now obviously wasn't a good time to talk about it.

Chapter Thirty-Eight

"Well, if you decide to stay, I'd love to have you," she said. "Are you going to fight night tonight, Liam?" Liam just shrugged. Talya sat in one of the barstools at the counter. Emma brought a plate of cinnamon rolls over. "You make the best cinnamon rolls," Talya said after her second bite.

Emma brought her drink to her and put a hot coffee on the counter for Liam. "I'm so glad you like them," she said with a smile. "Try the coffee. It's a new one I'm trying."

Talya opened the straw and put it into the drink. She closed her eyes after the first sip. "Oh, I've think I've died and gone to heaven. It tastes like I'm drinking chocolate cake!"

Emma laughed. "Good, that's what I was going for."

Talya took another bite of her cinnamon roll. "You're going to send me into a sugar coma," she told Emma. She put another bite on her fork and turned to Liam. "Here," she said.

Liam came and stood next to her. "You enjoy it," he said quietly as he put his hand on her back.

"Wow! Liam turning down cinnamon rolls! Who are you and what did you do with Liam?" Emma asked teasingly.

Talya glanced up at him. He gave a small smile to Emma, but it didn't reach his eyes.

The door to the shop opened. "Hey love," Emma greeted Garrett as he walked through the door.

Talya felt Liam stiffen next to her. She glanced between Garrett and Liam. Neither of them said a word as they stared at each other. Liam broke the stare first and moved towards the door. He disappeared a moment later. Talya stared after him, wondering if she should go after him or not.

Emma walked towards Garrett and wrapped her arms around him. He pulled her close and kissed the top of her head. "Hey sweetheart," he said in a heavy voice. He looked at Talya with a pained expression. "I'm afraid I might have lost my beta." Talya had no idea how to respond.

"He'll come around," Emma said softly.

"I don't know," Garrett said. "He's going to need you to help calm his wolf," he said, looking at Talya.

Talya nodded. "I don't know that I can really do anything, but I'll try." That was the second time today someone had told her that. "We need to find six more locations," Talya said bluntly.

It didn't faze Garrett. "Any leads on the next location?"

"No, but I'm working on it," she said. Garrett nodded. "I'm going to head back to Liam's house and see if he shows up there," she said quietly.

"Here," Garrett said, tossing her a set of keys. "You can take my car."

"Oh, that's okay. I can just walk," Talya said.

"Just humor me. Liam will appreciate it if you drive rather than walk back by yourself," Garrett said.

After a quick set of directions, Talya took her drink with her, said goodbye to Garrett and Emma and left the shop. She settled into Garrett's car for the quick drive back to Liam's house. Letting herself inside, she realized with disappointment that the house was empty. Liam hadn't come back yet. She plopped down on the couch, wondering what she should do next. She put her head back against the seat and closed her eyes as the last few days caught up with her.

She woke up sometime later. She sat up, and the blanket fell off of her to the floor. Liam must have come in while she was sleeping. She stood up and went in search of him. A few minutes later, she realized while he may have come back at one point, he was no longer here. She sighed and made her way to the kitchen. She opened the kitchen and frowned. Liam had gone back to his old ways while she was gone. There wasn't an ounce of food in the fridge or in the cupboards. It was almost five o'clock. Her eyes caught on a bag next to the couch that she hadn't seen earlier. She went towards it and opened it up. She smiled when she saw a container of food. She opened it and saw it was mashed potatoes, grilled chicken, and green beans. She sat back down on the couch and began eating.

After she finished, she went to her closet to figure out something to wear for the night. She had learned her lesson last time to dress accordingly. She searched her closet and finally settled on black skinny jeans with black heeled boots paired with a black top with a red leather jacket. She straightened her hair and left it down. She spent extra time with her makeup. When she was done, she stepped back from the mirror and surveyed herself. It would work for tonight.

The doorbell rang. She grabbed a pair of earrings and made her way out to answer the door.

"Hey, Talya," Madison said with a big smile. "You look fierce. I love it. Want a ride?" she asked.

"Yes," Talya said. She quickly grabbed her phone and followed Madison to the car.

"Hey Talya," Kyle said from the front seat.

"Hey," Talya said by way of greeting. Talya listened to Madison talk on the way there, but she didn't join in. She was too busy thinking about Liam. She wasn't sure if he would show up tonight or blow it off.

When they walked into the huge building, it was just as crazy and chaotic as it had been the last time she was here. Only this time, she didn't have the comfort of Liam at her side. She followed Kyle and Madison to the bleachers where the hundreds of pack members sat. Once Madison and Talya were seated, Kyle gave Madison a grin and a kiss and disappeared. "Is he fighting tonight?" Talya asked.

"No, he's emceeing tonight," Madison said.

"Oh," Talya said. That was usually Liam's job. She sighed and wondered again where he was and if he was okay. She looked around the room again, trying to see if he was here. She didn't see him, but she did see Garrett and Emma walk in, followed by Max. They came towards where she and Madison were sitting.

"Talya, have you seen Liam?" Garrett asked in a low voice.

Talya shook her head. "No, sorry. Not since the coffee shop."

"Okay, thanks," Garrett said. He turned to face Max, and they seemed to communicate with each other for a moment before Garrett bent to kiss his wife. Then they walked over to where Kyle was. Emma joined them on the bleachers.

"You doing okay, Talya?" Emma asked in concern. Talya shrugged. She wasn't really sure what to say.

"He's here," Madison said. Talya turned towards where Madison was looking and saw Liam. He strode towards where the guys were. He said something to Kyle and walked away. Talya's eyes followed him to the corner of the gymnasium. He stood off to the side of the door and stretched.

"Do you think I should go talk to him?" Talya asked Emma and Madison.

"I don't know," Emma said, watching Liam. "He's pretty upset."

Madison nodded. She looked back at Talya. "He's been like this ever since you left. I thought it would get better now that you're here, but I guess it's not."

"He's furious with Garrett," Emma said sadly. "Garrett said it's the first time Liam hasn't had his back since they were kids."

"I'm sorry," Talya said, feeling awful.

"It's not your fault," Emma said.

"It kind of feels like it is." Whatever they were going to say next was cut off when Kyle started getting the crowd warmed up and ready for fight night. Soon it was impossible to talk at all, so Talya sat back and watched the fights. She waited for

Liam's fight. She didn't have to wait long. Kyle announced Liam's name, and Liam strode towards the fight circle. His face was expressionless as he entered the circle. He took his shirt off and threw it to the side. Kyle gave the signal and Liam launched himself at his opponent. Talya cringed when he connected. His opponent went down on the first hit. A few seconds later, Kyle called the fight.

"Looks like he's over everything," Madison said dryly, shaking her head. Talya felt sick to her stomach. The rest of the night just got worse. Liam decimated each of his opponents. Talya couldn't get over watching him fight. He was insanely good. By the time they got to the last fight, Talya's stomach was in knots.

"I don't think I can watch this," Emma yelled next to her. Talya felt the same way. The last round was between Garrett and Liam. Talya wasn't sure what was going to happen, but she had a feeling it wasn't going to be good.

A frenzy came over the crowd when Kyle announced the last fight. She watched as Liam and Garrett stepped into the ring. "This isn't going to be good," Madison yelled over the crowd. Emma grabbed Talya's hand on her left side and Madison's hand on her right. She squeezed hard, but Talya didn't mind. She squeezed right back. She was terrified of what was going to happen.

Kyle gave the signal, and Liam launched himself at Garrett. Garrett defended it, barely. With that, the fight was on. Liam was full-on aggressive, but Garrett gave as good as he got. Talya winced every time either man took a hard hit.

"This is bad," Madison said. Emma and Talya didn't say anything. Talya couldn't look away from the train wreck in front of her. Neither man was backing down. Talya remembered how the guys had said that Garrett won every fight he ever had in the ring, and Liam had said it would stay that way. In his right mind, Talya knew Liam respected his Alpha. She had no idea what would happen if he beat him. She knew it wasn't an official challenge, but it could still be a big deal. Talya noticed that the volume in the place had dissipated considerably. She glanced around and saw people staring at the fight. Talya stood to her feet.

"What are you doing?" Madison asked her loudly. Emma didn't look away from the fight.

"I have to get him to stop," Talya said. "He can't beat Garrett in front of his entire pack."

Madison was shaking her head. "I don't think that's a good..."

Talya tuned her out. She climbed down the bleachers and made her way towards the fight. She saw Max standing next to the ring. She went that way. Max was watching the fight intently. "Liam needs to stop, doesn't he?" Talya asked in a voice loud enough that Max could hear. He didn't turn to her, but he nodded once. Talya took a breath. Nobody else could do this but her. She was the only one that might be able to get through to him. Honestly, she wasn't even sure is she could. Liam was so angry. Talya moved towards the ring, but a hand on her arm stopped her. She looked up at Max.

"I can't let you go in there. You will get hurt, and if that happens, Liam will never forgive Garrett," Max said earnestly. It was the most emotion Talya had ever seen in the man.

"I have to," Talya said. "I'm the only one who can get through to him." Max shook his head, but Talya dodged away from him and into the ring. She moved towards the two fighting men, trying to ignore her racing heart. "Liam, stop!" she called out. He either didn't hear her, or he ignored her. Talya hated what she was going to do next, but she didn't know how else to get his attention. She was counting on both men to be able to react fast enough to what she was about to do. If not, it was really going to hurt.

Chapter Thirty-Nine

Talya took a deep breath and stepped right up to the fight. When there was a space between them for a moment, Talya slid in between them and faced Garrett. She figured he wasn't as far gone as Liam. She saw his eyes widen as he came at her with a punch. In that millisecond, Talya knew he wasn't going to be able to pull it back in time. She prepared herself for the pain coming. Suddenly, her feet were swept out from under her and she rolled across the ring. When she stopped, she realized she was on top of Liam. An instant later, he rolled her off of him and stood up. He pulled her up to stand next to him. "What was that?" he said in fierce anger.

Garrett came and stood next to them. "You okay?" he asked Talya. Talya nodded. Garrett turned away and left the ring. Talya was vaguely aware of Kyle saying something into the mic and the pack cheering, but she tuned it all out. She stared at Liam, trying to figure out how in the world to help him.

"Did I hurt you?" Liam asked gruffly.

"No," Talya said quickly. Liam moved to turn away, but Talya put her hand on his arm. "Liam, stop. I'm here now," she said, not sure what else to say. Then she did the only thing she thought would get through to him. She reached up on tiptoe, put her hands behind his neck and pulled his lips down to hers. He didn't respond, and Talya felt like an idiot. Right as she began to pull away, he wrapped his arms around her and took control of the kiss, totally consuming her. Talya was glad his arms were around her to hold her up; otherwise, she would have fallen. She ran her hands through the back of his hair. He tugged her hair, angling her head so he could deepen the kiss. Then he gentled the kiss and pulled back.

Talya finally opened her eyes and saw startling blue eyes peering back at her. His eyes didn't seem as dark. "Are you back now?" she asked softly. Liam didn't answer; he just pulled her close again. "Can we go home now?" Talya asked.

Liam pulled back slightly and kissed her on the forehead. "Yeah, baby. Let's go home." He snagged her hand and led her through the crowd. Several people tried to stop and talk to them, but Liam just kept pushing through the crowd. Finally, they made it outside. Liam led her to his car and opened the passenger door for her.

"What can I do to help you?" Talya asked when he climbed in.

"Just be near me," he said. They drove to his house in silence. When they got there, neither of them made a move to get out.

"Are you still angry?" Talya asked hesitantly.

Liam turned his face towards her. "You know I'm not angry

at you right?" Talya nodded. He ran a hand over his face. "When they took you away," he began, his voice tight with anger. "I was so angry. I've never been that angry in my life. I tried to tell myself it was the best thing for you, but neither I nor my wolf believed that. When I called Sage, and she told me that you hadn't gotten out of bed for a few days, it just about broke me. Garrett had already given me the order, but we got into an argument again. It grew heated. He commanded me again to stay away from you. I thought it would be okay; it was just for a few weeks. I didn't take into account how much the man or the wolf would struggle without you at our side. Then when you finally came back to me, you were unconscious. I barely controlled my wolf to keep from ripping Paul apart. I could have dealt with all of that, and I did. But when you questioned my feelings for you, when you told me that you thought I had dropped from your life and wasn't interested in you anymore? That's what finally broke me. It makes me furious that you felt that way. That I let other people control me, and it ended up hurting you. The absolute last thing in the world I want to do is to hurt you."

Talya moved closer to him. "Liam, I didn't mean to make things worse for you," she started.

"Don't apologize. You didn't do anything wrong, Talya," Liam said in anger.

"Then can we put this behind us and move on? Because I really miss you. I miss the guy I fell in love with. The one with the easy smile and trouble in his eyes," Talya softly.

"What?" Liam asked, looking at her in shock. Talya stared right back at him. She hadn't meant to say that; it just sort of slipped out. But now that it was out, Talya realized she really was falling for Liam, hard.

"You love me?" Liam interrupted.

Talya smiled at him. "I do," she said. Liam closed the distance between them and kissed her. It wasn't slow and it wasn't gentle, and Talya loved it. He pulled back before she was ready for him to.

"I love you, Talya," he said in an emotion-filled voice. "I knew from the first day that you were going to turn my life upside down. I knew you were going to be trouble," he said with a smile.

"Was it when I said 'holy muscles'?" Talya said with a laugh. "That wasn't one of my brighter moments."

"Yep, I knew right then and there that you were the one for me," Liam said with a small laugh.

"I still love your muscles," Talya said in a sultry voice, running her hands up his arms and down his stomach muscles.

Liam grabbed both of her hands. "You'd better stop," he said in a low voice.

"Why? Can't handle the heat?" Talya asked, trying to get a rise out of him.

Liam shook his head. "Like I said—trouble."

Talya laughed then turned serious. "Are you okay now?"

Liam pulled her close. "I'm getting there. Maybe you need to touch me again," he said with a small smile that showed a trace of the Liam she remembered. Talya laughed and smacked him. His smile faded. "Will you let me mark you?" he asked in a low voice.

Talya hesitated. "What will happen?"

"Wolves mark their mate by biting them right here," he said as he pushed her hair gently away from her neck and rubbed the pad of his thumb over the spot between her neck and her shoulder blade. "The mark will remain permanent, telling other wolves that you're taken. Our scents will mix as well, another sign to other wolves that we're both unavailable. It's the next step towards making our bond complete."

"Yes," Talya said without an ounce of hesitation.

Liam blew out a breath and closed his eyes. He put his hand around the back of her neck and pulled her close to him. "Thank you," he breathed out. He pulled back. "Can we do it tonight?" he asked. Talya smiled and nodded. "I need to have Paul come over. Garrett told me Emma bled pretty badly." Liam frowned in concern.

Talya put her hand on his cheek. "I'll be okay. Paul will make sure of it," she said. "Now, contact him and have him come over."

"I already did," Liam said with a grin.

Talya laughed. "A little anxious, are we?" she said teasingly.

Liam shook his head, not smiling. "You have no idea."

"Well, let's get to it then," Talya said. Before Talya could blink, Liam was out of the car and opening her door. She just laughed, and he smiled.

"You have the best laugh," he said as he bent down and unbuckled her and pulled her out of the car and up and into his arms. He jogged up the front steps, unlocked the door, and carried her inside. He walked to her room and put her down. "You will need to lose the jacket. Do you have a top that you don't mind getting ruined" he asked.

"Yeah, I can just put a tank top on," Talya said.

Liam nodded. "That will work. Come to my room when you're done," he said. Then he disappeared from her room. Talya moved quickly. She changed out of her outfit from tonight and put on a pair of soft comfy shorts and a tank top. She took a few calming breaths before going to see Liam. She knocked on his door. "Come in," he called out.

Talya opened the door, and her breath caught in her throat. All around the room, candles flickered, and rose petals adorned everything... Her eyes sought out the sexy man standing across the room from her. He prowled towards her. Talya held her ground and didn't back up, even though she wanted to. His eyes skimmed down her body. "That's perfect," he said in a low growly voice. Talya glanced up at him and noticed his eyes were brighter than usual. Before she could ask him about it, he put his arms around her and pulled her close. Very slowly, he lowered his head. Talya's hands came up and wrapped around his neck, pulling him closer to her. He kissed her deeply. He pulled away from her lips and traced his lips over her jaw and down the side of her neck. Talya couldn't help the moan that slipped out. He walked them backwards until her legs hit the bed. He picked her up and placed her gently on the bed before climbing up onto the bed on top of her. He braced himself on his forearms, so his weight wouldn't crush her.

Then he continued where he left off. He kissed her again passionately. Talya lost all sense of reality and time. Liam took her to levels she had never experienced before. Suddenly, she felt a sharp pain in her neck. She cried out in pain. Liam quickly covered her lips with his and kissed her hard. After a few moments of intensity, he pulled back. Talya stared up at him in awe. "Your wolf," she whispered.

He looked down at her neck. "Are you okay?" he asked in a gruff voice, his wolf still very much present. He grabbed a towel from the side of the bed and put it gently on her wound. Talya flinched, even though she didn't mean to. "I'm sorry, baby. Paul's on his way." He kissed her gently on the lips.

"Oh, I'm probably getting blood all over everything," Talya said.

"It's fine," Liam said. Talya tried to focus on taking deep breaths. She always got light-headed after losing blood. She tried to push the darkness away that was threatening to overtake her. She hated this feeling; it was the worst feeling in the world. She was feeling sluggish, and the terrible nausea was building.

"Liam," she called out or tried to call out; her voice sounded far away. She heard him respond, but she couldn't focus on it. She felt herself slip into the darkness.

Talya found herself in her dream state. She knew what she had to do. So, she didn't wait around for the wolf. She envisioned herself right where she wanted to be. Unfortunately, she wasn't alone this time.

Chapter Forty

Talya stumbled backwards at the sight in front of her. There was a second vampire standing next to the creator vampire. The creator vampire let out a cold, humorless laugh. "Did you think that the wolf was the only one with creating powers? Meet my newest creation, my own dream walker," the vampire said.

Before Talya could even think the thought to dream walk to the wolf realm, the vampire was on top of her. He grabbed her hair and yanked her head backwards. Talya cried out in pain as her eyes watered. She tried to dream walk to the wolf realm, but she couldn't. It was as if her powers were gone. The vampire dragged her to where the vampire creator stood. Her head was held back, so she was looking right up at him. "I know what you're trying to do. You're trying to shut down my changing sites, but it's not going to happen." He leaned over her. "Want to know how I'm going to stop you?" he asked cruelly. He looked at the vampire who was holding her. "Turn her," he commanded.

Panic exploded in her chest. Before she could do anything, a sharp pain pierced her neck and she screamed. She felt her soul reach for Liam, her protector. "Liam," her heart cried out. Almost before Talya could process the thought, she was thrown aside and a massive brown wolf launched itself at her captor. She heard the snarls and fight. She watched as the wolf ripped the vampire's head clean off its body. The wolf turned and faced the vampire creator. The vampire just smiled cruelly at Liam. She watched as Liam's wolf launched itself at the vampire, but an invisible force kept him from getting too close. Three more times, Liam's wolf tried. He never even got close. "Liam!" Talya called out weakly to him. The wolf growled ferociously one more time, then moved to her side. Talya wasn't sure if this would work, but she was going to try. She wrapped her arms around the wolf's neck and dream walked them to the shifter realm. She fell immediately to the ground in her weakened state. Liam's wolf made a sound and nudged her with its body.

"Talya," she heard the wolf's voice. "You did good. You called Liam to you, the only one who could protect you. I'm going to send you back now. Rest. Good job, my child. I won't call you back until you've healed. Wrap your arms around Liam's wolf, so he will return with you." Talya lifted her weak arms and wrapped them around Liam's neck. The world around her faded.

Talya opened her eyes and gasped. She turned quickly to see Liam beside her in the bed. He shot up into a sitting position.

"Talya, what the-"

"What happened to you, both!"

"What is going on?"

It was Garrett's thundering the last question that caught Talya's attention the most. She could feel the power coming from him. "As much as I'd like to answer all your questions, maybe we could deal with the fact that I've been bitten by a freaking vampire!" she said, her panic rising with each word. She saw that both Paul's and Garrett's faces were thunderstruck. She also noticed for the first time that Max was in the room as well. "Great! You're all here for the show," she mumbled under her breath.

Paul finally snapped to it and grabbed supplies. "Lay down, Talya. Let's get this fixed." He eased her back onto the pillows.

"Don't touch her," Liam snapped at him.

Paul ignored him. He bent over Talya and put a cloth on her wound and pushed down. Talya cried out in pain. The next thing she knew, Paul was across the room, bleeding from the glass that had shattered when he hit the mirror.

Garrett turned to Liam. "Get yourself under control," he ordered. Paul walked back towards Talya. He bent over her again as if nothing had happened.

"You're bleeding," Talya felt the need to point out.

"So are you," Paul said. "But mine will heal in a few moments; yours won't." He pushed down on her neck again, and a low growl sounded next to them.

"Liam, I really need him to help me because this insanely hurts, okay? So, would you just cool it? If you can't, go over there!" she yelled at him. She was hurt and in pain, and she felt like her world had just imploded. Talya closed her eyes and took a breath.

"What happened?" Garrett ordered in a low voice.

Talya shook her head. "I don't know. One minute everything was fine; the next it went horribly wrong. I was looking for..." A sharp pain lanced her shoulder. "Ouch! What are you doing?"

"I'm giving you a shot of local anesthesia to numb your shoulder before I put stitches in," Paul said.

"Do you have to? I have a thing about needles," Talya said. She could feel her heart rate start to speed up. Talya closed her eyes. Could this night get any worse? Now she was going to have to sit here and watch herself get stitched up. She felt the bed shift. Without a word, Liam gently lifted her and put her in front of him between his legs.

"I've got you, baby" he said in a low voice. "Just relax against me." Talya let herself lean on him, needing his strength.

Talya looked up and saw Garrett staring at her intently, waiting for her to continue the story. She closed her eyes and leaned more fully against Liam. "I don't know how much you know about the dream stasis?" She posed it by way of a question. By the blank looks Garrett and Max were giving her, she figured they didn't know anything about it. "Okay, so when I dream walk, I end up in this dream stasis. Three realms exist there. The human realm, the wolf realm, and the vampire realm. The creator of the wolves stays in the wolf realm, and the creator of the vampires of the vampire realm stays in the vampire realm. I'm assuming it's the same for the human creator as well. Anyway, the wolf creator and the vampire creator cannot cross into each other's realms. Are you following me so far?" she asked. Neither Garrett nor Max so much as blinked. "Okay. Well, anyway, my job is two-fold. First, I'm like a liaison to your pack from the wolf creator. I can talk to you for him. The second part of my job is to cross into the vampire realm. While there, I'm supposed to sort through vampire dreams to find information. Right now, it's the locations of each of the sites they're using to try to turn humans."

"How?" Garrett asked.

"Within each realm is a place where all the dreams intertwine. It's called a melding." She went to explain what she's been doing. "This time, though, when I went back-Ouch!"

Paul grimaced from his position next to her. "I'm sorry, Talya. This is deeper than I thought. Try not to think about what I'm doing. Squeeze Liam's hand."

Liam put out his hand and took hers in his. Talya held on for dear life. She tried to continue, but she couldn't focus with what Paul was doing to her. She could literally feel him sewing her up, and it was not a good sensation. "Somehow, Talya pulled me into the dream with her," Liam continued in a steady voice. "When I got there, I was in wolf form. I killed the vampire who bit her," he said calmly, but Talya could hear the rage underneath the surface. She squeezed his hand harder. "She put her hand around my neck and transported us to the wolf realm where the wolf was. Then she brought us back here."

It was absolutely silent in the room. Talya was feeling lightheaded, so she closed her eyes and willed it to pass. "And I thought my power was cool." Emma's voice broke the silence. Garrett turned and held out an arm. Emma came and stood in front of him, against his chest. He bent and kissed her cheek.

"Are you okay, Talya? I can't believe all that you've been through. Garrett informed me of everything before I got here," Emma said.

"I'll be fine if the doctor here could stop using me as a human pincushion," she said in an irritated voice. Paul chuckled, apparently not bothered in the least by her words.

"I'm sure the guys have a million questions, but did you get enough at least for tonight so she can rest?" Emma asked, looking at Garrett.

"Yeah, get some rest, Talya and Liam," Garrett said. "Thank you, Talya, for the work you're doing. I don't take it lightly, what you're doing for our pack. Liam, check in with me tomorrow morning." She felt Liam nod behind her. "Thanks, Paul," Garrett said before leading Emma out of the room. Max followed without a sound.

"Okay, Talya," Paul said as he took a step back. "I think I've officially worked on you more than anybody in this pack," he said as he shook his head. "Liam, I think you've got your work cut out for you, keeping up with your mate. Let me get my stuff put away, and I'll get out of your hair." He disappeared for a moment into the bathroom.

"How are you doing, sweetheart?" Liam asked as he rubbed her side.

"I'm tired," Talya said, feeling totally depleted. Liam eased her forward slightly and climbed out from behind her.

"Let me get you some clean clothes to sleep in," he said. He climbed off the bed and disappeared a moment later. He came back moments later.

"Here, use this to clean off her shoulder. Try not to get the stitches wet; just clean up the blood," Paul told Liam. Liam took the rag and carefully cleaned her up. "Talya, here's some painkillers. The numbness in your shoulder should start to wear off in the next hour or so." Paul handed her a cup of water and some pills. "Now, get some rest, both of you. Liam, reach out during the night if you need me. Talya, take it easy. Let Liam do things for you, so your shoulder can heal nicely, okay?"

Talya nodded. "Thank you."

Paul nodded. "Okay. I'm out," he said with a wave. He grabbed his duffle bag and was gone.

"Let's get you ready for bed," Liam said. He stood next to the bed and reached forward to grasp the bottom of her shirt.

"What are you doing?" Talya asked.

"I'm helping you get dressed for bed. Please, just let me take care of you tonight," Liam said with a gentle tone. Talya gave in; she was too emotionally and physically exhausted to fight him. As soon as he saw she wasn't going to fight him, he pulled her shirt up and over her head, being careful of her wound. He pulled a soft tank top over her head and pulled it down. He turned her slightly and lifted her shirt in the back, so he could unsnap her bra. She finagled out of it and dropped it on the floor. "I think your shorts are fine unless you want to change them," Liam said.

"No, they're fine," Talya said. Each word felt slow and sluggish; she could feel her pills kicking in.

"Okay, let's get you settled," Liam said. He helped her lay down; then tucked her in. "Will you stay with me tonight?" Talya asked softly.

Chapter Forty-One

"You don't even have to ask," Liam said. "I have to do a few things; I'll be back in a minute or two." He walked into the bathroom, and Talya closed her eyes.

A few minutes later, she felt the bed shift. Liam crawled in next to her. She turned her head slightly to look at him. "You okay, beautiful?" he asked softly. Talya nodded, too depleted to do anything else. He kissed her on the forehead before wrapping his arms around her and holding her close. Talya fell asleep immediately.

Talya woke up the next morning and couldn't move. Her neck hurt and she felt stiff all over. She tried to move to a more comfortable position, but she couldn't seem to move.

"You okay, baby?" Liam asked in a sleepy voice. Talya nodded, grimacing at the pain it caused her. "You're in pain," Liam said before climbing out of bed. He was back a moment later.

"Here's some painkillers," he said as he helped her to sit up so she could take the pills. He eased her carefully back down onto the pillows. Paul showed up a few minutes later to check on her. He checked her stitches and asked her a few questions. She closed her eyes and willed herself to relax and let the painkillers kick in. She was aware that Paul and Liam were talking in low voices, but she ignored it. At some point, she fell asleep again.

Some time later, Talya opened her eyes slowly and looked around the room. She didn't see Liam anywhere. "Are you still in pain?" Liam asked, coming into the room.

Talya turned her head to look at him. "It's not as bad," she said.

Liam sat next to her on the bed. He pushed her hair away from her face. "I will never get that sight out of my head for as long as I live," he said in a gruff voice. "Talya, you can't go back there again," Liam began carefully.

Talya turned her head to look at him. "I have to," she said in a determined voice. "We have to find the locations of the other sites, or more girls are going to die. I'm not going to let that happen. It's not like I have a say, anyway. I don't decide if I'm going to show up in the dream stasis or not."

"Then we need to figure out a way to stop it; it's too dangerous," Liam protested.

"Liam," she began.

"No, Talya. You could have been killed. If you hadn't called to my wolf, they would have killed you," Liam said in a harsh voice.

"Then go with me; be my protector," Talya said.

Liam reached out and ran his hand over her cheek. "I will always be your protector, but what if I can't get there? What if it doesn't work? What if something happens to you? I can't let that happen, Talya," he said in a broken voice.

Talya put her hand over the top of his hand. "Nothing's going to happen to me."

Liam shook his head. "How did you pull me into your dream anyway?" he asked.

"I'm not exactly sure," she said.

"I wonder if it's because I marked you," Liam surmised.

"Liam," Talya began uncertainly. His eyes met hers. "Will I turn into a vampire?" she asked nervously.

"Oh baby, no," He gently climbed into bed beside her and carefully pulled her against his chest. "A bite won't turn you. They would have to drain you," his voice rumbled through his chest. "But let's not talk about it," he said, his voice gruff. "You're safe from being turned, sweetheart," he said as he ran his hand up and down on her back.

"What if I can't do it?" Talya asked. Liam's hand paused on her back. Talya continued. "It's my job as the dreamer to find the locations, but what if I can't? The vampire is already angry that I'm there. He said he is going to stop me. You killed his dream walker. I don't know if he's going to replace him. What if he creates more than one? And what if, once I find the locations, it doesn't stop? What if I have to just keep returning there every night studying dream after dream? What if I get hurt there or killed and nobody even knows? What if—"

"Talya," Liam's voice cut her off. He pulled back slightly and looked down into her eyes. "I won't let anything happen to you. I'm so sorry I didn't know what you were going through. But

I do now. You don't have to do it anymore by yourself. If you believe you need to do this," he paused and took a deep breath. "Then I will be with you every step of the way. If we have to sleep together every night, so you can be sure to pull me into your dream, then I will make the sacrifice," he said with a coy smile. Talya couldn't stop the smile from crossing her face. She shook her head at him. "Seriously, though," Liam continued. "We will make this work. I know that you are a Dreamer, and as much as a part of me hates that because of the danger, I also know that I am so proud to be your mate. You're so incredibly amazing! Garrett told me how you stood up to him and made them go to the first site. The fact that you figured that out is incredible, Talya. I will do everything I can as your mate to help you with your mission."

Talya wiped at the stray tear that slipped down her cheek. "Thank you. Can I ask you something?"

"Anything," he said, stroking her back once again.

"What happened to your family?" she asked softly.

"My father was killed by hunters," he said in a steady voice.

"I'm so sorry," Talya gasped. She put her hand on his chest.

"My mom never really recovered. She tried to raise me and take care of me, but it was mostly the other way around. She died when I was twelve," he said, sounding far away.

"I'm so sorry, Liam," Talya said quietly.

"What happened to your parents, baby?" Liam asked tenderly.

"Car accident when I was a baby," Talya said. "I never knew them. They went out one night on a date and left me with my grandparents. They were killed instantly in a head-on collision."

"I'm sorry, love," Liam said, pulling her closer to him.

"I really can't complain, though," Talya said from her position snuggled up to Liam's chest. "My grandparents are so amazing. They have been so good to me. I hate that I haven't been able to work to be able to help them more," she said in frustration.

"Do they need the money?" Liam asked gently.

Talya nodded. "My grandma's medication is really expensive. That's why I work as many hours as possible at the diner, so I can help pay for it," Talya said, feeling guilty.

Liam's arms tightened around her. "I'll take care of it."

"No, you can't do that Liam," Talya said pulling away from him.

"Why not?" he asked looking down at her.

"I can't ask you to do that," she said simply.

"You're not asking," Liam said. "You're my mate. They're my family too. I have plenty of money for us and to help them out too."

"What *do* you do for a job?" Talya asked.

"Garrett's bought up most of the land in town over the years. He owns an investment firm. I work for him. Along the way, I've invested a lot of money wisely over the years too. So, I'm pretty set. Our pack has a lot of money flowing through it," he said.

"Just how old are you?" Talya asked.

Liam laughed. "I'm twenty-one."

"How old is Garrett?" she asked next.

"Twenty-two," Liam said.

Talya scrunched up her face. "You guys seem so old."

Liam laughed. "I'm only three years older than you, Tally Bear," he said teasingly. Talya nudged him in the stomach. "I never thanked you by the way before everything got crazy."

"For what?" Talya asked in confusion.

"For letting me mark you. You can't begin to know how good it feels to have you wearing my mark," he said as he looked into her eyes.

Talya smiled at him. "You're welcome. What happens next?" she asked.

"Well, the next step is the last step," Liam said. "It's the equivalent of marrying in the human world. We don't normally do that as wolves, but things have been changing now that we're starting to mate humans," he said with a smile. "It's pretty simple. We pledge ourselves to each other in front of the Alpha. Whether the couple does that in private or in front of the pack is up to them. We always have a celebration at some point for the couple. Then once they complete the mating process, the couple is forever bonded. Neither of them can do anything to break the bond."

"Hmm," Talya said, thinking.

"Talya, I have no problem having a wedding; I know that's what you're used to," he said as he stroked her cheek softly. Talya didn't say anything. "Now there's something I've been waiting a long time to do," Liam said with a grin. "I have been trying to be patient and let you heal."

"What is it?" Talya asked.

You are so beautiful. Talya heard the words in her mind and looked at him in surprise. He had told her about this, but experiencing it was so much more than she thought it would be.

She wanted to say something back, but she wasn't sure how it worked. "How?" she asked simply.

Just think of something you want to say and think of me only, Liam said in her head.

Liam? Can you hear me? She sent to him. She didn't have to guess if he heard her or not. A big smile crossed his face. Talya shivered. She didn't think she would ever get over this sexy man. He chuckled and brushed her hair away from her shoulder.

I feel the exact same way about you, baby.

Talya felt her face heat up. "Did I say that to you?" she asked, mortified.

Liam grinned. "Yeah, you did. It's okay. You'll get used to it. I'm used to isolating my thoughts because of the pack link. But baby, you can send me thoughts like that any day, any time," he said with a grin. Then he bent down and kissed her gently. She knew he was being careful with her injuries—first from his bite and the vampire bite on her other side. Honestly his bite didn't hurt much anymore, but the vampire one still did.

"I have another question," Talya said, seriously.

"Shoot," Liam responded.

"Why don't you ever beat Garrett in a fight? Well, up until this last fight, that is. You could, couldn't you?" Talya asked.

Liam studied her face for a moment. "What makes you think I could beat him?" he asked.

"It was the way you responded when we were eating dinner with Steven and Wyatt. Something you said about *that's the way it's always going to be* when you referred to Garrett always win-ning," Talya said.

"I honestly don't know if I could beat him. It would be close," Liam began. "But I won't ever disrespect him by trying, well except for the other night," he said with a cringe. "If I wasn't with this pack, I could be an alpha. But this pack is my life. Garrett's the best alpha I know, and it's a privilege to serve as his beta."

"How do you know you could be an alpha?" Talya asked, curiously.

"By my alpha marks," he said simply.

When Talya looked at him in confusion, he sat up and pulled off his shirt. "The more marks, the more power the wolf and the man have. By the number of marks I have, I could be an alpha if I chose."

"I thought they were tattoos," Talya said.

"Nope. Those are my very own alpha marks. Feel free to touch them any time you want," he said with a grin. He jerked his head back suddenly. He gazed at a spot on the wall behind her.

"Liam? Is everything okay?" she asked.

"Vampires just breached pack lands. I have to get you to Garrett's house. That's where we gather the vulnerable women and children," he said. He picked her up quickly and jogged through the house to the front door. He opened it, and chaos ensued.

Chapter Forty-Two

Two blurs came towards them. Liam practically tossed her to the side. He launched himself into the air and shifted mid-leap. When he landed, he was a magnificent brown wolf. He took down the first vampire, but the second one appeared in front of Talya. Talya screamed at the man leering down at her. He gave a cocky smile before grabbing her. Then they were moving so fast, Talya couldn't even see anything. She heard a ferocious growl, and suddenly she was airborne. She tried to catch herself but landed with a thud on the ground. Pain flared through her as she tried to catch her breath. She turned to see Liam's wolf tearing into the vampire. Talya looked away, sick to her stomach. Her attention snagged on movement behind the house. A feeling of dread coiled through her.

There's more coming, she sent to Liam. His wolf finished off the vampire, ripping its head from its body. In one leap, he was in front of her. His wolf was growling, baring its teeth, with its hackles raised. If Talya hadn't known it was Liam, she would have been terrified.

Do not move from behind me, Liam sent to her. A rush of vampires came at them. Talya's heart slammed in her chest. Suddenly, several wolves came charging in. She recognized Garrett's black wolf at the helm. Right behind him was the dark gray wolf she knew to be Max. She saw several more wolves joining in the fight.

Talya wanted to look away from the gruesome sight, but she was afraid if she did for a moment, something bad would happen. Suddenly, everything froze in front of her. Talya stared around her. Nobody moved. "Quite a marvelous feat, isn't it?" Talya turned to face the voice she knew too well. Dread filled her when she saw the vampire creator walk through the gruesome scene all around them.

"How are you doing this?" Talya breathed out the question.

"I'm creating a dream stasis outside of the dream world. Complicated. Takes a lot of energy," he said with a cold smile.

"Why?" Talya asked simply.

"I wanted to get your attention." He nodded at the battle. "My vampires outnumber your wolves three to one. When I drop this hold, your precious wolves will be slaughtered. It may take a few minutes, but that will be the end result," he said as carelessly as if they were talking about the weather. "Unless..." he let the word hang.

Talya turned in a circle, viewing the battle scene. It was true. The wolves were greatly outnumbered. She saw the vampires she hadn't been able to see with the battle in front of her. They hadn't reached the fight yet, but they would as soon as the stasis lifted. There were dozens of them. Her eyes couldn't even count the number of them all. Horror gripped her, but she pushed for control of her emotions.

"Unless what?" Talya asked without emotion. She turned and faced the vampire head-on. "What do you want?"

"You," the vampire said simply.

"Why?" Talya asked; her mind scrambled to come up with an idea of what the vampire could possibly want with her.

"Doesn't matter. If you come with me willingly, I will call back my vampires," the vampire said.

Talya looked around her again, feeling sick. Her eyes sought and found Liam. He was frozen in the process of fighting two vampires in front of him. Two more were directly behind him. Did he know they were there? Would he see them in time? *Liam? Can you hear me?* She tried connecting with him, but there was no reply. "How do I know you will keep your word?" she asked in anger.

The vampire smiled slowly. "You don't, but is that a chance you're willing to take? Oh, I forgot to mention. I already have your friend."

A sick feeling settled in Talya's stomach. "Friend?" she managed to choke out.

"There's something special about her, but I haven't been able to put my finger on it yet. She put up quite a fight for a human. Lucky for us, there was nobody around to hear her screams. Just a simple human girl in a huge, empty house," he said sadistically.

Sage, her mind supplied as panic hit her. "Why are you doing this?" Talya asked, her voice shaky.

"Because you have the power to destroy what I want, and I am not about to let that happen. If you can't dream walk, you can't find the locations of my operations. It's simple really," the vampire said. "You come with me willingly, or your friend forfeits her life, and your pack faces decimation at the hands of my vampires."

Talya stared at him, the wheels in her mind turning. *He needs me to go willingly. Why?* Then it hit her. "You have no physical power in this realm." He said nothing, but his countenance darkened. Talya closed her eyes for a moment. There was no option in her mind. They had Sage, and they had an overwhelming number of vampires for this attack. Could the wolves still win? She wasn't sure, but she wasn't going to take the chance and lose lives because of it. Not when it was in her power to stop it. "I'll go with you willingly," Talya said. "But I want proof that you're going to call off the vampires."

"Little Dreamer, you are in no place to make demands," the vampire said.

"Then I'm not going with you," Talya said, lifting her head and looking him in the eye.

"Then the pack will die, and so will your friend," the vampire snapped. He put his hand up, and terror seized Talya.

"Stop!" she cried out. "I'll go with you." Her heart was slamming against her chest, but relief instantly flooded her when he lowered his hand. He reached out his hand to her, and Talya slowly put her hand in his. Revulsion filled her, but she made herself not follow her instinct to yank her hand back. A moment later, the scene in front of her was gone. When she opened her eyes and steadied herself, she was inside some sort of holding cell. The vampire walked out of the cell and slammed the iron door with a loud clang. He disappeared an instant later.

Talya checked the door; it was locked, just as she knew it would be. *Liam, can you hear me?* There was no response. She heard a soft groan and turned towards it. She couldn't see much in the darkness, but her eyes made out a huddled form in the cell next to hers. She walked that way slowly, unsure of what she would find. "Sage?" she whispered in the darkness.

It was quiet for a moment. Then she heard a stirring sound. "Talya?" she heard Sage's quiet whisper.

Talya fell to her knees at the edge of the cell. "Are you okay?" Talya asked.

It was quiet for a moment. "Are you really here?" Sage whispered.

"Yeah, it's me. How long have you been here?" Talya asked.

"I don't know," came Sage's despondent voice.

"I don't know how, but I'm going to get you out of here. I promise." Talya said. Sage didn't respond. "It's going to be all right, Sage. Liam will come for us," she said the words she believed with all her heart. Talya stood up and moved around her cell feeling every nook and cranny of the place, trying to find any weaknesses. She found nothing, but at least it helped to pass the time.

Time creeped by. She had no idea if it had been minutes, hours, or days when a door opened and a small amount of light entered. Talya stood and hurried over to the bars to see what was going on. Two vampires dragged somebody between them. They opened a cell and threw the person inside, closing the doors with a clang. A moment later, they were gone.

Silenced descended suddenly, and so did the darkness. Talya watched the other cell. "Hello?" she called out.

"Talya?" she heard a voice say, and her heart dropped.

"Emma?" she asked, hoping against hope she was wrong.

"It's me," Emma said in an angry voice.

"No! What happened?" Talya asked.

"I don't even know," Emma said with the same desperation that Talya felt. "Garrett said there was a vampire attack. He disappeared with most of the wolves. I-I don't even know what happened after that. I only woke up a few minutes ago. I tried reaching out to Garrett, but there's nothing there."

"I know. I tried with Liam. Somehow, they're blocking the connection," Talya said.

"Talya, we have to get out of here," Emma said, desperation in her voice.

"I know. I'm so sorry, Emma. This is all because of me. I will figure out a way to get you, me, and Sage out of here," Talya said, echoing the promise she had already made to Sage.

"Sage is here too?" Emma asked in surprise.

"Yeah; she's over on this side," Talya explained.

"Why would they take Sage?" Emma asked.

Talya shook her head. "I don't know." She'd been trying to figure that out herself. Talya heard Emma moving around for a while before she finally got frustrated and grew silent. Talya figured she'd probably been searching for a way out, just like she had.

"Sage," Talya said softly as she moved to the side of her cell. "Are you doing okay?" Sage didn't answer her, and Talya felt her heart beat faster. "Sage? Sage?" Talya felt desperation come over her. "Sage, answer me!"

"Are you sure it's Sage?" Emma asked from her cell.

"Yes, she talked to me briefly earlier. What did they do to her, Emma?" Talya asked in desperation.

"I don't know," Emma said softly. "But Garrett and Liam will come for us. They'll get us out of here, and we will get Sage too and make sure she's okay. And Talya, there's something else you should know."

"At this point, I don't even know if I want to hear it," Talya said with a grimace.

"Sage is one of us," Emma said softly. "I've been seeing glimpses but didn't put it all together until yesterday. But then this happened, and…" her voice trailed off.

"Wow," Talya said. "The vampire said there was something to her; he just didn't know what. I wonder what her gifting is."

"Yeah," Emma said.

Talya walked to the corner where Sage was. "Hang in there, Sage," she whispered. She slumped down next to the wall in defeat. Time dragged by. Talya talked on and off with Emma, both of them trying to take their minds off of their surroundings. At some point, Talya must have fallen asleep because she woke up in her dream stasis.

The scene that usually gave her such comfort held no such comfort now. She looked around for the wolf, calling out for him. He came into view, and Talya dropped to her knees. "Everything's a mess," she whispered as he drew close.

Chapter Forty-Three

"I know, child," the wolf said, sounding tired.

"What am I supposed to do? The vampire creator kidnapped me along with Sage and Emma. I don't know what they want with us, I can't get Sage to respond, Liam and Garrett are totally cut off from us... everything is really bad right now. What do I do?" Talya asked, desperate for answers.

"Right now, you get to work," the wolf said.

Talya stared at him, feeling like she'd been slapped. "I don't think you understand."

"I completely understand. I understand that right now, the vampire creator is busy trying to protect his work. Therefore, he is probably not guarding his dream realm. This is the perfect time to search for the cities," the wolf said calmly. "You are stronger than either of us realized. The vampire took you to keep you from entering this realm, but here you are. Somehow, your power was able to surpass his attempt to block your access to your power. You still have a purpose, Talya. You need to find those six cities, so that we can shut down the vampire's work or all *of this is for nothing. Use this time, Talya. They kidnapped you, think-ing to stop you from shutting their work down. Gain the upper hand. Find the cities, Talya; so, we can put an end to this once and for all."*

Talya opened her mouth and shut it. He did have a point; it wasn't like she was going anywhere in the near future. And he was right. If the vampire was busy, this could be the best time to find answers. "Okay," Talya said. She pushed her fear and feelings of the unknown aside and took a deep breath. She imagined the melding in the vampire realm. As soon as she stood in front of it, she waded inside and began the daunt-ing task of trying to find the locations of the vampires' sites.

Time seemed to pass differently in her dream world, so Talya was never quite sure how much time passed when she was here. But it seemed like a significant amount of time passed before she was flung suddenly back into her physical body.

Talya's eyes flew open, and she sat up quickly. "Talya! Thank God! I couldn't get you to wake up!" Emma's worried voice pen-etrated through her confusion.

"I'm sorry I scared you. I was in my dream world," Talya said.

"Are you okay?" Emma asked, worried.

"I'm fine. Did I miss anything?" she asked.

"No. I slept for a little bit. Sage hasn't woken up, I don't think. I haven't heard anything from her," Emma said.

Talya turned to face towards Sage's cell. "Sage, Sage, wake up. Can you hear me?" She received nothing in response. "I'm really worried about her."

"I know," came Emma's response. "Me too. But she's strong, Talya. She'll be okay."

She has to be, Talya thought to herself. Before she could say anything else, they heard a clang and the sound of a door opening. Talya stood quickly to her feet, blinking when the door opened and a small amount of light touched her cell. She watched warily as three men entered the holding area they were in. The man at the front stopped in front of Emma's cell and Talya didn't miss the gasp that came from her. Talya grabbed the bars to her cell, trying to see what was going on.

"Did you miss me?" the man asked with humor in his voice.

"What are you doing here, Alec?" Emma asked. Talya could hear the slight tremor in her voice, though her friend was trying to put on a brave front.

"Well, I heard my dear old sister was being detained, and I figured I would come to check on her," Alec said.

Talya moved to the side trying to get a look at his face. She glanced at the other two men. They were vampires. They stayed by the door. *Security maybe?* Talya thought to herself. Alec turned and faced Talya suddenly, and recognition flared inside of her. It was the man from the diner. He had been at her table the night Liam had taken her and fled. He came towards her with a cocky smile, and Talya stood her ground, staring him down. He turned towards Emma again. "Three down; one to go," he said.

"How are you a part of this?" Emma asked boldly. "Why would you work with vampires?" She asked the question Talya wanted to know as well. Talya could tell by looking at him that he wasn't a vampire. And if he was Emma's brother, why wasn't he helping her?

"It's simple really. You're worth a lot of money, little sister," he said, and Talya could hear the grin in his voice.

"Why?" Talya couldn't stop the question as it slipped from her lips. "Why would you turn your own sister over to vampires?" Now that she had started, she couldn't stop. Alec turned towards her with a cold smile. He walked towards Sage's cell for a moment before he came and stood in front of Talya's cell.

"Emma's worth a lot of money," he said.

"But why are you working with the vampires?" Talya asked, trying to wrap her mind around it.

He shrugged "They're the ones with the money," he said as if that justified his actions.

"So, you would sell out your own family for money?" Talya asked and couldn't keep the disgust out of her voice.

"She's not family," he spat the words at Talya.

Talya crossed her arms. "Why because she's not blood?"

"No, because she's an abomination, just like you!" Alec yelled at Talya. "None of you should be allowed to exist." His words were filled with hate. Talya shook her head. There was no reasoning with him. "You're born of wolf power but don't have a wolf inside of you. It's like being a human without a soul." He turned back to stand in front of Emma's cell. "I was going to kill you that day, the day you ran away," he said in a quiet voice. "I waited until you turned eighteen to be sure. When I realized you had no wolf inside of you, I knew what had to be done. Nothing like that should exist. But you escaped. Lucky for me, on my search for you, I heard about some vampires who were looking for a wolf girl without a wolf soul who were willing to pay top dollar to find you." He paused for a moment. "Imagine my surprise when I found out there were more of you. Since I was already familiar with your essence, they sent me to find the others. So far, I've done pretty good," he said cockily. "There's just one more of you abominations left out there," he said in disgust.

"What do the vampires want with us?" Emma asked.

"Don't know; don't care," Alec said. "I got what I came for— money," he said, drawing the word out. "Well, I would say it was good to see you, but that would be untrue." With that, he and the two vampires left, closing the door behind them. Darkness descended once again.

"Well, I guess you can't choose family, huh?" Talya asked. Emma didn't respond. "I'm sorry, Emma."

Emma sighed. "It's fine. I shouldn't be surprised. He's always been horrible." It was quiet for a few minutes before Emma asked, "What do you think they're going to do to us? Why haven't they come for us or done anything to us yet?" she asked.

"I think they are trying to find the fourth one of us, and at the same time trying to create vampires by turning girls. I think they need us out of the way. Well, at least me. With me out of the way, the vampire can continue doing what he's doing. I don't think he realizes I can still dream walk in this place. I can't contact Liam, so obviously there's something stopping that connection," Talya said.

"If that's true, you know what they're going to do when they find the last person, right?" Emma asked.

"Kill us," Talya said without hesitation. "We have to get out of here before that happens. You don't have any weapons on your person, do you?"

"No, they took my knife sometime while I was out of it," Emma responded.

"There's no way out of here," Talya said, shaking her head. Emma didn't answer. Exhaustion eventually plagued Talya, and she fell asleep.

"Dreamer," the wolf greeted her right away. "We must hasten and find those locations." Talya nodded. Without another word, she dream walked to the vampire realm. Hours later, she found something.

"I think I found it," Talya said when she appeared back in the wolf realm. She told him what she had found.

"Excellent work, Talya. I will pass it on to the wolves," the wolf said.

Talya stopped and stared at him. "You can communicate with them?" she asked.

"It is much easier having you as my interceder, but I will figure out a way," the wolf said.

"Can you tell them where we are so they can rescue us?" Talya asked hopefully.

"I'm sorry, Talya," the wolf said despondently. "I don't know where you are. I'm doing everything in my power to find that information out. As soon as I do, I will pass it on to the Northwoods Pack."

Disappointment flooded Talya. "Okay, thank you."

Moments later, she woke up back in her cell. She sat up. "Emma? Are you awake?" she asked softly.

"Oh good, Talya. I was worried about you. You were out for a long time this time," Emma's worried voice came to her.

"I'm sorry to worry you, but I found the next city," Talya said excitedly.

"Good," Emma said. "Where is it?"

"Phoenix, and I think I'm getting close to finding the next city. It's on the West Coast somewhere; I know that much," Talya said.

"Good work, Talya," Emma praised enthusiastically. "They brought some stale bread and water while you were sleeping. It's not great, but at least it's something."

Talya felt around in her cell until her hands touched the bread and the water bottle. She quickly opened the cap on the water bottle and drank it halfway down before capping it. She wanted to save some, as she had no idea when she would get any again. She glanced in the direction of Sage. "Did Sage wake up at all?"

"No," Emma responded.

Time slowed to a crawl in the cells. Talya existed somewhere in the midst of the prison cells of the vampires and the vampire dream stasis. When she was awake, the hours ticked away slowly, and she and Emma talked endlessly. Sage never responded.

When she was in her dream state, she spent every moment trying to find the locations. She found two more locations; the wolf promised he would let the wolves know. Talya was in the midst of the dream stasis when she was jerked back into her body. She opened her eyes and was startled to see angry vampires standing over her. She couldn't pull the scream that escaped her lips from their sudden appearance. They yanked her to her feet. "Talya!" Emma cried out, but Talya couldn't respond. They dragged her out of her cell and up a set of stairs. They walked a little bit before climbing another set of stairs. Talya blinked at the sudden light. She stumbled and had to close her eyes because her eyes couldn't adjust to the light. They continued walking, making twists and turns. Finally, they stopped walking. Talya opened her eyes slowly, blinking as her eyes watered. She glanced around the room. It was a small room with a desk and a chair. Before she could take anything else in, the door opened and slammed into the wall behind it.

Chapter Forty-Four

Talya jumped at the sudden noise. Her eyes widened in surprise, and she took a step backwards when she saw the angry vampire creator in front of her. "Three locations!" he yelled at her, slamming his hand on the desk. Talya tried to slow the thundering of her heart. "There is only one way those wolves knew those locations! It had to be you! How are you doing it? You are cut off from any kind of magic down there including the mate bond and dream walking. How are you still doing it?" he roared at her.

Talya didn't answer; she had no idea how she was still doing it. She wondered if the wolf was helping her somehow. But before she could think on that, another voice roared—in her mind.

Talya! Talya couldn't hold back the jolt of shock that went through her.

Liam?!

Where are you? Are you safe? Are you in pain? His words ran together, and Talya could hear the desperation in his voice.

I- before she could get anything out, the vampire leapt at her.

"No!" he screamed. His fist came at her so fast, she never even had a chance to dodge it. Pain exploded in her head.

Talya! What's happening? I feel your pain! Liam was freaking out in her mind, but she couldn't form one word to send back to him.

"You're talking to them! Get her out of here now!" the vampire roared. "Get her back in the cells!" Talya was yanked to her feet and dragged from the room. Her head was pounding, and her eyes were watering. She couldn't see where she was going, but she knew she only had seconds to talk to Liam.

Liam, she managed to get out. *They're taking me back down to my cell.*

Talya, where are you? Look around. Give me everything you see now! He demanded.

Talya opened her eyes, trying to push past the pain. *I don't know where I am. There's nothing,* she said desperately.

Talya, just tell me everything you see in front of you right now, Liam's voice came to her again.

The words began to pour out of Talya; she knew she had only moments before the connection was cut off. *Emma, Sage, and I are kept in cells underground. We came up two sets of staircases. We're in some kind of large building with offices.* She looked around desperately trying to find anything that would tell them where they were. *I've got nothing else,* she said to Liam, panicking now.

It's okay, baby. Just keep looking and tell me what you see. Liam's calm voice helped to keep the panic away. Talya looked everywhere, trying to find anything that would give her an idea of where she was. She saw the door ahead that led to the first set of stairs.

No! She screamed in her mind. *Find something! Find something!* But it was no use. She didn't see anything that would help her. *Liam, I can't find anything!* Even she could hear the helplessness in her voice.

I will find you, Talya!

Talya chocked back a sob at his words. The vampire on her left opened the door, and Talya turned to step back out of the way of the door. When she did, her eyes fell on a single item on a table in the room behind her. *Camilla's Coffee Roasters* she shouted in her mind to Liam. The door slammed behind her and she knew immediately that she was cut off from Liam. She had no idea if he had heard her or not. She really hoped that coffee cup was from around here; that it wasn't a false lead. It was all she had. She hoped it was enough.

Back in her cell, the time dragged by once again. She and Emma talked less and less. Talya seemed to be in the dream stasis longer than she was in her cell. Weakness and hunger plagued her. Somehow the weakness didn't translate to her body in the dream stasis.

She was able to work there endlessly without tiring. Finally, she found all the cities. Then, as if her body knew her work was done, she sank to her knees.

"Talya, you've done well. Rest now," she heard the voice of the wolf, *but she could no longer respond.* Darkness edged in and emptiness. She floated in the emptiness for a seemingly endless amount of time.

At some point, Talya began to be aware of sounds. She

couldn't place the sounds, but she knew she wasn't in her dream state any longer. She thought she heard Liam calling her name, but that couldn't be right. She must still be dreaming. Then hands touched her, and she jerked. She wanted to open her eyes, but she couldn't. "Talya, it's Liam. I'm going to get you out of here. It's going to be rough for a little bit, but I'll keep you safe." His words penetrated her mind, but she couldn't really make sense of them. She wanted to open her eyes to see if he was real, but she couldn't get them to open. She felt another pair of hands on her.

"Her heartrate is a little slow, but her breathing is steady. She's stable to move. Get her out of here." She recognized that voice, but she couldn't seem to place it. "Emma's stable too. Let's get them out of here." Suddenly, Talya remembered Sage. They couldn't leave her. She tried to open her eyes, but she couldn't. She tried to move, but Liam only held her tighter. "It's okay, Talya. I'm going to get you out of here." Talya used every ounce of strength she had left and willed her voice to work. "Sage!" She said in a raspy voice.

"Paul has Sage," Liam said.

Then they were moving. She heard Garrett barking out orders. She had heard him mad before, but nothing like this. At the top of the stairs, more wolves joined them. Liam was full-on running now, so Talya couldn't really see who was with them. When they got to the next door, they stopped.

"More vampires just hit the southern edge," she heard someone say.

"Everybody knows what to do." There was movement, and

Talya felt herself being handed off to somebody. She wanted to protest, but she was too weak. She managed to pry her eyes open. "Your mission is to get the girls into the helicopter and get them out of here. The rest of us will clear the path for you. Paul, you go with them to the helicopter. Wait." Talya wasn't sure what they were waiting for; she glanced up at the man carrying her. He looked familiar. She thought his name was Ricky or something. He didn't look down at her. He was watching Garrett, his face and body tense. As soon as Garrett gave the signal, somebody wrenched the door clean off its hinges and the group exploded forward. A second later, wolves surrounded them as they ran. Vampires came from everywhere towards them. Talya heard the vicious sounds of fighting. She tried to find Liam in the battle. It took her a moment before she saw his wolf. She watched as he and Garrett cleared the way in front of them, viciously attacking anything that came at them. Soon, the fighting was behind them and they were running towards the helicopter that sat about a few hundred yards away.

Suddenly, Talya was airborne. It happened so fast. One minute she was being carried; the next, she was on the ground. She looked up and saw the vampire creator looming over her. "Did you think I would let you escape, Little Dreamer?" he asked.

Adrenaline flooded Talya's body, and she was no longer weak. She scooted backwards away from him. The man that had carried her transformed into a wolf and launched himself at the vampire. In a movement faster than Talya could track, the vampire took a knife and slit the wolf's throat. "No!" Talya cried out, standing to her feet unsteadily. But it was too late. The wolf collapsed to the ground. Talya stared at the blood pouring into and soaking the ground, willing him to get back up. Two more wolves came at him and he did the same thing. "I can keep doing this all day," the vampire said. "The silver keeps them from healing, in case you were wondering," he said. He grabbed her hand; a moment later, they were far away from the battle.

"No!" Talya cried out as desperation flooded her.

The vampire stalked towards her. "I should have gotten rid of you a long time ago! You are destroying everything I have worked so hard for!" he shouted in his rage. Talya's heart was racing. She searched around her desperately, trying to find an escape. "There is no escape this time, Dreamer. No wolves to save you. It's just you and the creator of the vampire race. Who do you think is going to win this one?" he asked.

Talya looked at him and saw the rage in his black eyes; she knew in that moment that she was going to die. There was absolutely nothing she could do. *Talya, where are you?* She heard Liam's frantic voice in her head.

He took me; I don't know where I am. You won't get here in time this time. She heard him yell in her mind. Everything slowed down around her as she watched the vampire come towards her.

Talya stood tall. "You will not destroy any more lives!"

"Who's going to stop me? You?" the vampire asked with a cold laugh.

"You may defeat me and even kill me, but I've won," Talya said in a strong voice. "The Northwoods wolves know all the locations, and they will never stop until all of your sites are destroyed."

"No!" the vampire yelled in rage. "You will never stop me!" the vampire roared and grabbed her shoulder, holding her immobile. She couldn't loosen his hold. She watched as he raised his arm. "Goodbye, Dreamer!"

I love you, Liam. Please tell my grandparents I love them, Talya sent. Talya closed the link, so he wouldn't feel her pain but not before a howl that gutted her sounded. Talya closed her eyes and waited for the killing blow. A force shoved her back, and Talya fell to the ground. She stared in horror as the knife plunged into the wolf from her dream stasis. "No!" she screamed as the wolf stood for a moment longer before collapsing to the ground in front of her.

"No!" Talya cried out again, dropping to her knees beside him. Tears dripped from her eyes onto the wolf. She was no longer aware of the vampire. She could only see the red on the wolf in front of her. Her hands tried to stop the impossible stanch of blood in his side. "You shouldn't have done that," she cried.

"Talya, it's up to you now." The wolf said in a quiet but strong voice in her head. Talya lifted tear-filled eyes to look into his.

"I can't," she cried in her mind.

"You can. This is what you were created for. It's time to finish this. Take the knife."

Talya bit back a sob and reached out and yanked the knife from the wolf's side, crying at the pained sound he made. She stood to her feet shakily and held the knife behind her leg, so the vampire wouldn't see.

Chapter Forty-Five

He wasn't paying attention to her anyway. He was looking down at the wolf in disdain. "For the creator of the wolves, I was expecting a little more. That's all you've got? No wonder your wolves are such weak, pathetic creatures. Now, nothing is going to stop me from doing what I need to do. Not you, and certainly not your wolves. I just need to get back and kill the Alpha and his beta, and send in my vampires to finish off the rest of the pack." He continued to spew his hate-filled words without paying any attention to Talya.

His words fueled the rage already in Talya's heart. When she was close enough, she looked up at him. He looked down at her with eyes that were dark black with hate. "You're not going to hurt anybody else!"

"And you think you're going to be the one to stop me?" The vampire threw his head back and laughed. The moment his eyes were off of hers, she took the knife and slammed it into his heart. He threw her off of him before the knife could do any damage.

Talya landed a few feet away.

"You would try to kill me?" he roared at her.

Talya looked up as he came towards her, fury radiating from him. "Did you really think you could kill me?" he taunted. Talya looked around her frantically for the knife. She scooted backwards as the vampire came towards her. "I will kill you; then the Beta. Then I will kill the two friends that were with you in the cells and then your beloved grandparents. I will kill anyone you ever cared about!"

Talya's head jerked up at that. "You didn't think I knew about your family?" he asked coldly. He leaned over the top of her. "I will kill them slowly and agonizingly," he said right near her ear.

Talya's hand closed around the knife as she felt anger well up inside of her. Then she closed her eyes for a moment and opened herself to Liam, the way she had when she was in the vampire realm. She focused on the link between them. She found it and yanked on it hard; she would apologize for it later. She felt his power enter her, filling her. Her hands began shaking. "You should have killed me when you had the chance," she said with all the anger she felt. Then she took the knife and slammed it into his heart with the strength of a wolf.

He jerked violently, and she used every ounce of her strength to hold the knife there, knowing that the longer the knife stayed in, the more damage it would do because vampires couldn't do silver, just like wolves. The vampire stared down at his chest in shock and then at her. He was no longer laughing. Talya twisted it, entangling it in his heart even more. She didn't look at him; her body shook with the combination of Liam's power and her own. He tried to pull away from her, but she used all her strength to keep the knife there. The creator wolf joined her and pinned the vampire down with his weight. Talya grit her teeth and held on with all her strength while the vampire tried to remove the knife from his chest. Finally, the vampire's movement began to slow. Then he was still. Talya didn't release her hold. The wolf stepped back.

"You can release it now, Talya," the wolf said. Talya was frozen, staring at the vampire. The wolf nudged her and she dropped her hold on the knife. She stood and stumbled backwards, away from the body.

"You did what you needed to do," the wolf said.

"Is he..." she couldn't bring herself to say the word.

"He's dead," the wolf said. "Your wolves will need to dismember him and burn him, so he can never rise again." The wolf stumbled after that, and Talya rushed to his side.

"Are you okay?" she asked. She looked at his side. There was so much blood.

"I will be fine. I will have to recover for a time, but I will be as good as new soon. You got the silver out of me quickly," the wolf said.

Talya dropped to her knees at his side. "Thank you," she said.

The wolf nodded. "Wrap your arms around my neck, and I will take you back to your pack." A moment later, they stood in the midst of the battle between wolves and vampires. Talya swayed on her feet. The adrenaline that had kept her moving was gone. Her eyes searched for her wolf. She saw the moment he knew she was back. His wolf jerked its head in her direction.

Then he was running towards her. He shifted and pulled her into his arms.

"Talya," he breathed her name. He pulled back and bent down to look into her eyes. "Are you okay? I felt you pull on the bond. I tried to give you everything I had. Was it enough?" he asked.

"It was. Thank you." That's all she got out before she dropped like lead; she was absolutely depleted. He caught her. "It's okay. You're safe now. I've got you." His words were the only thing keeping her sane. She felt like she was coming apart from the inside out.

Liam ran towards the helicopter, holding her close to his chest. As soon as they were on board, he signaled for them to take off. He put her down while he pulled on a pair of pants then picked her back up again. Talya was too weak to do much but cling to him. He held her tightly, and she could feel the rigidness in his muscles. Liam made her drink some Gatorade. She drank about half of it before she couldn't do anymore. She leaned against Liam and closed her eyes.

———————

It took a week before Paul released Talya and Emma. She figured they could have been cleared to leave earlier, but Paul wasn't taking any chances. Though Paul had taken exceptional care of both Talya and Emma, he spent most of his time watching over Sage. Talya found out when she woke up that Sage was Paul's mate. He had known it instantly, the moment he stepped into the basement. Talya was shocked, but she knew that was nothing compared to the shock her friend would face when she finally woke up.

It took Sage several days to wake up. When she did, she wouldn't talk to anybody. Paul didn't tell her who he was, and neither did anybody else.

Talya figured she would give it a few days and then tell her. Right now, Sage was too traumatized to handle anything else. None of them were really sure what had happened to her before Talya and Emma had gotten there. Talya was worried about her, but she would give her a few days before dumping everything on her.

Sage opened her eyes from the nap she had taken and sat up in her bed. Talya walked over to her and sat on the bed next to her. "How are you feeling?" Talya asked.

Sage shrugged. "Okay." Talya wished for more, but she had agreed with Paul to let her come to grips with things on her own.

"Are you leaving?" Sage asked.

Talya nodded. "I got the all clear to leave." Sage nodded and didn't say anything. "So," Talya started. "Do you want to stay with me for the summer? I mean, you'd hate to lie to your parents." she said with a smile.

As soon as Sage had recovered enough to be alert, she had called her parents and said she had left for the summer to stay with Talya. She had apologized for not letting them know sooner. Thankfully, her parents had been traveling for most of the time she had been missing anyway and hadn't even missed her. Talya hated that for Sage's sake, but at least it hadn't caused an uproar when she had disappeared.

Sage didn't answer at first, and Talya's heart fell. "Yeah, I guess that would work."

Talya nodded, forcing herself to keep a smile on her face. She felt Paul's presence on the other side of the room. He never strayed far from Sage's side. Sage didn't even seem to notice him. "Sage, I want to keep you here another twenty-four hours and see if we can't get you to eat something. If you can keep it down and everything else checks out, you can go with Talya tomorrow," Paul said.

Sage didn't respond; she just lay back down on her pillow. Talya leaned over and hugged her friend. "It's going to be okay; I promise." Sage gave her a small smile. It wasn't much, but Talya would take it.

Liam came into the room a moment later. "You're back!" Talya said with gratitude

He smiled a tired smile. "I'm back." Talya hugged him tightly. He had just gotten back from destroying two of the vampire sites.

Talya nodded. "Thanks for everything, Paul."

"You're welcome," he said with a smile. "Don't worry about her," he said in a quiet voice. "I'll take care of her."

"I know," Talya said. "Just give her time; don't push her into anything," Talya cautioned.

Paul nodded. "I won't."

"Thanks, Paul," Liam said with a hand on his shoulder. Then he took Talya's hand and led her out to his car. It was quiet on the drive to his house.

Liam dropped her off in her room and gave her a kiss on the cheek. "You go ahead and get ready for bed. I'll be back in a while." He left a moment later. Talya stared after him. He wasn't okay, not in the least. She decided she would give him a few minutes; then she would go find him. She changed quickly into a tank top and sleeping shorts.

She lay down on her bed and waited for a little bit. After thirty minutes had passed, she decided to go track him down. She could have asked him where he was, but she wasn't sure if he was out in his wolf form and didn't want to be bothered. She left the room and walked towards the living room. She noticed the basement door slightly open. When she opened it and heard music coming from the basement, she made her way down the stairs. The music was thumping, and Liam was in the corner of the room beating a punching bag to death. Talya wondered what to say to him, how to connect with him.

She sat for probably another twenty minutes. When Liam showed no signs of slowing down, Talya stood and made her way towards him. Without stopping, she walked close to him and wrapped her arms around his waist under his arms, not caring that he was a sweaty mess. He pulled his punches and stood still. Talya tightened her arms around him. "Come back to me," she said loud enough for him to hear over the music. He turned, and she let go of him. He hit a button on his phone, and shut off the music. It was instantly quiet. Liam grabbed a towel and wiped himself off. Talya took a moment to appreciate the incredible masculinity of him.

"Are you okay?" she asked softly.

Liam's face hardened. He turned away from her and ran a hand through his hair. "I didn't protect you," he said gruffly.

"No, Liam. I chose to go with the vampires," Talya returned immediately. He stared at her. "The vampire didn't give me a choice. They would have killed everybody I love, including you." She had known this conversation was coming, but it didn't make it any easier.

"Are you telling me you let them take you?" he asked incredulously.

"I didn't have a choice," Talya said painfully. "It was either go with them, or they would kill everybody."

"You did have a choice!" Liam snapped at her in anger. Talya stared at him in surprise. He'd never snapped at her like that before. "You should have chosen to believe that I would keep you safe," he said, stepping in front of her and looking down at her.

"I did what I had to in the moment," Talya said, not backing down an inch. "And I would do it all over again if it meant keeping everybody else safe!"

"It's not your job to protect everybody, Talya!" Liam yelled at her.

Talya flinched. "You're not the Dreamer. You have no idea what it's like!"

"No, I don't know what being the Dreamer is like. But I do know what feeling the weight of the entire pack feels like. I know what trying to protect others is like. I get it, Talya. I really do, but I've also learned to trust others over the years. My pack has my back, and I trust them. Just like Garrett trusts me to have his back." Liam took a breath.

"I'm so sorry, Liam," Talya said. "I did what I thought I had to."

The fight went out of him. "I know," Liam said. They were both quiet for a moment, lost in their own thoughts.

"I will try to do better with trusting you," Talya said.

Liam nodded. "I'll do a better job of protecting you."

Talya wanted to argue with that but didn't want to start fighting again.

Talya sat on the weight bench. "You know," she began, "I should have been terrified out of my mind, and I was at times. But honestly, what scared me the most was when..." she paused for a moment. "When I thought I'd never see you again, when I thought we wouldn't have a future together." Her voice broke on the last few words. Liam sat down next to her pulled her gently from her seat and onto his lap. He wrapped his arms around her and held her close. "I guess I hadn't realized how deeply I care for you, and it kind of scares me," Talya admitted softly.

Chapter Forty-Six

"Look at me, Talya," Liam said and waited until she was looking at him. "I love you," he said simply. "Love is a powerful thing; it has the power to break us. It's terrifying to give somebody the power to destroy you. When you love with your whole being, you are giving somebody else the power to return that love or to crush you by not returning it. I want you to know that your love to me is a gift. It's not something I will ever take for granted. Not today, not fifty years from now. I love you more than I ever thought it possible to love somebody. You are my heart, body, and soul all wrapped up in one person. I know I won't always do things right. I know I will frustrate you and make you angry at times. We won't always see eye to eye on things, and that's okay. It's supposed to be that way. But know this—that every time we have an argument, it won't diminish my love for you. I may need time to cool off, but I will always return to you. I will always keep a tender heart towards you and love you. You are my heart, my very reason for existence. Without you, I am nothing. I don't want you to ever doubt my love for you, to ever feel like you're putting yourself out there and are unsure if I will reciprocate. Because I will, Talya. I will reciprocate with my whole heart. I love you, and you are the most precious thing to me in the world." Talya stared up at him with tears in her eyes. Liam gently wiped the tears from her cheeks with the pads of his thumbs. "What are you thinking, love?"

Talya swallowed, trying to get control of her emotions. "I love you too," she whispered softly. He bent and captured her lips in a kiss. "I don't know what I did to deserve you," she said when he pulled back. He grinned at her. "Liam, I want to be everything you want in a mate."

"You already are," he interrupted.

Talya put her finger on his lips. "Shh," she said. "I want to be the one you laugh with and cry with. I want to be the one you tell your burdens and secrets to. I want to be your safe place when you come home for the day. I want to be your encourager and cheerleader. I want you to share your dreams with me and your failures. I want to be the one to put a smile on your face across the room. I've watched my grandparents love each other with a deep, enduring love that's lasted over the decades. I want that with you."

"I want all of that too," Liam said with emotion in his voice. "But Talya, you are already all of those things to me." With that, he leaned forward and kissed her so tenderly. It was a kiss that was different from the other ones they shared. It was deeper than passion. It was a glimpse into their future, a future full of deep-abiding love.

"Will you stay in my room again tonight? If you dream walk tonight, make sure you take me with you," he said.

"I will," Talya agreed. They left the basement and walked back upstairs. Talya crawled under the covers and got comfortable while Liam took a shower.

"I'm serious about taking me with you," he reminded her again when he finished and crawled in beside her.

"I know," Talya replied.

"Give me your hand," Liam said. Talya rolled over and looked at him. "So, if you go, I'll go with you."

"I'm not sure it works that way," Talya said.

"I'm not taking any chances," came his response. He wrapped his long fingers around hers in a tight grip. Talya didn't say anything. If it gave him peace of mind so he could sleep, then she would hold his hand all night long.

Talya relaxed and closed her eyes. It took her a while to go to sleep. When she finally did, she opened her eyes and found herself in her dream state. *It worked," Liam said next to her, squeezing her hand. Talya looked around and didn't see the wolf anywhere. "It really is beautiful here," Liam said, looking all around. "Last time, I didn't exactly have a chance to look around."*

"Until recently, it always felt so peaceful here." Even as she said the words, she glanced around her nervously.

"I'll protect you," Liam said, tugging on her hand. He walked around, taking in the sights all around him, being careful not to let go of her hand.

Finally, the wolf showed up. Talya felt him before she ever saw him. He stopped a little distance away from them. "You're okay," Talya said with relief.

"I am." The wolf turned its head to Liam. "Protector, you made it back." Liam nodded.

"This is Liam," Talya said, uncertain of whether or not he needed an introduction.

"I know Liam as I know all of my wolves," the wolf said. "You are rested and recovered fully?"

"I am," Talya said. "And the next two sites have been destroyed."

"Good," the wolf responded. "Keep at them until they are all destroyed."

Talya nodded. "We will," Liam said next to her.

Talya let go of Liam's hand and walked over to the wolf. "Thank you for protecting me," she said as she hugged him tightly. She pulled back and wiped at the tears in her eyes.

"You're welcome," the wolf said simply. "Thank you for being my voice to my wolves."

Liam helped her up and kept a tight hold on her hand. "Thank you," he said to the wolf.

Chapter Forty-Seven

Before Talya could respond, the dream faded. Talya opened her eyes and realized she was back in Liam's room.

Liam rolled towards her and propped himself up on his arm. "You okay?" Talya nodded. "I'm meeting with the team this morning. We will probably be heading out tonight."

Talya sat up. "Okay. I'll go get ready."

"Talya, wait." Talya turned back to look at him.

"I'm going with," Talya said before he could say anything. "You need me there to direct you. If I'm there, I can help you find the site much faster."

"I know; Garrett told me. I just need you to promise to stay by me at all times and no more being the hero. Please let me protect you," Liam pleaded with her.

Talya smiled. "Deal. I have no desire to play the hero anymore. I am content to sit back and let you wolves do that."

"Thank you," he breathed out.

"My grandparents are asking when I'm going to come home."

Talya released the bombshell without looking at him. She called them every morning, and each day they pressured her more and more to come home.

"Talya, I can't lose you again. I won't do that to either of us," he said, his voice slightly deeper.

"I know, but I feel like I'm stuck between a rock and a hard place. I want to stay here with you; I really do. But they're my family. I need to be there to take care of them," Talya said with emotion.

"Talya, I want to spend the rest of my life with you. I need you by my side; my wolf needs you by our side. You're our mate. I can't let you go. But with all that said, if you want to live with them, I will go with you and live there as well," Liam said seriously.

"But what about your pack?" Talya asked.

"They'd pick a new beta. I would probably try to start my own pack. It's not wise to be alone and without a pack, and I could never join the pack that Brandon was a part of," he said with a shudder.

"I couldn't ask you to do that," Talya protested.

"Talya, you're my mate. If you need to go home to your grandparents; I will go too." He stood up and took off his shirt. "I think I'm going to let my wolf out for a run. I'll be back in a little bit." Without another word, he disappeared from the bedroom. Talya watched him go for a moment before heading to the shower. If his run was anything like last time, he was going to be awhile. Talya showered and got dressed for the day. She texted Emma to ask her for quick directions to the coffee shop.

It wasn't far; she just couldn't remember how to get there. She set her phone on the end table and went to finish getting ready.

A few minutes later, she heard a knock at the front door. Curious, she went to answer. When she opened the door, Madison stood there leaning against the door post.

"Hi," Talya responded. "What are you doing here?"

"I'm your ride to the coffee shop," she said. "Come on; let's get going. I need a coffee," Madison said grumpily.

Talya couldn't help but tease her. "You a little tired this morning, Madison?"

"Shut up. I just need coffee," Madison grumbled.

Talya grinned and grabbed her phone before following Madison to her car. "I always need coffee first thing in the morning too." Kyle was in the driver's seat. "Hey Kyle."

"Hey Talya," he responded with a grin.

"So not that I don't appreciate the ride, but why did you pick me up?" Talya asked.

"Emma texted me," Madison said.

"Nobody's supposed to go anywhere alone right now because of the threat of the vampires," Kyle explained from the front seat.

Talya nodded. That made sense. *Hey Liam, I'm heading to the coffee shop with Madison and Kyle,* Talya sent to him.

Stay safe. I'll be there soon, came his response.

Moments later, Talya walked into the shop behind Madison. "Morning," Emma called out.

"She's always way too chipper in the morning," Madison grumbled to Talya. That only made Emma grin more. "I need a caffeinated sugary drink," Madison said plopping into one of the high chairs in front of the counter. Talya tried to hide her smile. She glanced down at her phone, wondering what time it even was. She winced when she saw it was just after six. No wonder Madison was cranky.

The early morning hadn't bothered Talya; she was still on an energy-high from her dream. She had a feeling she would crash hard later. "So, I was serious about helping. Do you still want the help?" Talya asked as she approached the counter.

"Yes!" Emma said without delay. "Want to start now?"

"Sure," Talya responded. "I don't know how much I'll be around because I will be traveling with the pack to locate the vampire sites."

"I'll take whatever I can get," Emma said. "Want to start right now? I'm short on help today," Emma asked.

"Sure," Talya said as she stood and walked behind the counter. "You worked at a diner, right?" Emma asked. Talya nodded. "Well, this should be easy."

———————

The next two weeks flew as Talya fell into a pattern of working in the coffee shop and traveling with the wolves. They had successfully shut down two more sites. They were getting ready to leave soon to track down the next site. Talya felt good about that.

"Hey Sage," Talya called out as she knocked on the bedroom door. Sage had spent the last two weeks staying in the room next to Talya's in Liam's house.

"Come in," Sage called out.

Talya opened the door and stepped inside. "I'm heading over to the coffee shop for my shift. Want to come?"

"I'm good. Thanks," Sage said.

"I'll bring you back an iced coffee," Talya said, knowing it was Sage's favorite.

"Thanks," Sage responded with a small smile. Talya closed the door behind her, feeling guilty for leaving. She hated that she couldn't get Sage to come around, but both Liam and Paul kept telling her to let Sage come around on her own timing.

A few hours later, the door to the coffee shop opened, and Liam walked in. He caught her eye and smiled. "Can I steal you for a little bit?" he asked.

"Emma, I'm taking my break now," she called out.

"Sounds good," Emma responded from the back room.

"What's up?" Talya asked as she fell into step beside Liam.

"I have a surprise for you," he said. When he didn't say anything more, Talya looked up at him.

"What is it?" she asked.

"I can't tell you. It's a surprise," Liam said with a grin. He put his hand on her back and led her out of the shop towards his car.

"Where is it?" Talya asked, looking around.

"You do know how a surprise works, right?" he asked, amused.

"Fine," Talya huffed. He opened her door for her. Talya didn't ask any more questions, even though she desperately wanted too. A few minutes later, they pulled up in front of his house. Talya looked around but didn't see anything different.

She walked up the steps to the front porch and opened the door cautiously. When nothing popped out at her, she pushed it open the rest of the way. She walked into the house and didn't see anything. It wasn't until she walked by the kitchen that she stopped. "Grandma? Grandpop?" Tears immediately flooded her eyes as she ran to them and hugged them. "What are you doing here?" she asked when she finally got control of her emotions.

Her grandma was busy wiping her own eyes. "That boy of yours flew us here," Grandpop said gruffly.

"I can't believe you flew," Talya said in surprise.

"He sent a nice man to fly along with us. He took care of all the luggage for us and the tickets and helped us know where to go," Grandma said.

Of course he did, Talya thought to herself with a smile. "How long are you staying?" she asked. Grandma looked at Grandpop and neither of them said anything. "What?" Talya asked.

"Sweetheart, we aren't leaving. Liam asked us to live here with him and with you," Grandma said cautiously.

"Really?" Talya asked.

"Really," Grandma said, tearing up again.

Talya hugged them both again as tears came down her cheeks. "That makes me so happy," she said in a broken voice. *Thank you*, she sent to Liam. *Thank you so much! Thank you doesn't seem like enough, but it's all I have.*

You're welcome, he sent back to her. The door opened and Liam came in. Talya ran and threw herself into his arms. He caught her easily.

"Thank you!" she said again. He bent and kissed her gently. When he pulled back, he lowered her to the floor.

"They can live here with us; we can build an in-law suite for them, if that's what you want. If not, we pack up and move to their home." Liam asked.

Talya stared at him in surprise. "Really?"

"Really," he said with a smile.

Talya leaned towards him and spoke quietly. "You don't have to do this, Liam."

"I want to. Talya, you're my life now. Your family is my family. What do you want to do?"

"I want to stay here," Talya said with a smile.

"Are you sure?" he asked, looking into her eyes.

"Positive," Talya said. "Is that okay with you? Is that what you want?" Talya asked her grandparents.

"Yes, dear. That's what we want," Grandma said tenderly.

"Then, I'll have it done," Liam said simply and followed it with a kiss to her cheek. "We've got a pack meeting to go to in just a few minutes. Do you want to come or do you want to stay here?"

"I'll go with," Talya said decisively. "Do I have time to take a quick shower?"

"Yeah, go ahead," Liam said.

Talya hugged her grandparents again before heading back to her room. "I can't believe you're really here. Are you sure this is what you want?" she asked.

"Talya, all we've ever wanted to do was love you and take care of you. You're grown now, and you're an amazing, capable, beautiful woman. We realize that it's time to let you go. But if you would be okay with us living beside you, we would love nothing better!" Grandma said.

Talya turned to her grandpop. "What she said," he said gruffly. Talya hugged both of them again, wiping away the tears that slipped down her cheeks. When she finished hugging them, she turned towards Liam and pulled him with her down the hallway.

"I can't ever thank you enough," she said sincerely.

His expression was so tender and full of love when he looked down at her. "You don't need to, Talya. I love you."

Talya threw her arms around his waist and held on tightly. He wrapped his arms around her and held her securely against his chest. A few moments passed before Talya leaned back and looked at him. She took a deep breath. "Do you still want to mate with me?"

His face conveyed his surprise. "Yes!" he responded immediately. "Did you doubt that?" he asked in confusion.

"Well, we just haven't talked about it, and I wasn't sure how you felt about it," Talya said uncertainly.

Liam stared down at her. "Talya, I was ready to mate you the moment I first saw you. I told you that!" he said in a low, earnest voice.

"I know; I just wanted to make sure you didn't change your mind," Talya replied.

"No, baby," he replied tenderly. "Believe me, I will never change my mind about you," he said as he ran a finger down her cheek.

"Then let's do it this weekend," she said, watching his reaction carefully.

"Are you sure?" he asked simply.

"I am," Talya responded confidently. "My grandparents are here now and Sage. That's all I need. I mean, is it okay for my grandparents to come to the ceremony? To know about you?"

Liam nodded. "I already checked with Garrett. They're family now, and they will be living with us on pack lands." He wrapped his arms around her and brought her close to him. "I would love to mate with you this weekend, but only if you're sure. I've waited my entire life for you; I can wait a little bit longer."

"No more waiting. Let's do it Saturday night," Talya said.

"Good," Liam said blowing out the breath he was holding. "I was hoping you'd say that. I don't want to wait any longer." He lowered his lips and kissed her until she was breathless. He pulled back. "Now go take a quick shower; we're going to be late."

Chapter Forty-Eight

Twenty minutes later, she was back and ready to go. "Feel better?" Liam asked.

"Much," Talya said. They said goodbye to her grandparents and Sage, and Liam ushered her out the door.

Talya was anxious for the meeting. It was the first all-pack meeting since everything had happened. Before they walked into the building, Liam stopped her. "Talya, Garrett's going to be discussing the events of the last month with the pack. If at any time, it becomes too much, just tell me and I'll get you out of there."

"Thanks," Talya said. "I want to say that it will be fine, but I just don't know." Liam squeezed her hand.

They walked in and Talya immediately saw Garrett and Emma at the front. Emma caught her eye and smiled as she walked towards them. The bond between them was tighter now than it had been before.

Garrett came and stood beside Emma. "Talya, I haven't had a

chance to say thank you."

She felt Liam step close behind her. "Thank you for the work you have done as the Dreamer. I don't take it lightly what yo've done for this pack."

Talya wasn't really sure what to say. "You're welcome," she finally settled on.

A few moments later, Garrett called for the meeting to start. "It is with a grateful heart that I stand in front of you tonight with my mate back at my side," he began. Cheers rang out around the room and thunderous applause. "We are also grateful to have Talya, our beta's mate, back with us." More cheering and applause. When it died down, Garrett continued. "I want to thank each and every one of you that risked your lives to fight against the vampires, so we could bring our mates home. It was a long battle, and not one without loss. Thank you to each of you who fought by my and Liam's side. We will not soon forget it." Liam nodded beside Talya. "For those we lost, I would like to take a moment of silence to remember them." He read through a list of names. Some of them Talya knew, but most of them she did not. There was open weeping as Garrett read the list of names. When he finished, it was silent except for the soft crying sounds around the room.

After a few moments, Garrett lifted his head. "I value the lives of each one of my wolves, and I am grieving the loss of our pack members with you." Garrett looked out over his wolves. "We have had a month to grieve our losses, and I know that will never be enough time. Spend time remembering them, talking of them. We will honor their memories by not forgetting them." He paused and looked around the room. "Because of Talya, we have located and destroyed several vampire changing sites." Growling and cheering broke out simultaneously. "There are still more sites that must be destroyed. With kidnapping my mate and Liam's mate, the vampires have shown that there is no level that they will not stoop to. Even now, they are taking young human girls and trying to change them into vampires so that they can breed and produce more vampires." Angry growls and snarls ripped through the room. "We will not sit by and allow them to continue their evil work. "We have started a war with the vampires." It was deathly silent in the room now. "I am not naïve enough to think that it's a war that will end quickly. We took down their first four sites, but now they know we're coming for them. Things are going to get harder in the days to come. But that's okay. We are wolves. We were created to protect humanity, and that is what we will do. Spend this next week grieving your losses, loving your family, spending time with those you care about. Because after that, we fight. Other packs will begin to descend on our pack as we make plans to go forward. Be ready. I will have need of each and every one of you. We will stand strong because we will stand together. Remember, in the days to come, that we are the Northwoods Pack, the strongest pack in the country and we will not be defeated!" The room shook with thunderous applause and shouting. Garrett lifted his fist. "For the Pack!"

"For the Pack!" came the resounding cry.

Garrett pulled Liam into a meeting right away, so Talya sat and waited for him. Finally, he came towards her.

"Ready?" he asked.

Talya nodded. "Did you ask Garrett about Saturday?"

Liam nodded. "We're good to go. It's last minute, but with help, we can pull it off."

———————

The next morning, Talya sat upright in bed and shrieked as her door flew open and banged into the wall behind it. "Out of bed, girl!" Talya blinked and tried to calm her pounding heart.

"What in the world, Emma!" Talya said.

"You are having a mating ceremony in three days, Talya! Three days! Do you even know how much we have to do?" she asked.

Talya blinked again, trying to understand what was going on. Her eyes focused on Madison and Sage who came into the room much calmer than Emma. "She does have a point," Madison said. "Even though it's the crack of dawn!" she said, her eyes shooting daggers at Emma. Talya looked at Sage, but she didn't look ready to step in and save Talya any time soon.

"Drink your coffee!" Emma said to Madison. "Talya, get up and get dressed. I have hot coffee for you as soon as you're ready to go and not a moment before."

Liam appeared behind Madison and Emma with a grin on his face. When Talya caught sight of it and glared at him, he tried to keep a straight face but failed miserably. "You okay, baby?" he asked with a chuckle.

Talya glared at the man who was already showered and

dressed for the day and looked perfectly put together. "You can just take your grin and leave," she snapped at him. She tossed off her covers and moved towards the bathroom, muttering the entire time about early mornings and loud, obnoxious people. A hand stopped her from closing the bathroom door all the way, and Liam wrestled his way inside the bathroom. He closed the door behind him. "What?" Talya snapped.

He pulled out the coffee cup he had hidden behind his back. "I stole this when Emma wasn't looking," he said and held it out to her.

Talya snatched it out of his hand and took a drink. She closed her eyes and let the caffeine hit her. After a few more drinks, she opened her eyes and saw Liam watching her carefully. *"Have coffee available first thing every morning,"* he muttered to himself, but Talya saw the grin he was trying to hide.

"You can leave now," she said crankily.

He moved towards her instead. "You're adorable." She reached up to hit him, but he snagged her hand and kissed her palm instead. "You'd better get in the shower before she changes her mind and makes you go without a shower," he prodded her.

"Liam, I know you're in there, and I know you stole my coffee," Emma's voice sounded on the other side of the door.

"Busted," Talya sang out before she took another swig of coffee.

Liam stepped forward and kissed her suddenly, surprising her. "All right. I'm out of here for now. In three days, you won't be able to kick me out," he said with a wicked grin on his face.

Talya threw a towel at him. "Get out of here!" He left the

bathroom with a laugh. Talya quickly showered and got dressed for the day. She had a feeling it was going to be a day unlike any other.

Talya greatly underestimated how much needed to be done in three days. Somewhere along the way, she figured out that the wolves mating ceremony was pretty much comparable to a wedding. No wonder Emma had freaked out! But Emma, Madison, and Sage had been invaluable in helping pull everything together in such a short amount of time. Sage had even come around a little during the process and seemed to be smiling more.

Now here she was three days later. She stood still in front of a full-length mirror, gazing at the girl in the mirror. She didn't look anything like the girl she had been a year ago. So much of her life had changed. She turned slightly, taking in the whole picture. Madison had spent hours on her hair and makeup, and Talya had to admit every minute had been worth it. Her makeup was flawless, and the updo with braids Madison had created was stunning. Her eyes dropped to her dress. It was exquisite. While it wasn't exactly a wedding dress, it was pretty close.

The dress was a blush color with a tulle overlay that was embellished with glittering sequins, making it shimmer. It had a v-neck and thin straps. It fit around the waist, then dropped elegantly to the floor in layers of tulle. The back dipped down almost to her waist. The entire effect was breathtaking. Talya slipped on the matching soft slip-ons that Emma had given her.

Her grandparents had both cried when they saw her, and that of course had made Talya tear up. But a sharp word from Madison about ruining her makeup stopped her tears in her tracks.

Talya, I have something for you. Can I come see you? She heard Liam's voice in her head.

Isn't it bad luck to see me beforehand? She asked.

That's only for a wedding; luckily this isn't a wedding.

She smiled. *I'm in my room.*

She heard a knock on the door a few moments later, and she tried to settle the sudden nerves in her stomach. "Come in," she said softly and turned to face him.

He opened the door and froze. He stared at her as if he'd never seen her before. At first, Talya was flattered, but that quickly turned to nerves when he said nothing. "Do I look okay?" she asked nervously.

Liam shook his head and moved towards her. "Talya, I have no words."

Talya smiled at him. "So, I look okay then?"

He shook his head. "No, okay doesn't even begin to come close." He took both her hands in his. "There is nothing with which to even compare your beauty to. I got something for you," he said holding out a small box." Talya took it and opened it carefully. Inside was a gorgeous pair of rose gold earrings and matching necklace. "Emma helped me pick them out so they would match," he explained, watching her face carefully.

"They're perfect, Liam. Thank you. Will you help me put the necklace on?" she asked, turning around. He stepped close behind her and fastened the clasp. Talya put the earrings in; then looked in the mirror. "They're beautiful, Liam."

He held her hand up in the air and gently twirled her around. The tulle spread out around her as she spun. He smiled down at her. "*You're* beautiful, Talya," he said reverently. He spun her around again. "I only have one question." Talya looked up at him, waiting to hear his question. "How easy is it to get you out of that dress?" he asked with a gleam in his eye.

Epilogue

The ceremony was everything Talya dreamed it would be and more. Emma and Madison and the other women of the pack had outdone themselves. Every detail was absolutely perfect. Talya knew she would remember this day for the rest of her life.

In a rare moment, Talya found herself alone for the first time in days. Most of the well-wishers had gone back to their homes. Liam had left her for a moment to find Garrett and check in with him one last time before they disappeared for a few days. Talya enjoyed this moment, feeling as if she might burst from happiness.

"Hey, beautiful, can you tell me where Garrett is?" Talya turned to see a guy she didn't recognize standing in front of her.

"He's in a meeting right now," Talya replied. "Can I help you with something?" she asked politely.

He grinned and stepped closer to her. "I can think of a lot of things you could help me with," he said conspiratorially.

Talya kept the smile on her face but stepped back. "I have

somewhere I need to be," she said. Before she could step away, his hand shot out and grabbed her wrist. Her eyes shot to his. "Let go of me," she said. *Liam!*

I see him, she heard his low angry voice. "I suggest you get your hand off of my mate immediately if you want to have two hands tomorrow." The guy in front of her immediately dropped her hand and put both hands up in sign of a surrender. Liam stepped in front of her, effectively blocking her from the man's view.

"Sorry, man, I didn't know," the man said.

"You didn't know?" Liam repeated icily. "You didn't guess that the gorgeous girl, who is clearly marked and wearing a beautiful dress at a mating ceremony wasn't the one who was mated? Who are you?" Liam barked at him.

"Maverick Benson. I'm the beta of the Orlando pack. Our pack just got into town, and my Alpha sent me to check in with Garrett," the man said.

"It's Alpha, not Garrett," Liam said sternly.

Maverick cracked a smile but didn't argue with Liam. Talya stepped up beside Liam and studied the man. He turned to look back at her. When he caught her looking at him, he winked. Before Talya could do anything to stop him, Liam launched forward and punched him. Talya heard the crack and watched as blood sprayed from the man's nose. The man yelled and grabbed his nose.

"You broke my nose!" he shouted in anger.

"What's going on?" Garrett's voice entered the fray.

"This crazy man broke my nose!" Maverick said.

Garrett crossed his arms over his chest. "This man is my beta," he said. "Who are you and why are you on our pack land?"

"I'm Maverick, the beta from the Orlando Pack," the man said before cursing.

Garrett shot a look at Liam. "Welcome," he said, turning back to Maverick. "I'm sorry it started out this way. Where is your alpha?"

"He's outside. He sent me in to check in with you," Maverick said.

"Liam, take Maverick to Paul," he said and turned away.

"Are you kidding me? It's my mating ceremony," Liam said in anger.

"Maybe you shouldn't have broken his nose then," Garrett said smoothly. Turning back to Maverick, he said, "Liam will take you to our healer. I apologize on my beta's behalf." With that, he strode away, leaving Maverick and Liam glaring at each other.

"Come on," Talya said. "Let's go find Paul." She tugged on Liam's hand as she said it. Liam mumbled something under his breath. She didn't catch it, nor did she want to. A quick peek behind her told her that Maverick was following.

Talya saw Sage sitting by herself at a table near the back of the room. "Hey, Sage," Talya called out.

Sage stood up and gave Talya a hug. "Everything was beautiful. Congratulations," she said quietly.

"Thank you," Talya said. Talya saw the exact moment Sage saw Maverick.

"What happened?" she asked, seeing the blood. She started

moving towards Maverick.

"He broke my nose," Maverick said nodding to Liam.

Sage's eyebrows raised when she looked at Liam, but she didn't say anything, "Let me get you something to clean it up with," she said before disappearing. She came back a moment later with some paper towels. "Here," she said. She handed Maverick the towels and watched him for a moment before sighing. "Let me help. Sit down," she said, nodding to a chair.

Maverick surprisingly did as she commanded him. She grabbed another towel and wet it with a water bottle. Then she started cleaning the blood off his face. He watched her silently. When all the blood was cleaned, she gently touched his nose. "What are you doing?" he asked cautiously.

"I'm trying to feel where the break is," Sage said distractedly. She felt where the break was and put her hand over it. A moment later, they heard a popping sound and Maverick yelled in pain. Then he shook himself. Talya stared at him; she could feel Liam beside her doing the same thing.

"You're a healer," Maverick said in awe as he stood up and took a step closer to Sage. He reached out like he was going to touch her face.

"Don't touch her," an angry voice commanded from behind them. Talya turned to see the normally mild-mannered doctor walking towards them. He made his way over to where Sage stood and stepped in front of her.

Maverick stepped back slightly. "Thanks, Healer," he said with a smile, ignoring Paul. Without another word, he strode away from them.

Talya stared after him in shock. Then she looked back at Paul. He moved and Sage stepped out from behind him. Sage didn't look as surprised as Talya thought she would be. Paul, however...that was a different story. Talya could see the shock on his face. She wasn't sure when he had gotten there or how much he had seen, but he had obviously seen enough. "Sage, what was that?" Talya finally found her voice.

Sage shrugged. "I've done it before." Then without another word, she walked away.

Talya met Liam's surprised gaze before she looked back at Paul. "My mate's a healer?" Paul asked in a whisper. Talya had no idea what to say.

Liam clasped Paul's shoulder. "Well, we knew she was going to have a gift." He cocked his head. That's one doozy of a gift," he said.

Paul nodded, even though his face was still in shock. "She pretty much just ignores me," Paul said, turning to Liam. "What do I do about that?"

"Win her over," Liam said with a grin. Then he pulled Talya up and into his arms. "I believe I've waited long enough," he said in a low voice near her ear as he strode out of the clinic and to his car.

"What have you waited for?" Talya asked innocently, trying and failing to keep the grin off her face.

"To spend the rest of my life with the most precious gift I've ever been given...the woman I love," he said with such love in his eyes that Talya felt tears come to her eyes. Liam settled her carefully in the front seat of his car before closing the door and moving to the driver's side.

Talya looked out the window with a smile on her face. She couldn't believe that this man was hers now. Wariness touched her mind for just a moment before she pushed it away. She wasn't naïve; she knew this wasn't a storybook ending. There was more dream walking to do, more fights to be fought, and a war to be won. But right now, in this moment, they could put all that aside, for this moment before them. She was with her mate, the man she loved, and that was enough for today.

Several hours later, they arrived at the cabin Liam had rented for them. Since her grandparents stayed with them right now until the renovations were done, Liam thought this would be best. She climbed out of the car and smiled at the cabin, surrounded by woods on all sides. "This is perfect." Her words were followed with a shriek as Liam picked her up. "What are you doing?" she asked him with a laugh.

"Gotta carry my wife across the threshold," he said with a grin.

"Do people still do that?" Talya asked.

"They do now," he said.

"Don't we need to grab all our stuff?" Talya asked, looking back at the car.

"Nope. We're not going to need anything over the next few days. The fridge is stocked, the pantry is full, and the linens are provided. What else could we possibly need?" he asked.

"Oh, I don't know. Clothes maybe?"

He looked down at her with a wicked grin. "Baby, you're not going to need any clothes while we're here."

Talya laughed. "Right."

He grinned again and took the three steps up to the front porch in a single leap. He unlocked the door and closed it behind them. "Oh, Liam. This is perfect." He didn't comment; he walked steadily towards a door that was closed. When he opened it, Talya gasped in surprise. "Liam." The entire room was swathed in the flickering light of candles. Rose petals adorned the bed and the floor. There were snacks and drinks on a side table. Talya grinned at Liam. "Are we not leaving the room the entire time we're here?"

"That's the plan," he said. He set her done on the bed and took off her shoes. When he moved to her dress, she stopped him.

"Wait. I have something special I want to change into," she said.

"Is it in the car?" he asked, leaning back.

"Nope. I came prepared. It's in my purse." She stood up and kissed him, pulling away before they got too into it. "I'll be back in a minute," she whispered. She disappeared into the bathroom and took the bag out of her purse. She carefully slipped into the special outfit she had picked out for tonight with Emma's help. She didn't bother looking in the mirror; she finger brushed her hair and walked out of the bathroom. She stood by the door, waiting for him to turn around.

His reaction was everything she was hoping it would be and more. The look on his face said it all. "You are so beautiful," he breathed in awe. He led her by the hand to the bed. "I love you more than you will ever know," he said as he tenderly ran his finger down her cheek. "Let me show you just how much." He bent his head and spent the rest of the night and the following days doing just that.

Far too soon, it was time to pack up and head home. After they packed everything and climbed into the car, Liam leaned across the seat and kissed her deeply. "Talya, those were by far the best days of my life."

"Me too," Talya said in between kisses.

"Are you ready to head back?" he asked.

Talya nodded. "I'm ready to begin our life together. "

"Me too, baby," he said and took her hand in his.

"How do you think Sage is doing? Do you think Paul is making any headway with her?" Talya asked, glancing at him.

"Probably," Liam said with a grin.

"How can you be so sure?" Talya asked.

He squeezed her hand. "Because he's a wolf, and wolves always get their girl."

Talya leaned her head back and smiled. *Yeah, Sage will be just fine.*

THE END... for now

The storyline will continue on in Paul and Sage's story

Want a Chapter from Liam's Point-of-View? Join my email list to get the

BONUS CHAPTER.

Ajmanneybooks.com/bonuses

About the Author

Amanda lives outside of Philadelphia with her husband and four kids. Some of her favorite things to do include reading, family days, being a pastor's wife, and watching football on Sunday afternoons with her family.

Connecting with A.J. Manney:
If you enjoyed this book, would you consider leaving me a review on Amazon? I would greatly appreciate it!

I would love to connect with you! You can find me on Facebook and Instagram at A. J. Manney Books. Follow me to stay updated for new book releases at AJManneyBooks.com!

Acknowledgments

Thank you to my editor, Caryn. Thank you for countless hours to help this book be the best it can be. I so appreciate you!

Thank you to my cover designer, Les. I love everything you create! Thanks for an amazing cover!

Thank you to my kids for being patient and allowing me the time to write!

Thank you to my biggest fan- Matthew, my husband. Thanks for believing in me and being behind my dreams. Thanks for spending hours formatting my book!

**Special thanks to you, my reader! Thank you for sticking with me. I've enjoyed starting this new series and hope you've enjoyed reading it! Thank you!

While you're waiting for the next book in the Wolves of the Northwoods Series, check out my True Marks Series.

Visit:
AJManneyBooks.com

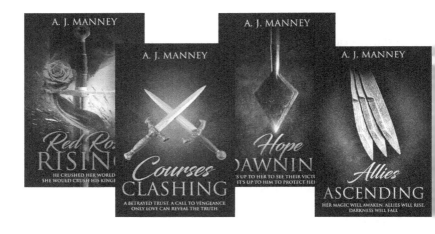

AJManneyBooks.com

 facebook.com / ajmanneybooks

 @ajmanneybooks

Made in the USA
Middletown, DE
09 September 2024